GIFTS from the SEA

Jane Goodger

A SIGNET BOOK

SIGNET
Published by New American Library, a division of
Penguin Putnam Inc., 375 Hudson Street,
New York, New York 10014, U.S.A.
Penguin Books Ltd, 80 Strand,
London WC2R ORL, England
Penguin Books Australia Ltd, Ringwood,
Victoria, Australia
Penguin Books Canada Ltd, 10 Alcorn Avenue,
Toronto, Ontario, Canada M4V 3B2
Penguin Books (N.Z.) Ltd, 182–190 Wairau Road,
Auckland 10, New Zealand

Penguin Books Ltd, Registered Offices:
Harmondsworth, Middlesex, England

First Published by Signet, an imprint of New American Library,
a division of Penguin Putnam Inc.

First Printing, December 2001
10 9 8 7 6 5 4 3 2 1

REGISTERED TRADEMARK—MARCA REGISTRADA

Printed in the United States of America

PUBLISHER'S NOTE
This is a work of fiction. Names, characters, places, and incidents either
are the product of the author's imagination or are used fictitiously,
and any resemblance to actual persons, living or dead, business
establishments, events, or locales is entirely coincidental.

BOOKS ARE AVAILABLE AT QUANTITY DISCOUNTS WHEN USED TO PROMOTE
PRODUCTS OR SERVICES. FOR INFORMATION PLEASE WRITE TO PREMIUM
MARKETING DIVISION, PENGUIN PUTNAM INC., 375 HUDSON STREET, NEW YORK,
NEW YORK 10014.

Chapter One

He came ashore, half-dead, on an incoming tide in late October, his battered boat pushed along by an unrelenting current. He lay in a whaleboat unmoving, hardly breathing, letting the waves guide him where they might, his mind long ago made up that dying on the churning ocean would be a fitting death for a man whose every joy and every despair was born on the sea.

On a high bluff above the Atlantic, Capt. Jared Mitchell's unwelcome savior trudged along the soft sands, her skirts whipping in the incessant wind, her hair flying back like a signal flag shredded in a mighty gale. The boat was small, and still too far away for the young woman to see yet. Rachel Best, lost in thought and memories as she walked along the desolate beach, would curse a hundred times the tide that brought Jared Mitchell into her life and into her reluctant heart.

Each day, Rachel walked along the bluffs of Truro, the wind making her cheeks, nose, and chin cherry red, like old man Withers who drank too much of the rum from bottles he'd found washed up on the beach two summers ago. She would make her way from her parents' cottage nestled behind the dunes and walk the quarter mile to the bluffs that rose above the beach's white sands and the pounding surf. Even on calm days, when the Atlantic Ocean lay flat and blue, the waves ripped at the shore, sucking at sand and pebbles only to cast them back with the next wave.

Her booted feet sank into the soft sand that ran along the high bluff, and by the time she reached her spot near the lighthouse her calves ached. She did not keep her eyes riveted on the ocean, glancing up only now and again, searching with awful intensity as she always did for some sign of Richard. Each time she did, her pulse would pound a bit harder, that hope she fed with her daily wanderings coming alive in her heart.

A man like Richard Best simply did not die in the surf he'd grown up with, especially not when the seas were relatively calm, in spite of the fact that thirteen other men had perished. Her Richard was alive. She simply refused to believe anything else. It had been long enough so that Rachel knew, in some small part of her mind she refused to acknowledge openly, that she was being foolish. She had grown up hearing tales of men missing for years only to turn up alive and glad to be home. But she'd decided long ago that they were just tales, not true stories of real men. If Richard had somehow survived the daring rescue of the foundering bark, if in the end he had fought hard to live and had been plucked from the sea by some passing ship, surely he would have been able to send a message to her, if not made his way back home. As weeks turned into months, she pretended, at least to those around her, that she was not still searching the waters of Cape Cod for her husband. But she was.

Because Rachel knew he was alive. It was as simple as that. The alternative—that he had drowned—was nearly as impossible to believe.

"Where are you, Richard?" she whispered, her dark blue eyes scanning the horizon with the skill of a salty old captain. In the distance, two ships seemed to glide across the seas, the full brilliant white sails pushing them northward toward Boston. With a sigh and a glance at the old lighthouse, Rachel turned back toward home. That was when she saw the boat bobbing gently in the ocean, a black spot in the distance, but clearly a boat laden with something, for it sat low in the water. She couldn't be sure from this distance, but Rachel thought it was a lifeboat or whaleboat making its steady way toward the beach.

It seemed she stood there for hours staring at the boat, her heart beating so painfully in her chest she could hardly breathe. A man lay prone in that boat; she was almost certain she could make out a human form lying there. His name pounded in her head in time with her heart: *Richard, Richard, Richard.*

Lifting her skirts, Rachel ran along the bluff, stumbling more than once in the fine sand, heading toward the lighthouse and Donald Small, the keeper. Thank God he was here and not at the Mews Tavern, where he'd been seen so often of late. She could see him, a small, dark form walking along the base of the whitewashed light, more than likely watching over his mums that struggled to grow in the sandy soil.

"Mr. Small," she called, even when she knew she was too far for him to hear. But inside she felt a rush of excitement: a boat was coming to shore laden with a man. Certainly it *could* be Richard, who, weary from rowing, had decided to lie down in the boat hoping to sleep before struggling to beach the boat. Perhaps a passing ship, not willing to stop at a local port, had agreed to cast him off. It was not as fantastical as all that, she told herself as she plunged through the scraggly brush that surrounded the light, her feet crunching loudly over the stunted growth.

Donald Small looked up from his flowers and Rachel waved. The small, wiry man became instantly alert, immediately sensing that Rachel was not simply calling out a hello. Rachel lifted her long skirts, heedless of the thorny branches that tugged at her stockings. Out of breath, filled with hope, she gasped out, "A boat, a man. To the south."

Small lifted his head sharply, his nostrils quivering as if he could somehow smell the boat. Then his brown eyes narrowed. "I'll get my claw," he said, and ran back to a small shed beside the lighthouse that contained his lifesaving equipment. When he returned he dragged a gurney behind him that carried blankets, a rope, and a claw that he would use to hook the boat and drag it safely onto the beach.

"You didn't see a ship? Or another boat?"

"No. Just this one."

Small saw the hope in her eyes and turned away from it. He'd not be a party to this girl's fantasy. And now here he was three months later walking beside a woman whose face glowed with the expectation that her long-lost husband had returned to her. Touched in the head, some said. And maybe they were right.

"Looks like a whaleboat," he said, and Rachel nodded.

As they approached the spot on the bluff where they would make their descent, Rachel noticed two other men making their way toward them. Word of a boat floating free, a ship in distress, moved quickly in Truro. Likely someone saw the boat and passed the word. Rachel's heart filled—they would need help carrying him home. Whoever he was, she amended quickly, trying not to hope too much, trying to tell herself, even as her hope grew to painful proportions, that the man in the boat would not be Richard.

But he could be, couldn't he?

"Oren. Obed." Small greeted the two men heartily. The Cobb brothers, just home from a fishing trip on George's Bank, nodded in unison. They weren't twins, being all of eleven months apart, but they might as well have been. The two looked and acted identically, the only difference being that Oren could be known to carry on something closely resembling a conversation. But certainly never in the presence of a woman.

"Whaleboat," Oren said.

Small grunted. "Looks to have a bit of a load in her. Hard to say, but I believe there's a man lying on the bottom. Not moving, from what I can see."

Oren answered by moving down the embankment, his boots sliding deep into the sand. Obed stepped down next, surefooted and deft on the steep bank. Small gave Rachel a look, as if he were about to tell her to stay put, but apparently changed his mind when he saw the determined look on her face. Rachel lifted her skirts and took a plunging step down the bluff, as proficient at negotiating her way down the bluff as the Cobb brothers.

By the time the four were standing at the edge of the beach, the boat was beginning to bob in and out of the surf. It was a low tide rising on a calm day, so pulling the boat to shore would be a relatively easy prospect. The undertow, usually so treacherous, was less so on this day, making the men's task of getting close to the boat an easy one. Rachel stood just at the edge of the tide, where the sea sank harmlessly into the sand, clutching her hands together and repeating over and over in her head, *It's not him. It's not. Oh, please, God, let it be him.*

She could see a booted leg propped up and well salted, moving in time to the gentle swell, but it was impossible to tell if they were the same boots Richard had worn that last day. The man's pants were of an indiscernible dark color. One hand was draped over the side of the boat, fingers dipping into the water when the waves tossed the boat with enough violence. Richard's hand? Rachel stared, desperately trying to remember what her husband's hands had looked like. The hand that dangled listlessly, lifelessly over the side was large and finely formed.

Small threw the hook and rope, snagging the bow of the boat with a single try, and began dragging it to shore with the help of Obed. They were up to their knees in the surf, the waves sometimes splashing their thighs with seawater. Oren plunged deeper to grasp the boat as it neared the beach.

"What color hair?" Rachel shouted, aware of how desperately hopeful she sounded.

Obed turned to her, his eyes expressionless, giving no hint of what he'd found in that whaleboat. "Brown."

Brown. Not Richard. Not her beautiful blond husband. Disappointment flooded her, made everything around her disappear for a fleeting moment. Not Richard. She wanted to rage against the heavens for giving her hope, that terrible bit of faith that had overcome reason.

"Alive?"

Small's voice shook her from her own misery. There was a man in that boat, someone else's husband or father, someone else who might be going home after a nightmarish ordeal. Or into a grave dug by Truro men. The raging disappointment was swept away, and Rachel found herself praying with all that she possessed that this man, whoever he was, was alive.

"Barely," came the grave answer.

Rachel shuffled back to allow the men to drag the boat ashore.

"Whoever he is, he's been to hell and back. And

apparently had fun along the way," Small said, after getting his first good look at the boat's passenger.

"What's that smell?" Rachel said, wrinkling her nose. The air had suddenly been fouled with a stench as offensive as had ever touched her nose.

"Him," Oren said, nodding toward the man, a small grin playing about his solemn features.

Rachel peered cautiously into the boat, her eyes widening. A bear of a man lay sprawled at the bottom of the boat, his face so covered with grime and hair it was impossible to discern his features. His clothes, hair, and skin were covered with a film of sorts, and Rachel decided that whatever it was that coated him was likely the source of the horrid smell.

"Whale oil," Small said. "Rancid. Urine, vomit. Whiskey."

"That'd do it," Oren said, waving his hand in front of his face. For a man who worked the sea, who came home smelling of fish, it was quite a thing to be offended by another's scent. But this . . . this was just too, too much, Rachel thought, covering her mouth and nose with one hand.

"It's horrible," she said in a gasp, backing away from the boat. "Are you certain he's alive?" She certainly didn't want to get close enough to find out.

"He's breathing," Oren said, humor entering his eyes as he looked over the contents of the boat.

"I don't know how," Small said, chuckling.

Rachel furrowed her brow. "What do you mean? Is he injured?" She took a step forward again, holding her breath, and got a closer look at the giant who lay in the whaleboat. He didn't appear to have an injury, though with all the grime it was difficult to tell. His hair was so long and thick and matted, it was possible there was blood caked in it, though Rachel didn't want to get close enough to determine that fact.

"Ain't injured."

The man in the boat let out a loud snore, and for the first time Rachel noticed the contents of the boat. At least five amber bottles, all empty, lay at the bottom of the boat—one still nestled lovingly in the man's left hand.

Rachel let out a gasp of outrage. "He's drunk!"

"Seems to be," Small said, this time letting out a full-fledged laugh. He forced a sober look. "But that don't mean he doesn't need saving and nursing as much as the next man. More than likely he's suffering from more than drunkenness. Man can't last long at sea without food and water. Likely as sick as he is drunk."

"I hardly think that possible," Rachel said dryly, and to her surprise the Cobb brothers laughed.

With a sigh, Small said, "Let's get him on the gurney and up to your place, Mrs. Best."

Rachel opened her mouth to argue, then reluctantly clamped her mouth shut. Her parents' cottage was the closest house, and the man, despite everything, would certainly require nursing—a job always delegated to the women of Truro.

"Very well, Mr. Small. Let's bring him home."

Chapter Two

Jared Mitchell was aware he was conscious long before he could bring himself to open his eyes. Vague images flashed through his tired brain, of women and men hovering over him, of soft lamplight and softer hands. He wasn't on the *Huntress*, that was for certain, he thought as he struggled to make sense of where he was. It was as if he were floating in a thick, pea-soup fog that thinned only enough to see the vaguest of images before swirling mist shrouded his mind once again.

Beneath him was a smooth, crisp sheet. His head lay upon a feather pillow, and draped over him were heavy blankets tucked tight beneath a feather mattress, making him, oddly, feel more secure than trapped. He heard soft movements in another room, and smelled coffee and bacon. Jared would have smiled had he been able to garner the energy to do so. Wherever the hell he was, it was a nice place to be.

For a few moments he struggled to remember why he wasn't on the *Huntress*. *Why, why, why*, his mind lazily whirred. With a mental shrug, he decided he didn't care, though for the life of him he didn't know why he didn't. *I should care*, he thought. *I should won-*

der what fate befell my ship. Instead, he luxuriated in the feeling of a soft bed and breakfast smells and opened his eyes.

Not six inches away, wide, clear, little-girl brown eyes peered at him from beneath a precisely cut fringe of soft blond bangs. "Hello." A crystal voice came out of that perfect little face.

Jared growled and watched with idle amusement as the girl's eyes grew big. He thought for certain she would scream, and some wretched part of him wanted her to be frightened. But then her sparkling eyes turned to half-moons and the blond cherub giggled, raising one hand over her lips as if she were aware that laughing was not the response he was looking for.

"Are you a giant?" she whispered, sobering.

"Yes. And I eat little children for breakfast," he said through a throat gone rough from disuse. He closed his eyes again, exhausted by this exchange already.

The little girl giggled again. "You're funny," she said. "You can't eat me. I'm a fairy princess and I live in a castle and giants aren't allowed. And if you try, I have a dragon who I found and he'll eat you first."

What an odd, fearless child, Jared thought, his eyes still closed. He knew his appearance would frighten the bravest grown man, never mind this little wisp of a girl. He must be losing his touch. The one thing he had cultivated in the past six years was the ability to make people go away. He was quite good at it, with an instinct for knowing just what to do to create the largest distance between himself and humanity. It was why he so enjoyed being on the *Huntress.* No one could accuse any of his motley thirty-six-member crew of being anything resembling humanity.

And now he couldn't even discourage this small child.

"Mama!" She let out an ear-piercing yell. "He's away-ake."

Jared's eyes fluttered open long enough to see a brown skirt covered by a yellow apron move into his range of vision. "Well, if he wasn't awake before, he certainly is now." A sigh. "Belle, look, honey, he's still asleep."

"He was awake, Mama. He told me he was a giant and was going to eat me."

Jared heard another sigh, followed by a musical laugh. "He did, did he?"

"Yes, Mama."

He could almost picture the little girl's earnest face gazing up at her mother. He forced his eyes open, curious to see this woman with the soft voice and laugh.

"Ah. He is awake, Belle. Hello, sir," said a blurry female form. He felt a strong hand behind his head, a cool mug held to his parched lips, and blessedly cold water against his mouth. His eyes drifted shut as he drank, sputtering, drooling down his chin and neck, until she drew the cup away. "Not too much, sir. I fear it will come right back up."

Jared blinked to clear his vision, but when he opened his eyes, all he saw was the butter-yellow apron. All he felt was a cool hand on his brow.

"You've still a bit of a fever, sir." She took her hand away, and Jared frowned. "Do you know where you are, then?"

He swallowed. "No."

"You're in Truro. Cape Cod. Near Highland Light."

Confusing images filled his mind: of the sea, endless nights, torturous days, his ship in the distance. Shouts and yells and hoots of laughter. "How?" he muttered, more to himself than to the apron standing in front of him.

"You came ashore four days ago on a whaleboat.

We could only make out the letters R-E-S-S on it, and no ship has foundered in a fortnight. At least not along the Cape."

"*Huntress*," he said. "Whaler." He shook his head back and forth as if trying to jostle his brain to clearer thought. A cool hand pressed against his forehead, and her soft breath hit the side of his face. "Shh. Don't think too much. You've been ill, sir, for these four days."

He closed his eyes, the feel of her hand on his fevered skin soothing him, drugging him.

"Is he gonna die, Mama?"

Jared was vaguely aware of listening for her answer, but he drifted away to blackness before she uttered a word.

"No, Belle, he'll not die." Though Rachel wondered just what had kept this man alive these past days. His fever had raged for four days, his body racked with seizures so violent, it took her and both parents to wrestle him to the bed. His skin hung on him like drying leather, forcing Rachel and her mother to tediously spoon water down his parched throat. And then last night his raspy breathing had cleared and he'd slept a normal sleep for the first time since they'd brought his stinking person into their home.

Rachel turned to see her mother standing in the doorway, a question in her eyes. "He was awake and spoke, but he's so exhausted he fell back to sleep before I could ask him his name."

"Poor lamb," Mabel Newcomb said, shaking her head sadly.

"Oh, Mama, this poor lamb nearly drank himself to death."

"But I thought he needed water," Belle said, her brown eyes wide with concern for the stranger in her bed.

Rachel grimaced inwardly. She'd forgotten that her curious little daughter was still in the room guarding over their patient, as she had been since Donald Small and the Cobb brothers had deposited him there. "Go eat your breakfast, Belle." When the little girl hesitated, her worried gaze shifting to her "giant," Rachel added, "He's fine, darling. Just tired."

When she was gone, Rachel turned and scowled at the man. "I don't understand her attachment. He still stinks to high heaven for all the bathing we gave him. And he does look like a giant."

She would care for him, make him well, and send him on his way. *Good riddance.* Rachel gritted her teeth at the thought of how much longer it might be before he was gone. He was a reminder of her foolishness, of her hope. Of her painful disappointment. And if ever there was a man who was unlike Richard, it was this man, this hairy, huge man lying on her daughter's bed.

Richard, as strapping a lad as he was, had been small compared to this behemoth. Richard, with his silky blond hair, his deep brown eyes, and his pale skin, looked like an angel. Her patient, with his long, curling hair, matted and dirty, his long beard, also matted and dirty, and his deeply tanned skin, would have made Richard look like a delicate flower. Big, hairy, dirty. Rachel suppressed a shudder. She loathed big, hairy, dirty men.

"I imagine he'll return home as soon as he's able," Mabel said. "No doubt there are people out there worried about him."

Looking down at him, Rachel couldn't imagine such a thing. He was the picture of a man who'd lost any desire to maintain even the semblance of civilization. His clothes, which they'd boiled in lye and then boiled again, were finely made garments of expensive fabrics and intricately carved bone buttons with solid gold inlay, and had a Boston tailor's label.

Clearly they were his garments and not items he'd confiscated from another soul, for very few men would have fit into them. But they were as neglected as the man himself, in such poor condition surely the man who wore them had not cared a whit about himself or the clothes on his back for some time.

Then she remembered his first fevered night in their cottage, his nearly incoherent ramblings that made no more sense than if he were speaking in a foreign language. Only a handful of words had made sense, and now that she thought of them, the way he'd sounded when he'd uttered them, her heart softened. "Abby," he'd said, his voice low and desperate. "I'm so damned sorry."

Jared's nose twitched. He was awake, and he knew he was in a clean bed, but he could distinctly smell the three-day-old carcass of a whale. The woman, the young one with the red-gold hair, sat in the corner sewing, her foot tapping lightly on the small rag rug beneath her feet as she rocked back and forth, the skids of the chair creaking against the wood floor. She wore sturdy boots and a practical dress of brown. The dress's drab shade made the rest of her appear to glow with color—the faint pink blush on her cheeks, the redness of her full lips, that glorious curling hair. She wore no adornment, not even a comb in her hair, but for the thin gold band on her left hand. She was clean and unrumpled, her face serene.

"What's that god-awful smell?" he grumbled, and watched with a small amount of satisfaction when the woman jumped.

"I believe, sir, that it is you." Her expression was serious, but her eyes, a remarkable mix of deepest blue fringed with gold, were lit with amusement. "We did our best to bathe you, but some of the stench clings still."

"Good Christ."

She stiffened. "Sir, we do not curse in this—"

"Yes, yes. I'm certain you don't," he said with no apology in his tone. "Where the hell—" He stopped, muttering another curse under his breath. He hadn't had to watch his language in years. "And where might I be, madam?" he asked with mock gentility.

All amusement disappeared from her eyes. "Truro. Cape Cod. Near the Highland Light."

He realized he'd already asked that question and had it answered. "Yes. Cape Cod. I washed up on a whaleboat." He spoke as if telling a tale about another person.

The woman stood and strode toward the bed, one hand extended. When he moved his head away, she spoke calmly. "I want to see if you still have a fever."

Jared lay stock-still as she laid her hand upon his brow, his eyes pinned to the whitewashed ceiling. "It's nearly normal," she said brightly, withdrawing her hand. "You've been here six days now. We don't know your name. I'm sure there are people who are worried about you."

"Jared Mitchell. Captain of the whaler *Huntress*." He squeezed his eyes shut, thinking of how he could have ended up on a whaleboat in Truro when the last he remembered the ship was passing Block Island on the way to New Bedford. And then it came to him like a cold Atlantic wave.

"Oh, good God," he said, covering his face with his hands.

"Captain Mitchell, what is wrong?"

She touched his arm. Why did she keep touching him like that? *Bothersome woman.* He wanted her to go away; he wanted everything to go away, including and especially himself.

The *Huntress* had been just one day out of New Bedford, and he and his world-weary crew had been celebrating mightily. In the ship's hold was a full load of fine whale oil; in their bellies was enough whiskey and rum to leave the entire population of New Bedford drunk for a day. The ship had left port nearly four and a half years ago, one of the longest whaling voyages ever recorded. The men were eager to step foot in the city they still called home, but their captain was not. At least, after swigging down a full bottle of whiskey he was not. The more he drank, the less he wanted to see the city of his youth, filled as it was with its cursed happy memories. He wanted none of it.

Stumbling toward the mainmast, he called his men together and announced that the crew was free to go home, but his voyage was not over yet. Amid shouts of laughter, he ordered his men to ready a whaleboat for a long voyage. To the well-soused sailors, that simply meant heaving aboard a case of whiskey with much fanfare and joviality. Jared, long past caring, flung himself aboard the whaleboat and ordered it be lowered, which the men did, laughing and calling down to the captain as he happily waved a full bottle of whiskey.

"To hell with New Bedford," he called out, taking a long drink. "To hell with everything," he'd muttered, looking at the blessedly full bottle in his hand. "To hell with me."

More sober than he'd been in two years, Jared pulled down his hands and looked at the woman standing over him, concern etched in her face. The realization that he hadn't cared whether he lived or died filled him with bottomless shame, made worse in that he wasn't certain yet whether he was glad he had lived.

"What is your name?" he asked, his voice soft and devoid of any real interest.

"Rachel Best."

"Rachel Best, I'd like you to leave me alone."

She looked at him another long moment before nodding and turning away.

Rachel softly closed the door feeling an inexplicable knot in her throat. She didn't want to feel sorry for Jared Mitchell. She didn't want to feel anything at all. But something in his eyes—or something not there at all—hurt her heart.

Chapter Three

∽

Truro was a desolate strip of land, twelve miles long and four miles across at its widest point, made up of rolling hills, sand dunes, and endless beaches on the ocean side, and marshes and meadowlands on the bay side. It was said that the people of Truro rarely smiled, had faces carved from the wind, and, if a stranger should happen upon them, spoke sparingly. From the time they took their first breaths out of the womb until the day they were buried in the sandy soil, they breathed salt-tinged air. The sea was what defined them, and it dictated nearly every facet of their lives. They were fishermen and boatbuilders and, like Rachel Best and her family, lifesavers and wreckers—people who plucked stranded sailors from their foundering ships, then profited from the salvaged cargo.

They were hearty, fearless folk who had stood fast against an incessant wind, stinging sand, and a land so barren it hurt the eye. A covering of tough, scraggly bushes growing no higher than a man's shin marked much of the town, as if the hearty plants of blueberry, huckleberry, and beach plum knew better than to try to grow tall. A few scrub pine, leaning as if perpetually pushed by the wind, were all that remained of the trees long ago cut down for houses and firewood.

Rachel Best loved every single bit of her Truro, even the sea that had swept her husband away. She stood staring at the lighthouse, cursing it for not doing its job the night Richard disappeared. She knew better, of course, than to blame the light. A hundred lights that night could not have prevented that ship from being drawn closer and closer to shore, the captain helpless against the driving currents and ever-shifting sandbars. She allowed herself to wish, foolishly she knew, that the whaleboat carrying that stinking, hairy behemoth had instead carried her husband home to her.

"Rachel Best, shame on you," she said aloud. After leaving her patient she'd gone immediately outside in an attempt to rid herself of the sudden urge to comfort him. It was testament to just how soft her heart was that an irritable man such as Jared Mitchell could garner such a sentiment. Her family had doctored dozens of men, all of whom had been suitably thankful to have been plucked from the sea. Perhaps it was that this man had been so very ill, she thought charitably, that he could not gather the strength to seem grateful.

But that wasn't it. Rachel was not so small-minded as to think ill of someone because he hadn't gushed his thanks. Something about the captain was untouchable, unfathomable. It hurt, somehow, to look into his eyes and see absolutely nothing. He was like her Truro, barren and unapproachable to a stranger but loved by those who knew it best. She smiled at her fanciful thoughts, wondering who had ever loved Jared Mitchell. She had seen something in his eyes for a fleeting moment, a glimpse into a place she was quite certain she didn't want to go.

Rachel let out a sigh and turned back toward

home. Captain Mitchell would be gone within a week or two and there would be another stranded sailor and then another. This stretch of the cape could see dozens of wrecks a year, and that meant someone had to look after those stranded sailors and passengers. There were so many shipwrecks that the Massachusetts Humane Society had built along the barren beaches dozens of charity houses containing foodstuffs and a fireplace and fuel for men and women who survived the wrecks. Two or three ships foundered somewhere on the cape every month, and a single storm could drive half a dozen ships ashore. He was just one man, one of many, Rachel reminded herself.

This man who seemed to dominate their little household would become a faint memory, someone she would think of sometimes and wonder about when she looked out at sea and saw a whaling bark.

At the door Rachel emptied her boots of sand by knocking them hard together, unconsciously keeping her back to the tiny cottage where she once lived with Richard. It had been too difficult for her to live there alone with Belle, so she had moved back in with her parents. She pulled on her boots, not bothering to lace them, and pushed open the plank door.

The Newcomb house was actually two buildings attached together. The original structure was a small cottage her father's parents had built more than fifty years before. It was a large, single room with a kitchen and sitting area divided by her mother's pride and joy, her Royal cookstove. Twenty years later, her own father had built a two-story saltbox behind the original cottage, cut a hole in the wall, and connected the two buildings with a short hall. Two bedrooms made up the bottom floor, and a third, with a severely slanting ceiling, made up the second floor.

Once, there had been more than enough children to fill those bedrooms—two brothers, dead now fourteen years, and four little ones who died before their first birthday. But the two sons, fishermen like their father, had died back in 'forty-one—among fifty-seven men who died in that terrible storm in George's Bank. Richard's father and brother had been among the dead, and so the orphaned ten-year-old boy had come to live with the Newcombs. Rachel had been just eight years old when Richard became a part of their family. He was a little boy who needed a mother and father, and the Newcombs were parents who desperately needed a son. It was inevitable that Rachel and Richard marry. On Rachel's eighteenth birthday she became Mrs. Richard Best. A year later she was a mother. And now, to everyone on Truro, a young widow.

"How is the captain?" she asked her mother as she bent to tie her boots. Mabel stepped from the sink where she'd been washing the morning dishes, her white apron spotted with dishwater. She nodded toward the stack of dripping dishes and turned back to the sink to continue scrubbing an iron pan that had fried their eggs since Rachel was a little girl. Rachel walked to the counter, grabbed her apron from her hook and tied it on, then took up a rag and began swiping at the drying dishes.

"Your father went in to check on him," Mabel said.

Just then the sound of loud cursing came from their patient's room, and then Ambrose's voice boomed: "By God, I don't like wiping another man's arse any more than you like another man wiping your arse." He continued in a softer tone, apparently aware of just how loud he'd been shouting, for all the two women could hear then was muffled words. Rachel and her mother looked at each other, their eyes twinkling in good humor. They immediately sobered and went about their business when they heard the door open.

"The captain wants a bath," Ambrose said with a scowl. "About to faint dead away, but he wants a bath." He continued mumbling under his breath as he took up a deep bucket and went outside to the outdoor pump.

When he returned, Mabel said, "Well, you can't fault a man for wanting a bath."

Her father grunted and poured a good portion of the water into an enormous pot, then opened the stove and stoked the coals.

"I'll be needing far more than that to get our man Captain Mitchell smelling sweet," he grumbled, eyeing the inadequate pot.

Rachel wrinkled her nose at the memory of the captain's stench and laughed. "Do you need help with the bath, Papa?"

Ambrose raised his eyebrows, and Rachel blushed hotly when she realized her father had misunderstood her. "I meant do you need help lugging the tub into his room."

He waved a hand at her as he left the room, and Rachel sighed. "He thinks he's still a young man."

"Oh, he knows exactly what he is, Rachel," her mother said softly. "He just doesn't want to give in to it."

There were days when Ambrose's joints were so swollen and painful he could hardly walk. It hurt to see him in such pain, and hurt even more when he refused to admit he needed help. But when Ambrose rolled the large brass-and-oak tub down the hall and to her daughter's room, he did so with ease. That brass tub was another treasure found on the beach, once part of a wealthy captain's stateroom. It—and hundreds of other items—had washed up onshore from a wreck off Truro four years before. Rachel still remembered the glow in her mother's eyes when

Ambrose pulled their handcart into the yard, the gleaming tub in the back. The ship's name—the *Georgina*—was engraved along the rim.

The Newcomb house was practically furnished with items found on Truro's beaches, including their mahogany dining table, which Rachel's mother polished each Saturday. It had once had a large hole cut into one end for the mizzen mast to fit through, but her father had cut the mast down. Around the rich table was hodgepodge of chairs, some of which they had actually paid for. Only two were gifts from the sea.

To Jared, the sight of that large brass-and-oak bathtub was as thrilling as the sight of a sperm whale's fluke twenty yards off the leeward bow. Well, perhaps not. But he was damned sick of smelling his own stench and could only imagine what he must smell like to the amazingly clean inhabitants of this house. He'd never in his life seen a pack of cleaner, healthier folk. They bristled with energy, with skin that glowed with good health, and eyes that were clear and lively. Next to them he felt like a filthy, lumbering, sickly bear in a house of sprightly, sparkly elves. And far older than the man now shoving the tub into the center of the room.

"I'm heating up the water," Ambrose said, moving his sharp-eyed gaze over Jared's head. "Didn't see any vermin in that mass on your head."

Jared felt his cheeks grow hot under the old man's perusal and hated his weakness. He hadn't given a damn what anyone thought of him in years. But for some reason this little old man with his homespun shirt and baggy pants made him feel ashamed. He stared at the ceiling.

"Would you object to a haircut and shave, then?"

"No."

"I'll go get the shears and razor. Can you make it to that chair on your own?"

"Yes," Jared said, even though he realized he

might not be able to. Hell, he hadn't been able to wipe himself, he'd been so weak. After Ambrose left the room, Jared eyed the chair. Getting into it meant taking perhaps three steps. Small steps, at that. He sat up slowly, keeping a blanket about him in case one of the women entered the room. He willed the room to stop spinning and silently commanded his body to stop shaking. He swung his legs over the side of the bed and rested, almost laughing that he even needed to rest. In all his life, Jared had never felt this weak. He'd spent four years on a whaler working until he'd thought he'd drop, and then working more. Through fevers and coughs that racked his body he worked, never giving in to exhaustion, never failing to captain his ship. Now he wasn't certain he could make it to a chair that was nearly close enough to touch.

Hell and damnation.

Perhaps if he reached out far enough, he could grasp the back of the chair and fall into it, he thought. Jared leaned forward and touched the seat with his fingertips, his other hand clutching the mattress for support. Sweat began to drip from his forehead, down his face, to his chin, and to the floor, and the shaking grew to an almost violent tremor that racked his body.

"You're a stubborn one," Ambrose said, dropping the shears and shaving paraphernalia next to the chair.

He stood there staring at Jared, hands on hips, until Jared growled out, "Well, are you going to help me, old man?"

Strong, wiry arms were thrust beneath his arms, and Jared felt himself lifted from the bed. He had just enough strength to help the old man, for he doubted Ambrose could have lifted him entirely. When he reached the chair, he fell into it with a shaking breath.

Without a word, Ambrose began cutting away the long strands of matted hair.

"Have to go short to get all this out," he said finally.

"Do it. Please." Jared closed his eyes and tried to forget the last time he'd had his hair cut for him, but could not. He still remembered her fingers, cool on his neck and on his cheek as she moved his head this way and that, her face growing more and more horrified the larger the pile of hair around him grew. Abigail had done a terrible job, leaving one side longer than the other, cutting his bangs at an odd angle that gave him a rather deranged look. They'd laughed so hard that tears had squeezed from his eyes and she'd nearly busted her whalebone busk. How Abigail could laugh. And then he'd tried his best to repair the damage, not even pretending she'd done well.

It had been the last time she'd cut his hair. The last time he'd laughed until he cried.

"Now the beard," Ambrose said, pulling and tugging on his whiskers, cutting with the shears until it was close enough to shave.

"Want a mustache? Muttonchops?"

He shook his head. "Sideburns to here," he said, pointing a dirt-encrusted finger to about a half inch below his earlobe. He wanted it all off.

Ambrose worked quickly, but even so, Jared was beginning to feel exhaustion seep into his bones. He could hardly keep his head steady as Ambrose shaved away the last of his beard. The old man stood back and stared at the result. "You look human," he pronounced, and Jared felt a smile tug at his lips.

Ambrose disappeared to fill up the tub, coming and going four times—two buckets of hot, two of cold—before helping him into the tub. Getting into the tub was far more difficult than moving to the chair, but the two finally managed it, sloshing only a bit of water over the side when Jared fell rather heavily into the bath.

"Christ," he muttered, disgusted by his weakness. He didn't think he'd have the strength to wash his own body, but he couldn't bring himself to ask for more help. When Ambrose held out the soap and cloth to him, Jared stared at the items as if they were a hundred miles away and completely unattainable. He willed himself to raise his arm, to take the offering, but he could not do it.

Without a word, Ambrose dunked the cloth into the water and soaped it up. Jared could feel his cheeks heat, the humiliation of another man washing him unmanning. And yet he was grateful it was this man bathing him and not the young woman, with her blue-and-gold eyes that seemed to so easily see beyond his carefully erected shield. The soap created a floral-scented white lather, and Jared's nostrils twitched.

"A hundred crates of scented soaps washed up last winter. Never saw so many happy women," Ambrose said, chuckling as he moved the cloth to Jared's back. He scrubbed mercilessly and impersonally, attacking his charge as if he were sanding the bottom of a skiff. When he was finished scouring every inch of flesh, he took out his penknife and pared and cleaned Jared's fingernails and toenails. Jared hadn't been so clean since the day he left New Bedford more than four years ago. He was as weak as a baby and now as clean.

"Can you stand?"

The feeling of helplessness must have shown clearly in Jared's eyes, for Ambrose moved behind him and put his arms beneath Jared's. "On the count of three. Ready." Jared nodded even though he was not ready. He was exhausted, ready to slump forward into the now-cool water, but he knew this little old man would not have the strength to lift him as deadweight. He took a deep breath and tried to heave himself up on the count of three, but he felt the blood rush to his head, the room spin crazily, before everything went black.

The two women in the kitchen froze when they heard the crash, then rushed as one to the bedroom, looking down when their shoes sloshed into water seeping beneath the door. Mabel opened the door to find Captain Mitchell faceup and flat out on top of her husband, who lay pinned to the floor in a pool of water.

"Need help?"

"A bit."

Her mother stood there awhile, enjoying the sight of her husband so helpless and in such an awkward position before quickly covering the captain's middle with a blanket. "How on earth did this happen?" she said, her voice laced with laughter.

"He's as weak as a newborn but thought he could make it to that bed. Got enough pride to fill an empty hull, that man."

While her mother went about trying to heave the captain off her husband, Rachel stood in the doorway, rooted to the spot, staring at the most beautiful male body she'd ever seen. It was true that the only other man she'd seen in his altogether was her husband. But she instinctively knew she was looking at something few women had ever seen—perfection in the male form. He was all muscle and fine, sunbronzed skin except for a sharp tan line where his pants began, peeking just above the blanket her mother had so hastily thrown. Rachel darted her eyes away quickly from that area to let them travel down his finely formed legs and to his highly arched feet. He did indeed look like a giant felled. A perfectly sculpted, well-muscled giant.

"Rachel. We could use your help, dear," her mother said, giving her a knowing and slightly censorious look that made her cheeks redden instantly.

"Oh. Of course," she said, moving quickly to the other side of Captain Mitchell. And that was when her breath stopped. This man lying on her daughter's bedroom floor could not be the same man who had washed up onto their beach. It wasn't quite fair that a man with such a body could have been blessed with such a face. With his hair short and his beard gone, a man who was beyond handsome had emerged from her father's ministrations. Beneath the grime that had made his hair appear black were softly curling chocolate brown locks. His cheeks were lean, his lashes long and straight. His nose was straight, his mouth . . . She looked away. Why she suddenly found looking at a man's mouth forbidden, she didn't know.

Her hand fluttered above him; she was suddenly unwilling to touch him. In an instant he'd gone from a patient to a man.

"I'll likely die under here if you don't get him off," her father said in a growl. Rachel blinked and blushed again, knowing she'd been caught staring.

"I hardly recognize him," she said to explain her sudden interest in the captain.

"You turned him human, Ambrose," Mabel said. "No doubt we'll be getting a fair amount of female visitors." She chuckled, and Rachel had to force herself to join in the laughter. She didn't find the thought of women ogling the captain at all amusing.

Like her mother, she placed one hand beneath his shoulders and the other at midback, telling herself she didn't notice how warm and smooth his skin felt beneath her hands, how solid he seemed. He had not a single ounce of excess flesh despite his large size.

"Let's pick him up," Mabel said, and she and Rachel lifted with all their strength, getting him just high enough for her father to wriggle out from underneath him. Jared mumbled something indiscernible when his head thunked rather loudly back to the floor.

"He's a solid one," Ambrose said, gazing down at the man sprawled on the floor. "Do you think you girls are up to getting him into that bed? I'll get his torso; you two get his legs."

Rachel flushed. The thought of wrapping her arms around one of his solid, hairy thighs so close to his male member made her feel intensely uncomfortable.

"I've a better idea. I'll get one arm, Papa, you the other. We'll drag him onto the bed and then swing his legs on."

Ambrose grunted his agreement and the two struggled to get a good hold on him, for he was still slippery from the soapy water he lay in. Mabel moved frantically behind them to make certain the bedcovers were protected by old blankets. With much tugging, the family finally had him on the bed, if a bit cockeyed.

Rachel ended up on the bed, having dragged while her father pushed him onto the mattress. She was crawling over him when he opened his eyes, his startlingly green eyes. He seemed to look right through her.

"She's crying," he said quite clearly, before his eyes fluttered closed and he fell into a sound sleep.

Rachel furrowed her brows and crawled over him and off the bed, holding her father's forearm for assistance. She was still puzzling over his words when she heard her daughter's heart-wrenching sobs.

Chapter Four

✐

Rachel kissed her daughter's knee just above the bandage that hid a scrape a twelve-year-old boy would have been proud of.

"All better," she said, looking up into her daughter's tearstained face. "Now perhaps you won't try to climb any more trees with Darius Paine."

When Rachel had come upon her daughter, the girl had only recently discovered that her knee was streaming blood. It was the sight of that blood more than any pain she felt that brought forth the cries of pure terror. It was all Rachel could do not to smile at her daughter's horrified expression as she pointed to her bloody leg.

"But then Darius will call me a sissy," Belle complained.

"It's all right for a girl to be a sissy," Mabel called over from the counter where she was pounding a large blob of dough into submission.

Rachel kissed her daughter's nose. "Just try to be more careful." Rachel had grown up the youngest, a lone girl amidst two rambunctious boys, so she knew even girls could take affront at being called a sissy.

"How is the giant?" Belle asked.

"Captain Mitchell," Rachel corrected. "And he's sleeping."

"He's still sleeping?" She moaned the words as if saying, *Santa's not coming this year?*

"He's taken a bath and gotten all worn out."

"Oh, goody. Then he won't stink anymore," Belle said as she hopped off the table and immediately headed to their patient.

"Oh, no, you don't, young lady. Let Captain Mitchell sleep."

Belle looked as if she was about to argue, then swung around, her silky blond hair flying about her head. "I'm going upstairs to play," she announced, and stomped up the stairs.

The two women worked silently together for several minutes, kneading the dough and forming loaves.

"Belle is certainly taken with him," Mabel said.

"She thinks he's a giant. He told her so himself, so she says." Rachel opened the oven to check the temperature, then added half a shovelful of coal. "I'll be glad when he's gone, that one."

"When who's gone?" Belle said, running through the room toward the front door. The little girl's effort to braid her own hair was already coming undone, and Rachel felt a fresh wave of love for her child. "Captain Mitchell's not gone, is he?"

"Isabelle," Rachel said in a long-beleaguered voice. "Captain Mitchell is still here and he's sleeping. He's not going anywhere for some time. I don't want you in there bothering him like before."

Belle looked at her mother solemnly. "I wasn't bothering him. I was just visiting."

"I know, Belle. But sometimes a visit can bother."

Belle thought about that for a minute. "I think he almost smiled at me." With that, she ran out the door again.

Rachel heaved a sigh.

"She's just like you, you know," Mabel said fondly. "I remember one night just before Christmas there was a wreck off the lighthouse. It wasn't much of a blow, but so bitter cold. My goodness, I can still remember how my cheeks burned that night. We saved a shipful of men, brought them to shore, warmed them up. Each family took one or two. We brought home Elmer Primmel and you fell in love at first sight."

"Mama, I've heard this story a hundred times. Elmer Primmel was nothing like Captain Mitchell. He was a gentleman."

"Bit of a fop, if you ask me. Those dandy clothes of his."

"He was a passenger, not a seaman," Rachel said, feeling herself being drawn into an argument she'd had with her mother at least a dozen times. "And I was seven, for goodness' sake."

"Belle is five. This is her Elmer."

Rachel's father came into the room, sweeping off his hat to reveal a mostly bald head. He was a small man, but tough and with a face so lively, you could tell a tale from every wrinkle. Which was fortunate, for Ambrose Newcomb rarely spoke more than a few words at a time. "Getting colder," he said, peeling off his coat.

"Getting older," came Mabel's oft-said reply.

"Still sleeping?" he said, shooting a glance toward the bedrooms.

"Still." When Mabel spoke with her husband, she tended to mimic his style of speech. Rachel didn't know whether it was intentional or unconscious, but there were times when they would hardly exchange more than a few words but volumes were spoken.

"Chances are Mr. Small will be by later," Mabel

said. "No doubt the whole town's near to bursting with curiosity about the captain. Not every day a lone man washes ashore."

Ambrose grunted. Rachel smiled, struck suddenly by how wonderful sameness could be, and just as suddenly she felt that emptiness that had started years ago bloom inside her. She and Richard had never been so easy with each other. Their silences were painful, obvious, leaving Rachel feeling somehow lacking and slightly bewildered. Before their marriage, she and Richard had been the grandest friends. But after, she'd found herself trying to fill the silences with chatter and could see her husband turning inward. Sometimes, when she was feeling particularly low, she'd imagine that Richard hadn't gone into the surf at all, but had simply disappeared while she was talking to him.

She wanted—needed—for him to come back so she could prove to him that she could be whatever he needed her to be. Her Richard, with his wispy blond hair, his solemn brown eyes, and his faraway looks. He always seemed so unhappy, a sadness she couldn't begin to touch, and she once asked in frustrated anger if he wished he'd been with his brother and father the day they had died in 'forty-one. It was the only time she'd seen Richard truly angry. He'd screamed at her that she didn't know him, that she knew nothing of what was in his heart, and he'd slammed out the door. Later he'd returned and said he was sorry for shouting. But he hadn't said he was sorry for his words.

A loud thump coming from their patient's room shook her memories away. "I'll go," she said, taking up a cloth and wiping her hands free of flour and dough. When she opened the door to the sickroom, she found Jared sitting on the floor, a sheet blessedly covering him, looking frustrated and angry and as weary as a man could and still have his eyes open.

Jared nearly groaned when he looked up and saw that yellow apron standing in front of him. He was shaking and trying not to show it. All he'd wanted to do was relieve himself, but he'd discovered he couldn't even manage that.

"Oh, Captain, what on earth were you trying to do?"

He watched her sturdy-booted feet step toward him, heard the rustle of her crisply clean skirt, smelled the intoxicating odor of flour and yeast and home, and wanted to growl at her like a wounded grizzly. So that was what he did.

"I was trying to take a piss," he said, purposely blunt. *Go away, pretty, clean woman.* He breathed in deeply just to torture himself.

He could almost feel the anger emanating from her, though he hadn't even looked up at her yet.

"Should I get my father?" Her voice was even, painfully controlled.

"If you could slide the pot over to me, I can manage," he said, knowing it came out sounding like an order. He heard her puff out a sigh before doing as he asked.

"Are you certain I shouldn't get my father to help you?" Jared half suspected she was trying to goad him.

His eyes still staring at her crisp yellow apron, he ground out, "As I said, I can manage." And he did manage once she left, though his show of independence cost him a great deal. He was shaking like a palsied old man by the time he hoisted himself back onto the bed, and was just covering himself when he heard the knock.

"May I come in?"

The young woman again. He couldn't remember her name, only that she smelled like heaven might.

"Enter."

He never would have called out that word had he known that in her wake would be that little girl. He immediately turned his head toward the wall. Good God, was she trying to torture him? He closed his eyes and willed them both away.

"Hello." That small voice cut a hole in his gut.

"I'm sleeping," he said, keeping his voice low and menacing.

The little thing giggled. "You're not. You're talking."

"Belle, I think he wants to be alone. Come along now."

He felt a cool, small hand on his forearm, then a tiny whisper close to his ear. "You don't really want me to go, do you, Mr. Giant?"

Jared swallowed hard. *Go away. Go away.* He squeezed his eyes shut and fought the urge to put his hands over his ears even though he knew he couldn't muffle the screams he heard in his head. His hand fisted, bunching the blanket beneath his palm.

"Belle, leave Captain Mitchell be."

He heard an urgency in the woman's voice, almost as if she was frightened for her daughter. As if he would harm her child. He turned his head and couldn't help but smile when he saw Belle's face not three inches away, her eyes large and curious, her little nose perfect. She had not a smidgen of fear. They stared at each other for a long moment, the girl's mother obviously nervous and undecided hovering behind.

"He wants me to stay, Mama," Belle said, and her eyes turned into half-moons.

"It's all right," he said, finally looking past the girl to her mother. She stood there, her eyes filled with worry and indecision. He closed his eyes briefly. "Truly, let her stay."

He watched with amazement as the woman's mouth curved up into the gentlest of smiles. She bent to Belle, placing a hand on her little girl's shoulder. "Not too long. Even giants get tired." She gave him a look of thanks, one that melted a bit of the ice around his heart.

"All right, Mama."

He fell asleep to a little girl's chatter.

Rachel could tell he was awake by the way he clutched the bedcovers, his knuckles white, the muscles in his arm bunched and straining. He looked ridiculously big in her daughter's bed, his wide shoulders nearly as broad as the feather mattress beneath him.

"I've brought you your clothes, Captain." She watched as his fist grew tighter, then relaxed. "I'm afraid they are in terrible condition, but we did our best to clean and repair them." He didn't turn to look at her offering, and Rachel grew uncomfortable standing there, holding the clothes out to a man who had not yet acknowledged her presence. "I've begun sewing another shirt for you so you'll have something decent to wear when you return home."

He turned toward her finally, his eyes steady on hers, making Rachel fight a sudden and nearly overpowering urge to flee. He frightened her, she realized, and she wondered fleetingly if he enjoyed his ability to do so.

"I've forgotten your name," he said.

She cleared her throat unnecessarily. "Rachel Best."

"Thank you, Rachel Best." He turned his head to stare at the ceiling.

"I'll just put your things on this chair. I don't expect you need help." Silence.

Rachel stared at him, the beginnings of a rare flare of temper growing. For some reason his silence made her want to talk more, and she realized guiltily that she'd done the same thing to Richard a hundred times. The more silent her husband became, the more talkative she became. Once she'd tried to play his game and didn't utter a meaningful word for an entire day. By the time it was night, she was about to burst at the seams and let forth a rush of angry words to a husband who had been completely oblivious to the fact that she'd been uncommonly quiet.

"Why do you feel the need to express aloud every single thought that comes into your head?" he'd asked with real curiosity.

As she recognized where her anger came from, Rachel did her best to tamp it down. This man might be big and strong as an ox when well, but there was also something about him that made her already soft heart turn to mush.

"Do you want something to eat? Ma's made a nice fish chowder. My father caught some bass earlier today out on the sand bank." She stopped and waited and watched his great chest rise and fall, his hand clutching the bedcovers once again.

"Is it always so damned windy here?" he asked abruptly.

"Well, yes. I hardly notice it, but yes, there's always a fair wind blowing."

"It never stops," he whispered.

Rachel moved to the bedside and knelt down, hesitating only a moment before placing a hand on his. "What is wrong, Captain?" He clutched at her hand so hard, Rachel winced. She watched as his throat convulsed.

"I need a drink," he said at last, and with a harshness that surprised Rachel. "I need a damn drink now."

Rachel removed her hand from his, struck hard by how disappointed she was by his demand. "We have no spirits in this house."

Jared rubbed his eyes with the heels of his hands as if overcome with weariness. "Surely I had some left in my whaleboat."

"There were two bottles left. Obed and Oren, men who helped drag you ashore, took the bottles."

He sat up with a violence that sent Rachel skittering to the door. "They had no right," he said, his voice snapping like a sail in a gale.

"They saved your life," Rachel said softly, listening in vain for her mother's footsteps before remembering that she and Belle gone visiting old Mrs. Potter bearing a gift of steaming fish chowder.

"They had no right to do that either," he said, but much of the bluster was gone, and he almost seemed embarrassed.

Rachel moved a hand behind her to search for the latch. When she found it, she swiftly opened the door and turned quickly to leave.

"Mrs. Best."

She closed her eyes, her body poised to flee. "Yes, Captain?"

"Please turn around."

She did, but her hand remained on the door.

"I've been at sea for nearly five years. It's not an excuse for my poor behavior. I . . ." He moved his hands in a helpless gesture. "I didn't mean to frighten you."

She didn't deny that he had, and he offered her the smallest of smiles.

"I'm simply a mean cuss. Captain of the roughest, meanest crew on the seven seas, with a reputation that would send most ladies running."

"He's right," her father said, entering the room. "Just talked with Donald Small. He's the lightkeep here. Said you're a legend in New Bedford. Said you brought in more sperm oil in a year than any captain before you."

A grin split the captain's face, and Rachel was stunned by the change it made in his appearance, even if the smile didn't quite touch his eyes. He went from handsome to mesmerizing. "I can smell a whale from ten miles out," he said, his smile revealing startlingly even white teeth.

"No doubt they could smell you, too," Rachel said, then instantly snapped her mouth shut, horrified that she'd said aloud something so rude.

His smile disappeared and he stared at her, a look that would have made a less hardy soul quake. "That was my secret, Mrs. Best," he said softly, and a shiver traveled up her spine.

"Would you like to know what happened to your ship and crew, Captain?" Ambrose asked, darting a quick look between his daughter and the captain before tossing Jared his drawers and pants. He settled himself into the chair with a weary groan.

"I would, sir."

"Mr. Small telegraphed New Bedford inquiring about your ship. Got a message back today that it made port a week ago with a hull full of whale oil. All the men are well and accounted for, but for their captain." Ambrose reached inside his pocket. " 'Captain's whereabouts unknown,' " he read.

Jared frowned, knowing he had a duty now to let his family know he was alive. No doubt West had gotten his mother in a frenzy with tales of how his big brother had turned mean like their father, how he'd grown so reckless some of his crew wondered if he enjoyed dancing with the Grim Reaper. The last time he'd seen West was in the middle of the Atlantic. He was home now, probably married to that girl he so obviously loved. The truth was, Jared's conscience—he did still have one—told him to contact his family, and he was only slightly irritated that the light-keeper had shot off that telegram. The man was only doing his duty by inquiring about a ship whose captain had washed ashore. He certainly couldn't take Jared's word that the ship was safe and heading to port.

"Have you a pen and paper?" he asked. "I have to send a telegram after all."

"I'll get it," Rachel said, and left the room.

When she returned, Jared was alone in the room and standing a bit shakily. He had his drawers and pants on and was frowning at their loose fit. "I think I'll be needing a dish of that chowder, Mrs. Best, if you don't mind." He looked up to find her staring at him. Or rather, staring *up* at him.

"I'm taller standing up," he said, dipping his head slightly, an unconscious attempt to put her at ease. Because he was feeling a bit unsteady on his feet, he sat on the edge of the bed before quickly pulling his shirt on and buttoning it.

She handed him a small lap desk. "There's paper, pen, and ink inside."

He opened the desk, taking out what he needed, and wrote, *Mother am well in Truro Cape Cod Jared.*

He handed over the note to Rachel. "If you could bring this to the telegraph office."

Rachel glanced at the cryptic note. "That's all you're going to write?"

"My mother likely thinks me dead. When she receives this note, she will realize she's been mistaken. It is sufficient."

The woman gave him a look of disbelief. "She'll be insane with worry. Perhaps . . ." She grabbed up the pen, dipped it in the ink, and scribbled something along the bottom. "Here."

With narrowed eyes, Jared took the note. She'd written, *Love to all. Be home soon.*

"No." His good humor was gone, taken quite efficiently by this meddlesome woman. "The pen, please." He couldn't quite believe it when she backed away from him and shoved the pen behind her back.

"When your child is missing, when you think they are dead, it's a terrible thing. Two of my brothers died at sea and it nearly destroyed my parents. First came the hope that they might be alive, then the horror that they had died. Nothing could be worse than losing a child or even believing you have."

Jared's entire body grew hot and his eyes became hard. "Don't lecture me on my obligations. And don't presume to believe I need a lecture. Now give me the cursed pen," he said in a low, menacing voice.

Rachel, her eyes wide and again filled with wariness, held out the pen in a hand that trembled. Jared let out an irritated sigh. "You needn't fear me," he nearly shouted.

Rachel blinked. "Then stop frightening me."

He scratched out her words, anger in every stroke.

"You like frightening people," Rachel persisted, and Jared nearly let out a groan. "You, Captain Mitchell, are a bully."

He nodded. "Yes, I am."

"And bullies are always cowards," she said, and her eyes widened as if she knew she'd stepped over a line. What a brave, foolish woman.

Jared grew still. "You have found me out, Mrs. Best. How very perceptive of you. Now that we understand each other, perhaps you will leave me be, as I have asked on more than one occasion."

"I'm sorry. I didn't mean—"

Jared shook his head. "Ah, but you did mean what you said. And I'll not argue with you." He handed over the piece of paper, looking at the scratched-out part and disliking intensely the sense of shame that washed over him. Rachel took it from him in blessed silence, slowly departing from the room and closing the door quietly behind her.

Chapter Five

≈

He hadn't seen the woman—Rachel—in three days, but he could still hear her outraged voice daring to tell him what it was like to lose a child. As if he would have to imagine such a thing. As if when the wind shrieked over the dunes and swirled around this drafty old house he didn't hear his daughter's screams.

It had been a blessing, really, when little Mary died, when her cries of pain diminished to whimpers, when finally, finally there was silence.

They had been out to sea nearly two years, he and Abigail and their new daughter, when he harpooned the largest sperm whale God had created. He'd been so full of himself, so proud, so damn ready to show off to his delicate little wife and happy little daughter what a big, important man he was. So he'd done something he never should have—he allowed them on deck to watch the boiling of the blubber. He knew it was dangerous, so he'd cautioned Abigail to stand back, away from the slickest part of the deck, away from the tryworks where great chunks of blubber were placed. But Abigail didn't know of the dangers, and she'd always had more curiosity than sense. And she'd been trying to show him that this whaling life, this life she'd begun to hate, was still an adventure to her. Abigail never saw her own limitations. She was so tiny a good wind would have ripped her from the deck. But she pictured herself at the helm in the middle of a gale, climbing masts and dropping sails. He loved this in her, loved her courage even as he feared it.

On that day the seas were rough, making the boiling even more hazardous than usual. He should have banned her from the deck, but he liked having her there, liked knowing her eyes followed him about the deck. It happened quickly, a large chunk of blubber, a pitching ship, a great splash of scorching hot whale oil. And then screams of agony from his wife and six-month-old daughter. Mary died after four days; Abigail lingered for three weeks, begging him and God to end her life. The day he slid that tiny little shape into the depths of the Pacific, Jared ceased to live. He could still remember standing on the deck, his face buffeted by the wind, as he watched his daughter's body fall into the sea, feeling as if his very soul were being ripped from him.

He could not drink his pain away, or work it away, or scream it away. It lived with him, filling up the place where his soul used to be, eating at him, beating him down. Because he'd known better than to allow Abigail and their little baby on deck during a boiling. His pride had killed them. He had killed them.

For as long as he could remember, he had been the responsible one. Even when his father was captain and he the cabin boy, he had taken it upon himself to stop his father from his cruelties. He'd been the only one to take on his father head-on, the only one his father would listen to, the only one his father loved. He'd protected the crew, his own brother, his mother, from a father no one understood but him.

He'd grown big and burly, a strapping young man who had captained his own whaler when only twenty. It was not self-pity that drove Jared to blame himself for the deaths of his wife and child, but the law of the sea. A captain was responsible for everything that happened on his ship, and it shamed him that he had failed in this simplest of duties. It was a weight he would carry for the rest of his life, a burden of grief and guilt he didn't even want to shake off. It was his penance.

Mary would have been seven years old this spring. She would have had his green eyes, her mother's light brown hair. She would have flung her arms about his neck, clutching him with all her little might. He hadn't thought about her grown up; Mary had stayed as she was in his mind, a chubby little baby who smiled at him when he made funny faces. But seeing Belle every day created a picture in his mind of what Mary might have looked like had she lived. Belle had become his bedside companion, her constant chatter a source of wonder to him. He knew he looked fierce with his scowls and beard-darkened face, but she was dauntless.

The day she'd placed her hand in his something deep inside him gave way, like a sturdy sail finally tearing in a fearsome wind. She led him to the dinner table, all full of importance, and told him to sit beside her. He felt like some big oaf, the lumbering giant her vivid imagination had created.

Jared looked about him, feeling awkward to be dining with this family, and noticing for the first time that Mrs. Best's husband was not among them. He assumed that he was a fisherman out to sea for a few days.

"Glad to see you up and about, Captain," Mabel said.

Jared nodded at the woman in answer. She was a

stout lady with iron-gray hair and fading brown eyes that held a smile in them even when she scowled. The family joined hands and Jared felt a tug on his wrist, giving up his hand reluctantly to the persistent Belle. His other hand remained in his lap.

"You're supposed to join hands, Captain," Belle said in a whisper loud enough for all to hear.

Rachel felt her cheeks redden. She hadn't seen the captain since her ridiculous lecture to him, managing to be conveniently out of the house whenever he required nursing. She offered up her thanks to God when he recovered enough to care for himself. It would be only a matter of days before he was gone forever. She didn't know why, but his presence in their home made her feel distinctly uneasy, and holding his hand even for grace felt unseemly. She had seen him naked, after all. She had touched his warm, solid flesh with her bare hand, let her eyes drift slowly down the glorious expanse of smooth, unclothed, bronzed man. If she reacted to him, it meant only that she was a woman and he a man. A beautiful man.

Jared raised his hand with obvious reluctance and she hesitated, darting a look to him, and pausing when she saw one of his dark eyebrows quirk up in question. *Why aren't you holding my hand, Mrs. Best?* he seemed to say. *What are you afraid of?*

Stiffening her back, she placed her hand in his and was immediately beset by the most horrifying of physical reactions. She nearly jerked her hand away but his grasp tightened slightly, his warm, solid, manly grasp. Rachel swallowed.

"Mommy. Say grace."

"For that which we are about to receive we thank you, Lord, amen," she said in a rush, pulling her hand away the moment her tongue pressed out the *n* in *amen.*

Rachel dared a look to the captain and wished immediately she had not. His expression was so intense, so blatantly male, Rachel felt her face flush once again. It was almost as if he knew exactly what her body had done when she touched his hand.

Her mother began scooping dumplings out of the pot to reveal her thick chicken stew, plopping them on their plates. "Got your appetite back, Captain Mitchell?"

From the corner of her eye, she saw him rub a tanned hand across his flat stomach. "Yes, ma'am, I believe it has returned." He held out his plate with a steady hand, though Rachel sensed it took an effort to do so.

"Mommy. Do I have to eat the carrots?"

"Yes, Belle."

"They're mushy."

"Eat your carrots."

Poor Belle did as she was told, but put on a great show of gagging after every bite. Jared leaned over to her.

"If you bury them in the dumpling, you hardly notice them," he said, then demonstrated his technique. Belle watched, her brow furrowed in concentration. Rachel watched, too, until she realized she'd become entirely too fascinated by the way his mouth closed over his spoon.

"It's warm in here," Rachel said in an attempt to explain her pink cheeks. What the devil was wrong with her?

"You do look a bit warm," Mabel said over the gagging sounds of her granddaughter.

"It didn't work," Belle complained. "I can still taste them."

"Oh, Belle, just eat around them, then," Rachel said, sounding harassed.

"But then I'll go blind," Belle said, popping in another of the offending vegetables and scrunching up her face. Rachel was thankful her daughter's plate was now carrot-free.

"I expect you'll be heading home soon, Captain," Rachel said to break the silence that formed.

"Rachel, the poor man can hardly make it to the dinner table," Mabel said, clearly chastising her daughter.

"I wasn't suggesting he leave tonight. I believe I said 'soon.'"

Mabel gave her daughter a cross look, which Rachel chose to ignore. She was feeling out of sorts, and she wanted the captain to leave so her mind could be at peace. She didn't like that she noticed his hands, that he made her blush. What would Richard think of her now if he knew? That thought only made her mood darker.

"Too bad Daddy won't ever get to meet the captain," Belle said, and the silence that hit the table was almost tangible.

"Where is Mr. Best?" Jared inquired politely, looking from one downcast face to the next.

"In heaven," Belle said sadly. "He got killed trying to save the sailors."

Rachel stood abruptly, her chair scraping back on the plank floor. "Mama!" Rachel said, glaring at Mabel.

"It's not right, what you're doing, Rachel," Mabel said, staring into her chicken and dumplings. "Tell her, Ambrose."

Ambrose looked mighty uncomfortable at being pitted between mother and daughter. "Your mother's got a point," he mumbled, then scooped up a large mouthful.

"Mama pretends Daddy's still alive," Belle said to Jared, who was looking more and more uncomfortable with each word uttered by this family. "She was looking for Daddy, but found you instead."

Oh, my God. Rachel had never in her life felt more humiliated. "I must apologize, Captain. My daughter—"

Jared held up a hand to stop her. "No need to explain, Mrs. Best."

"Did I do something bad?" Belle asked, her eyes wide with worry. She was such a sensitive little girl, and Rachel felt terrible about what she'd been inadvertently doing to her daughter. She hadn't told Belle her daddy was dead; she'd refused to attend the funeral service her parents had insisted on. But how could she tell her daughter that her daddy was dead if Rachel believed that he might be alive? What if Richard walked through the door one evening? It hadn't been that long. Only three months. He could be alive, she thought. Rachel hadn't known that Belle was aware of her daily vigils on the beach, or that she'd held on to a thread of hope that Richard was still alive. Neither had she gone to her daughter and told her the truth of what had happened. She simply could not bring herself to do what her mother had obviously done.

"No, Belle. Of course you did nothing bad."

Her little face screwed up the way it always did before she let out a torrent of tears. "I want Daddy," she wailed, and Rachel's heart broke, even though she knew Belle was putting on a bit of a show. It didn't help that her mother was shooting her a look that said, *Do you see what you've done to your little girl?*

She thought she heard Jared mutter something like "Aw, hell" under his breath as he listened to Belle's heart-wrenching sobs, his face taking on a slightly panicked look. Rachel rushed to Belle's side and hugged her close.

"Daddy is up in heaven, honey, just like Grandma said. He . . . he died that day and God took him home." It was the hardest thing Rachel had ever said, because for some reason it felt like a lie. "When I walk along the beach I'm not looking for Daddy; I'm remembering him." Rachel picked her up, cuddling her close as she used to when Belle was tiny, and walked her to the room they shared. "Do you remember how Daddy used to fish? How he'd take a big ol' bullfrog and throw it into the water and come back with a fish for supper?"

She could feel her daughter's head nod, and she continued her soothing talk all the way up the stairs.

After Belle had settled down and fallen asleep, Rachel walked down the hall, feeling her way in the dark, and paused when she saw a light coming from the captain's room. Closing her eyes, she summoned the courage to knock. As always, he called out a gruff "Enter."

He was sitting up in bed, fully clothed, a book in his lap—*Moby-Dick* of all things. He held it up and chuckled. She liked the sound and almost told him so before coming to her senses.

"I got that for my father for Christmas two years ago. It took me almost that long to read it to him. His eyes are so bad, he can't read that small print." Rachel sat in the room's only chair, her hands folded in her lap. "I want to apologize for that scene."

"There's no need."

"It's been three months and I still look," she said, opening her palms on her lap, a gesture that told him she knew that part of her was a bit crazy.

"Is what your daughter said true? Did you find me?"

"Yes."

"And you thought perhaps I was . . ."

Rachel let out a puff of air. "Yes. Perhaps."

Jared was silent for a long moment, his long, blunt fingers moving along the edge of the book. She watched, fascinated that hands so big would appear somehow graceful and refined when holding a book.

"Well, I'll let you read." Rachel stood. "Good night."

She was at the door when he spoke.

"Sometimes, even when we know they are dead, even when we've seen their bodies, a part of us hopes that it's all been a lie, some hoax played on us by God or the devil." He looked up at her and she felt pulled into the green depths of his eyes.

"Good night, Captain," she said, and let herself out the door.

Her mother and father were sitting by the stove when she entered the kitchen. "Sorry I didn't help clean up," she said. "I'm going outside for a bit." She walked out the door before either could say a word, feeling an overwhelming need to be alone. Rachel would talk to her mother later, tell her she was grateful that she'd told Belle her father was dead.

It was pitch dark out and the coldest night thus far, but Rachel was only vaguely aware of the frigid wind as she walked along the short, sandy path that connected her parents' house to the one she'd shared with Richard and Belle. Her little cottage always looked so mournful at night, dark and deserted. Rachel walked to the front door and pushed. It was much as she'd left it, but it was so cold inside, a cold that seeped into her bones and made her shiver.

It still seemed impossible to her that Richard was gone and that he would never return. Why couldn't everything have remained the same? She closed her eyes and tried to imagine how it was, hating that her stomach twisted with unhappy memories rather than the joyful ones she longed for. For though she wanted to recall happy evenings cozied up by the fire, the truth was that Richard patrolled the beach four nights a week, and spent the other three nights with his pals at the Mews Tavern. He rarely drank, but would sit and talk and smoke his pipe, cutting Rachel so completely out of his life that they'd become virtual strangers. And Rachel would tell herself things could be far worse: he could be a drunkard, or brutal and cruel. How could she complain when her husband's only sin was that he did not love her?

She could not remember what Richard looked like when he smiled, or how his voice sounded when he said he loved her.

Because he had never said those words. Never.

Once she had confided in her mother that she feared Richard didn't love her, and Mabel had simply smiled. "Your father doesn't need to say the words for me to know, Rachel." Rachel didn't say it then, but her mind screamed that she didn't know whether Richard loved her. And she was too frightened to come out and ask him for fear of what he would say.

Rachel stepped farther into their cottage. She sat at her little table, her hands folded in front of her, and stared blindly at the chair where her husband always sat, willing him to be there. "You're not coming back, are you, Richard?" she whispered. Rachel let out a long breath, then flattened her hands on the table and pushed herself up, wanting to cry because she knew even as she said those words aloud that she couldn't bring herself to believe them.

Chapter Six

When he had thought Rachel married, when Jared had pictured a husband somewhere waiting for his wife to come to him, it had been easy to shut off that part of him that desired her. Jared drew a sharp line at seducing another man's wife, though he'd never had a problem bedding a willing woman no matter her marital state. It had been so long since he'd bedded any woman, he would have had to be a eunuch not to react to her.

A whaling ship, out at sea for months at a time, was not the place to find members of the fairer sex, so it had been nearly a year since he had lain with a woman. He hadn't been with a white woman since his wife.

Rachel was not beautiful, as Abigail had been. She was not petite, or even overly feminine. He would not worry about Rachel Best trudging along in a strong northerly wind. She would simply dip her head against the wind and keep going. Rachel appealed to him, though he didn't quite know why. He liked to lock at her, to watch her as she sewed some garment or moved about his room with quick efficiency. Or laid a gentle hand upon her daughter's head. He liked the fire in her eyes when she was angry, the way she pressed her lips together when she was afraid, pretending not to be. He liked that she spoke aloud what most people would only think, then pretended to be shocked by what she'd said.

There was something both indomitable and vulnerable about her, and for some reason that odd combination made her seem more desirable than any woman he'd known. He would not worry about hurting her when they tussled about in bed, but he might worry about wounding her heart.

Ah, Rachel naked in my bed, Jared thought, a smile on his lips. He knew such a thing would never happen but enjoyed such lurid thoughts nonetheless. He wondered what Mrs. Best would think if she knew where his thoughts had inevitably drifted these past days.

And all because she'd gone from married to available. If she had been skittish around him before, now she was downright terrified. Jared didn't understand why he enjoyed her terror, but he did. He stood too close to her, grasped her hand at grace a bit too tightly, let his eyes drift over her far too much. Almost daily she managed to comment about his burgeoning health and how fortunate it was that he would be able to go home soon.

Jared had no intention of going anywhere, a decision that had little to do with his growing attraction to Rachel. Such an attraction he felt certain would pass, but this odd feeling in his gut when he thought of leaving scared the hell out of him. For the first time in his life, he didn't know what to do. He knew only that he didn't want to go home. On a whaler, just the word *home* could make the stoutest man weep. A letter from home, a gift, was cherished more than a pocketful of gold. But for most of his life, his ship had been his home, the only place he'd felt comfortable. His skin had been coated with salt spray far longer than his boots had touched soil. He was as much a part of the sea as the whales he'd hunted since he was a boy.

For the first time in his life, he didn't long to feel a deck swaying beneath his feet. He didn't miss the snap of the sails, the thrill of the chase, the camaraderie of his men.

Jared stepped along the high bluff overlooking the Atlantic, his eyes on the lighthouse ahead. On the horizon, a clipper ship raced with the wind toward Boston harbor, and closer to shore a fishing skiff battled a choppy sea. He felt weaker than he wanted to, but stronger than he had in nearly a month.

"Hey, there," a man called from the base of the lighthouse. "Captain Mitchell, is it?"

"It is," Jared called out as he moved from the sandy bluff to the brush-covered ground near the whitewashed light.

The man looked behind him and smiled. "I see you, Isabelle Best."

Jared turned to find a smiling little girl trying unsuccessfully to hide behind a blueberry bush. She stood. "Hello, Captain."

Jared gave her his deepest scowl. She held out her hand for him to take, a gesture he ignored. "I followed you," she said.

"Shouldn't you be home?" Jared grumbled.

"No. I'd rather be with you," she said, smiling so widely, so obviously, it dawned on Jared that she was hiding some sort of secret. He stared at her, his green eyes narrowing, until he realized she was hiding something behind her back.

"What are you hiding back there, my fair princess?" he demanded, his expression serious.

She rolled her eyes and giggled before thrusting out her hand. "It is a gift for my brave knight," she said, holding out a gingerbread man—with one missing arm.

He looked sternly at the missing limb until Belle

fessed up that it fell off and she had to eat it so it wouldn't go to waste.

"I see you have a shadow," Donald Small said, smiling at Belle. He nodded behind Jared. "Two shadows."

Again Jared found himself looking behind him. Rachel, her skirt whipping in the wind, marched toward them looking the picture of a mother who was about to chastise her errant child. Belle, full of drama, grasped his pant leg and moved a bit behind him, as if he would protect her from the wrath of her mother. Jared felt a fierce and almost painful rush of protectiveness, and pushed her a bit further behind him, looking as if he were ready to defend the little girl with his life.

Rachel growled like a bear, hunched over and menacing, and grabbed her daughter, tickling her until the air was split by little-girl giggles. Then she stood, hands on hips, and said, "Isabelle Best, I told you to stop following Captain Mitchell about, didn't I?"

Belle lowered her eyes, but Jared had the distinct feeling she wasn't nearly as downtrodden as she appeared. "Yes, Mama."

Then Rachel lifted her head and Jared felt his entire body react to her. He understood the tightening in his groin, but he was rather perplexed about the odd little feeling in his gut. If Donald Small hadn't been standing there, he wasn't at all certain he could have resisted kissing her. She huddled deeper into her jacket, stuffing her hands into the large pockets of what appeared to be a man's coat. Her husband's coat.

Jared looked away, disliking the sharp twinge he recognized as jealousy. He was suddenly glad she was wearing that coat, that reminder she was a widow who still looked to the sea for her husband.

He wanted to press his mouth against hers, knowing that if he did, she would push him away in shock. A hard slap to his face would be even better. It would end right now the strange fascination he had with this woman, this carnal need that overwhelmed him at the oddest moments. Just that morning she had been washing the breakfast dishes, her back to him, and he had the most lurid image of himself coming up behind her and lifting her skirts. He'd pictured her smooth, rounded buttocks, imagined laying his mouth against her soft skin. He'd left the house abruptly without a word and let the cold November wind burn his cheeks and cool his ardor.

"Why don't you all come in for some nice warm cider," Small said, turning to go before getting an answer. Belle grabbed Jared's hand, then held out her other to her mother. Jared disengaged his own hand—too roughly, he knew—but he could not stand to have her little hand in his, warm and trusting. He wasn't part of them and never would be. Ignoring Belle's little pout and Rachel's sharp look, he moved ahead of the two, following behind Small as he walked toward his tiny house.

Rachel watched him stalk away and wondered at his withdrawal, hurting for Belle, who had simply wanted to hold his hand. She couldn't begin to understand such a man—a man who had forsaken civilization for years hunting whale and losing himself in a world completely foreign to her. Even with his hair trimmed and his beard shaved off, he exuded a wildness that frightened her—and fascinated her. She'd planned to ask him today about patrolling the beach. Her father was getting too lame to be out in the raw, chilled air late at night. Ambrose had taken over on beach patrol when Richard disappeared, but the nights walking the cold beach took their toll. Rachel looked to the horizon and hugged her free arm about herself as she looked at the ships sailing safely from shore. At night, this serene picture too often became nightmarish for those sailors who now enjoyed a fine wind and warm sun on their backs.

Each night from dusk to dawn, volunteers would walk up and down the beach carrying their costen signals. If ships came too close to shore, the men would wave the flares to warn ships away from the treacherous sandbanks. It was an uncommon month that saw not a single wreck on Truro's twelve-mile stretch of beach, even when the weather was fair. Jared was strong enough, she thought, to take her father's place, if only for this single night.

"Captain Mitchell, if I could have a word with you." She watched him stop, reluctance in his manner. "You go on with Mr. Small, Belle, and get some of that cider in your tummy."

Rachel walked to Jared, hating that he loomed so high above her. She disliked feeling small and delicate. "You seem much improved, Captain."

"I am."

"My father suffers from rheumatism, which only gets worse when the weather is damp." Rachel looked pointedly out at a fog bank building in the east. "He's supposed to patrol the beach tonight from midnight to dawn."

Jared nodded, apparently already knowing of the Cape Codder's practice of patrolling the beaches at night and in foul weather. "I'll take his place, if he'll let me."

Rachel smiled at his understanding of her father's stubborn ways. "Perhaps you could say you wanted to have such an experience. His pride, you see."

"I'll speak to him."

His expression, his voice, remained hard, despite the kindness that Rachel thought must lurk inside him and gave her the courage to gently chastise him. "My daughter can be a pest, I know. But I believe she has decided you're some sort of hero."

"You may inform her of her mistake."

Rachel stiffened, immediately deciding that kindness had nothing at all to do with his volunteering for patrol. "I shall do that. And I shall insist she keep her distance from you if that is what you want."

His eyes took on an almost murderous glint. At that very moment Belle giggled, her laughter dancing on the wind like thistledown. He dropped his head as if to study the sand beneath his boot and stuffed his hands deeply into his pant pockets.

"Belle does not bother me," he said, his voice low. He raised his head and stared at Rachel a long moment, making her pulse quicken. "*You* bother me, Mrs. Best."

She let out a small breath and pointed a finger to her own chest. "I do?"

"Aye."

It was the most ridiculous thing for him to say. So ridiculous that Rachel found herself laughing, even as he narrowed his eyes.

"What is so amusing?"

"I have made a point of *not* bothering you, Captain. I have gone out of my way to avoid you. I should say that you, sir, are easily bothered."

"Why have you avoided me?" he asked like an inquisitor at a trial.

"Well, because you . . . because I . . ." Rachel felt her skin flush pink. "You are rather disagreeable, Captain. Please do not take offense."

To Rachel's surprise, he smiled. Without saying a word he turned and strolled toward the lighthouse, leaving her to wonder what had just made this enigmatic man so pleased with himself.

She found him disagreeable. *Good*, he thought as he walked into the keeper's small house. He ignored that insistent part of him that wanted to go back to her and ravish her until she thought him highly agreeable.

Not finding anyone in the tiny house, Jared made his way down a narrow passageway that connected the house to the light. A spiral of iron stairs led to the light, and the smell of oil and lamp smoke grew thicker as he ascended the stairs. The trapdoor leading to the top was open, and Jared poked his head through to see Belle peering out the lighthouse's thick glass enclosure.

"Welcome to Highland Light," Small said with obvious pride.

Jared stepped fully into the small room, which left little space between the rows of argand lights and the windows, his eyes immediately going to the sea, where several ships could be seen.

"I'm supposed to document the number of ships passing, but 'tain't as easy as it looks. Sometimes I count 'em twice. Sometimes not at all. Hard to tell which is coming and which is going, 'cause there's so many of 'em. I get most of 'em in the log, though."

Jared silently counted six ships.

"I see six," Belle piped up, then counted them off.

"That's just the number I got," Small said, patting Belle's head. She ducked beneath his hand and moved to the now-dark light.

"Mr. Small lights these lamps every night," Belle announced. "We can see it from our house."

The light consisted of fifteen lamps placed within two rows of reflectors, one above the other.

"Do you need to monitor them all night?"

"No need. I fill the lamps every morning, trim the wicks, and light 'em at night. Trim 'em once during the night and that's about it. Allows me to get to the Mews, most nights at least for an hour or two. But when it gets real cold, so cold your tears freeze on your cheeks, the flame burns low. You can hardly tell it's lit. One night last year I got surprised. Cold snap come on in during the wee hours and light near went out. Never was so scared in all my days. All I could think was a ship out there headin' for shore because there was no light. I have to heat the oil downstairs and lug it up here. Damn nuisance. All because the government got cheap and won't buy good oil."

"Damn nuisance." Belle nodded smartly.

"Ah, hell," Small muttered.

Jared chuckled beneath his breath.

"S'pose you'll be headin' home soon," Small said as he jotted something in his logbook.

"I'm in no hurry."

"Well, then. I keep boarders at my house, not a mile from here. Three dollars and fifty cents a week. Got no boarders now, so you'd have the place to yourself. Winter's not a time to attract a great number of folks to these parts."

Jared nodded noncommittally, but he was thinking of that tiny cottage near the Newcomb house. He'd peeked inside that morning, finding a cozy but obviously abandoned dwelling.

"Captain Mitchell's staying with us," Belle said, giving Jared a look of such adoration he wanted to run down the spiral stairs. Perhaps he would board at the keeper's house.

He hunkered down so he was at eye level with Belle. "I cannot overstay my welcome, Belle. It would be rude, you see. And what if another sailor needs help? Would you turn another man away?"

She shook her head. "But you could stay until another shipwreck."

Rachel called to her daughter from below, ending the debate. Belle disappeared down the hatch, her booted feet sounding like distant bells as she made her way down the iron stairs.

"I'll be patrolling tonight," Jared said. "Anything I should know?"

Small shook his head. "It's easy enough. Just walk your two-mile stretch, lamp in hand. Can get a mite cold at night, so I warn you to bundle up." Small smiled. "Here I am telling a sea captain to dress warm."

"I'll heed your advice, sir." Jared gazed out the window. "As much time as I spent at sea, I never gave much thought to the men on land watching us."

"It's a living," Small said. "Boring as a two-hour sermon most of the time. But when we've got a wreck, by God, it'll get your blood running fast. Had a good one in July. Saved every last man on a bark scuttled on a sandbank just north of the Pamet River."

"Were you there the night Mrs. Best's husband died?"

Small turned and busied himself trimming the lamps' wicks. "By the time I arrived, the men had all been lost. Drowned."

"And Mr. Best?"

"Didn't see him there. Not one body washed ashore. Current around here is fierce. A ship of thirty men can go down a few hundred yards from shore and not one body will wash up. By the time I got there, Best was missing and the boys were already stripping her down." He paused to snip a wick. "Didn't get nothing worth a damn, neither. But that July wreck," he said, turning, his face animated. "Now, that was something. The locals, including

your Newcombs, made a fast profit shipping the
cargo back to the shipping company."

"They're wreckers?" Jared asked. He'd heard of
such people who benefited by others' misfortune.
When a ship foundered, the wreckers salvaged every
last bit of the ship, including the cargo, and charged
the shipping company for its own goods. Some had
even been known to charge the shipping company
for saving the crew. His tone conveyed what he
thought of such a living.

"They're honorable folk," Small said. "And there's
not a man in Truro who would go after a cargo of
gold if there was a single man to save. They're doing
a service, they are, and should get paid for it."

"And I imagine every bit of cargo makes it back
to the shipping company."

Small chuckled. "Well, perhaps not all." He gave
Jared a wink. "I've been told that every time there's
whiskey or rum aboard, all the cargo is lost at sea.
A pity, for certain."

Jared suspected a great deal of cargo never found
its way to its rightful owners.

"I know what it looks like to mainlanders," Small
said, sensing Jared's disapproval.

"Like stealing?"

Small gave him a jerk of his head. "Just payment
is what it is."

Jared wondered how just it would seem to Small if
he were a shipowner and about to lose his livelihood
because of the wreckers.

"Stay around here long enough, Captain, and
you'll come to my way of thinking. You'll see."

But Jared was no longer listening. His eyes had
found a splash of color among the brown brush
below. Belle skipped beside her mother, and he could
tell from the way they walked, from the way Rachel
moved her hands in the air, that they were singing

a song. And then Rachel stopped and peered out to sea, her daughter skipping on ahead. She shaded her eyes with one hand, scanning the horizon. He watched, with an odd tightening in his chest, as she brought that hand down to fist it into her skirts before she began again walking toward home.

Chapter Seven

~~~

In the three weeks he'd been with the Newcombs, he'd never seen Rachel angry. Now he was getting an eyeful. She stood, hands on hips, in the threshold of the little cottage, her eyes spitting pure venom.

"What do you think you're doing, Captain?"

Jared continued to sweep the floor of the kitchen, moving a small pile of dust and sand toward the angry woman who stood in his way. He'd known the Newcombs would honor his request to live in this cottage, just as he'd known their lovely daughter would vehemently protest. It was a cruelty to her, he knew, and he was not a cruel man, no matter that he made himself out to be one. A cruel man did not have twinges of conscience at his misdeeds, and this was certainly a misdeed.

"I am sweeping, Mrs. Best," Jared said.

"You've no right. No right at all to be here. I want you to leave."

Jared continued to sweep, even though he was achingly aware that she was on the verge of tears. And angry tears or not, he could not abide a woman crying. It simply made him crazy.

"Your father gave me permission."

"It was not my father's place to give you permission. This is *my* home and I say you cannot move in here." He could hear the anger and frustration in her voice, and so was not surprised when she said, "Why don't you just go home?"

He stopped sweeping when he noticed he was getting the toes of her brown boots dusty, and he stared at the woman whose eyes glittered with unshed tears, who appeared to be about to scream or attack him, he wasn't certain which.

"I'm growing attached to this barren spit of land," he said, purposely goading her, though he didn't know why he did. The tears in her eyes served only to magnify their stunning blue. Her hair was tamed into a small, tight knot, but softly curling wisps of windswept hair fluttered about her face. Her cheeks were red—from anger or the cold November wind—and she wore that oversize coat of her husband's like a shield against marauding giants. She was so damned lovely, so feminine and tough and sturdy and delicate. God, he was going to go insane staying here, seeing this woman every day, dreaming about her every night. A sweet torture.

She took a deep, calming breath. "Mr. Small has a house he lets. It's not far from the light."

"I prefer it here. If you'll excuse me, I'd like to sweep this dirt out the door."

Rachel looked down at the small, silty pile by her feet, and he could almost see her thinking that the dirt he was so blithely sweeping away was *her* dirt. Instead of backing out the door, she stepped over the pile and farther into the room.

"I don't want anyone living here. It's our home."

"He's not coming back, Mrs. Best."

He saw the slap coming long before he shot a hand up to stop it from making its mark. He saw it in the way her mouth grew hard, the way her eyes turned to ice. His large hand wrapped around her wrist, her glittering eyes not a foot from his. His eyes drifted down until they rested briefly on her lips, slightly parted as she panted out her rage. "I hit back," he said, then slowly released her arm.

"I'm certain you do," Rachel said, her voice full of contempt and shaking with emotion. She took a step back from him, and a part of Jared regretted that he had again frightened her. He'd never hit a woman in his life and hadn't the foggiest idea why he was letting this woman believe he had.

When Ambrose had suggested he settle into the cottage, his instinct had told him to say no. Something perverse in him had made him say yes. As if he wanted to torture himself by staying near her, as if he wanted to drive into her skull that her husband was dead. And Jared was not. Ah, that was it, wasn't it? It made Jared feel better, finding himself on familiar ground. Lust. That was something he recognized and understood.

"This is my home."

A weaker man would have given in to those softly spoken words that held a volume of emotion. He ignored that small plea and the part of his heart that felt a pinprick of shame. "I am a very wealthy man, Mrs. Best. Your father will be well compensated for renting out this cottage to me. Certainly you cannot deprive your father of the opportunity to provide for his family." He watched with fascinated horror as one tear escaped her eye.

"I don't care about your money."

Jared shrugged, struggling to appear unaffected by that blasted tear. "Apparently your father does."

Rachel sniffed, but did not argue, swiping at that single tear in an angry gesture. She did not want him in her house, in the one place she could go to escape him. Now, even when he was gone from Truro, she would always remember him standing in her kitchen, broomstick in hand, cuffs rolled to his elbows, revealing the strength of his forearms. He looked as if he could lift the little cottage and shake the sand and dust from it. *Go home, go home,* she wanted to shout.

Just as strongly, something inside her wanted him to stay. She was not a young girl anymore; she'd been married for six years. She recognized what was happening to her, the feelings he evoked from her body whenever they were near. But she was unprepared, completely so, for the strength of those feelings. They were distracting and annoying and . . . pleasant. For the first time in her life, she was attracted to a man she did not love. Rachel told herself there likely wasn't a woman alive who wouldn't be attracted to him, this handsome, strapping man whose face, on the rare occasions when he smiled, could knock the breath from a body. She wanted him to go away, for she feared that if he stayed she would be foolish someday. She would sway into him as she longed to do and would beg him to hold her. It had been so very long since she'd been held by a lover. Far, far longer than Richard's disappearance. Years and years.

Richard had not wanted her after she'd gotten pregnant. They had lived as brother and sister, but with a hurt between them only a husband and wife could know.

Now Jared would be staying in her home, sleeping in the bed where she'd so often slept alone, his large body sprawled atop it like a slumbering giant. And she would picture herself curled up beside him, touching him, kissing him.

It was shocking to Rachel to feel this way, almost as if another's soul had entered her body, and a sinful soul at that. For nowhere in her thoughts did she find herself married to Jared Mitchell, he a wealthy sea captain, and she the daughter of a wrecker. It wasn't worth the effort to dream about even if she were inclined to do so. His presence was nearly as large as the emptiness left by Richard—and that alone filled her with shame and guilt. She shouldn't be attracted to another man, not when her heart still had not said good-bye to Richard.

"I will not stay here long, Mrs. Best."

"Why are you staying here at all, Captain? Why not go home to your family or to your ship?"

The grip he had on the broom handle tightened. "I've been at sea so long, my home is my ship. I no longer have a home. I gave up my ship."

Rachel saw something flicker in his eyes, something raw and hot. "What do you mean, you gave up your ship?"

He laughed without humor. "How do you think I ended up here when my ship is safely in port? I abandoned my ship. My duty. I abandoned everything." He turned abruptly and began putting the table and chairs back into place.

Rachel made a small sound of protest. "You were escaping your ship?" she asked, still confused about what events had led up to the captain's drifting aimlessly.

"I was escaping myself," he spat. "I was not so drunk I didn't know the consequences of what I was doing. I knew." He placed a chair at the table with a thunk, then gripped the top of the chair fiercely.

"You knew you might die?"

"I more than knew."

Rachel felt as if something heavy lay on her breast. What could make a man who'd seemed so strong come to such a state? What pain did he hide inside that was so awful that death seemed like solace? "I'm sorry."

Again that bitter laugh. "Don't be. I don't need your pity any more than I need to pity myself. Now, if you don't mind, Mrs. Best, I'd like to finish up here."

He stared at her, making her feel as if she were the one trespassing, until she turned and left.

"How could you? How could you let that man stay in my house?"

Ambrose ducked his head and rubbed the back of his neck with one gnarled hand. "Seemed the right thing to do."

"Papa. It was the absolutely wrong thing to do. He is a stranger to us. And that is *my* house."

"Don't you go yelling at your father, missy," Mabel said crossly.

"Yelling isn't nice, is it, Grammy?" Belle said, looking up from her sad attempt at knitting herself a scarf. Rachel gave her daughter a cross look and was rewarded with a wide grin.

Rachel wanted to scream, but instead took a long, deep breath. It seemed everyone was against her in this. She was going to lose this fight, and Jared would live in her home.

"It seemed the Christian thing to do," Ambrose mumbled.

Rachel nearly rolled her eyes, for Ambrose Newcomb hadn't stepped foot in a church since Belle's baptism at the Methodist meetinghouse. "He hardly needs our charity."

"Charity's got nothing to do with it," her mother said softly. "He's paying for the privilege of living there, and the good Lord knows we could use the money. Since Richard's been gone, things have gotten a bit tight around here." Mabel lowered her voice. "You can pretend away some things, Rachel, but you can't pretend we don't need the money. Besides, it is the Christian thing to do. Can't you see that the man is damaged?"

Rachel didn't like the small tug she felt at her heart. "He's nearly well. He's patrolling tonight, isn't he?"

"That's not what I mean, and I think you know it. A man doesn't abandon his ship for no reason."

"He's simply foolish and bad-tempered," Rachel insisted.

Mabel gave her husband a questioning look, and Ambrose must have conveyed something, for Mabel sat down at the kitchen table and nodded at Rachel to join her. "Belle, why don't you go play with your dolls."

Belle made a little face, but did as her grandmother asked without complaint.

"Donald Small told your father something today that I think might help you understand the captain a little better. And help you to understand why we've allowed him to stay here. The captain had a wife and daughter. They died at sea. It was years ago, but a man doesn't get over something like that."

The image rushed back of Jared walking ahead as Belle offered her hand to him, and Rachel's heart turned to mush. Her eyes moved to her father, who was looking blindly out the kitchen window, no doubt remembering his own boys taken by the sea. And though she'd been wrapped up in her own grief since Richard's disappearance, she had not been blind to her father's physical decline since that night.

Rachel didn't want to feel compassion for the captain. She didn't want to feel anything at all. "Did he say how long he plans to stay?"

Ambrose cleared his throat. "Leave him be."

"I only wanted to know because—"

"Leave the man be, Rachel."

Rachel clamped her mouth shut, feeling a tinge of betrayal. They were so worried about Jared Mitchell and his pain; what of their own daughter's suffering?

What about the pain of seeing a strange man in her house, when she longed to see Richard? Rachel knew that was only part of the reason she wanted him gone, and likely a smaller part than even she was willing to admit to herself. Jared frightened her in a way that had nothing to do with his fearsome looks and mocking cruelty. He made her afraid of herself. And so she stopped arguing with her parents, wondering silently if her parents would want him to stay knowing their daughter was fighting a terrifying attraction.

Chapter Eight

As Jared made his way down to the beach to relieve Ambrose, he could see the ships in the distance, lights dancing on the water, and he could imagine the captain and mates looking into the blackness, a tiny bit of fear slicing into their guts. He'd never cared for sailing along the coast, for he didn't trust the charts nor even the eyes of his best mate.

"Not much moon tonight," Ambrose said, jerking his chin at the pale silver sliver in the eastern night sky. He handed over his costen, a ten-inch rod that when struck glowed hot and bright. "If you see a ship heading too close, you strike your costen and wave it. It's fair weather tonight, but out there it's black as pitch and you can't tell the land from the sea. It's the kind of night the mooncussers like, damn their rotten souls."

Jared had, of course, heard of such scalawags, men who would lure a ship to shore only to murder the crew and pillage the cargo. Cape Codders were adamant in their protestations that such vermin had never existed on their curling peninsula, though stories of such men sometimes rippled along the towns strung along the cape. Those corrupt men, they said, roamed the coast of the Carolinas. By swinging a lamp, the mooncussers would imitate a ship bobbing at anchor in safe harbor. A confused captain would head to that phantom harbor and run aground, where certain death awaited them at the hands of the murdering mooncussers, so named because they cursed the moon when it shined brightly. Rumors of mooncussers ebbed and flowed like the tide. Lately such talk had been loud, Jared learned from Donald, after a ship foundered and the captain claimed to have been heading to what looked like a safe harbor. No one put much stock in the story, for the only souls to reach the beach were those there to save the crew. In fact, the ship remained intact, the cargo safe.

"Would take a hard man to do such a thing," Jared said.

Ambrose grunted his agreement. "Good night to you. You're done when the sky turns pink. These legs are about given in."

Jared began his patrol, enjoying the bracing feel of the cold wind on his face. He could almost imagine himself near the helm of his ship, hearing the creak of the ropes, the ruffle of the sails, the low singing of the crew. In the distance, Jared saw the light of another patrol and felt an unexpected sense of camaraderie with this unknown man who also felt the sting of the frigid air, whose toes were likely as cold as his own, whose ears burned and whose cheeks were raw from the wind. Jared nearly laughed aloud. A strange, foreign feeling came over him in the dark of the night, one that took an inordinate amount of time to recognize. He was enveloped in a sense of well-being that lasted perhaps three heartbeats before he was able to tamp it down. For what was he doing, after all, but walking up and down a beach holding a torch? He greeted the man with a curt "Evening," and saw in the dim lamplight of the man's lantern that the man gave a nod. Then he turned and walked in the opposite direction, heading toward another man patrolling his two-mile stretch.

By the time the eastern sky glowed a pale pink-yellow, Jared felt about as done in as he'd felt in his life. He looked at the bluff he knew he must climb as if it were a jagged mountain and not simply a sloping bank of sand. With a sigh, he waded through the soft sand, refusing to give in to the exhaustion that weakened him. With shaking limbs, he finally crested the bluff, dropped his lamp, and placed his hands on his knees, trying to regain his breath. Even in the frigid air, sweat dripped from his nose and soaked the shirt beneath his coat.

When he finally recovered, he glanced up to see Rachel standing a dozen yards away looking as if she were about to flee.

"Are you—"

"I'm fine," he said brusquely.

"Yes. I can see that."

He narrowed his eyes and bent to retrieve his lantern, feeling weak and shaky, then began walking toward Rachel, who stood there bundled up against the cold, her cheeks red, her eyes sparkling with good humor, and found himself even more irritated. He never trusted anyone who was cheerful before the sun fully rose.

"There's coffee and breakfast for you in the house, if you like."

"I can fend for myself, as I've said." The words came out as surly and as downright mean as he felt. Jared intended to simply walk by her. He didn't want to be polite and nice and cheerful. He didn't want to have anyone see him when he trembled in weakness. He didn't want a woman cooking for him, looking after him, smiling at him. But as if his eyes had a will of their own, he shot a glance toward her as he went by. He stopped and gazed down at her, knowing he looked fierce and dangerous, knowing that grown men had quaked under such a stare. Hell, this woman had skittered away from him half a dozen times when he looked at her just this way. But for some reason, this time she lifted her chin and had a look of compassion or pity or some such warm ex-. pression in her pretty blue eyes. For a moment he was confused by that look, and mightily suspicious.

"I'm sorry about your wife and child," she said softly.

He looked away in disgust. Donald Small, that cursed, gossipy man, had told the Newcombs about his lost family.

"And I suppose you think that's why I'm so ornery. So damned disagreeable," he said, emphasizing the curse.

The warmth in her eyes disappeared. "Perhaps."

"Or perhaps I'm just mean."

"You're not as mean as you pretend to be."

Blast this woman, with her rosy cheeks and bright eyes, her lush lips, her stubborn jaw, her—*ah, Lord above*—her figure that made a man want to drop to his knees and beg her to be his. "You're giving me those cow eyes again," he said in a growl.

"Cow eyes?"

"I'm not blind. Nor stupid."

She thrust her hands onto her hips. "I have not been giving you cow eyes."

"And what were you just doing, looking up at me with those pretty blue eyes of yours?"

"I made the terrible mistake of thinking you deserved some sympathy. You know, Captain, it is not a weakness to be kind or pleasant. It is not a human failing to mourn a wife and child."

He suddenly found Mrs. Best to be a completely unappealing woman. "Once again, Mrs. Best, you presume to know something of which you know nothing." Jared looked past her, wondering at the insanity of staying in a place where he was not wanted, in a place he wasn't certain he even wanted to be. Hell, he should go home or go somewhere. He was just about to do that, stalk to the little cottage and gather his few belongings, when she spoke.

"I have a terrible habit," she said softly, drawing his eyes back to her. Despite that acid tongue, she was lovely to look at, he conceded. And at the moment she looked downright pathetic.

"Only one?" he asked, cocking one brow.

Rachel pursed her lips. "I'm certain I have several, but my worst habit is that I cannot keep my mouth closed when it is painfully apparent that I should."

"Is that an apology, Mrs. Best?"

"An explanation."

"Ah." He was silent for a long moment. "If you are waiting for me to confess my own failings, I'm afraid you'll be waiting a long time."

He was delighted when her eyes narrowed again. It was so easy to rankle this woman. "You are about to reveal another flaw, Mrs. Best."

"And that is?" she asked tightly.

"Your temper."

Hands were again thrust onto her slim hips. "I do not have a temper. I am the most mild-mannered of women."

Jared began walking toward his cottage, his long-legged strides forcing Rachel to run to keep up with him.

"You are the only person I know who can incite such anger. You enjoy baiting me," she said, pointing an accusing finger at him.

He stopped so suddenly that Rachel stumbled. "That I do, Mrs. Best. That I do."

"Why?"

Jared found himself looking down at her, his body

throbbing with desire, and he realized the only thing he was fighting at the moment was the urge to kiss her. She must have seen something in his expression, for her eyes widened slightly and she stepped back from him. A slow, knowing smile spread over his mouth. He dipped his head slightly. "You're making those cow eyes again," he said in a near-whisper.

She blinked, and he watched her face turn red. "I don't even know what that means. Cow-eyed. And I certainly don't look at you that way."

He grinned. "You do. But it's to be expected. I'm a handsome man, after all."

Rachel snorted. *What an arrogant man*, she thought. Arrogant and handsome and exasperating.

"You don't think me handsome?" And he gave her a smile that sucked the breath from her lungs. Good heavens above, he was beautiful.

"I imagine some women would think so."

"But not you?"

"Perhaps."

Jared's grin widened. "What if I told you that I thought you beautiful?"

She shook her head and gave a little laugh. "I'd think you somehow got to that whiskey of yours." Rachel began walking toward the house again, but found herself blocked by a large male form. She looked up at him, his face awash in the soft pink glow of the new day. His eyes drifted to her mouth, and Rachel's insides turned jittery and light. It was a terrifying feeling.

"I'm not looking for a man in my life, Captain," she forced herself to say. "You should know that."

"Well, then, Mrs. Best, we are at odds. For I am most definitely looking for a woman. But I'm afraid not the sort of prudish woman who blushes when I say the word 'damn,' nor the kind who gets all uppity if I stare a bit too long at her mouth."

His eyes drifted there again, and Rachel could almost imagine what his kiss would feel like. "I'm not a prude," she said, wondering why she was arguing with this man whom she didn't want in her life, who she wished would sail off to New Bedford with the setting sun.

As quick as that, he bent his head and kissed her, roughly, and disappointingly quickly. Her face turned scarlet and her hand shot to her mouth in horror. He had the audacity to throw back his head and laugh.

"Good God, if you could see your face," he said between the gales of laughter.

"How . . . how dare you!"

Still chuckling, he began walking toward his cottage. "I'm a daring man, Mrs. Best. You'll find that if you issue me a challenge, I'm one to take it."

Rachel found herself running to catch up to him, knowing that part of her was reluctantly fascinated by their teasing. "I issued no challenge. I merely said I was not a prude. That does not give you the right to kiss me. I want an apology."

"You'll not get it," he said easily.

"I don't like you."

He shrugged his shoulders and kept walking.

"You're rude. And crude and a big oaf." She was a little behind him and so didn't see his face, only his shoulders shaking with mirth, which only served to heighten her anger.

"And you don't know how to kiss."

He turned instantly, his eyes alight with humor and something dangerous. "Is that a challenge?" he asked silkily.

She balked immediately. "Simply an observation."

He stood before her, his massive arms crossed in front of him, gazing down at her with a bemused look. "Ah, too bad," he said wistfully. "Perhaps I am a bit out of practice with this kissing business. Is there a tavern in Truro Center?"

Rachel blinked at what appeared at first to be an abrupt change of subject. Then she had a sudden and not-so-pleasant image of Jared sitting at a table with a pretty tavern girl on his lap, kissing the daylights out of her. "The best is the Mews," she said, knowing that the only person serving drinks there was old Sam Travist's daughter, Esther, a quiet, unassuming girl. "I know it only because my husband would go there from time to time. Besides, it's the closest."

"Then that's where I'll be. Give this to your father, will you?" he asked, handing Rachel the costen flare.

"Won't you be eating that breakfast?" Rachel called after him.

"I'll be drinking my breakfast this morning."

Jared sipped some wonderfully strong coffee before filling his mouth with some of the best sausage he'd tasted in years. Eating, apparently, would be the only physical pleasure he'd receive this day. Truro Center was not the bustling place Jared had hoped for. It consisted of a meetinghouse, a combination general store and post office, and two taverns—one that was now open and one that opened only in the evenings. He made a quick stop at the post office on the chance that the package of personal items he'd telegraphed his brother to send had arrived, and found it had not.

Mews Tavern, the one recommended by Rachel, was nearly empty. It was not a rollicking place stuffed full of ladies easy on the eyes or easy anywhere else. He half believed Rachel had sent him here because the one woman in the place was timid as a mouse and the owner's daughter. No one spoke but for the girl, though he knew the few patrons must have been curious about his presence. In a place like Truro, a stranger in winter was an uncommon thing.

After his late breakfast, he wandered about a bit, walking to the marshlands to the west. The few people he passed stared and nodded when he did, but he had the distinct feeling that if he had ignored them, they would have done the same. The talkative Donald Small must be an anomaly, he thought, as he sat leaning up against a scrub pine tree and gazed out onto the marsh. The day was unseasonably warm, fooling a few flying insects into coming out and dancing in the sun. Jared wondered when he'd felt so entirely alone. He'd grown up on a whaler, where you could hear a man snoring or yelling or coughing every hour of the day. To be here in utter silence but for the soft sound of the wind rushing through the pines and birds calling out was as foreign to him as being on a ship would be to most people. A drowsy smile tugged on his lips. This was nice. Quiet. Alone. He idly watched a tiny swarm of gnats, his head drooping lower and lower until he succumbed to the exhaustion that seeped into his bones. When he awoke two hours later, the sun already sinking low on the horizon, he walked back to town, feeling aimless, oddly content, and voraciously hungry.

He was in the middle of his second meal at the Mews that day when Donald Small entered the small tavern. He immediately came over to Jared and sat down. After a day of near silence, Jared was happy to have someone to talk to.

"Esther," Small called to the plain young woman who was wiping a table nearby. "How is the beef stew this evening?" He turned to Jared. "Esther here makes the best beef stew on the cape. Maybe in all of Massachusetts." Small beamed up at the girl, who smiled politely at Small's compliment. "I eat here nearly every night. Best food around. And the best service," he said overloudly.

Jared suspected Small might have had a bit of a crush on the poor girl, and he felt a twinge of compassion for both of them. Esther had seemed more embarrassed than flattered by Small, while Small's affection was so transparent, it was nearly painful to watch.

"Would you like some stew, sir?"

"That'd be fine, Miss Travist." She gave Jared the very same polite smile, and he found himself wishing she hadn't when he saw the pained look on Small's face.

Small looked from Esther to Jared. "You two know each other?" he asked, smiling widely and revealing uneven, yellowed teeth.

"I ate here this morning."

"That's two stews," Esther said, before turning away. Jared had no doubt that the girl hadn't a clue Small was infatuated with her.

"Here I thought lightkeepers were chained to the light," Jared said good-naturedly, hoping to get the hangdog expression off Small's face.

"Once the light's lit, it's good for five, six hours. Course, I can't imbibe," Small said, eyeing Jared's whiskey.

"More pity to you," Jared said, lifting the whiskey and taking a healthy drink.

Small nodded to the drink. "That stuff nearly killed you."

"What doesn't kill you makes you stronger," Jared said lightly, refusing to give in to Small's unusually gloomy mood. He took another long drink, then motioned to Esther to bring him another. "I haven't had a drink in nearly a month. This tastes damn good."

Esther brought the stew along with the whiskey. She smiled again at Jared when she asked the men if they needed anything else, and he could see Small's ears turn red. Normally Jared would have had a little fun at a man's expense when he was so obvious about his affections. But something told him that Small wouldn't think it amusing if he called Esther *darling* or returned her smile with one of his own. He knew what his smile could do to the ladies—at least some ladies, he thought darkly, thinking of Rachel.

He gave his thanks politely and immediately turned to his stew. It was mouthwatering. "You'd better hurry and marry that lady," Jared said to assure Small he had no interest in Esther himself. "A cook this good won't be available long. Wonder why no one's snapped Esther up?"

Small's cheeks pinkened and he stared at his bowl. "She had a beau for a long time. But he's gone now." Small shoveled the stew in like a starving man, and Jared, who was used to mannerless sailors, couldn't help but think a quiet, pretty girl like Esther wouldn't see Small as the man of her dreams. Poor sap.

Rachel let out an impatient sigh. Jared hadn't yet returned, and as it grew dark outside, she found herself looking out the window to her cottage to see if a lamp had been lit.

"Not back yet, is he?" Mabel called as she set the dishes on the table for supper.

"Not yet, fool man."

"On a bender, no doubt. Frankly, given how we found him, I'm surprised it hasn't happened before this, with him here near a month."

Rachel bit her thumbnail. "Oh, I don't care if he drinks himself into a coma. But he's not fully recovered. He was shaking like a leaf just this morning after patrol. And he must be exhausted. Lord knows he didn't get any sleep last night."

Mabel smiled at her daughter. "No, I can tell you're not worried at all."

"And that's another thing. He should know we'd be worried."

"He's a man used to looking after himself," Ambrose said, puffing on his pipe.

Rachel forced herself to step from the window, forced herself to stop picturing the man who'd kissed her just that morning passed out on some sandy path between the Mews and the cottage. Or worse, picturing him in bed with some woman. She'd suggested the Mews, but that didn't mean that was where he ended up. Rachel didn't even pretend to be concerned about his immortal soul for cavorting with a woman. She knew that hot, uncomfortable feeling that made her stomach feel slightly sick was one thing: jealousy.

The shame of it, feeling such a thing with her husband gone not even four months, and thinking about a kiss that was really nothing, that hadn't lasted longer than a heartbeat. To find herself developing an attraction to a such a man was baffling. She'd thought he was the sort of man she disliked. He was large, rough, and looked at her as no gentleman would, not even the men of Truro, whom no one would confuse with gentlemen.

Two months after Richard disappeared, they began appearing at her door, these weathered Truro men who smelled faintly of fish no matter how many times they bathed, a tentative smile on their faces, hair combed, shirts clean and tucked in. Rachel pretended to not know why they were visiting her, treating them with the same friendly politeness she always had and sending them on their way looking a bit confused. There were many more men in Truro than women, and so the one year of mourning for a widow was often ignored. Hadn't Hope Willis married Trevor Granger only one month after her husband died?

Rachel had no interest in remarrying. None at all. She ignored her mother, who would sometimes look at her sadly and say, "I hate to see you alone after we're gone."

"Ma, you're only forty-six years old. Mrs. Baxter lived to be eighty-five."

"My own mother died at thirty-seven," Mabel would say, and look at the window as if she expected to see the Grim Reaper stalking her. "And don't think you'll have Belle in your old age. She'll go off and marry and you'll be alone."

That seemed so far away that Rachel could only laugh. No, there wasn't a man in Truro whom she could imagine marrying. Each time she pictured herself carrying out her marital duties with one of them, she either cringed or chuckled.

Rachel went to search for Belle to stop her mind from thinking about marital duties and Captain Mitchell.

She awoke with heart-pounding abruptness, her entire body taut. It was so quiet in Truro but for the wind that any other sound could wrench Rachel from the deepest sleep. She got out of bed and peered out the window just in time to watch a large manlike shape tumble to the ground. Jared had finally made it home. Well, almost.

She watched, waiting for him to rouse himself, but he stayed where he was, flat on his back. With a huff of disgust, she swung open her window and stuck her head out.

"Captain," she said in the loudest whisper she could manage. "Are you awake?"

"It's a beautiful night, Mrs. Best," he said in a smooth, rich baritone. "If I close my eyes, I can feel the ship rolling beneath me. Fine old crate, the *Huntress.*"

Rachel smiled. "I think you should go to bed, Captain."

"There's a fair wind blowing tonight, but the seas are calm."

"Good Lord," Rachel mumbled to herself, before slipping on her boots and throwing her coat over her nightgown. She walked as quietly as possible out of the house, but when she reached the outside, her mother called down from the second floor.

"Do you need help, Rachel?"

Her mother's face was pale in the night, the cap on her head and her nightgown glowing white. "I'll let you know if I do." Her mother disappeared and the window shut behind her.

"I hope you're happy, Captain; you've awoken the entire household."

He'd hoisted himself up on his elbows and looked at her with a wide grin on his face. "Hello, Mrs. Best."

"Hello, yourself. Can you make it the rest of the way to the cottage?" He was nothing more than a dark shape in the sand, but for the whites of his eyes and his startlingly white teeth. He was smiling, the ridiculous man.

"Well, I can't leave you out here. It's freezing tonight and you'll die of exposure."

"We wouldn't want that," he said good-naturedly, heaving himself up and stumbling just a little. "Rougher seas than I thought," he muttered to himself.

Rachel stood there with her arms crossed, her disapproval glaring, even to a man as apparently soused as the captain.

"You think I'm drunk."

"Aren't you?"

He swayed as if he were indeed on the deck of his ship in rough seas. Again she saw that flash of white that told her he was smiling. "I've been drunker."

"I'm certain you have. And I'm certain you gave no thought that there were people here worried about you, thinking that perhaps you knocked your head and lay dead."

She saw, even in the darkness, his brows furrow. He scratched his head, as if confused about something. "You were worried."

"Well, we all were. A bit. If we do find you dead upon the path, do you want to be buried here or shipped home?" Rachel couldn't believe what she was seeing, but it was clear he was smiling again.

"Mrs. Best, you do make me smile." He took a step toward her, and Rachel took a step back; he frowned down at her. "Why do you do that? Step away from me," he asked.

If he'd known how gruff he sounded, how very angry, he would know, Rachel thought.

"Are you afraid I'll steal another kiss? Is that it?" His voice had gone soft again, low and smooth, like an unexpected pocket of warm air on a cold winter's night. She'd never met a man who could do so much with the timbre of his voice.

"I . . ." She cleared her throat. "I think I'll go in now. I just wanted to be certain you made it safely home." She backed away a few steps.

"Mrs. Best? You're the first woman I've kissed since my wife. Can you believe that?"

"I've heard tales of whalers," she said, still moving away from him.

"Oh," he said with a negligent shrug. "I've had plenty of women. More than I can count, by God. But a kiss? Not a one."

Rachel blushed and was thankful for the dark night.

"What do you say to that, Mrs. Best?"

"I say they were lucky women to have escaped your sorry attempt, Captain."

He laughed, a hearty, deep, happy sound. "If I were a little more drunk or a little more sober, I'd show you how unlucky those poor women were."

"Your arrogance is astonishing. Good night, Captain."

"It has been, hasn't it?" He walked the short distance to the cottage, swaying only a bit, like a seasoned seaman walking on the deck of a ship on smooth seas.

Chapter Nine

 ~

Capt. Francis Calhoun knew he was losing his ship long before the *Isaac Small* smashed into a sand-bar that the fierce current around the cape had carved during a July tempest. The wind and tide drove the ship and its crew of twenty-four men relentlessly toward the shore, a looming dark gray shadow on the horizon. The men were afraid, and, by God, so was he. Two men pulled on the helm, hoping to steer the ship away from shore, arms shaking from the effort, hands nearly frozen to the wheel, faces reddened by the stinging sleet and raging gale.

The canvas was reefed as much as he dared, for without sails the helm would give up all control. Captain Calhoun dragged himself to the ship's bow, squinting his eyes against the wind and sleet, and felt his heart drop from his chest just moments before a great wave lifted the *Isaac Small* high, then slammed it down onto the bar, throwing him and the men to the deck with a bone-jarring, timber-rattling impact. He knew that if the ship was not lifted free, all would be lost, for not even the sturdiest of vessels could withstand the power of the punishing sea beating it down, down upon the sand. The ship tilted precariously, driven by yet another monstrous wave, but it remained fast on the bar. Heaving himself up, Captain Calhoun looked to shore and saw, through the foulest weather, the figures of men and women gathering on a beach that moments before had looked perilously near but that now looked impossibly far away. With the waves crashing broadside, he issued a fateful order: "To the mainmast, men. God save our souls."

It had been Jared who ran to the Highland Light to alert Donald Small of an impending wreck. He had been watching the ship all night, he and others waving their costens knowing that the captain was helpless to stop the ship from being driven closer and closer to shore by a wind that only got stronger as the night wore on. When daylight came, dull and gray, Jared took off for the lighthouse and Small, who loaded his two-wheeled cart with his lifesaving equipment and drove the two miles southward as Jared ran to alert the townspeople.

Within an hour, it seemed as if every Truro resident was upon the beach, eyes pinned to the foundering ship. Many held cedar shingles in front of them to stop the stinging sand from pelting them. It was a sobering thought that these people were so used to such scenes that they could think to remember to bring their shingles.

"She's too far away for the cannon," Small said, even as he readied the contraption that would fire a lifeline to the ship's rigging. Jared, still an outsider, watched as the Truro men readied the cannon, faces set, expressions hard with determination. They worked without speaking, efficiency borne of practice, and with an urgency that spoke of the men's respect for the power of the sea. The wind blew in on them, sleet and sand slashing at their faces, and carrying with it the sounds of the *Isaac Small*'s crew crying for help. The ship was close enough so that they could see the whites of the seamen's frightened eyes, close enough to hear them scream when a wave ripped at them as they clung to the rigging, even over the roar of the surf.

Jared could not have imagined such a surf. It was a wild, raging thing as it ripped at the beach, crashing down like thunder he could feel deep in his chest, sucking at the sand like some starving beast. He'd been in storms more violent than this, with seas far rougher. But a ship would roll and pitch and cut through seas that looked like they would swallow a ship whole. This ship could not cut through the waves, could not roll and pitch safely over them. It could only submit to the power and devastation; it could only be torn apart. Above the roar, he could still hear the men as they were battered by the sea. His eyes were pinned on the ship and the men, but he was acutely aware of Rachel when she came to stand beside him. He looked down and saw the pain and horror on her face that he saw on those of all the residents who were gathering on the beach, but with an emotion that went deeper.

She pulled at his sleeve to bring his head down, and he heard and felt her speak near his ear. "Have they tried the cannon yet?"

He shook his head no just as the air was split by the sound of the cannon, and the townspeople watched helplessly as the heavy brass window weight fell far short of the ship.

"Too far." Rachel moaned, shaking her head, and Jared fought the urge to draw her to him, knowing it would have been a selfish gesture. He had watched whaleboats crushed beneath the fluke of a powerful sperm whale; he had heard the cries of his men before the sea sucked them down. It was, of course, horrific. But it had always been quick. He'd had the comfort of knowing the men had died quickly. But this . . . this was nightmarish.

"Try again," said one young man. Jared looked at the man, little more than a boy, and could almost see the panic growing in his gut.

"Ain't no use, Eb. Waste of powder," Donald said, his eyes weary and resigned.

"We got to try again," Eb said, a desperate note to his voice. "We can't just let them die out there. And they will. By God, if you don't try, I will."

To Jared's surprise, Donald stepped back, giving him a shake of his head. The young man named Eb was joined by another strapping lad, and the two adjusted the cannon in a vain hope of reaching the ship and its men. Again the cannon fired. Again the line fell far short. The screams—*good God*—the screams of those poor souls stranded on the ship were enough to drive a sane man mad. Jared wanted to howl out his own frustration, but remained still, outwardly calm, watching the boy's panic grow each time the wind carried with it the sounds of the seamen.

He knew what the boy was feeling, what every man and woman on that beach was feeling: that something must be done. How could they simply stand there, within sight of those sailors, and do nothing? Eb paced the beach, mindless of the wind and stinging sleet, as his friend watched. Another, younger boy walked up to him, but Eb pushed him away roughly. For an hour the boy paced and the townspeople stood silent. A few left, for it was achingly cold and it was obvious there would be no rescue. Rachel stayed on the beach beside him, her eyes, like his, pinned on the ship, on the waves that battered it. He found strength in her quiet presence. Not for an instant did he think to send her home, did he believe she did not belong on that beach. She leaned against the wind, not against him, and for some strange reason that made her seem more vulnerable.

"If only the sea would die down," she said. But as the day grew old, the seas only got stronger.

When the foremast snapped, the cries from the men still clinging to the mainmast heightened, and those still on the beach felt a surge of impotent urgency.

Eb stood alone, his hands fisted by his sides as he stared at the ship a long, long moment. When he turned, his face was set and his eyes blazed with determination.

"Let's get the dory," Eb said to his friend, then stared at Donald like a man ready to take on the world.

"I wouldn't do it, boys," Donald said, straining his voice to be heard above the roar of the surf. "She's blowin' too hard, and those combers will capsize you for certain."

The boys ignored the lightkeeper, turned, and ran up the bluff, returning within an hour with a small dory.

"Sweet mercy," Jared said beneath his breath. He turned to Donald, who had become a friend these past weeks. "You can't let them do it, Don."

"Can't stop 'em either. Stubborn to the bone. And hell, they just might do it. They grew up here. They know this surf better than I do."

Jared was stunned to see hope in the lightkeeper's eyes and knew it was misplaced. The crowd cleared a path for the boys, and Jared heard several people wish them well: "By God, someone is finally doing something." "Good luck, boys, and God be with you." He could see the hope in their eyes, and couldn't help but think some sort of insanity had gripped this crowd. For even if those boys made it through the surf, the waves crashing about the ship would certainly dash their tiny boat against the hull and shatter it.

"It's suicide," Jared shouted, ignoring the hostile looks from the crowd as he stepped to the edge of the surf and put a hand on Eb's shoulder to stop him.

It seemed as if in that moment the screams of the crew were amplified, and Jared could see desperation bloom in the young man's body.

"We can't just let them die," Eb shouted to the crowd gathering around them. "Me and John are going in."

"Don't do it, son," Jared commanded. "That surf will turn your boat to splinters. Don't be fools."

"You got no rights here, Captain. Talk is you abandoned your ship like a coward. Me and John here ain't cowards. Move aside."

Jared heard the rumbling of approval from the townspeople, even as his face turned ruddy from the boy's insult. But he wouldn't back down. "Look at that surf. You'll never get past it. You'll die as sure as you're standing here."

"I've been in surf twice that big. I ain't afraid." Eb turned to his friend, who was looking a bit unsure. "Let's go, John."

Jared gripped the other boy's arm and looked into a face impossibly young, his blue eyes filled with fear. "Don't do it, son."

The boy instantly became hostile. "Hands off. I ain't no coward."

Jared watched in helpless frustration as the boys dragged the boat to the surf, well-wishers urging them on, calling out for them to be careful. Fools, who were about to let two of their men die. He stood alone by the cannon as the rest of the crowd, including Donald, moved to the edge of the surf, his eyes seeking out and finding Rachel, who appeared to be comforting an older woman.

They started out strong, heading into that hellish surf, and for an instant Jared thought—he hoped and prayed—that he was wrong. The oars dipped, their strong backs bent, and they pulled the dory into the surf. "Come on," Jared whispered. "Come on, boys."

They'd gone not fifty yards, rowing against the violent sea, when a huge, curling wave smashed into the small dory, overturning it with an ease that was horrifying to watch.

"Ah, Christ," Jared said, running toward the water as his eyes swept the incoming waves for a sign of the boys.

"There!" Two heads bobbed up, two dark spots against the foaming sea, then disappeared beneath another wave.

Every eye was on the surf; every heart pounded with hope. Five seconds, ten, thirty. And then the sick realization came that they were gone, swept out to sea.

The woman Rachel had been talking with let out a scream of denial and crumpled to the beach. The only sounds were the driving surf and the woman's cries, for the men stranded on the ship had seen what had happened and for a moment forgot about their own terror.

Rachel held Eb's mother, who stared stonily out to sea as if God's hand would gift her with her son. Rachel's grief was riddled with guilt, for she'd fallen in with the rest of the crowd, urging the young men on, foolishly allowing them to risk their lives for a hopeless cause. But it had been impossible to remain unmoved by the plaintive cries of the men. Impossible for everyone but Jared.

"I'll take her home." Rachel looked up to see Eb's father. "C'mon, Mattie. He's not coming back." The words were said with an underlying tenderness that broke Rachel's heart. This man might not shed a tear, but he would grieve hard, and tonight he would hold his wife to him and let her cry for him.

As the day wore on, the situation became only more desperate. The seas were unrelenting, crashing into the fragile ship again and again until it began to break apart. The foremast was torn away completely, the main cabin shattered, and still the men clung to the rigging of the mainmast.

"They can't last much longer," Jared said, coming up next to Rachel.

Rachel looked at him, searching for some emotion in his hard eyes, and saw only cold assessment. She watched as the ship was again engulfed in a wave that pummeled the poor souls stranded there. It was getting dark and more difficult to see the men, to know whether the same number held fast to the rigging.

"They ought to move to the mizzen," he said, as if to himself. "The ship's being torn apart from the bow." Rachel dragged her gaze from the ship and stared at Jared a long moment, watching as he blinked when a man cried out, watching his fists clench and unclench in rhythm with the waves pounding the ship. His ears were bright red from the cold; his dark hair was frozen at the ends and wet near his scalp. Slowly Rachel unwound the scarf wrapped snugly around her neck. She moved in front of him and offered her scarf.

Jared looked down at her, then at the scarf in her hands. His face tightened briefly before he took the offering.

"You need a hat," Rachel said needlessly. "But this scarf will do for now."

"Aye." He fingered the material briefly before swinging it about his neck and lifting it up until it covered his ears, his eyes once again going to the *Isaac Small*.

Rachel huddled further into her coat, not wanting to even think about how very cold those men were on the ship.

"Have them light fires, Mrs. Best," Jared said. "Those men need to know we're still here watching over them."

Rachel didn't question why he didn't call out himself for the fires, but simply gathered a few bystanders and set them to work. All night they fed the fires, even when they could no longer see the ship or hear the men. Rachel went home once to eat and check on her daughter, who had already been tucked into bed by her grandmother. As the night wore on, nearly all went home, resigned to the fact that nothing could be done until morning, and then only if the seas had subsided. Jared stood like a sentinel silently watching over the fires, moving in to throw on a piece of driftwood if the flames got too low.

Rachel walked up to him and handed him a jar of warm barley and broth. He took it without comment and drank it down quickly. "Thank you," he said finally, handing her back the jar. "The seas have calmed a bit, but I fear it is too late." The men were silent, no longer torturing the few who stood solemnly on the beach with their plaintive cries.

The ship slowly emerged in the dawn's light, a broken skeleton with a single mast still standing amidst a calming sea. The mizzenmast stood alone, jutting into the brightening sky. The mainmast—and the men who had clung to it—were gone. With the dawn, several boats were launched, and Rachel watched as Jared stepped aboard the first, her heart aching for him. He'd been right, of course, about the rescue, about the masts. There was no sign of life from shore, no sign of the men who had so tenaciously clung to a mainmast that had been ripped from the ship sometime in the night. By the end of the day, every bit of salvage would be torn from the ill-fated ship. Any remaining cargo would be removed, the shipowners contacted, a price for recovery negotiated.

As the edge of the sun reached the horizon, the ship's outline became clearer, and Rachel watched with disbelief as the shape of a man high in the mizzenmast became discernable. One of the small boats had reached the ship, and Rachel watched as a man heaved himself onto the foundered ship and immediately began climbing the mast.

"That's our captain, by God," Ambrose said, pulling down his spyglass and handing it to Rachel.

Rachel looked through the glass and watched as Jared climbed the rigging, as he wrapped his arms around the man and tore him from the mast. It was clear, even from the beach, that the man did not live. Jared handed the body down to the waiting men and stayed where he was for a long moment. Rachel could no longer see, for tears filled her eyes, blurring the ship and Jared.

"I'm going home, Papa." She wanted to cry her heart out for those poor men, for the boys who died foolishly trying a rescue, for herself and Richard. And for Jared. She didn't know why seeing Jared climb that mast made her weepy, but it did. Perhaps because she alone knew he'd cared far, far more than he let on.

When Rachel reached the top of the bluff, she looked back at the damaged ship. Several boats had tied up to the *Isaac Small*, and men were no doubt trying to salvage what they could from the wreck. Jared sat alone at the ship's stern gazing out to sea, and Rachel felt that tug at her heart again.

When she returned home, her daughter was up and eating her breakfast of molasses-sweetened porridge. "Did all the men die, Mama?"

"I'm afraid so, Belle," Rachel said, hanging up her coat. "Everyone is going to be very sad for a while."

"Is the captain home yet?"

Rachel sat down, weary to her bones. "I don't want you bothering the captain today, Belle. He's been up more than a day now, and worked hard last night."

Mabel walked into the kitchen and Rachel shook her head, telling her silently that no one on the ship had survived the night. She sat down next to her daughter. "There was a wreck in Nauset when I was a girl. The men abandoned ship, and all were lost. The next morning the ship was high and dry, and there was a fire still lit in the cabin. It's almost more than a soul can bear, sometimes."

"We save a lot, too, Mama."

"I know. I know."

The women were silent, both thinking about the tragedies they'd each suffered at the hands of a cruel sea, the only sound Belle's spoon clinking at the bottom of her bowl.

"Grandpa said the captain acted bravely. Did he, Mama?"

Rachel thought of Jared standing up against the townspeople when those two boys wanted to try a rescue, of him keeping the fires burning, of him climbing that mast only to find a dead man. "He did. All the men were brave."

"But the captain especially?"

At the hopeful note in her daughter's voice, Rachel smiled. "I suppose you could say that."

Belle smiled. "May I be excused?"

"You may."

Rachel watched her daughter bound out of the chair and head for the door. "You need a coat, young lady." In a flash, she jerked her coat from the peg and disappeared out the door.

"I don't understand that man," Rachel said.

"The captain?"

"I've never met anyone like him. He seems so hard, and yet . . ."

Mabel gave her daughter an understanding smile. "Your father is the same way, dear. He's got a heart so soft, he's had to create a shell around it to protect it. But it's so easy to poke holes through that shell. I don't know if you remember when your brothers died, but it nearly destroyed your father. Richard saved his life, I think. Gave him a reason to go on."

"I remember." In many ways, her father had been closer to Richard than to his own sons. They'd clung to each other in their grief—a boy who'd lost his father and a father who'd lost his sons. Though Richard had pulled away from her, he had never pulled away from her father, and the two had remained close until the day he'd disappeared.

Died, Rachel forced herself to think. *Until the day Richard died.*

"Your father lit the captain's stove this morning. Why don't you go fix him some coffee before you get some rest yourself," Mabel suggested.

"The last time you suggested making him breakfast, he wasn't entirely pleased."

"Oh?"

"I think he said something about being able to take care of himself. But I think just this time, I will. He's got to be exhausted. Too tired to get too surly about coffee and fried eggs."

Mabel chuckled, then stood and picked three eggs from their basket and handed them to Rachel.

Rachel tucked the eggs in her yellow apron and walked the short distance between the houses without bothering with a coat. She knocked, then walked in to find the cottage cozy and warm. "Hello?"

Glad to find herself alone, Rachel went about making coffee and heating an iron pan that hung against the wall. She smiled, feeling a sense of nostalgia to be cooking on her old stove, using her own pan. Cooking for a man. Rachel shrugged. There was nothing wrong with feeling good about cooking a meal for someone. Taking a spoonful of lard from the earthenware pot, she plopped it in the pan, where it sizzled and glided, like a stone on a frozen pond. The door opened just as she was about to crack the first egg.

"I thought I'd make you breakfast. I know you don't want anyone looking after you," she said in a rush. "But you've been up more than a day now, and it's really the neighborly thing to do, so if you'll just sit down right there, I'll have some eggs for you in a jiffy and be right out."

He stared at her a long moment, making her want to explain all over again what she was doing in his— no, her—cottage, but she held her tongue.

"I don't mind. Thank you." He sat down at the table, then slowly unwrapped the scarf from his neck and held it in front him, fingering the soft material. He pushed the scarf away, as if realizing what he was doing, then leaned back in the chair. "I'm really not up to fending for myself."

Rachel gave him a tentative smile, then turned back to the stove, expertly cracking the eggs into the hot pan. "Over easy?"

"That's fine."

Rachel wanted to say something to him, wanted to tell him that she thought he'd acted honorably, that she didn't think him the coward that boy had named him just before plunging into the surf and to his death. Instead she poured some scalding coffee into a thick mug, remembering he took it black.

She placed it in front of him and was startled when he covered one of her hands with his. She wasn't certain what he would do—kiss her hand? drag her to him?—but she wasn't at all prepared when he turned her hand this way and that, examining it, touching it in a dispassionate way. He seemed almost to be in a trance, his breathing audible, his grip on her hand not quite gentle, though far from rough. Then he brought the back of her hand to his beard-roughened cheek and pressed it against him, his eyes closing briefly before looking up at her, something achingly beseeching in his gaze.

"I . . . I can't," Rachel whispered, drawing back, and not knowing quite what she was refusing. She turned back to the stove and hurriedly removed the pan from the heat. She was afraid to look back at him. He'd been asking for comfort, she was certain, and she hadn't been able to give even that, because when he'd held her hand she'd felt something more than heartache, more than a twinge of physical attraction. She'd felt something deep and unshakable grip her heart.

Rachel felt sick inside. With a trembling hand she scooped the eggs from the pan to a plate, cut a slab of bread her mother must have sent over, and turned to him. He was sitting, hands around his mug, his eyes looking into his coffee as if it fascinated him.

Silently Rachel placed the plate before him and sat down next to him. He got up, muttering, "Fork," then returned to simply stare at the egg-laden plate, his fork still in hand.

"I wish you would leave," he said finally.

"Oh." Rachel felt horrid. Now if she embraced him, as her heart screamed for her to do, it would seem she did so out of pity. She wasn't certain if it was because she was so tired, because she had witnessed the deaths of twenty-four men, or because she'd hurt a man she didn't realize could be hurt, but Rachel burst into tears, a ridiculous deluge that soaked her face. She sobbed into her hands, shaking her head, all the time stupidly saying, "I'm not crying, I'm not crying."

Quickly the torrent was over, and she wiped her face on her apron, and laughed when she saw the look of bemused panic on Jared's face. "I don't cry often, but when I do, it's rather copious."

"It's been a trying day," Jared said. He started to cut his egg, but this time it was Rachel who placed her hand on his. She pulled the fork from his hand and placed the palm of his hand against her soft cheek, pressing it there, her eyes wide and uncertain.

Jared moved his thumb downward so that it brushed over those lips he so wanted to kiss and watched as her eyes fluttered closed. He felt the shaky breath she released, and his body reacted to her response, his groin tightening from a simple shattered puff of air.

He leaned toward her, his eyes open, afraid that if she opened her eyes and saw the raw desire in his own, she would pull away. When his lips finally touched hers, he smiled, and her eyes shot open.

"You're smiling," she said, her mouth moving against his.

"I've said before that you make me smile, Rachel." Then he kissed her again, this time possessively, moving his lips against hers, mouthing her, nipping her full lower lip, his hand still on her face, his thumb hovering near her mouth. Gently he pulled down on her jaw, opening her mouth, and tasted her. She let out a sound, a little squeak of surprise, as he moved his tongue gently against hers.

She pulled back, her cheeks flushed, her breathing a bit unsteady, and he dropped his hand.

"Why did you do that?" she asked, a little crease forming between her brows.

Perhaps, Jared thought, *I am a bit out of practice if*

the only response I evoke with my kiss is curiosity. "I thought," he said coolly, "that you wanted me to."

"No. Yes. No."

"Well, which is it, Mrs. Best?" he said, unknowingly switching to her formal address, unwittingly reminding her that her husband had died less than five months ago.

"It's no."

She rubbed a hand against her forehead, staring at him as if he'd somehow offended her fine sensibilities. Hell, he couldn't have misread her that much. She'd closed her damn eyes when he'd touched her cheek, and if that wasn't a sign that a woman was pleased, he didn't know what was.

Unless it was pity she'd felt for him. Pity because he'd laid his soul bare before her and she'd pulled away, then regretted hurting him. Hell, it had hurt. Everything hurt. Especially the look in her eyes of regret and alarm, as if she expected her husband to walk in on them at any moment. Suddenly Jared felt the control he'd had over his life, over every emotion he'd felt for the past five years, slipping out of his grasp because of this woman looking at him like some kissing monster sprung from the bowels of hell. He didn't like that his heart felt as if it were being squeezed, as if his throat had something hot lodged in it.

He stared at his now-cold eggs. Next to him, she rose and made a grab for his plate.

"I'll heat them for you," she said.

He pulled the plate back from her, feeling childish and not giving a damn. "They're fine," he said sharply, then proceeded to shovel a huge mouthful into his mouth. Cold. He *hated* cold eggs.

"Well, I don't know why you're so angry with me."

"I'm not angry," he said, knowing full well he sounded very angry.

"I'm leaving."

"Good-bye."

She stood at the door, staring at him. "It's just that no one's ever . . . Oh, forget it." And she slammed out the door.

Jared stared at the door a full second before bounding out of his chair and striding to the door. "Rachel," he shouted to her quickly retreating back. "Get back here." She crossed her arms and remained where she was.

"Please," he said in a growl, then managed to give her something like a smile. She walked to him, belligerence tinged with wariness, a charming combination, Jared thought. When she was within arm's length, Jared gave a quick look to make certain no one was about, then dragged her inside, ignoring her squeal of anger as he slammed the door shut.

And then he kissed her. Hard and long, pressing her against the closed door, both hands buried in her hair, his tongue buried in her mouth, his body hard against hers. He was a physical man, who made love with every inch of his body. He could be infinitely gentle, as he had been with his delicate little wife, or savage, as he had been with countless other women. With Rachel, he sensed he could be something in between.

He pulled back, his breathing harsh, his arousal creating an obvious bulge in his pants.

Rachel lifted a trembling hand to lips kissed pink by his lovemaking, her eyes darting nervously and growing wide when she saw his obvious need.

"You know I want to make love to you."

Rachel nodded.

Something of her uncertainty and fear must have shown in her eyes, for his entire body, held taut, slowly relaxed.

"I'm damned tired," he said, his voice rough and

low. "When I close my eyes, I feel like I'm on my ship. You must be tired, too. Go home, Mrs. Best."

Rachel looked at him, torn about what she was feeling, her heart saying one thing, her body saying something quite different. She wanted to make love to him, wanted to feel his body heavy and hot above hers, wanted to know what it felt like to have him slide inside her and move and kiss her as he'd just done. Over and over.

She opened the door and walked out, but before she closed the door behind her, she poked her head back in.

"Call me Rachel."

She shut the door quickly, picked up her skirts, and ran home.

Chapter Ten

After every storm that blasted by the cape, a handful of townspeople would walk along the endless miles of soft sand searching for treasures that would sometimes wash ashore. They would gather driftwood, the most common find, pile it high in carts, and use it for firewood throughout the bitter winter months. Indeed, the Newcombs had a huge pile of wood—some obviously ripped from a stranded ship—on one side of their home. A ship's mast could heat a home for most of the winter, or be cut up and used as shingles. Jared was beginning to understand Truro's complex relationship with hardship. There was not a soul in Truro who didn't mourn for those fallen sailors, and hardly a home that didn't have a bit of the *Isaac Small* in its woodpile.

Like many Cape Codders, Donald Small had a collection of quarterboards, long, narrow boards with ship's names carved into them, some simple and some elaborate. Jared chuckled and shook his head when he spied the *Isaac Small*'s quarterboard tacked onto one of the lighthouse's outbuildings.

"Oren gave me that one 'cause of the last name and all," Small said, a bit embarrassed by the gift. Small was carrying five-gallon barrels of oil from the shed to the lighthouse, and Jared pulled up two, placing one beneath each arm.

Jared enjoyed visiting with Small, a talkative man who loved to tell tales of wrecks, of the cabin boy found still alive and lashed to the mainmast, the only survivor in a wreck off Chatham, of the crew who perished after abandoning a ship that never sank. There were endless stories, all joyfully told by Donald Small. Lightkeeper was a lonely profession, and so Small didn't mind that Jared visited almost daily. Small would light his pipe and lean back in his chair, his log always within reach, and spin a tale. Jared would have been hard-pressed to explain why he enjoyed the older man's company. There was something soothing about sitting in his tiny and stiflingly hot kitchen and hearing the man drone on and on. As a whaling captain, he was used to long hours of idleness interrupted by a great frenzy of activity. But here life had a gentle ebb and flow, an almost soporific cadence that Jared found, to his growing dismay, comforting.

Christmas was nearing, but Jared felt no urge to return home. Other than two telegrams and a package from home containing clothing and other personal items, he'd had no contact with his family. He hadn't celebrated the holiday in years, except to give his crew rum and the day off.

Even though he knew his mother would like him home for Christmas, he had no plans to leave Truro. He didn't want anything to pull him away, to bring him back to a world he wanted to forget. Donald Small, with his penchant for talking rather than listening, was good company to Jared. He followed the lightkeeper about as he did his duties, as he heated the oil on his kitchen stove on particularly cold nights so the lamps would burn brighter. It was Small's greatest fear, he admitted, that during a frigid night the light would dim and a ship would founder. The last keeper lost his job that way, so Small was diligent about keeping his light lit and bright.

Small rarely imbibed, but Jared would sometimes nip at a bottle from a crate of whiskey Small had discovered on the beach a year before, surprising himself by stopping before he got drunk. He would stay there for supper or eat with Small at the tavern, believing Small when he said he enjoyed the company. He'd arrive at his own cottage long after the sun disappeared, long after he knew Rachel had gone to bed.

He walked home, his pants scraping against the barren berry bushes that lined the thin path cut through the sand, thinking of Rachel, of her quiet strength, of her need to explain every thought that came into her head. He stopped on a rise and looked down at the two cottages, dark and huddled together in a tiny hollow, picturing her sleeping and wondering if she felt half as lonely as he did. Jared let out a short, impatient breath, wondering why after being alone for six years, he had decided only now that he was lonely.

They'd been skittish around each other since those kisses, since he'd told her he wanted to make love to her, and now he found he missed her.

God! What an idiot he was to say something like that aloud. Certainly she knew enough about a man to know what he wanted, but to say it, to point it out, had been foolish in the extreme. He couldn't act on his desire, not with her wary and half-afraid of him. He was glad of her fear, glad she didn't look at him all the time as she had that morning, her lips parted, her eyes drowsy, her body languid and arching toward him. Lord knew he was no saint, but he hated feeling as if her husband would walk through the door at any moment and catch them. The man was dead, but he was alive and well in Rachel's heart, and that was what had stopped him that morning.

Though he called her Rachel to himself, he called her Mrs. Best to her face, ignoring her request, erecting a wall he wasn't certain he wanted to scale. He pretended those kisses never happened, that those words had never been spoken. Jared walked toward his cottage, the wind in his face, his hands jammed deep into his pockets. Tomorrow night he'd be on patrol. He'd have the entire night to walk and drive himself mad thinking about her.

Jared had completely taken over beach patrol for Ambrose, whose joints had become even more painful with the damp, frigid air that swept in from the Atlantic. On the nights he wasn't with Small, he patrolled the shore, costen in hand. On one calm, moonless night, he'd warned a ship away by waving his costen. He'd looked up and down the beach automatically to see if any other patrol had spotted the ship, and saw only a light above him that quickly disappeared. He'd wanted to whoop for joy when he saw that ship tack off and head safely away from shore, wanted to tell someone, to share his euphoria. For a man who'd spent nearly every moment of his life within spitting distance from another man, it had been strange to realize he was utterly alone.

Jared pushed open the cottage door and saw a lamp glowing low in his bedroom. He leaned against the doorjamb and frowned, not because he disliked the intrusion, but because he found he liked it too damn much. This feeling of contentment was swallowing him—a not entirely pleasant sensation, but one he did nothing to stop. Never in his life had Jared felt contented. He'd lived on the edge since he was six years old and a cabin boy on his father's whaler. He'd been brash and loud and crude and defiant his entire life. This feeling of well-being was as uncomfortable as new boots, as foreign to him as formal wear, but satisfying in a way he found slightly baffling.

"Jared, my good man," he said to himself, "you are starting to like it here entirely too much."

As the days passed, the only thing that jarred him out of his contented state was the unexpected sight of Rachel. He could not control the sudden pounding of his heart, the way he would awaken hard and sweating from a particularly vivid and erotic dream. He could not help but search for her familiar form as he trudged along the beach. During the day, Jared had taken to walking the beach like countless others, his eyes seeking out some treasure he could bring to the Newcombs. He felt like a child on holiday, and not at all like himself. One day something glittered in the sand, and Jared hurried over to find a silver hand mirror. He, a man who could have bought the finest etched-gold mirror, had presented it to Mabel as if handing her a rare treasure. She'd blushed and thanked him, and he'd grinned like a fool, hoping Rachel would think him gallant. But these days Rachel hardly glanced his way, and they were never alone.

Christmas was just a week away when Jared found on the beach a clear glass buoy that fishermen used to float their nets. The often colorful glass balls were a particular treasure to Cape Codders, often gracing walls like oversized Christmas ornaments. On his long voyages, Jared, like many whaling captains, would carve whalebone. His particular expertise had been in creating ships in bottles from the thin and pliable baleen. So when he found that perfectly clear ball, he kept his find to himself, knowing instantly what he would create with it. He worked at night, tediously carving from wood each delicate piece before gingerly placing it in the glass ball, sometimes working well past midnight on his gift for Belle.

He bought a painting of Highland Light for the Newcombs at the general store, a scene done by one of the many artists who visited the cape during the summer months. For Rachel, he had nothing. Truro's general store had very little other than the practical. He couldn't very well give her a bolt of gingham. He hadn't bought a present for a woman in years, and hadn't the slightest idea what this particular woman would want. It couldn't be something too extravagant, as his pocketbook could certainly afford. Nor something too personal, as he found he wanted to do. He thought of her hands, those capable, beautiful hands, and discarded the idea of buying her fine embroidered silk gloves. She didn't seem to need anything. Every notion he had, he discarded, and then he became irritated that he was spending so much time thinking about a gift for a woman.

"Why are you mad?" Belle had come upon him just as he was pondering the gift-giving business.

"I'm not mad, little girl. I'm hungry!" He lurched at her like the giant she pretended he was, and Belle gave a squeal of delight before remembering she was a brave princess who could slay mean giants.

"I cast you from my kingdom," she said regally, and Jared bowed down to one knee.

"Your servant," he said.

Belle giggled. She wore bright red mittens, a misshapen red muffler, and a red woolen hat, so that only her bright eyes and nose were showing. It was icy cold out and the sand was crusty from the morning frost. It had yet to snow any amount, so the ground was bleak and brown, covered with the low, scraggly brush that had long ago lost its foliage.

"Grandma sent me out to ask if you're going to the Christmas supper at the meetinghouse. She says you can go even if you are an Episcopal."

"Episcopalian."

"Will you go? You can sit next to me."

Belle looked so hopeful, Jared couldn't say no. He wondered how anyone could say no to such a child. She had bored a hole into his heart from the beginning, and Jared had no resistance to her. He'd stopped trying weeks ago. She was his little darling.

"With such an invitation, I can hardly say no."

She grinned.

Jared's eyes widened. "You've lost a tooth!"

Belle immediately closed her mouth. "It fell out this morning. It was loose but I didn't tell anyone. Darius Paine's father yanked his out when he told, so I kept it a secret. But it fell out anyway."

"That's what happens." Suddenly Belle's eyes filled with tears. "What's wrong, princess?"

"I'm s'pose to keep it and put it under my pillow for the tooth fairy, but I lost it," she wailed mournfully. "And now the tooth fairy won't come."

She flung herself against him, and Jared, looking a bit bemused to find a crying five-year-old in his arms, patted her back with one hesitant hand.

"We'll find your tooth," he said.

Belle pulled back. "But we looked everywhere."

"Giants have special powers."

Belle smiled, amazing Jared with her mercurial mood swings. "Really?"

"Really. Now smile for me so that I know just what I'm looking for." Belle gave him a wide smile. "I'll find your tooth before it's dark. Just in time for the tooth fairy."

"I'm going to tell Darius about my tooth. Bye."

Jared watched her go, a smile on his face. Then he

went into his cottage, picked out a piece of whalebone, and carved a little tooth. By the time Belle returned, he was finished. She accepted the not-quite-perfect tooth without question.

"You go in the house right now and put it under your pillow," he said sternly.

"I will."

Belle skipped home, the tooth held tightly inside her mitten. "Mama, look. Captain Mitchell found my tooth."

Rachel turned to see her daughter holding up something that looked very much like her tooth. When she held it in her hand, however, she knew immediately it was not her daughter's tooth at all. Rachel felt something hot behind her eyes, something that felt ridiculously like threatening tears.

"He said giants have special powers and can find tooths."

"Teeth."

"But I only lost one tooth."

Rachel sighed, deciding to forgo her grammar lesson for the moment. "Then that makes this tooth even more special, don't you think? I wonder what the tooth fairy will bring you?"

"A new penny?"

"You never know," Rachel said, giving Belle a little kiss.

"Where ever did that man find Belle's tooth?" Mabel asked after Belle went off to place the tooth under her pillow.

"He didn't. He carved one for her."

"Well, I'll be."

Rachel took up her muffler and coat. "I'm going to go thank him. I'll be right back."

Rachel braced herself against the bitter wind, thankful that the cottage was so near. This thank-you was simply an excuse, she knew. In her head, she could hear him say, over and over, *I want to make love to you*. Oh, just thinking about his voice, gruff and low, and his eyes, burning with desire, as if she were beautiful and the most desirable woman in the world, would make her feel as if her entire body were blushing.

She found him outside, sitting on a simple bench her father had built, facing the sun and out of the wind. It was almost warm there. He was straddling the bench, bending his head at some task. When he saw her he lifted his head and smiled, and Rachel had to fight to breathe. It had been days and days since she'd been alone with him, but it seemed like yesterday he had pressed her against his door and kissed her.

"That tooth is sure something," she said, fighting not to dip her gaze to his mouth.

"I'm not the carver my brother is, but I thought it was close enough."

Rachel rocked to her toes and back. "It's warm here. Compared to out in the wind."

"That's why I'm sitting here."

She let out a nervous laugh. "Yes. That's what I thought."

Jared folded up his pocketknife and gazed up at her. "Your daughter invited me to the Christmas supper."

Rachel studied the ground. "You're coming?"

"I said I would."

Rachel felt like stamping her foot in frustration. They were acting like strangers to one another. She hated this, hated that a single kiss—well, a few kisses—would turn them wary. She wished it had never happened. She wished he would kiss her again. Oh, she didn't know what she wished.

Rachel forced a smile. "I must warn you that you'll

likely be surrounded by the single girls. I don't know how many have come up to me every Sunday after meeting and asked about you."

He raised one eyebrow. "Oh? And what have you told them?"

Rachel hated that her face flushed red. She'd addressed such inquiries coolly, hoping to deflect any interest in him, a fierce possessiveness enveloping her each time one of the Truro girls coyly asked about him. She shouldn't have mentioned their interest, she realized. "I've told them only that you are well." She didn't tell him that some of the women had turned him into a hero for trying to stop those two boys from going into the surf.

Jared fiddled with the small object in his hand; it appeared to be another "tooth." He held it up. "Just in case she loses another," he said, to explain the carving. He squinted past her to the setting sun and inhaled a deep breath before swinging his leg around and motioning for her to sit next to him.

Rachel sat, her stomach a jumble of nerves at being so near him.

"I lied to you," he said, his eyes still on the carving held between his thumb and forefinger. He let out a sharp puff of air. "About that kiss." He looked at her then, gauging her reaction, studying her, and Rachel did her best to act only mildly interested in what he was about to say.

"Oh?"

"It wasn't a purposeful thing, the lie. I just forgot." He tossed the tooth away in what appeared to be an angry gesture. "The last woman I kissed wasn't my wife. It was my brother's wife." Jared let out a humorless laugh at the shock Rachel couldn't hide.

"Oh, they weren't married at the time. I'm not as bad as all that. But I kissed her. Against her will. I was drunk and she was there, and I didn't realize until later that I'd forced myself on her, that she didn't welcome my advances. She was there, and I suppose I was lonely for a woman, and so I kissed her."

During the speech, Jared kept his head down, his eyes hard on the ground. Rachel knew what he was implying: that the kiss between them meant nothing to him, that he was sorry.

"You weren't drunk that morning," Rachel said softly, watching as he clenched his jaw.

"No."

But it was still a mistake. Rachel bent her head so she could better see his expression. "I let you kiss me. I wanted you to. Then." She let out a nervous little laugh. "Of course, we were both tired, and it just happened. I don't want you to think I've been mooning over you because of it. I haven't. I haven't even thought about it. Well, perhaps a bit. Just wondering what you were thinking. Not that I want you to think about it, although I expect it would only be natural for a person to think about a kiss when they saw the person they'd kissed." Rachel pressed her lips together, willing herself to shut up.

Jared's hands gripped the edge of the bench on either side of him, squeezing even more tightly before he turned to look at her, amusement and something hot in his gaze.

"I've thought about little else but that damned kiss. You consume me, Rachel," he said so softly she barely heard him. "I know you've only been widowed a few months. I know that. And I know that I'm going to leave this place. Soon. Hell, I don't even know what I'm still doing here." He looked around, as if looking for the reason he felt so anchored to Truro. "It's this place," he said, his nostrils flaring as he breathed in the salt-tinged air. "I don't understand why I'm still here."

"I've never known anything but Truro," Rachel said, grasping onto the most mundane of what he'd said. *You consume me, Rachel.* She swallowed, feeling she had to explain why she'd backed away from him, why she'd been so afraid of what she'd been feeling. "And I've never known any man but Richard."

The impossibility of the situation hit Jared full force. He didn't belong here with these good people, with a woman like Rachel, who was still fighting the truth that her husband was dead. He'd kissed her on lips that had only brushed against her husband's, and though he told himself he'd done nothing wrong, a part of him felt as if he'd somehow soiled her. That was why, when he felt her hand on his nape, when she pulled him down to kiss her, he resisted for three heartbeats before giving in to his aching need to feel her lips against his.

He wanted to fill his hands with her breasts; he wanted to lift her skirts and touch a creamy thigh; he wanted to drive himself into her. Oh, God, if she knew what was going through his head when she touched her mouth against his, she would pull away and run home. His grip on the bench only tightened, for he knew that if he released his hands, he would pull her to him, carry her into his cottage and to that bed where she'd made love with her husband. It was only a simple kiss, nearly as innocent as a child's, but he'd mentally made love to her, touched her breast and felt it swell beneath his palm, nuzzled her belly, felt her heat around his member, touched every moist and warm place she possessed. When she pulled away, he knew she had no idea what that kiss had done to him, where it had sent him, how much effort it had taken to accept that innocent offering and seize nothing more.

"Now we're even," she said, a soft smile on her lips.

He smiled back even as his heart pounded madly in his chest, even as he hurt from not having her.

"Are you truly leaving soon?"

Jared pushed a hand through his hair, thankful to have his mind on something other than making love to her. "I got a letter today from my mother asking me to come home. It seems as if my little brother's crew mutinied off the California coast. I can hardly believe Gardner is old enough to captain a ship, never mind drive a crew to mutiny." His father, as cruel as he was, had never had a problem with his crew. Not because he inspired loyalty, but because he'd made certain no one on the ship knew how to navigate but him. Those poor sailors feared the endless ocean, believing the gruesome tales his father told of what lurked in the deep far more than they feared his father.

"Has anyone heard from him?" Rachel asked.

"Apparently not. But the first mate said they put him off safely." Jared chuckled. "I half believe the little idiot deserved his fate, if the mate went along with the mutiny. The last time I saw Gardner, he was fifteen years old and already full of himself."

"Aren't you worried about him?"

Jared shrugged. "Worrying about him isn't going to bring him home safely."

"Your mother wants you to go get him?"

Jared nodded. "My other brother would go, but his wife is expecting their firstborn."

"You're going, then?"

Something in her voice made him look sharply at her, but all he saw in her eyes was curiosity, certainly not the disappointment he thought he heard in her voice. "Not right away."

"I'm glad," she said, then quickly added, "You've been such a help to my father, you see. And, of course, Belle would be devastated to lose her giant."

Jared gave her a wink. "And who would you steal kisses from if I were gone?"

Rachel laughed, her blue eyes lighting up, clearly delighted with his teasing, and Jared's heart did a slow flip-flop. "If you keep looking at me like that, I might never leave," he said, sounding far more serious than he'd planned. He knew, suddenly, that it was true.

Chapter Eleven

⁓

Jared looked at his gift to Rachel with a critical eye, thinking that the tiny little cottage in the old whiskey bottle looked silly. Or charming. He couldn't decide which. To his mind's eye, a ship would look far better. But the cottage, a whimsical, near-exact replica of the one he now sat inside, might just make a woman smile. It was becoming far too important to him to make Rachel smile. Everything in Truro was becoming far too important, he realized.

Letting out a sigh of irritation, he set the bottle high atop the large hutch next to Belle's gift, noticing for the first time that the wind outside was rattling the windows. Though the cottage was almost overly warm, ice coated the outside of the multipaned windows, half melting from the heat inside and leaving a clear oval of clean glass in each rectangle.

Jared opened the door and was hit by a bitterly sharp blast of air. Damn, it was cold, the kind of cold that took your breath away, that hurt your lungs to breathe it in. He'd whaled the waters near the Arctic, so Jared knew what cold felt like, and the air whipping around the cottage was frigid. Jared closed the door quickly, wondering if a storm was brewing offshore. He padded to the window that faced the lighthouse and looked out . . . and saw nothing.

"Bloody hell," he whispered, his eyes searching the blackness for the beacon that shone so brightly that ships twenty miles out to sea could see it. *There!* Dimly glowing was the light, but Jared knew something was wrong, that the light should be shining brightly on a night such as this.

Pulling on his boots and grabbing his coat, Jared rushed from the cottage to the Newcombs' and banged on the door. Mabel answered, her face already filled with concern, for a visitor in the evening always meant something was wrong somewhere.

"A ship?"

Jared looked past her to Ambrose, who was getting up slowly from his spot near the fire. "The light is nearly out," Jared said. "Something must have happened to Don. I may need your help."

"It's the cold," Ambrose said in his clipped manner.

As Jared watched Ambrose hobble painfully to retrieve his boots, he knew the old man would be of little help, though he couldn't bring himself to speak his thoughts aloud.

"Papa. I'll go."

Jared turned to see Rachel, her coat and boots already on. Ambrose clenched a fist against the wall, but said, "Be careful."

"I want to go, too," Belle said, peeking her head around the corner.

"You're supposed to be in bed, young lady," Rachel said sternly. Belle frowned, a full-fledged, face-scrunching scowl. "To bed." Rachel pointed a finger, and Belle turned around muttering something, but obeying without further argument.

Rachel let out a sigh, then handed Jared a scarf, wrapped her own head, and headed out the door. "Belle announced today that she was big enough to go everywhere by herself. You should have seen her, stretching that little body up and thinking she could convince me that all five-year-olds should be allowed to go to town alone."

"I wonder where she gets that stubborn, independent streak," Jared said, as if he knew full well where Belle got it. Rachel ignored him.

"My father's worse than ever tonight," Rachel said when they were a few steps from the house. "It kills him that he can't do what he used to do."

"This damned New England weather's to blame," Jared said, squinting his watering eyes against the bitter wind. It was so cold, his exposed skin ached. "I hope Don's all right. He looked a bit pale earlier today. Said he was coming down with a cold. Hell, if he was sick, he should have told me, the fool."

"Men never like to admit they're sick."

The two walked hurriedly to the lighthouse, both knowing it was critical they do whatever possible to get the lamps burning brightly. Ships at sea looked to the light to guide them around the cape—without it, disaster was almost certain.

When they reached the rise by the lighthouse, Jared let out a curse upon seeing Don's darkened cottage. "This doesn't look good. Something's got to be wrong. Don would die before he let that light go out." Unexpected fear ate at Jared's gut. He'd come to like the old man in the past weeks. He should have known he was sicker than he was letting on; he should have stayed with him.

When they reached the lighthouse, Jared entered the house without knocking and nearly stumbled over the lightkeeper, who lay prone and moaning on the floor.

"Aw, hell, Don," Jared said, kneeling beside the shivering older man as Rachel lit a lamp. "Come on, you old fool," he said kindly. "Let's get you to your bed."

"The light. I passed out," Small rasped.

"Taken care of. Don't worry. It's bright as daylight out there," Jared lied. Then to Rachel in a tone that brooked no argument, "Get that fire stoked hot."

He picked up Small with ease, laid the old man on his bed, and tucked the covers around him. "You thirsty, Don? You need anything?"

"Thirsty."

"I'll be right back." Jared went back to the kitchen to work the pump.

"It's frozen; I already tried it. But there's a bucket of ice in the corner there. Once this fire's going, I'll melt some."

Rachel looked at Jared as if she'd never before seen him. He was in complete control, his movements economical, his face taut, his words clipped. He was the epitome of a sea captain, bigger than life, tougher than rawhide, cooler than the ice in that bucket. She hated doing it, but she found herself comparing Jared to Richard, who had not been the calmest man when under duress. When Belle had gotten terribly sick after eating a raw mussel, she'd spent nearly as much time comforting and calming Richard as she had Belle.

"The water can wait. We need to heat up the oil. Is that fire going yet?"

Rachel felt the top of the stove. It was just getting hot to the touch. "Nearly."

Jared disappeared and returned a moment later with a small cask in his hands. He hefted a huge kettle on top of the stove and poured the oil in. It was thick from the cold. As he watched it pour into the pot, Jared clenched his jaw.

"Don said the government gave him cheap oil to save money. Look at this oil. It's as thick as molasses." When he was finished, he dropped the cask with disgust. "I'm going to check on the light. You keep that fire going," he said.

Rachel smiled after he left, thinking about how his crew must have jumped when he issued an order. She found herself complacently following orders like a cabin boy. By the time he returned, the oil was thinning in the kettle. "Are the lamps still lit?"

"Barely. How's that oil?"

"Almost ready, sir," Rachel said in mock sternness.

Jared chuckled, then gave her his darkest scowl, though she could see by the light in his eyes that he was teasing her. "Are you being insubordinate, sailor?"

"Never, sir!" Rachel tried to be serious, but broke into a fit of giggles. A moan from Small sobered her immediately. "How is he?"

"He's got a fever; that's all I know."

Jared went to check on the lightkeeper while Rachel stirred the oil, which was now thin and nearly hot. When Jared returned, she said, "I think the oil is ready now. It's hot."

"Let's put the oil into something smaller. You ladle; I'll hold the pot."

Rachel grabbed the large ladle and began scooping the oil from the kettle and into the pot as quickly as possible, knowing that with each passing minute, a ship could be moving closer to danger. The pot was nearly full when she accidentally hit the ladle hard against the side, causing a small amount of oil to splash onto her hand.

"Ouch!" she yelled, dropping the ladle onto the floor and shaking her hand.

Rachel would never know how Jared was able to put the pot down and grab her as quickly as he did without spilling a drop, but before she could even look at her hand, he had pulled her away from the stove in a frenzy of movement.

"Christ, oh, Christ, are you all right?" He looked at her hand as if he expected it to be horribly disfigured, when in fact it hardly hurt at all. "Rachel,

honey, I'm so sorry. Oh, God. I never should have
let you help. Damn it, what the hell was I thinking?"

"Will you please stop all that cursing and let my
hand go?" Rachel pulled her hand forcibly away.
"I'm fine, Jared. I was just startled. Look. It's not
even red." Rachel held up her hand to his panic-
filled eyes. He took several long, deep, shuddering
breaths before abruptly turning away to retrieve the
pot. He bent to pick it up, his hand visibly shaking.
Letting out yet another curse, he straightened and
fisted his hands by his side before calmly picking the
pot up off the floor.

"I'll be in the light," he said without turning to
her.

Rachel closed her eyes briefly before going to the
sink for a cloth to wipe her hand, which was only a
tiny bit pink from the hot oil. Brow furrowed, she
wondered at Jared's reaction to what had been a simple accident. Perhaps as a whaling captain he was
overly cautious when it came to oil. Giving a mental
shrug, she went in to check on Donald Small, laying
a cool cloth over his forehead.

"The light."

"Jared's taking care of it, Mr. Small." He closed
his eyes, obviously trusting his friend to make
things right.

Rachel put some ice on the stove to melt before
making her way down the long, narrow, covered
passageway that led to the lighthouse and climbing
the winding iron staircase that led to the light. She
wrinkled her nose at the strong smell of oil and
smoke. Looking up, she could see a square of bright
light coming from the trapdoor, and she smiled,
knowing Jared had successfully lit the lamps. She
poked her head up cautiously, not knowing whether
he would be glad or annoyed that she'd followed
him up. His back was to her as he leaned on the

iron railing and looked past his reflection out to the dark Atlantic.

"Hello." Jared turned and looked at her briefly before turning back to the sea. He was clearly still upset about what had happened in the kitchen, Rachel thought as she squinted her eyes at the brightness, noting that each of the argand lamps was burning brightly. Fans of light cut into the night air through the light snow that was beginning to fall.

Jared seemed so very alone standing there, and Rachel wished she could simply go up to him and wrap her arms about his waist, rest her head against his back. She could kiss him; she could give him release from the desire she saw when he looked at her, but she could not give him comfort. Always he held something back, something hidden, a hurt or a memory that scarred him, as if joy and happiness were simply words to him and not something he'd personally experienced. Even when he was with Belle and laughing, Rachel sensed a deep sadness that went beyond simple grief, and an aloneness that went beyond loneliness.

"My wife and little girl died from burns. Hot oil from the tryworks splashed on them."

Rachel's eyes instantly filled with tears as understanding and compassion flooded her. "Oh, Jared, how awful."

"Yes," he said softly. "It was awful."

Rachel looked at her undamaged hand again, now understanding why Jared had reacted as he had. "Look, Jared." She held up her hand to show him that she was unharmed. He turned, his eyes filled with a despair that slammed into Rachel's heart and made it hurt. He slowly held up his own hand and grasped hers, pulling it to his mouth and kissing her palm, his eyes tightly closed. It seemed the most natural thing to step into his arms, to raise her head for his kiss, to wrap her arms around him as she longed to do. He let out a low sound that rumbled from his chest as his mouth came down upon hers.

He kissed her with ferocity and a possessiveness that was almost frightening. He held her face between his hands in a way that made her feel cherished, his eyes traveling over each of her features and lingering on her mouth. "I think about this all the time, you know. Your mouth. Kissing you." To prove it, he kissed her again, long enough to make Rachel's knees weak with the desire raging through her veins. And then he pushed her away almost angrily. "Half of Truro could see us. Or at least our shadows." He gave her a tight smile. "I lose myself when I'm with you."

"Is that good or bad?"

She'd asked the question lightly, because suddenly everything was too serious, because her heart was pounding and her body was shaking. But he looked at her, his gaze penetrating, and he didn't smile. "I'm not certain yet."

"Perhaps we shouldn't kiss anymore." She hoped that he'd immediately protest, and fully expected him to. She hoped that her challenge would cause him to dip his head and prove that he wanted to kiss her. So when he nodded, she barely stifled a gasp of disappointment.

"I wasn't really serious about not kissing," she said, grinning at him.

"This isn't a game anymore," he nearly growled.

Rachel stiffened. "I never thought it was."

He made a gesture of impatience. "You're not the kind of girl a man kisses for fun. If you don't know that, I do."

Rachel suddenly found the light unbearably warm and glaringly bright. The smoke was choking her. "Then what kind of girl am I?"

Jared muttered a curse, then repeated it loudly when he saw her expression. "For one thing, you're not a girl. You're a woman," he said angrily, grasping her upper arms. "For another thing, I think I'm . . ." *Falling in love with you.* He was so surprised by the thought, by what he'd almost said aloud, that he dropped his hands and stepped back.

"You think you're what?" she demanded.

Jared stared at her, stared at this woman he loved, a carefully blank expression on his face. "I think I'm going to check on Don."

He moved past her, brushing by her in the narrow space between the lamps and the railing.

"That's not what you were going to say."

He ignored her and moved down the hatch, then stopped. "Can you manage that with those skirts?" he called up.

"Quite well," came the clipped reply.

"I'm sure you can," he said angrily. Hell, he didn't know why he loved her. She was too independent. Too tough. As he made his way back to the ill lightkeeper, it kept pounding at him, relentless and almost painful: *You love her.*

Jared remembered loving Abigail. It had been an uncomplicated thing with only joy and happiness. He'd known her since he was a boy, decided to marry her when he was eighteen and home for four months between whaling trips. He'd courted her, then left her. And when he returned, Abigail was standing on the dock waiting for him, tears in her eyes. They were married two months later, and on a ship two months after that.

The moment he'd known he loved Abigail, he told her, and she'd flung herself into his arms shouting that she loved him, too. They had hardly discussed whether Abigail should accompany him on a ship, and never did Jared feel the raw fear that she could be in danger. He was young, strong, and brash, and loved his girl so. What could possibly go wrong?

Abigail, the poor thing, had no idea, none at all, what she was getting herself into when she walked aboard that ship. She couldn't know of the terrible loneliness, the endless seasickness, the stench, the vermin, the men who swore and spit and scratched. Jared knew it would take some adjustment, but he'd been completely unprepared for just how frightened Abigail had been. She confessed one night when the seas were rough and the wind blasting sleet and snow that she knew she'd made a mistake. It had crushed Jared. This was his world, and he wanted his wife to be part of it. He set about teaching her about the ship, about whaling, hoping to change her mind.

And that was why she'd been topside for the boiling, a place any sane man would have known was fraught with danger. She hadn't wanted to watch, not really, but he'd smiled and charmed her and sentenced her to die.

He moved down the narrow corridor toward Small's cottage, ducking his head at the entryway. The man's small bedroom was lit by the light, a sharp shaft of it streaking across the foot of the bed.

"You got her lit," he said, sounding weak and raspy.

"We did." He placed his hand on the older man's forehead. It was hot and dry. "How are you feeling?"

"Better now. Better." He swallowed and winced. "Thank God you came, Captain. Thank God."

"Someone would have come. The patrols would have seen the light was out."

"I just couldn't make it. Couldn't."

"Get some rest," Jared said, dismissing his words with a shake of his head. "I'll stay here tonight. You needn't worry about the light. Rest now."

Small's eyes drifted closed, and Jared made certain he was well covered before entering the kitchen. Rachel was there, stoking the stove.

"How is he?"

"Resting. I'm staying here tonight. You might as well go on home. It's late."

Rachel nodded but didn't move from her place by the stove. She looked so damned pretty with her cheeks flushed and that red-gold hair of hers flying about her face. Jared swallowed and made an attempt at a smile. "I'll walk you back. Donald'll be all right for now. And the light's well lit."

The wind moaned against the lighthouse, a mournful, low sound that sometimes carried all the way to the Newcomb house. Rachel huddled further into the coat even though it was quite warm in the kitchen. "I hate to go out there again. It's so cold. But I suppose my mother's getting worried. I'd be happy for the company, if you don't mind."

Just then the door flew open and Mabel Newcomb rushed through. It took one look to see something was desperately wrong. "Is she here? Is she?"

"Not Belle," Rachel said, fear washing over her face. Her mother began crying.

"Oh, have mercy. She's not here?"

"Mama, where is Belle?"

Chapter Twelve

〜

"She left the house. She must have seen you leave and wanted to follow. Oh, God, Rachel, she didn't take her coat. I thought for certain she was coming here. She knows the way." Mabel dissolved into sobs, muttering about the cold and coats and how Belle knew better than to leave the house without a coat, while Rachel stood there, stunned, looking from Jared to her mother as if beseeching someone to tell her it was all a horrid mistake.

"Where is Ambrose?" Jared said, the command in his voice instantly calming Mabel, if not Rachel.

"Out looking."

"Where? Precisely."

"I came here; he went south, along the beach."

"Good. Rachel, you head toward Truro Center. I'll look on the beach from here to the bluff below your house. Call for her. Keep calling and listen." Jared's gut clenched as he gathered up every lamp in the lighthouse and lit them, raising the flames high. "Did she have on her shoes or slippers?"

Mabel looked about to dissolve into tears again. She shook her head. "I don't know. I can't imagine she would have gone out without shoes."

It was so damned cold out there. He knew it

wouldn't take long for a little girl without a coat to fall into a slumberous state. "We have to find her quickly. Go. Now. And keep calling." Jared handed the women a lamp. They were about to leave when he thought to give them a blanket in case they found her. Shoving the rough wool blanket into their arms, he grabbed up his own lantern and blanket and headed out the door.

"Jared," Rachel said, looking up at him, looking for hope that he knew he shouldn't give.

He set his jaw. "We'll find her." Then he turned and walked toward the beach.

With every cold blast that stung his cheeks, his fear grew. He knew what the cold could do to a grown man. He'd seen men nearly die without even knowing they were in danger. He once pulled a young man from the crow's nest, his face pale and tinged blue, and the entire time the fool was mumbling how he was fine. His own father had told him a tale of a man who came back from the dead after being nearly frozen. They'd put him in the hold, wrapped in a blanket, and when the time came to slide him into the sea, his father noticed the man's hand move. But that was one of the grand stories his father told, and he'd never known which were true and which were simply tall tales.

His lungs ached from the frigid air and his eyes watered as he searched in vain for a sign of Belle. The lamp was turned down low, for he found it easier to see into the distance without it, even without a moon. Every shadow, every bit of beach debris he saw made his heart bloom with hope. And he called over and over, until his throat was raw. In his heart he knew that even if the little girl heard his cries for her, she would likely be unable to respond. With each minute that passed, his fear grew, his cries became more desperate, his thoughts more tormented with memories of his own little girl, dying, silently beseeching her daddy to stop the hurt. Sharp and raw, the memory of Belle hugging him, so soft and little, stabbed into his heart. Somehow she'd gotten in there, nestled deep inside that cold place where his grief and pain lived, and made him love her as if she were his own.

"Please, God," he said in a ragged whisper, squeezing his eyes closed. "Don't let her die."

Cold. God, it was so cold. Rachel was a mindless creature, dissolving slowly into a grief so deep it was all she could do to keep calling out her little girl's name. She tormented herself with visions of Belle huddled against the cold, calling out for her in an ever-weakening voice, wondering where her mommy was.

"I'm here, baby," she said aloud, her voice thick with tears that fell and froze on her cheeks. She searched the path that led to Truro Center, calling out, begging God, praying, cursing the cold. In the distance she thought she heard her mother, and she looked back at Highland Light. She turned and stared for a long, long time and knew, suddenly and with certainty, that Belle never would have ventured this way, toward the dark. She would have gone toward the light; she would have been trying to find her mother.

A sense of calm stole over her. Her mother in her frantic search must have walked right by Belle. She must have. Belle would have gone toward the lighthouse, fearless and foolish, thinking that she was too big to wear a coat if she didn't want to. And maybe she realized quickly that she needed her coat and started heading home. Perhaps she was home right now, being fed warm broth by her grandmother.

Rachel shot a quick look back into the darkness,

fear and doubt suddenly blooming in her chest. What if she turned around now and Belle was just over the next rise, or over the next? What if she was a few feet away? If she turned back now, she would miss her and Belle would surely freeze to death. For the rest of her life, guilt would gnaw at her, rip her apart. Wasn't her heart already ravaged by guilt over Richard?

"Richard, I don't know what to do," she whispered. "I don't know what to do!" she screamed, hurting her throat. She wanted to collapse, to drown in her grief and anger. Instead she turned toward the light, toward her cottage, believing—knowing—that Belle had walked toward the lighthouse. She prayed she was right.

Jared stood at the base of the bluff beneath the path that led to the Newcomb cottage. The tide was in, so the beach was simply a thin strip of sand. He couldn't have missed her, walked on past as she huddled against the cold. Could he have?

"Where are you, Belle?" he said aloud. He stood at the base of the bluff debating whether to continue down the beach or scour the path between the bluff and the cottage, keenly aware that Belle's time was running out. The wind carried the sound of someone calling out, and he tensed, thinking perhaps she'd been found. But no, it was simply Rachel or Mabel, calling over and over.

The cold seeped through his coat, through his thick sweater, and a feeling of dread washed over him. A little girl could not live long in such temperatures. A little girl would die, would simply curl up and fall asleep.

Jared swallowed past a growing lump in his throat, and his hands balled into fists. He wanted to scream out his frustration, as if screaming would somehow bring Belle to him. He was just about to trudge up the bluff when something caught his eye, a flash of white, a fluttering in the wind. Slowly he raised the flame in the lamp and held it high. A little foot, as white as the sand it rested upon, peeked out from behind a drift of sand.

"Oh, God." He rushed over to her, laying the lamp by her head and bringing her up into his arms. "Belle, honey, it's the captain." She was stiff and icy, her lips blue, her skin so pale it, too, had taken on a bluish cast.

"Daddy," she said, her voice soft and muffled.

"Oh, Belle," Jared said, his voice breaking as he hugged her tightly to him. "You'll be all right, baby. I'm going to get you warm."

"I *am* warm," she said, and actually tried to push him away.

"I know. You're warm," Jared said as he wrapped the woolen blanket about her. One little pink slipper still clung to her foot. He covered her from head to foot, then opened his jacket and nestled her against his body, shocked at how cold she felt.

Holding his bundle tightly against him, he made his way up the steep bluff. When he reached the top, he began yelling, "I found her. I found Belle." And then to the bundle he held against him, he said, "I found you, baby. You're safe now."

"I know, Daddy."

Jared pressed his cheek against the top of her head. She was hallucinating, of course. He'd seen it happen before; men who'd been out in the cold too long would suddenly see their wives or children. To the superstitious sailors, it was a frightening thing for one of their own to claim to see a relative who had passed on. They thought it portended death, and they would spit or flee or make the sign of the cross, depending upon their religious beliefs.

Ambrose was the only one at the Newcomb cottage when he reached the house.

"She alive?" he asked, his voice gruff but his eyes filled with fear.

Jared nodded and brushed past the old man and toward Belle's room. "She's nearly frozen, though."

"I've got water heating. We'll dunk her in."

Jared ripped back the covers and laid Belle down, then piled all the blankets atop her. "No. We've got to warm her slowly. Heat some bricks. We'll wrap them and lay them around her."

"She's not shivering," Ambrose said, hovering by the door, worry etched into his face.

"She's past that. She'll shiver. Then we'll know she's getting warmed up."

Rachel burst into the room, tears flowing freely down her face. "Oh, Belle, my baby," she said, rushing to her daughter's side.

"Mama." Belle smiled through blue lips. "I forgot my coat," she slurred.

"I know, honey. It's all right."

"Oh, thank the Lord," Mabel said from the door. "Where was she?"

"At the base of the bluff." Jared swallowed hard. "I'd walked right past her. Right on past." He stared hard at the little girl in the bed, at her perfect face, which was just beginning to regain some natural color. She would have died. She would still be huddled behind that windswept drift if Jared hadn't seen her white nightgown fluttering in the wind, if he hadn't turned to look down the beach one last time. He felt as if a giant fist were squeezing his heart.

"I'll be in the cottage," he said, whirling around, brushing roughly past Rachel and her mother. "Just keep her warm. Put the bricks around her."

Belle began shivering. "Oh, Mama, I'm so cold."

"That's a good sign, according to the captain,"

Ambrose said, his hand filled with hot bricks wrapped in some of his old flannel shirts. "Said it meant she was warming up. Let's get these around her. Warm you up good, eh?"

Belle managed to nod, even though her little body began to quake almost violently. Rachel lifted the covers and lay down next to her daughter, to hold her, to make her warm. "My toes hurt," Belle said, and began crying.

After an hour, the shivering stopped and Belle drifted off to sleep, her breathing soft and even. Rachel brushed the hair from her daughter's forehead and kissed her now-rosy cheek, closing her eyes at the softness, the warmth of her skin.

"I almost lost her," she said to her mother, who'd come in to say good night.

"It's a terrible thing to lose a child."

Rachel nodded. "I don't know how you went on. I truly don't."

"You just do, that's all. You just go on breathing, living."

Rachel looked at her mother. "Did you ever think you couldn't go on? Did you ever wish—"

"No. I never did. I had you. I had your father. You go on. You live."

Rachel nodded. "It's funny. Jared told me about his little girl tonight, about how she died. I thought I understood, but I didn't. I suppose I still don't. But I understand better, that kind of pain. I don't know if I could go on, if . . ." Her eyes filled with tears.

"You just do," Mabel said with Yankee finality. "Good night."

"Good night." Rachel hugged her arms about herself and stared at Belle sleeping. And stared and stared as silent tears coursed down her cheeks. Finally she wiped her cheeks with her apron and moved to the window to look out. Jared's cottage was still lit from within. She walked to the kitchen, pulled on her coat, and went outside, crossing to his cottage before giving such a late-night visit much thought. Before she could knock, the door opened.

"I saw you coming," he said, stepping back to let her in. "Hell of a night."

Rachel walked in, welcoming the blast of warm air that hit her. It was one thing she'd always loved about her cottage—it was so small, it warmed quickly and stayed toasty even on the coldest winter nights.

"I know it's late. I wanted to thank you for finding Belle."

"How is she?"

"Sleeping. Warm." She stood in the middle of his kitchen feeling tense and awful. And so alone. She didn't want to feel alone. "Oh, Jared." Her eyes filled with tears. He opened his arms and she ran into them, hugging him to her fiercely.

"It's all right. She's all right," he said against her hair as he crushed her to him.

"But . . . but . . ." She hiccupped. She looked up at him. "Oh, how did you bear it? How did you?"

His eyes filled with pain. "I didn't." He stepped back from her, and Rachel wished she'd never said such a thing to him. Of course he hadn't "gone on," as her mother said she had. He'd tried to drown himself in whiskey, then hoped the cold Atlantic would do the job for him.

"When my wife and baby died, I wanted to die. I prayed to die. I thought I deserved to die. Every time I saw the sun rise, every time I felt the pure joy of living, I'd remind myself I didn't deserve to feel that way. I killed my family." He ignored Rachel's small sound of protest. "Belle. Looking for Belle, thinking she was dead." His eyes moved over her face as if searching for something, understanding or shock or anger. "I couldn't bear it again, Rachel. She's not even mine and I . . ." He closed his eyes briefly. "This man," he said, jabbing a thumb into his chest so hard, Rachel winced. "This man cannot lose another child."

She knew he was warning her away from him, telling her straight out that they could have no future. "I told you before that I'm not looking for a man," she said. Yes, she'd said it before, but this time she knew she was lying to both of them.

Chapter Thirteen

Rachel, to her great annoyance, found herself surrounded by three of Truro's eligible men, none of whom were saying much to her. They were talking to one another of fish and weather, the two main topics of conversation at any Truro gathering. They even smelled of fish and weather, that briny scent a fisherman carried with him even after a good, hot bath. Each, at one time or another in the past three months, had visited her with the specific intention of courting her. The visits had been awkward meetings in which Richard had been the topic of stilted conversation, making their attempts at courting strained, solemn affairs. Rachel didn't think ill of the men—they simply wanted a wife, and she was available. How could they know that Rachel considered herself decidedly unavailable when she was too polite to tell them directly to go home? They were her friends and she liked them all.

Rachel looked between the shoulders of her admirers, not even pretending not to look for Jared. She smiled when she found him sitting on the side of the meetinghouse with Belle on his lap. All evening, just as she had predicted, a covert parade of Truro's single women had filed past Jared. At first it was all

Rachel could do not to rush to his side. But then she
noticed that her daughter was doing a fine job of
staking her claim and was far less tactful than Rachel
would have been. Each time a lady came to say hello,
Belle would direct Jared's attention immediately to
herself. At this moment, they were talking earnestly
about something; he was nodding and she was ges-
turing, her face alight with happiness. Belle had one
hand about his neck, and her booted feet were swinging, banging against his shin so hard, Rachel winced.
She wondered when he'd gone from not wanting to
hold Belle's hand to allowing her, crumbs and jam
and all, onto his lap. Despite his fervent declaration
that he wanted nothing to do with any child, Belle
was ever more his shadow. He didn't push her away.
Truth be told, he seemed to welcome her attention.
She couldn't count the number of times she'd seen
the two of them walking along, more often than not
Belle's hand tucked into his large one. He'd hoist her
onto his shoulders and she'd laugh and shriek to be
up so high. No, he didn't ignore Belle. *He's ignoring
me,* Rachel thought, telling herself it was ridiculous
to feel jealous of the attention he was lavishing on
her own daughter.

It was silly on her part, but ever since his grief-
filled declaration that surely was meant to tell her
they had no future together, she'd begun to think of
him as something permanent in her life. She'd begun
to think that she was perhaps—just perhaps—falling
in love with him.

She watched as Belle kissed his cheek, as he pretended to wipe away the slobber, making Belle giggle. Belle would be devastated when Jared left. And
he would leave. He would, she told herself. In some
ways Belle would mourn his loss more than that of
her own father. Richard was more like Ambrose, a
gruff, crusty Cape Codder who felt extremely uncom-

fortable around little girls. Richard would ruffle Belle's hair as if she were a scrappy puppy, and mutter something about her new Sunday dress, blushing as if he'd gushed, and Rachel's heart would swell.

She'd thought Jared much the same, yet there he was looking quite content to have a five-year-old entertaining him. Belle looked so tiny sitting on his lap. It didn't matter that he could look fierce, or that he towered above most men. He held an elusive quality that obviously Belle felt. She'd never seen Belle on Richard's lap; she'd never seen her even ask to be picked up. Yet there she was, her eyes wide and earnest, sitting on her giant's lap.

Rachel looked about the room, at the people she'd known her entire life. The meetinghouse's benches had been cleared from the center of the room and moved to the perimeter, where the married women, widows, and elderly sat. Boughs of evergreen had been strung about the room, and sprigs of holly adorned the windows. In the room's center, the young people gathered, a sharp imaginary line dividing the girls and boys, though they eyed one another often enough. Running among them were the children, polished shoes scuffed, shirts untucked, pinafores wrinkled and stained with sweets. Rachel fit somewhere the middle, for she was a young widow. Her girlhood friends, those women who now sat on the benches with babies on their knees or sleeping on their shoulders, looked at her with a mixture of fear and pity. Pity that she'd been left alone so young, and fear that the same might happen to them. Many of their husbands were fishermen and were at this moment fishing off George's Bank, getting in one last trip before Christmas.

Rachel was close to none of them, for her home was isolated, a good walk from the bayside, where most of Truro's residents had built their homes. Her best friend—her only friend—had been Richard. Standing with these three men, Rachel felt oddly alone, and the longing for Richard—the Richard of her girlhood—came on sudden and strong.

Her eyes drifted to Jared. He was not her friend. She was uncertain what he was, other than a man she thought of too much, wanted far too much. The thought of kissing any of the men standing near her was enough to send her into a fit of giggles. Oren, who became animated only when discussing the size of a cod, and Obed, who never became animated. Samuel Roberts had teeth missing and foul breath, though he was the best-looking of the lot until he smiled.

"Gentlemen, if you'll excuse me. I think I'll rescue Captain Mitchell."

All three looked at her as if they'd forgotten she was standing among them. They probably had.

As she neared Jared and Belle, he looked up, and Rachel felt that now-familiar jolt, a frisson of sensation from her scalp to her toes, and she looked away fearing he would see in her eyes what she was thinking. Always with such feelings would come the guilt that Richard had disappeared not even six months ago and the knowledge that never, not even when she was a giddy sixteen-year-old, had she felt anything close to the way she felt when she looked at Jared.

"Where are all the ladies you promised me?" Jared asked, his eyes lit with good humor.

"Ah, the parade of single ladies is over? I suppose now they are simply mooning from afar."

"What's mooning?" Belle asked, resting her head sleepily against Jared's shoulder.

"The way your mama looks at me," Jared whispered overloudly.

Rachel shot him a look of exasperation, but inside she was glad that he was teasing her again.

"Oh," Belle said, satisfied with the explanation, and Rachel turned red, thinking that somehow she'd been so transparent that even her five-year-old daughter had recognized where her thoughts strayed.

Rachel laid her hand on the side of Belle's face. "Tired, hon?"

Belle nodded, closing her eyes and snuggling against Jared.

"I can carry her home," he said, and Belle smiled, her eyes still closed.

Jared stood, shifting Belle so that her head lay upon his shoulder. She wrapped her arms about his neck, contented as a kitten curling up in the sun. Rachel couldn't help but think that next year Jared wouldn't be around to carry her sleeping daughter home. Her heart ached for Belle—and for herself, she admitted. She and Belle would be alone, truly alone. It was the first year Rachel could remember that her parents had stayed home from the Christmas supper, and for the first time she took seriously her mother's dire warnings that they wouldn't be around forever. Hadn't she thought Richard would be with her forever?

Rachel looked over to the man striding next to her. He seemed invincible, but he'd nearly died. Rachel gave herself a mental shake to rid herself of such maudlin thoughts. It must be the Christmas season, her first without Richard, that was making her so melancholy.

"Don't you want to be home for Christmas?" she asked.

Jared seemed taken aback by the question. "I haven't been home for Christmas in more than ten years." He said it without a hint of sadness.

Rachel couldn't imagine such a thing, such a life as a whaler led. To her, family and home life was everything. It was unthinkable to her not to be home for the holidays. "Did you ever get lonely for home?"

Jared let out a small chuckle. "As a lad I did. But whaling is the only life I've ever known. To me it's strange to be on land."

"And will you be going back to sea?" Rachel ignored the hollowness in her heart at the thought that he would go to sea. For some reason, it was more disagreeable to imagine him on a whaler than in New Bedford. She waited for him to answer as they made their way up a sandy bluff. When they reached the top, they could see the ocean, the moon's reflection wavering on the surface. He stopped and stared out over the Atlantic. "You miss it."

He shook his head. "No. Not at all. I've been at sea but for a few months a year since I was six years old and a cabin boy for my father. I loved it, everything about it."

"I think I should hate it," Rachel said. "I'd miss home too much."

Jared felt the weight of Belle on his shoulder, her moist little-girl breath against his neck, and couldn't imagine being anyplace on earth other than where he was at that moment. If he could freeze time, he would have done it right then, with Rachel standing next to him looking lovely in the moonlight, and Belle sleeping trustingly on his shoulder. Safe. He knew he couldn't have borne losing Belle. But walking away, saying good-bye as he knew he someday would, seemed nearly as difficult. Jared had never been a man to examine his own feelings too closely. Things were what they were. He was either happy or not. The most troubling thing was, lately he'd been happy, happier than he'd been in his life. And for some reason that he found rather bemusing, all this happiness scared him. What he really needed, he decided, was a swift kick in the head. Maybe that would knock some sense back in and purge him of all this damn *thinking*.

"It's a different world at sea. A man's world, and certainly not a gentleman's world," he said, remembering some of the more unsavory activities he and his men engaged in.

"And yet your wife went with you."

"Aye. She did. My father warned me a hundred times: 'Ye don't take a female on your ship, lad,'" Jared said, imitating his father's rough voice. "Many captains bring their wives. Some enjoy the life. Abigail didn't, though she tried."

He began walking again, shortening his steps to accommodate Rachel's slower pace. "I won't be going back to sea."

"Why not?"

"It'll kill me, that life, and I've decided death isn't something I want to experience yet. I'm thirty-two years old and I've looked death in the face more than most men do in a lifetime." Jared knew he sounded bitter, and was actually surprised that he was revealing so much to himself and to Rachel. Until he'd spoken the words aloud, he hadn't come to a decision about returning to his ship. But now that he'd uttered the words, it felt right. *He* felt right. Patrolling the beach at night made him feel good. Waving that costen flare and turning that ship from shore had had him walking on clouds for a day. When was the last time he felt like that?

Rachel let him in the house and led him to Belle's room, watching silently as he laid her little girl on the bed and kissed her forehead. Belle had slept on his shoulder all the way home, stirring only a bit when Jared laid her down. Belle loved Jared in the pure, open way only a child could, and Rachel's heart already ached for the time when he would leave and crush Belle's heart.

And mine.

Her mind whirled crazily, and she ached to ask

him how long he planned to live in the cottage. A part of her hoped that if she never broached the subject of his leaving, he would stay forever. Over and over she asked him silently: *Why are you still here, Captain Mitchell?*

Why would a man, a wealthy sea captain, hang about a place like Truro? Such a man would pay his debts, and when they were paid, he would leave. She realized with sickening clarity that she had allowed herself to hope that she was the reason he was staying, that he would fall in love with her and marry her. Rachel resolutely decided that what happened at the lighthouse had more to do with his own painful memories than any real care or concern for her.

Rachel simply wanted to curl up and lose herself in self-pity. What had she been thinking? That he would stay? That a man who'd seen the most exotic places on earth would decide to make Truro his home? She almost laughed aloud. And what of her? Did he pity her, too? The poor widow whose husband didn't love her, who had never been properly kissed, who practically threw herself at him?

In her world, if a man kissed a woman it meant they were courting. And certainly if a man declared he wanted to make love, it was tantamount to a marriage proposal. But Rachel instinctively knew then—and was even more convinced now—that Jared was from a world where the rules were far different. They had kissed more than once, and in a way that was just one step away from making love. Did it mean nothing?

Rachel brushed that thought away, growing angry with herself as they walked out to the kitchen. She lit a lamp so they wouldn't be stumbling about in the dark. "Thank you for carrying Belle home," she said, feeling foolish and intensely aware of just how alone they were.

He grunted a reply, seemingly lost in thought, and judging by his expression, those thoughts were wreaking havoc. "Those men at the social. Are any of them courting you?"

She smiled. "Actually, I think all three are."

"All three?" He was clearly stunned, and Rachel wasn't certain whether she should be amused or insulted by his reaction.

"Well, Wally Peterson wasn't at the social tonight," she said, tapping a finger against her chin. "If you count him, that makes four."

Jared gave her a dark look. "And you warned me about the Truro women. It's the Truro men who need looking after," he grumbled.

Rachel gave him a brilliant smile. "Jealous?"

He tipped her chin up with his thumb and forefinger. "Insanely," he said, peering hard into her eyes.

She thought he was about to kiss her, but he dropped his hand and walked to the door.

"Good night, Rachel."

"Good night." He closed the door behind him. "Jared."

As Rachel tiptoed about the house, readying herself for bed, her parents lay wide-awake. "He'll take her away, May," Ambrose whispered. "He's here now, but he's not the kind who'll stay, a man like that. I thought . . . well, never mind what I thought."

"Oh, Ambrose, I'm sure you're worrying about nothing. The captain will leave, and without Rachel, and no hearts will be broken. Richard's been gone only five months now. You've seen how she's been with the other boys."

Ambrose gave a grunt. "I wish she would set her cap for a local boy. There's been enough of them bangin' on the door to make any woman happy."

They were silent for a long moment before Ambrose let out an impatient hiss. "I should never have let that cottage to him."

"Rachel wouldn't marry him if it meant leaving. And we need the money now that Richard's gone."

"If he asks, she'll leave. And take herself and Belle off to the city."

Mabel turned to her husband, a sharp twinge of fear gripping her heart. "I think you're imagining things."

"You could light a fire with their looks," he grumbled.

Mabel lay back again and stared at the ceiling, her stomach twisting with worry. Ambrose was right, she thought. The captain was not like Richard, content to stay, happy to be their son, willing to do almost anything to please them, including marrying Rachel. She'd felt only a small amount of guilt asking that of him and knowing Richard saw Rachel as a little sister. But she'd known Ambrose couldn't bear to lose another son. Never had her husband been so happy as the day they announced their engagement and their plans to build a little cottage a stone's throw away.

Mabel sighed inwardly. It hadn't mattered. All her planning had been for naught when Richard died. Ambrose lost yet another son, his most favored son. He'd given up that day, and his health had deteriorated ever since. Though Ambrose hadn't paid much attention to Rachel, Mabel knew he couldn't bear losing another child—if only to a marriage that would take her away. But she also suspected her daughter's heart couldn't bear to be broken again.

Chapter Fourteen

When Jared was five years old, his father, in a rare event, was in port for the Christmas holiday. His little brother West was one year old, just beginning to toddle about, and he remembered his father commenting how Jared had been walking at nine months—long before his younger brother. Jared hadn't known it then, but he realized now that his father had been drunk—quite drunk that Christmas. He recalled only that his father, his large, sea-captain father, was favoring him over his crybaby little brother. He'd said, just to please his father, that for the next Christmas, he wished he could be his father's cabin boy. The old man, with a great roar of pleasure, promised Jared then and there that he would indeed be cabin boy in one year's time, ignoring his mother's pleas that six was far too young to go to sea.

"By God, woman, I promised the boy, and I'll be damned if I'll go back on my word because of some female caterwauling. Now shut that mouth and stop that brat from crying." West had started screaming the minute his father began to yell.

Jared remembered feeling both fear and excitement, for he knew without a doubt that his father would make good on his promise. He also remembered looking over at his mother, seeing her eyes glitter with tears, and wishing he'd never made such a wish. It was his most vivid memory of Christmas.

As he sat in the Newcombs' cozy house, the smell of bayberry candles mingling with evergreen and the roasting turkey, he felt distinctly removed from the others. He imagined that when the Newcomb boys were alive, it must have been a boisterously happy crowd that filled this small space that was now, if not subdued, certainly not happy.

This was their first Christmas without Richard, and Jared could see that the adults were trying to make this holiday festive for Belle's sake. His absence made Jared's presence even more evident, as if he were already taking the man's place at the table and in their life. He had the distinct feeling, particularly from Rachel's parents, that his presence was not entirely welcome. It was a damned uncomfortable thing, for he suspected he knew just what Rachel's parents were finding so objectionable: their mutual attraction.

Rachel and he could not hide the smoldering thing that made the air crackle whenever they glanced at each other, though by unspoken agreement they did try. It was after an innocent but flirtatious exchange with Rachel that he noted Ambrose peering at him with suspicion. The old man had scratched his cheek and pressed his mouth tightly closed as he exchanged a look with Mabel that Jared interpreted as surprisingly hostile.

Jared's attention shifted to Belle, a much safer female to rest his eyes upon. She wore her new mittens and scarf and held her Christmas orange in her hand as if she held a treasure. The minute Jared had knocked on the door, Belle was there to show off her gifts, and to show him that yet another tooth was coming loose.

Rachel, in her yellow apron, bent and put the potatoes in the oven, and the air was filled with the wonderful scent of cooking turkey. The turkey was a gift from Obed, who, with a sharp jerk of his head and a darting look toward Rachel, declined an invitation to Christmas dinner.

Jared's gifts to the family were at his feet, and more than once Belle had wandered over and stared at the cloth-covered gifts. She didn't say a word, apparently having been warned by Rachel not to bother him about the presents, for she pressed her lips together tightly, and Jared could almost hear her fervent wish that he give her hers.

Rachel let out a sigh. "Belle, please leave the captain alone. Gift opening is after dinner."

Belle gave her mother a tragic look, and Jared simply could not take another second of this child's plaintive yearning. "I suppose it wouldn't hurt anything to let Belle open hers." He grinned at the dazzling smile the little girl bestowed upon him. She turned and began hopping up and down in front of her mother, unable to contain her hopeful excitement.

"Oh, if the captain doesn't mind," Rachel said. Then to him, softly: "You know, you didn't have to bring gifts."

His voice low so only she could hear, he said, "With the looks your father has been giving me, it's a good thing I came bearing gifts."

She looked embarrassed and apologetic at once. "It's Richard," she said.

"I know."

"Mama," Belle whined, tugging on her mother's apron.

Rachel laughed at her daughter's antics.

Jared picked up Belle's gift gingerly, admonishing the little girl to be careful. She sat on the rag rug in front of him, her best dress flowing about her, and

Jared smiled. She tugged on the rough string that held the cloth closed, revealing the clear glass net buoy, a tiny but enchanting castle inside.

Belle let out a breathy "Ooohh."

"Jared, it's beautiful," Rachel said, her eyes slightly shinier than normal.

"How did it get in there?" Belle asked in awe.

"Magic," Jared said, making his voice low and mysterious. "You see, that very castle once sat high upon a cliff in Scotland, when a wicked witch cast a spell and shrank it down, and all the people in it, and put it in that glass ball to keep it forever."

"Until the spell is broken," Belle said, her eyes bright.

"That's right," Jared said.

"How can the spell be broken?" she asked, her eyes looking at the castle as if searching for its tiny inhabitants.

"A prince, of course," Jared said. "He was a very unhappy prince until he met the princess. That witch was jealous and cast a spell upon the princess and her castle. The prince has been searching for her ever since. And when he finds her, he'll set her free." Jared looked up at Rachel, and he actually blushed that he should be so transparent in the telling of his story. He cleared his throat.

"You might as well open yours," he said, bending down and picking up Rachel's gift. He thrust it toward her and looked away while she opened it.

"Oh, Jared," she said, her voice filled with emotion. She held the bottle in her hands and inside was a replica of her cottage.

"I wanted to give you your cottage back," he said gruffly.

"Oh, Mama. It's our house!" Belle said. "Did a witch shrink that, too?"

Jared realized he'd ruin his story of a castle princess if he admitted he'd built the cottage in the bottle. "A good witch," Jared said. "And as there was no one inside, no harm was done."

Belle smiled and climbed up onto his lap. "Thank you, Captain," she said, and kissed his cheek. Then she wrapped her arms about his neck and whispered, "I love you."

She scrambled down, carefully picked up her gift, and hurried to her grandmother to show her the castle. Something hard clogged Jared's throat, making any response impossible. *I love you.* It had been so long since he'd heard those words, he found he was nearly unmanned by them.

"Thank you. For both gifts," Rachel said. She glanced over her shoulder before bending quickly and kissing his cheek precisely where her daughter had. She walked over to the tree and gathered up a large, brightly covered package. The color on Jared's cheeks darkened.

"Thank you."

Rachel laughed. "You haven't even opened it yet."

Jared pulled on the ribbon and removed the wrapping, revealing a small bundle of knitted items. One by one he lifted them out: gloves, a muffler, a hat, woolen socks, and something he couldn't quite tell what it was. He lifted it out, a question in his eyes.

"Belle's offering, I'm afraid." She lowered her voice to a whisper. "It's supposed to be a mitten. She's still working on the other one."

Jared looked down at that almost-mitten, his fingers running over the oddly shaped object, and again he felt that annoying knot grow in his throat. It was far too small, but he slipped his hand in anyway and called Belle over to him.

Belle skipped to him, grinning widely when she saw her creation on Jared's hand. "This is the nicest present I have ever received," he said solemnly.

"When you finish the other, I shall be the warmest man on patrol."

"Mommy made gloves, but I think mittens are warmer. My fingers get cold in gloves."

"Mine, too." He kissed her forehead.

"Belle, come help me set the table. And I could use some help from you, too, Rachel," Mabel called, and Jared thought he detected a bit of testiness.

He had the distinct feeling he had worn out his welcome.

West Mitchell thought perhaps the coach that had brought him from the train station in Hyannis had dumped him in a desert. A damned cold desert. It wasn't the last place on earth he wanted to be—that most assuredly would have been a whaling ship somewhere in the Arctic Ocean—but Truro was a close second. He hardly noticed the stark beauty of the place, instead giving himself over to think that he would much rather be home, in bed, with his wife.

As West trudged along the winding path one of the locals said would lead him to the Newcomb cottage, a wave of anxiety washed over him. He felt, at times, that he was the only sane Mitchell family member. Gardner, a brash, young, foolhardy kid, had gotten himself thrown off his ship somewhere off the California coast. It would be a fool's errand to look for Gardner, something his mother knew as well as he. But his mother, Julia, had hoped that such dire news would have brought Jared home. Julia was slowly coming undone, and West would be damned if he'd allow that to happen. Jared, the oldest, but by far the most lost of his brothers, could be dead or dying for all they knew. A single cryptic telegram informing them he was alive and another requesting his personal goods were all the evidence they had that Jared was all right.

Stories from the *Huntress* crew chilled West's blood. Clearly Jared was a man with a death wish; he'd known that already. But to cast off from his ship with no provisions but a case of whiskey was somehow more telling than a quick act of suicide would have been. Thank God he'd been rescued. He hadn't the slightest idea what he'd find when he saw Jared, but he'd had plenty of time to let his mind draw vivid and ugly pictures.

No doubt he'd be drunk and unkempt, surly and mean. Like his father. If he had to bathe him himself, if he had to chain him up and tie him down to keep him from drinking, he'd get his brother home to give their mother some peace of mind.

And so when West Mitchell saw his brother for the first time, he blinked his eyes and blinked them again—hard—for surely his eyes were playing tricks. He had just reached the two cottages nestled behind the dunes when he saw a man walking over a bluff, a child on his shoulders, booming out a sailor's ditty and accompanied, quite well, by a high-pitched little-girl voice. The man was well-groomed and exuded health and an energy that was unmistakable.

"Jared?"

The man who had to be Jared stopped in his tracks. "Good God, is that you, West?"

"Who's West?" piped up the little urchin still on his shoulders. Jared slowly brought the girl down, a smile spreading on his face. He strode toward West, strong, sturdy, full of life. West found himself in a bear-hug embrace, his back being slapped almost painfully hard. Then Jared jerked back, his face filled with concern.

"What happened? Mother? Gardner?"

"No, no. Nothing like that. I . . ."

Jared's attention was drawn down to the little girl, who was tugging on his jacket. West was momen-

tarily ignored as Jared hunkered down to her level.
"This is my brother, West. West, this is Isabelle Best."

"Hello," Belle said shyly.

West took her hand and bowed over it formally.
"Miss Isabelle." Belle giggled, her sparkling eyes
darting to Jared to make certain he was watching.

"Belle, why don't you go tell your mother all
about West."

"Bye," Belle said, giving a small wave before rushing home to tell her mama about the handsome
stranger who called her Miss Isabelle.

Jared led West to the cottage, aware that his little
brother was looking at him strangely. "I'm renting
this cottage from the people who live in the other
house," he explained as he let West through the door.

"Belle's parents?"

"Her grandparents."

"Is she an orphan then?"

Jared felt his cheeks flush for no other reason than
that he was thinking of Rachel. "Her mother lives
there, too," he said rather too gruffly, and made himself busy stoking the fire. "Want some coffee?"

"Only if it's strong and black."

Jared ground the coffee and its scent filled the
small cottage. He knew West was likely curious
about what he'd been doing here all this time, and
that he'd have to come up with some sort of intelligent answer.

Finally Jared could take the silence no longer.
"Why are you here, West?"

"I came to rescue you," he said with a self-
effacing smile.

Jared let out a low chuckle. "Someone's already
done the deed."

"I can see that. Whom should I thank?"

"Rachel." He cleared his throat. "Mrs. Best. Belle's
mother." Jared clamped his mouth shut, fearing he
was giving too much away.

"Are you coming home, Jared? Between Gardner and you, Mother's rather in a frazzle."

"Of course I'm coming home," Jared said automatically. Then he sat down opposite West. "Hell, I'm not certain what I'm going to do. This place has bewitched me."

West gave his brother a long, hard look. "I don't mind running things. You know I don't. But with Gardner God knows where, and you giving up whaling—at least for now—I've either got to hire two new captains or sell one of our ships. And there is Mother. She's driving me crazy. She knows we can't go running after Gardner, but she knew we could go running after you."

Jared rubbed his hands through his hair, guilt washing over him. Everything had been left to his younger brother to handle while he'd been wallowing in self-pity. He stood and poured the coffee to give him time to think, as if thinking about what he was going to do with the rest of his life hadn't been nagging at him every day for weeks. He placed the mugs of steaming coffee on the table and sat down heavily.

"I know you've been through a lot, Jared, and I can't say that I blame you for escaping for a bit. . . ." Jared held up one hand to stop West's words.

"Enough," he said abruptly, hating the pity he saw in West's eyes. He knew what he must look like, hiding away in this godforsaken little town on the edge of the world. How could he tell West that he'd never been happier, that he wasn't hiding from life; he'd found it? Hadn't he? He knew what his brother would see: a man who'd cast himself off to die on the sea, the same man who'd put the barrel of a pistol between his teeth and begged his brother to pull the trigger.

Unbidden, memories of his greatest shame swept through his mind. He'd been drunk, of course, and on his brother's ship, the *Julia*. The brothers hadn't seen each other in years, years in which Jared had systematically ripped his soul from his body. Sara Dawes, West's future wife, had been on board ship, and in his drunken state, he'd imagined she was a doxy, free pickings for a man who hadn't been with a woman in months. West had even claimed not to have touched her, and Jared had cruelly laughed.

He'd cornered the girl and kissed her. He was so big, so oblivious to her fear. With a jerk, she turned her head to escape his mouth, letting out a sound of protest. And he'd laughed. Laughed, thinking she was playing a game. Then he'd felt the solid, cold barrel of a pistol hard against his skull.

"You bastard," West had said, pushing the gun hard against Jared's temple. Jared hadn't even winced, but kept his eyes straight ahead. He stood there as if he were in no danger. He almost felt . . . relieved.

"Miss Dawes is quite delectable. Quite tempting. I think Father was right about you," Jared said slowly, deliberately. "Perhaps you do like boys better."

West's hand began to shake. "Go to hell."

With one quick movement, Jared turned his head so that he stared down the barrel of the pistol and grasped West's wrist with one hand. Jared opened his mouth and forced the gun between his lips.

"Oh, God, no," Sara had whispered.

"Jared, sweet Jesus," West said, his voice harsh, his eyes filled with anguished disbelief.

"Do it, West." Jared's grip on West's wrist tightened. "Do it!"

West had looked at his brother in horror, shaking his head in denial, his breath coming out in short pants, while Jared stood still. And waited.

West pulled the gun away, then grabbed the back of his brother's head and held him, his hand clawing through Jared's tangled hair. "What the hell is wrong with you?"

Suddenly Jared pushed away, letting out a strangled sound. "Leave me the hell alone," he'd growled, as he stumbled toward the stairs to escape the coward he'd become.

Disgust and shame filled him at the memory, at the knowledge that his brother pitied him, doubted him—even if he had good reasons to.

"I know what I am doing," he said, sounding angry. "And I know my obligations. I have never forgotten them, West."

Jared was a bit surprised when West said quietly, "I think you have."

Jared's eyes flashed rage, and just as quickly crinkled with good humor. "You're getting a bit cocky, West," he said, leaning back and tipping his chair on two legs with careless ease. "You've got some of the old man in you after all."

West grinned back. "More than I care to admit."

Jared let the chair fall back and took a large gulp of coffee. "I'll go home to appease our mother. But I can't promise to stay. There's nothing in New Bedford I care to revisit."

"Only your family."

"Yes," he said softly. "My family."

"Well, West, come to take your brother home, have you?"

West looked up from his ham to Ambrose Newcomb, and became aware that everyone around the table was waiting expectantly for his answer. The little girl, Isabelle, looked adorably worried, her pretty mother pensive, the parents . . . pleased as punch.

"No," he said cautiously, aware that Jared was scowling. "I just wanted to see for myself that Jared has recovered. His telegrams were a bit . . ."

"Terse?" Rachel said, giving Jared a pointed look.

"To say the least." He'd taken one look at Rachel

Best and suspected that she was a large part of the reason his big brother remained in Truro. It didn't take long before his suspicions were realized: his brother couldn't keep his eyes off her.

"Captain's going to live here forever," Belle said, her tone shaky and a tiny bit desperate. "Aren't you?"

West watched with fascination as his brother's hard face softened to something he'd never seen. Ah, hell, he'd be lucky if Jared ever came home. If he was correct, he not only loved Rachel, he loved her little girl, too.

"He's got to go home," Ambrose said rather sharply. Belle turned to her grandfather, her mouth opened in shock and her eyes glittering with tears.

"Papa," Rachel said, clearly upset by her father's insensitivity.

"Well, it's the truth," he grumbled.

Belle looked beseechingly up at Jared. "You're not going, are you?"

Jared shifted in his chair, obviously trying to come up with something that wasn't an outright lie but that also wouldn't cause those tears glittering in her big brown eyes to fall. "No, Belle. I'm not leaving. At least not right away."

"But I don't want you to ever leave."

Jared looked around the table, his expression clearly one of desperation. West coughed into his hand to stop himself from chuckling at his brother's discomfiture.

"The captain's mother is very worried about him, Belle. Do you remember how worried I was when I couldn't find you?"

Two big teardrops fell from Belle's eyes. She sniffed and nodded her head.

West could almost see the panic growing in Jared's chest at the sight of those two teardrops, and so he wasn't surprised when he turned to Belle and said, "I'm not going anywhere for a long time, pumpkin."

"Oh, good." The little girl threw her arms around Jared, who gave West a look that told him, *This is the reason I am still here.* Jared ignored the puff of impatience from Ambrose, the worried look in Rachel's eyes, and hugged the little girl close. West had the most difficult time trying to recall that the last time he'd seen Jared, he had been as lost as a man could be. He could not ask Jared to leave this place; he knew that now.

West shifted his eyes from Jared to Rachel's parents, who glared angrily at Jared, making West distinctly uncomfortable. He'd no idea what he was witnessing, but the undercurrents swirling about the table were enough to bring a weaker man down. Jared, however, pointedly ignored those glares and gave Belle another squeeze before setting her back at her own place. Then he gave Rachel a look so searing, a monk could have interpreted it.

"How long will you be visiting, Captain Mitchell?" Rachel asked West politely.

"I'm leaving tomorrow. My wife is expecting our first child and I don't want to be away too long."

"How wonderful. Are you hoping for a girl or a boy?"

"The men in our family are all a bit ornery. I'm hoping for a girl."

The talk turned to children and names and other safe topics. Rachel kept darting looks to Jared, wondering if he'd meant what he'd said about not leaving or if he was simply trying to appease Belle. She couldn't help but wish he would stay. *Stay, stay. Forever. Or leave now.* It was a subtle torture not knowing what he would do.

Each night since Christmas, she would look at the miniature cottage he'd made and try to imagine Jared

building it with those large hands of his. The cottage
and the castle were so fanciful, so impractical. So
unlike what she'd thought Jared was like. She held
close to her heart the image of him working alone,
silently, like a gift she didn't want to open yet. He
was not entirely what she thought he was—a gruff,
good man trying to scrape away the heartbreaking
memories that nearly crushed him.

The meal ended, bringing Rachel from her
thoughts. West bowed and thanked her parents for
the meal, and Jared gave his brother an amused look
at his good manners—a look West pointedly ignored.
She watched as they strode through the door, her
heart singing when Jared turned to her just as he
was about to close the door and gave her a smile.

"Can I go outside, Mama?" Belle asked, already
wrapping her scarf around her throat.

"Yes, but let the captain and his brother be, Belle."

Belle pursed her lips, letting Rachel know she had
planned to visit with the captain. "All right, Mama,"
she said finally, and allowed her mother to button
up her coat and slip her red mittens on.

"Not too long. It's awfully cold out there."

The door slammed behind her daughter and Rachel let out a sigh.

"If he's going to go, I just wish he'd get it over
with," her mother said, sounding tired.

"Perhaps he'll stay," Rachel said, ignoring the way
her heart began pounding in her chest at the thought
of Jared going.

She felt her mother come up behind her and closed
her eyes, not wanting to hear what her mother
planned to say.

"He's going to go, Rachel. And he's going to break
Belle's heart when he does."

Rachel relaxed slightly. Her mother must not know
how she felt about Jared, how she thought about him
nearly constantly. How she noticed how strong his

hands were and imagined them touching her. Sometimes she wished she'd never seen Jared's naked body, but the glorious image was seared into her head. She could close her eyes and imagine her hand on his brawny chest, on his flat stomach. Rachel let out a shaky sigh. "I know. Belle loves him."

"You love him, too, don't you, Rachel?"

Rachel jerked her head and looked at her mother. "I . . ."

Something must have shown on her face, for her mother's entire body sagged in defeat. "Oh, Rachel. He'll not stay. I think he might just be staying on to pay us back for saving him. I don't think we could have made it through this winter if not for the rent he's paying on that cottage. If you've got it in your head that he's staying on because of you—"

"I don't," she said sharply, feeling anger at her mother and at Jared.

Mabel pressed her lips together and shifted her eyes away from her daughter. Drawing in a deep breath, she said, "He may ask you to go with him. He may want to take you and Belle away."

Mabel's voice shook slightly, startling Rachel. She'd never thought of such a thing. Always in her mind it had been a matter of Jared staying. Never had she imagined Jared asking her to go with him. Then she shook her head, a frown marring her face. "He wouldn't ask me to go with him," she said with conviction. "He's never spoken of such a thing." *He doesn't love me.*

Rachel tried to picture herself packing up her things and leaving Truro behind, but she couldn't. She'd never been farther than Provincetown, never thought beyond someday visiting Boston. But leave Truro and her parents forever?

"What would you say if he asked?" her mother demanded.

Rachel shook her head slowly. "I don't know."

Her answer seemed to satisfy her mother, for she even managed a smile. "Perhaps you don't care for him quite as much as you think you do, then," she said.

West and Jared walked along the beach, invigorated by the sharply cold wind blowing against them. Jared told West of the patrol, how he'd walked this beach dozens of times, how he'd waved his costen, how he'd watched a crew of men die just a few hundred feet from shore.

"Sometimes I think I could do this forever," he said, more to himself than to his brother. "Live here. Forever."

"And other times?"

Jared shrugged. "Other times I don't know what the hell I want." Jared stopped walking and gazed out onto the cold, gray Atlantic. "You've always known what you wanted, haven't you?"

West chuckled. "I didn't always get what I wanted. I spent ten years longer on a whaler than I wanted to. But yes, I had a plan." Jared could feel West's scrutiny. "Why don't you just ask her to marry you?"

Jared studied the sand beneath his feet. "It's not that easy. Her husband just died. And she hasn't let go. It's too soon for her, and he died under mysterious circumstances, apparently drowned in fairly calm seas. His body was never found. Besides, I don't think . . ." He stopped. "She doesn't love me," he said finally.

"I see. Then perhaps the best thing to do would be to leave," West said softly.

"I've thought of that." *A hundred times I've thought of that.* "How is your wife?"

West smiled, allowing his brother to change the subject. "Very pregnant and very irritable." West filled him in on life in New Bedford, about the house he was building, about the ships and the business. And every once in a while, he said, "You'll see for yourself when you come home."

He would have to return to New Bedford, Jared knew. For once in his life, he'd have to act the eldest son. But not yet. He'd go back in a week, a month. He would.

But not just yet.

"Why are you still here?" Rachel demanded, crossing her arms. West had left that morning and Rachel had come over with freshly baked bread, still steaming beneath the cloth.

He looked confused, but Jared knew damn well what she was asking. "You want me to leave your cabin? I thought we settled that."

"No, no. I meant, why are you still here in Truro?"

Jared settled into his kitchen chair and folded his big hands in front of him. "I don't know," he said finally.

"I think I do know," Rachel said, sitting across from him. "And if you think we need your money, you're wrong." The moment it was out of her mouth, she knew she had been completely wrong, for the look on his face was one of surprise.

"You do need my money, but that is not why I'm still here." Something in his voice had changed, grown hard and cynical. Rachel didn't like it. "I'm hardly that honorable, though I thank you for thinking me so."

"I think that if you're going to leave, you should do so soon. Belle has come to care for you," Rachel said, knowing with a feeling close to dread that she was really talking about herself. "When you go it will break her heart."

Jared stared at the lamplight and took a deep breath. "So you're saying go now or stay forever."

Panic bubbled up inside Rachel. That was not at all what she was saying. Oh, God, what was she saying? She hadn't thought it through, once again speaking without thinking. She wasn't ready for him to leave, and yet she'd somehow forced him to make a decision.

"No. I just wanted to know why you were still here. You see, I got it in my head that you felt sorry for us, and I suppose that made me angry and just a bit afraid about what would happen when you did leave and how dependent we were all becoming on you, and I . . ." She made a helpless gesture with her hands. "I never thought you'd leave. Not right away."

He gave her a smile. "You do go on, don't you, Mrs. Best."

"Richard always said it was my biggest flaw. I never had a thought in my head I didn't say out loud. It's gotten me into all kinds of trouble."

"I imagine so." He laid his hands flat upon the table. "Even so, you are right. My family wants me home, and I can't stay here forever."

Why not?

"Why not?" Rachel cringed, knowing again it was one of those thoughts that was better left unspoken, because she really didn't want to hear why it would be so easy for him to go.

He leaned back in his chair and flashed her his most charming smile, shielding her from what he was truly thinking. "Because if I stayed, Mrs. Best, I would have to marry you."

Rachel was quite certain her heart stopped beating for just a moment. "I . . ." She cleared her throat and prayed her tone matched his negligent one. "I don't see why that should be a condition."

"Well, this is how I see it. I was brought up in a home where if a man makes love to a woman, he should at least have designs on marrying her, and I assure you that if I stay, we will make love. The rules change, of course, if it's her given trade; then marriage is not preconditioned." His tone was casual, almost playful, but his eyes never left hers, and he'd gone very still.

"I was brought up to believe you shouldn't marry someone you don't love."

Jared blinked hard, then gave her another smile. "Well, then. The wedding's off," he said grandly and with good humor. He stood, scraping the chair back, and bowed. "Good day, Mrs. Best. You may rest easy tonight, for I leave tomorrow."

He escorted her politely to his door, and Rachel compliantly went. For the first time in her life, she hadn't the slightest idea what to say.

Chapter Fifteen

Rachel lay awake for hours thinking of Jared and his offhand proposal—if indeed that was what it was. She'd almost torn back the covers more than once, ready to bang on his door and demand whether he'd been serious or not. Did he truly want to marry her? He hadn't quite said so, and yet when she'd left she thought she saw—or at least imagined she saw— a flicker of something in his eyes that could have been disappointment that she'd not asked him to stay.

She banged her pillow in frustration, trying to re- call precisely what he'd said and how he'd said it. Something about making love and that leading to marriage. Didn't he say that if he stayed they would make love, and that would mean they must marry? Was he proposing to her or warning her? The one thing he'd been completely clear about was his desire to leave.

"You insufferable man," she said, the pillow jammed over her head so that no one in the house- hold would hear her. She sat up and lowered the pillow, fisting her hands into the soft down. "I don't want you to leave," she whispered, and was shocked to feel her eyes burning with tears. A slow smile formed on her lips. "I don't want him to leave." Just as quickly she frowned, fiercely, for she didn't like the next wave of emotion that washed over her. It felt distinctly and uncomfortably like love, that giddy, light-headed way she'd felt when she was sixteen. Back then it had come on her slowly, her love for Richard turning from friendship to something more. This time she felt as if she'd been hit by a cold tidal wave that knocked the breath out of her.

The last thought she had before finally drifting off to sleep was that she'd gone and done it again: fallen in love with a man who didn't love her.

Rachel slept far later than usual and awoke feeling tired and grumpy, with something awful nagging at her. Something was bothering her. Something she needed to do. Something . . . something.

She sat up with a start and immediately looked at the bright sunshine outside.

"Oh, my God." She flung back the covers, tore off her nightdress, and dressed as quickly as she could, not even bothering to finish tying her stays. She grabbed her navy blue everyday dress, cursing the multitude of buttons down the front.

"Boots, boots," she muttered, not seeing them where they should be, then spying them partially underneath the covers that fell from the bed. She tugged them on, not caring that she'd gone without stockings, and rushed out of her room.

"Oh!" She hurried back into her bedroom and peered quickly at her reflection. Her hair was still in her night braid, and bed-messy, but she hardly saw just how frazzled it was. She could think only one thing: Jared was leaving today and might already be gone.

Her mother was at the stove when she rushed into the kitchen.

"You slept late this morning," Mabel said, turning and eyeing curiously her daughter's unkempt appearance.

"Has the captain come by this morning yet?"

"He was here earlier. He's—"

But Rachel was already out the door and running toward his cottage. Her heart nearly stopped when she saw Belle near the door drawing in the sand, sniffling and looking heartbroken.

"Belle, honey, what's wrong?" Rachel said, kneeling down near her daughter.

"The captain said he was going and he wouldn't let me come," Belle said.

Rachel gathered her daughter in her arms. "Oh, Belle. Honey, we knew he was going to leave."

"But he lets me go with him to the lighthouse sometimes," Belle wailed into her shoulder.

Rachel gave Belle another squeeze. "Tell you what. I'm going to try to find him. You stay here and help Grandma. I thought I smelled some of her muffins baking."

Belle managed a small smile before discarding her stick and heading home. Rachel watched her daughter skip to the house for a moment before tearing off for the lighthouse. By the time she reached it, her lungs burned and her legs ached.

"Here and gone, Mrs. Best," Donald Small said, his nose red from his lingering illness. "Saw him head to the beach."

Rachel, her frustration growing, waved a thanks. Walking the beach was far more expeditious than traveling on the road, for the sand along the shore was firmer. Though a coach went through town periodically, it was notoriously slow, getting bogged down in the sand again and again. Most men traveling alone went either by horse or by foot. She decided Jared must be walking to Hyannis, where he would be able to take the train to Boston. If she ran, she could perhaps catch up to him. She hadn't the slightest idea what she would say to him when she reached him, but Rachel knew she had to say goodbye. If she was making a fool of herself, at that moment she didn't care. Certainly she wouldn't blurt out that she loved him, even if it meant biting her tongue in half. She knew only that she couldn't let him leave without seeing him first.

Rachel half ran, half walked along the narrow, windy sand path that cut though the thick brush and led to the bluff overlooking the beach. Winded, she reached the bluff, nearly sobbing when she looked down the beach and saw nothing but sand and sea. Surely he couldn't have gone so far that he was out of sight around the curve of the beach, but he must have. With a sigh of resolve, Rachel picked up her skirts and trudged down the bluff. When she finally reached the bend, again she saw nothing but a long strip of deserted beach. She was too late. He was gone.

Jared stood atop the bluff near his cottage and stared at the sea that had drawn him ever since he could remember. That lure, that feeling that would come over him when he'd been on land too long, was gone. He stood there, eyes closed, feeling the wind beat upon his face, and tried to call it back. He tried to recall the sharp crack of canvas, the feel of the deck moving beneath his feet, that rush of exhilaration when he heard the lookout call from above: "There she blows. She blows to starboard!" The only thing that made him feel that way nowadays was Rachel. He would have told her if it hadn't been such a very unromantic image. "You make me feel the way I do when I spot the spout of a sperm whale, darling." He had to chuckle.

All he could think of as he gazed at the sea was how good it had felt the night of the social to have Rachel walking beside him as he carried a sleeping Belle on his shoulder all the way home. He'd let himself imagine they were a family. It was so unlike him to allow such thoughts into his head and into his heart. His family was dead. The last few days, for the first time since Abigail and his daughter died, he saw himself as a husband and father. He saw himself surrounded by children; he pictured a dining table full of food, and sitting around it were children with messy faces and loud, high-pitched voices, and a wife looking on with sweet indulgence. Rachel, of course. Their children, without a doubt.

He'd truly meant to say good-bye to everyone that morning, but the damned words wouldn't escape his throat. Looking at the sea did nothing but make him glad he was on land. He wondered what Rachel would say if he asked her to marry him, as he'd almost done yesterday. He knew she didn't love him. He knew that. But the thought of leaving her, leaving behind this imaginary family he'd built in his head, was getting more and more difficult to do with each passing day.

"Damn you, Richard Best," he whispered, his eyes hard on the cold Atlantic.

He turned and walked back to the cottage, feeling in his heart that tonight he would say good-bye. Though it was cold, he left his door ajar as he straightened up the house, an invitation for Belle to stop by if she happened past. Even as he'd made her stay behind while he went to the lighthouse, he was thinking that perhaps he'd just keep walking. But he hadn't, of course.

He heard something outside, and he turned just in time to see Rachel take a harmless tumble just outside his door. By the time she'd recovered and was brushing sand from her skirt, his heart was beating at a more normal pace—or at least not racing like some lovestruck fool's. He waited for her, drinking in the sight of her, so very glad to see her he couldn't help but smile.

She was a mess. Her hair was in a braid, though much had escaped. She wore her dead husband's coat, but it was open, revealing that she'd misbuttoned her dress. And when she'd taken that tumble into the sand, she'd exposed a flash of flesh that told Jared she'd forgotten her stockings.

"Lord, Mrs. Best, you do look pretty this morning," he said sincerely.

She tucked one of the many errant strands behind an ear and gave him a tentative smile. "I happened to be walking outside and I saw your door open," she said, slightly breathless, "and so I thought I'd mosey on over to see if you were still around and . . ." Her voice faded and she gave him a sheepish grin. "I just ran up and down the beach like a madwoman looking for you. I didn't want you to leave without saying good-bye."

Jared rubbed his beard-roughened jaw, realizing he hadn't taken the time to shave that morning, and looked behind her and up at the vividly blue sky before studying her again. "The thing is, I decided not to leave just now."

"No?"

Lord, why did he feel so damned nervous? "I know what you said about loving the person you marry. I was hoping you could put aside that rule of yours." He sounded like an idiot.

Rachel ducked her head, and he watched as she swallowed. He was putting her in a spot. He was forcing her to reject him again. Wasn't once enough?

"Just forget it," he said sharply, turning away and looking about desperately for something to do. The room was immaculate. "I'll stay on another week. That'll give Belle time to get used to the idea." He heard the door close behind him and he stiffened, thinking that perhaps she'd gone.

"It's a good rule, about loving the person you marry," Rachel said, ignoring the rest of what he'd said.

"Yeah. It probably is." Hell, he couldn't even look at her now. He wanted to run as far and as fast as he could down to the beach, and on and on until he was somewhere far from her. He wanted to hit something. Hard. "Like I said, just forget it."

"Richard never loved me," she blurted. "I can't do that again, you see. It's awful loving someone and them not loving you back. I'm sorry, Jared. But I just won't do it."

Jared jerked his head to stare at her. "Are you saying that you love me?"

"Isn't that what I've been saying all along?"

She looked so confused, so completely baffled, that Jared had to laugh out loud. He wasn't certain, but he didn't think he'd ever felt so giddily happy in his life. He put his hand on one side of her face and drew her near.

"Rachel, that might have been what you were saying, but it's not at all what I was hearing." He swallowed past something hard in his throat. "*I* love *you*."

To his bewilderment, Rachel began shaking her head in denial. "No, no. You can't. Oh, but do you? Do you, really? Because if you do, if you do, then—"

He stopped her with his kiss. "Shut up," he said softly, "and just let me kiss you."

He loved to kiss her. Loved the way her lips were soft and warm against his, pliant and slightly moist. Her cheeks were cold from the sharp January wind, and so he kissed them warm, smiling when he realized her nose was like ice. He kissed there, too. Then her reddened ears, her neck, the underside of her jaw. He took off her husband's coat and flung it away to the floor. "You need a new coat," he muttered against her neck. He was achingly aware that they were in the home she'd shared with her husband, that he intended to make love to her in their bed. He wanted to erase his memory, wanted to love her until she forgot she was ever married before. *Selfish, selfish man,* he thought, but didn't care.

"We're going to make love," he said.

"Yes."

Rachel wanted this, wanted to see him above her, wanted him to kiss her forever. When she felt his hand on her breast, it was no tentative caress; it was bold and firm and screamed *I want you.* Nothing about Jared was shy and tentative. He attacked her buttons with determination, exposing her with a grunt of pure male satisfaction. He gazed at her, his eyes on fire, looking at her breasts as if he'd never seen anything quite so beautiful in his life. It was heady, and it was incredibly sensuous. Never in her life had Rachel felt all wobbly-legged from just a look. He peeled off her dress and made short work of her stays, and Rachel blushed at knowing just how little time she'd taken to dress that morning, as if somehow anticipating what was to come later.

She stood amidst her discarded clothing in broad daylight, her body singing and throbbing as she watched him undress. It had been chilly in the room, but the fire in the stove had quickly turned the room warm and cozy. And then they were both standing in her old kitchen without a stitch of clothing, silly grins on their faces.

"Come here," he said, his voice low and intoxicating. He didn't wait for her. He stepped forward, pulling her almost roughly against him, his large body hard and big, his chest wonderfully hairy. She decided she adored big, hairy men. She laughed, remembering what she'd thought of him when she first laid eyes on him.

"You laugh," he said like a crazed pirate, kissing her breast with relish.

"I was just thinking that perhaps you are a giant," she said, blushing to the roots of her hair, feeling his arousal hard against her.

"I love when you do that," he said, noting her flush. "And now I know everywhere you blush." He kissed her breasts again, nuzzling her, growling, licking, then biting gently upon the very tips. At her gasp of pleasure, Jared picked her up and carried her to the bed. It was colder in the bedroom, so he quickly covered her with his body.

Rachel tried not to think of Richard, tried not to let the thoughts come: *Richard did not do that, he did not touch me that way, he did not make those sounds.* Even as her body responded, even as she felt things happening that she'd never before experienced, she couldn't stop her thoughts that loving this man was so, so much better. Guilt washed over her.

Jared lifted his head. "What's wrong?"

She was startled that he'd detected anything, and now she felt guilty about that, as well. She gazed up at him, at his perfect, beautiful, all-male face—at Jared. Jared, the only man who'd ever loved her. She smiled. "Oh, Jared, nothing. Nothing at all." She drew his head to her and kissed him, trying with all her being to rid herself of anything but how wonderful Jared was, how loving, tender, rough. Oh, my, but he knew how to touch her.

He came into her slowly, letting her feel every sensation, letting her guide him. He began moving and Rachel lost herself in what he was doing, how he was making her body sing in a way it had never done before. Rachel opened her eyes, stunned by what was happening, realizing that there was more and more to feel, that there was something wonderful and mysterious and joyous happening to her. She arched her back and cried out as her body was filled with a shot of pure pleasure that ran from her breasts to her toes. Rachel clutched Jared hard to her as he found his release, her mouth pressed against his shoulder.

He kissed her over and over, told her over and over how he loved her, how happy he was. He even laughed as he withdrew and gathered her near, never realizing that she'd begun crying hot, bitter tears. She shuddered, and he sat halfway up as she turned away and buried her head in her hands.

"Rachel, honey. What's wrong?"

"I don't know," she sobbed.

"I know I'm out of practice. . . ." She sobbed anew at the humor in his voice. Oh, how she loved this man.

"It's not you. Oh, Jared. Richard never loved me. He never did. Never, never. And I think hearing you say it just made all that come back." She turned and looked at him.

Jared felt as if she'd just taken his heart and squeezed it. "I can't say I like talking about another man when I've just finished making love," he said, then took a short, angry breath. "Do you still love Richard?"

Rachel lifted her chin. "Do you still love your wife?"

"It's not the same. I know Abigail's dead. I don't stand up there hoping to see her come sailing home." Jared's entire body was taut and angry.

"That's not fair. Abigail's been gone for years. You saw her. I never saw Richard's body. And we're in our bed."

Jared let out a curse and saw Rachel's eyes widen. "Yes. I curse. I drink too much sometimes. But, damnit, I love you, Rachel. But I'll not share you. I won't do it."

Rachel pulled up her knees and rested her forehead against them, crying anew.

"Stop crying," he said, all frustration and guilty anger.

"I can't help it if I feel guilty," she said, her voice muffled by tears and her knees. "I don't want to, truly I don't." She lifted her face. She looked so damned sad, so confused.

"You weren't ready," he said, his voice harder than he'd intended.

"I thought I was." Rachel twisted the blanket with her hand.

"If Richard walked through that door right now . . ."

Rachel shook her head back and forth. "Don't," she pleaded.

"If he walked through that door, Rachel," he said, ignoring her plea, "who would you choose?"

"You're not being fair."

"Maybe not. Hell, no, I'm not being fair at all. I don't want to be fair." He forced himself to relax, to calm his voice. "It's soon for you. I know that. And I know it's not a question of who you would choose; it's that you haven't said good-bye. He's dead. Richard is dead."

She winced and his heart nearly broke. "Ah, Rachel. I need for you to give me your heart. All of it, love."

She shook her head, and he thought for a moment she would deny him the one thing he wanted most in the world. "Oh, Jared, you have my heart. I think that's why I feel so guilty. I've given it away so easily."

"This has not been easy."

She let out a small laugh. "No, I suppose not."

"Loving me doesn't mean you didn't love Richard," he forced himself to say. He was selfish enough to wish she hadn't loved her husband.

"I know that."

They lay back down, and he dragged her against him, squeezing her almost painfully close.

"I love you," he whispered, and she hugged his arm tight in answer. It was only then that he realized that she hadn't said the words *I love you* aloud.

He kissed the top of her head and her eyes drifted shut. Outside, the wind blew, whipping up sand, buffeting the cottage, rattling the windows. He lay there awake long after Rachel's breathing had softened, savoring the feel of her next to him, the way her hair tickled his shoulder, the way her feet pressed against his calves. Rachel had loved him with her body freely and joyfully. But he knew, no matter her words, that she had not given him her heart, that she might never be able to. His embrace tightened and she moved sleepily against him. God, he loved her so damn much.

But he knew it wasn't enough.

Chapter Sixteen

~~~

"Tell me about Richard."

Ambrose looked up from the hull he was sanding and stared long and hard at Jared. He set his jaw mulishly and went back to work on the boat's bottom. Jared stood there, bemused more than irritated by the man's actions. Ambrose, he suspected, knew damn well he wasn't going to leave him be until he had an answer. Finally Ambrose straightened and let out a sigh.

"What do you want to know?"

"I want to know if there is any chance he is alive. And if not, I want to know why Rachel is still holding out hope."

Ambrose threw down the sharkskin he was using to smooth the hull. Then he pulled out his pipe, fished for his tobacco pouch, tamped in a pinch or two, and lit it, puffing slowly, deliberately. Jared was a patient man. If Ambrose was trying to purposely irritate him, he'd find he had failed. A man who sailed for months without spotting a whale certainly could wait for an old man to fill his pipe.

"He's dead," he said, then clamped his mouth tight over the pipe's stem. "Though I can understand Rachel's doubts." Ambrose looked toward the cottages as if making certain they were alone and in no danger of interruption. "Richard grew up here. He knew that surf," he said, jerking his head toward the sounds of the waves rushing ashore. "It wasn't calm that night, but 'twern't rough, neither. At first, when Don told me he must have drowned, I didn't believe it. Not Richard. Maybe I just didn't want to believe it. He was a strong swimmer." He shook his head, shaking off the grief. "Something must have hit him on the head."

"The other sailors, the ones on the ship, they all died. Perhaps the surf was worse than you think."

Ambrose scowled, dismissing his theory, and spat.

"What happened that night, Ambrose?"

Jared watched as Ambrose's grip on the pipe stem tightened, as the old man set his jaw. He wanted to take him by the collar and make him talk, shake him until he coughed up every piece of the story.

"All I know is that a ship foundered and men died, Richard one of them. Now leave it be," he said, squinting one eye closed and giving him a glare with the other, like some gnarly sea dog.

Jared studied the man's face. Instinct told him that Ambrose wasn't telling him the full story. A ship of men didn't die in calm seas; a ship didn't come close to shore unless it was driven there by raging currents. Or unless it was lured to shore. Jared recalled seeing a light above him the night he waved that ship away from shore. He'd dismissed it, but now he wondered if a band of mooncussers lived in this quiet little town.

"You said yourself the seas weren't really rough that night. How did the sailors die? It was summer. The water would have been warm."

"All I know is that they died. And Richard died." Ambrose turned away and snatched up the sharkskin, apparently intending to go back to work. Jared refused to be dismissed.

"Mooncussers," Jared said softly and with certainty.

He watched with satisfaction as Ambrose stiffened. He jerked around, anger distorting his features. "If you're saying Richard was part of a band of mooncussers, you're dead wrong. He would never kill a man. Never."

"And yet all those men died on a warm summer night in moderate seas."

"You ever meet a sailor who knew how to swim?"

The old man had a point. He knew better than most that the vast majority of men aboard any ship would sink like rocks if thrown overboard. "All right. But what about Richard? You said he was a strong swimmer."

Ambrose closed his eyes. "No one but Don could recall seeing him, and even he wasn't sure. Richard was on patrol; he would have been the one to see the ship first, the one to call out the alarm. But there was no alarm that night."

"What are you saying?"

Ambrose leaned against the boat's hull and fiddled with his pipe. "You wanted to know why Rachel thought Richard might be alive. Well, for a damn long time I thought he might be, too, but for different reasons. I thought he'd run away. But it's been too long. He's dead. I'm sure it of now. Don must have been right all along."

Jared felt his gut knot with the realization that Richard's death might not have been a simple drowning, and that Rachel's confusion about his disappearance was warranted, not simply a mourning woman's foolish hope. "Why would Richard run away?"

"He was in love with another woman. I found out about it." Ambrose shook his head and let out a bitter chuckle. "I was up in the light when I saw them. I wanted to beat the tar out of him for cheatin' on my Rachel. I told him to break it off, told him he would no longer be my son if he didn't. I thought he had. But when he disappeared a week later . . ."

"You thought he'd run away with her."

"He hadn't. The girl is still here and Richard is gone."

Jared let out a curse and grabbed a handful of his own hair, pulling until it hurt. "He could still be alive. He could be hiding somewhere, waiting for the girl." Jared felt as if he would vomit.

"No. He's dead," Ambrose said with absolute certainty.

"How can you be so sure?" Jared demanded, knowing he sounded desperate.

"It's been more than five months. If he loved that girl—and I know he did—he would have sent for her by now. And she wouldn't be going about the way she has, as if the world has ended. Richard was a good boy, a good son."

"He was a rotten husband."

Ambrose grunted his agreement. "That boy would have done anything for me. But this thing he had for that woman, it was tearing him apart, making him act and do things—"

"Who is she?"

Ambrose shook his head. "Esther Travist, not that it matters." He took a deep breath. "I blame myself. He told me before he agreed to marry Rachel that he had feelings for another girl. I told him he'd get over her, that once he and Rachel were married he could be my true son." Ambrose swallowed convulsively, and Jared looked away from the man's grief. "They'd been carrying on for years. *Years*. Rachel never knew and she never will," he said, recovered enough to give Jared another of his glares.

"Of course not," Jared said, his heart aching for

Rachel. She'd known Richard hadn't loved her, but it would be far worse to know he'd loved another. "I would never do anything to hurt Rachel."

"You love her, then, do you?"

"Yes, sir, I do."

Ambrose spat out a bit of tobacco. "Truro's all she's ever known."

"I'm becoming rather fond of the place myself," Jared said, smiling at the old man's concern for his daughter. "If you're asking if I'd take her away from here, the answer is no. I've no desire to return to New Bedford."

Ambrose tapped out his pipe and took up the sharkskin. "You asking permission to marry my daughter, Captain?"

A wide grin split Jared's face. "I am, sir."

Ambrose made Jared wait six strokes of the shark-skin before giving him an answer. "You have my blessing," he said, all gruff and cross.

"Thank you, sir," Jared said.

He walked away from his future father-in-law, thinking that asking his permission to marry Rachel had been far less harrowing than asking his daughter would be.

Jared stood next to Donald Small as they gazed out over the Atlantic and the ships that dotted the horizon. "Light traffic today," Small said, squinting his eyes. The sun was so bright, it hurt the eyes to look out to sea. "It's been an easy winter, thank the good Lord. Had a wreck in Orleans 'bout a week ago. No one lost, and they got quite a haul of coffee beans fresh from Colombia, dry and good as new. Charged the company a hefty sum to ship it back to them. Well, most of 'em anyhow." He jerked his head to the south. "That ship coming or going?"

"Coming."

Small let out a curse and turned back to the light. "Might as well fill the lamps. You coming?"

Jared walked next to Small, sensing that the older man was spitting mad about something. He knew it wouldn't be long before he had an earful, and he was right. Small had just started filling the lamps when he started.

"Man puts in fifteen years. Fifteen years and gets sick once, and all of a sudden he's a detriment to the service. Hell and damnation, who am I telling tales to? No one's forcing me out. I know I'm getting too old. Putting ships in danger." He straightened from his job of filling the lamps, placing the oil container on the iron floor. Holding out his hands, he demanded, "Look at these hands."

To Jared's surprise, they trembled noticeably.

"I know I'm gettin' old. Just didn't think it was going to happen overnight! That sickness lingered like never before. I've still got a cough in the mornings."

"Are you telling me the government is asking that you resign?"

"Naw." Small hung his head. "I'm telling you that I'm asking myself. I got a letter from the service commending me for keeping the light lit that night. Guess lights went out all up and down the coast." He stuffed his hands in his pocket. "I wrote back saying it was you they should thank and recommending you as next lightkeeper."

Jared was stunned. "You *what*?"

"Well, I figure you and Mrs. Best plan to get married." At Jared's look of disbelief, Small said, "Hell, everyone in Truro's had the two of you married weeks ago. Poor Oren got so drunk, he nearly drowned. Man's not a drinker. So I wrote that you, with your experience on the sea, would be a good choice."

Six months ago, Jared would have rejected such an idea out of hand. But now the idea of being lightkeeper on this barren strip of land was immensely appealing. The house, of course, was much too small for a family, something that could be easily remedied. Small himself had a larger house not a mile away that he sometimes rented, especially in the summer months. Jared hadn't given much thought to what he would do after he and Rachel married. The only life he knew was at sea, hunting whale, and it was a life he had no desire to return to. He suddenly could picture himself tending the light, filling the lamps, counting the ships that passed by. For an instant fear wrapped itself around his heart, for the life he'd begun imagining was becoming too real, too vital to his existence.

"I'll think about it," he said, looking around him with new intensity. *This could be mine. This life could be mine.* Such a thought would have been suffocating not too long ago. But he'd realized something about himself in the last few weeks—he had been tired of life, of all the ugliness he'd seen. The air was sweet here. *Life* was sweet here.

"You don't have to decide until spring. I'm not retiring until the end of June. I've lost heart for this job." He grew silent, his expression pensive and anxious. He laughed. "Too many ghosts, I'm thinking. Too many men dead in those waters."

"But you've saved more than have died, surely."

"Yes. But the dead ones haunt you. Their screams, the look of terror on their faces." Small pressed his lips together until they whitened. "In the meantime, I can teach you the ropes," he said, again good-natured, as if he hadn't just been talking about death and ghosts and terror. "Hell, you know most everything already. I'll give you a lesson on the breech buoy, fire off a few mortars so you get a feel for the contraption. Too bad you never saw it in action. It's something to see some poor soul clinging to that line as we drag him from a foundered ship."

Jared's brows furrowed; he was not taken in by Small's false cheerfulness. "You ever suspect mooncussers around these parts?"

"No, no," he said absently. He peered up at Jared. "What makes you ask?"

"Nothing much. Just one night when I was on patrol I waved off a ship and thought I saw a light above me." He paused, his gaze never leaving the lightkeeper's face. "And then there's the mystery surrounding the sinking of the *Merry Maid*. And Richard Best's death."

Small gave Jared a speculative look. "You think it was mooncussers that night?"

"I think it's possible."

Small stroked his stubbled chin as if deep in thought. Finally he shook his head. "I don't think so, Cap'n. Don't forget, I was there that night. Granted, it was after those poor souls drowned, but I know the men who were at that wreck. All good local boys. I can't imagine any one of 'em getting involved in such a thing."

"You're probably right." Jared looked out over the ocean, watching as the clouds' shadows created bits of gray amidst the startling blue, as if a giant whale lumbered beneath the surface. It was difficult to imagine the sea turning violent enough to founder one of those great ships skidding along the horizon. But he'd seen with his own eyes ships dragged to shore by the vicious currents. Who knew why that ship had foundered, or why Richard Best had died? He wouldn't have given a damn about Best if he hadn't destroyed Rachel's life the night he disappeared.

"You sure you want to give all this up, Don?"

Jared asked, forcing thoughts of Richard Best from his mind.

"No, I ain't. But I know I have to. It's a damn hard thing, getting old. A damn hard thing."

"Sometimes, old man, it's a damn hard thing being young, too."

Small gave him a wave of dismissal. "You think on it, Captain."

Jared assured him he would.

Chapter Seventeen

~~~~~

It was a glorious day, as if the world had decided the poor souls of Truro had suffered enough winter and needed relief from the endless wind and cold. A soft breeze blew in warm air, bringing out some foolish bugs who thought perhaps spring had come. It was a day for being young and carefree—for being in love. Rachel wanted to whirl around, to swing Belle into the air, to shout to the world that she was happy.

If there remained a small twinge of doubt and guilt for feeling so wonderful, then she pushed it away. *I'm in love*, she thought forcefully. She believed it. She had to believe it. Rachel swallowed down the bit of despair that gripped her heart, miserable that even when she was so happy, sadness could touch her. With that ridiculous thought, Rachel laughed.

"I've gone completely mad, Mama," she announced as she strode into the kitchen.

"Love will do that," Mabel said.

Rachel grinned, grabbed up an egg, and cracked it into a bowl. "Belle did a fine job collecting eggs this morning," she said, eyeing the half dozen eggs in her daughter's basket. They were beautiful eggs, perfect, from their lovely, perfect chickens. Rachel let out another contented sigh.

"My goodness, Rachel, you could take the sun's place for the day with that smile. Did something happen yesterday?"

Rachel felt her cheeks grow warm. *I made love to Jared yesterday. I reached the stars; I held them in my hand.* "Yesterday?"

"Yes. Yesterday. While your father, Belle, and I went to town."

Through her happy haze, Rachel became slowly aware that her mother's voice had grown stern. Never in a thousand years could she tell her mother what had happened. Just thinking of such a thing made her cheeks grow even warmer, and her mother's gaze grow even sharper.

"He kissed me," she said finally, giving a silent prayer that her mother would believe her.

"He didn't . . . ask you anything, did he?"

Rachel knew precisely what her mother was hinting at. That single question, one that truly hadn't occurred to her, managed to drain away some of her joy. Jared *hadn't* asked her to marry him. She'd simply assumed, given what he'd said to her before, that they would marry.

"No, Mama. He didn't," she said.

Mabel let out a harrumph. "I'm sure he will."

Rachel nodded, but suddenly she was not sure. Suddenly that great lack of asking her loomed large. Why hadn't he mentioned marriage? A brisk knock on the door stopped her panicked thoughts. It was Jared's knock, authoritative, impatient. She smiled and thought, *This is it.*

Marry me. Please marry me, darling. Will you marry me? "Will you promise to love me and only me and put your damned husband in a grave where he belongs?" Jared muttered as he crossed the small distance between his cottage and the Newcombs'. He wasn't sure of her answer. Shouldn't a man who was about to ask a woman to be his wife be certain of her answer? He stopped halfway to the cottage, clenching his fist, his entire body, against his doubts. Of course she would say yes. She had to.

But what if she didn't? What if she looked into his eyes and she slowly shook her head? What if she laughed? Stupid thought. Rachel wouldn't laugh. What the hell was wrong with him? When did his world revolve around whether or not he had a woman? *Now*, his mind screamed. "Stop thinking," Jared softly chastised.

He stopped before the door and rapped on it twice, consciously unclenching his jaw. It would not do to look as though he wanted to murder her. That thought made him smile. So when Rachel opened the door, she saw a smiling man, a man sure of himself. A man in love.

"Good morning," she said, grinning up at him. She looked so happy to see him, so clean and bright. So ready to say yes.

"Walk with me?"

She bit her lip, and Jared right then wanted to drag her into his arms.

"Good morning, Captain," came Mabel's rather stern greeting.

"Morning, Mrs. Newcomb."

"Let me get my coat," Rachel said, grabbing one coat, replacing it, then taking another. Her husband's coat. She'd left it behind, he realized when he saw her pulling on a light green wool coat.

She closed the door and walked next to him, seeming shy and uncertain.

"How long do I have to wait before I can kiss you?" he asked, and was rewarded by her musical laughter. She put on a show of considering his question, then pursed her lips and closed her eyes.

"Wanton," he said sternly, before giving her a chaste kiss on her cheek.

She batted him playfully on the arm, clearly disappointed by his kiss. "You need more practice, just as I suspected."

They walked along the sandy path toward the bluffs, the sun kissing their faces, two people with their hearts on their sleeves. When they reached the top of the bluff, Jared held out his hand.

"Come on," he said, feeling like a young boy, feeling as if he could fly down to the beach on wings. They stepped down, laughing and sliding, getting sandy and not caring. It was a bit cooler right by the water, and Jared pulled Rachel's collar around her neck, then left his hands there, his thumbs moving along her jaw, caressing her smooth skin.

"You are beautiful." He saw the doubt in her eyes. "You are," he said forcefully, so that she would believe him. He let out a breath that shook, and he kissed her lightly on the lips so she wouldn't see the desperate love in his eyes. He'd never been so afraid in his life.

"Rachel." A deep breath. A silent prayer.

Something behind him must have caught her eye, for suddenly she looked over his shoulder, her brows furrowing. Then her eyes widened, and she let out a small gasp, the kind a person emits when caught by surprise by a jagged flash of lightning. Jared looked over his shoulder, curious, and saw a man walking along the beach. He was tall and slim with blond hair, and he held up a hand in greeting.

"Oren," she said, closing her eyes. "Oren."

Something in her voice shook Jared to the core. "What did Richard look like?" he asked, pretending a nonchalance he didn't feel.

"Oh, Jared, I'm sorry."

Jared gripped her arms, hating her response. "What did he look like?"

Rachel shook her head, her eyes filling with tears. "I will not be moved by your tears," he said harshly, softly, so Oren Cobb couldn't hear. As the blond man walked by, Jared waved a hand in greeting and even managed a smile.

Rachel stared out to sea, trying in vain to blink back her tears. She didn't care what Oren would think of her turning away. *Oh, God, what have I done? What have I done?* If she could have turned back the clock, she would have done so. Even she was surprised by her reaction. Her foolish reaction. *Richard is dead. He is dead.*

"Rachel."

Rachel turned to him, feeling a dread as cold as his voice wash over her. How different he sounded now from the last time he'd said her name, as if another man entirely had called out to her.

"I know he's dead," she said, hoping to meet him head-on.

"You don't."

Rachel glanced up at him, terrified at what she would see. "Please, Jared. I'm sorry. But you don't know what it's been like for me. Richard—"

"I don't care about Richard," he said between clenched teeth. "Saint Richard can rot in hell."

Rachel winced. "Are you purposely trying to be hurtful? Because if that is what you are trying to do, you are succeeding. I cannot turn off what I feel." More tears escaped her eyes, and she wiped them away angrily.

Jared dropped his head and put his hands on his hips. "I know that." He stared at the sand a long time in silence. "It only makes what I've asked you here to say easier. I'm going home."

His words hit her like a blow to her heart. "For how long?"

He scuffed the sand with his boot and stared hard at the small hole he was creating. "I guess for good."

"Oh." Rachel's mind swirled with a hundred things she wanted to say to him, to ask him. She tried to remain silent, knowing that whatever more she said would only force him to say over and over again that he was leaving. With an inner shrug, Rachel conceded to the voice inside her that demanded she not let him go without a fight. "Are you saying you don't love me anymore?"

His head snapped up and his eyes were so filled with hurt and anger that Rachel let out an involuntary sound.

"I love you. But I'll be damned if I'll share you with another man. I can't."

Tears welled up in Rachel's eyes, and this time she let them fall unheeded. Her throat felt as though someone were squeezing it, her heart as if it had been pierced with something hot and jagged. "It was a mistake. I saw Oren and I thought—"

"That it was Richard. I know," Jared said. "Damn you, Rachel, you wanted it to be him. He's dead. He drowned that night; you know he did."

Rachel wanted to cover her ears to block out the truth of what he said. She felt as if her head would explode. "Richard didn't drown! He could be out there somewhere, wanting to come home to us, wanting me to be a good and faithful wife when all I've done is forsaken him with another man." She gasped and slapped a hand over her mouth, horrified by what she'd just said.

She shook her head back and forth, trying to deny she'd just uttered those damning words. But they were out there; she could not call them back. "Oh, Jared."

"I can't do this, Rachel," he said, his voice sounding strange. "I'm sorry. I love you too damn much."

"You don't have to leave. Stay. Be patient with me. Please, Jared."

Again anger flared in his eyes, but his voice remained calm, even cool. "I have to leave," he said, the words precise and clipped. "I'll say good-bye to your parents and Belle and then I'll go."

Rachel bit the inside of her lip, but nodded her head. He looked tightly coiled, as if one more word from her would unleash the violence that he held in check with his iron will. She wasn't afraid he would physically harm her, but she was desperately afraid she would unleash the anger growing just beneath his cool surface.

"It'll break Belle's heart, you know." She watched as the anger dissolved, replaced by something even more painful to see.

He smiled sadly. "Mine, too." He lifted one hand to the side of her face and gazed down at her, his eyes sweeping over each feature, finally coming to rest on her mouth. He lowered his head and kissed her softly before pulling her head to his shoulder, roughly, desperately. She felt his lips move against her hair, but she didn't hear his words.

"I love you, too," she whispered, not knowing if he heard her, knowing only that it didn't make a difference if he did or not.

Chapter Eighteen

◁∽◁

New Bedford

Julia Mitchell stood in her grand hallway listening to the loud ticking of the grandfather clock and wondering whether she should approach her oldest son, who, as far as she knew, was still in the back parlor. He'd arrived from Cape Cod just three hours earlier and had been in the parlor ever since.

She loved all her sons, but Jared, with his brooding dark looks, sometimes frightened her. She knew it was because he looked so much like her dead husband, a man she had feared and grown to hate. When she was a young bride, Julia would sometimes stand in this very spot and listen to the sounds of her house. She could stand there in a square of pale sunlight coming through the high window above her, and allow herself some peace. She would stand quite still and watch the sunlight fade to darkness and listen, missing nothing—not the muffled sounds of seagulls coming from the harbor, not the clatter of pans being washed in the kitchen, nor the endless ticking of the hall clock.

It was that clock, she realized long ago, that drew her to this spot more than anything. In her younger years it was a reminder of time, a quiet marking of the years of having her husband blessedly at sea, the pendulum swinging its joyous reminder: *A million times will you hear this sound before he returns.*

West had said he feared Jared was becoming like their father, but deep in her heart Julia knew better. Inside that imposing blatant maleness, Jared was as gentle as West, as carefree as Gardner. He was a good man. But when he was vexed, when he shut down and glared at her, she couldn't help that tingling of fear that crept up her scalp. She hardly knew him. Jared had been taken from her by his father when he was just six years old. Her husband had tried his best to mold his oldest into the image of himself, but in the end he'd failed. Jared, for all his bluster and fearful anger, had a soft heart. Perhaps, she thought, it was that soft heart that made the rest of him appear to be so hard. Perhaps he was protecting that soft inner core.

Julia wiped her hands on her skirt and gave herself a mental shake. She was about to head toward the parlor when West trudged down the stairs, a wooden toy in his hands. He'd been up to the nursery in search of some of his old things to give to his little son. Boys. Julia sighed. That was all this family needed was more boys.

In his hand was a small horse on wheels, a pull-toy that Julia remembered had been a favorite of West's. West lifted the toy up sheepishly, showing his mother what he'd come for. "I thought Thomas might like this," he said.

Julia clutched her hands together at her waist, and West's expression grew concerned. "What's wrong, Mother?"

"It's Jared. He's been in that parlor since he returned. He hardly even greeted me before he went storming in there."

"I don't think it was you he was escaping. Things turned sour when I mentioned Mrs. Best." When Jared walked through the door as if he'd only been gone for the workday and not five years, Julia had nearly swooned. Then she'd thrown herself into her oldest son's arms. To West's annoyance, Jared had hugged his mother, but with a reserve that would wound a mother's heart. He'd been so damned polite to both of them, West wanted to give his brother a good kick in the ass. Instead he'd asked about Rachel, and that had worked better than any ass-kicking West would have dealt out.

"Obviously something happened between the two of them," West said wearily.

"Why don't you go in and talk to him?"

West chuckled. "Mother, he won't bite off your head, you know."

Julia flushed, disliking that she'd been so transparent, and disliking even more that she felt so uncomfortable being alone with her oldest son. "Just go talk to him," she said, holding out her hand for him to give her the toy.

West thrust it to her good-naturedly, and headed down the hall as if he were taking a leisurely stroll about the house. Inside, his stomach clenched nervously. He and his brother were closer now than they had been growing up, but he still couldn't help but feel a bit intimidated by him. He was so damned big, and when his temper was up, West liked to stay out of his way. He took a deep breath and walked through the parlor door.

At first he didn't see Jared, but the telltale smell of pipe smoke was in the air, and a small cloud of smoke billowed above a high-backed wing chair at the far end of the room.

"Jared?"

Silence.

"Mother's desperately worried," he said, keeping his tone light. He paused in case his brother wanted to say something. Grimacing slightly, he asked, "What happened with Rachel?"

"Damned if I know."

Jared was being obtuse, West decided. "Did she tell you to go?"

"No."

How very helpful his brother was being. "You two have an argument?"

His brother shifted in his chair. "No."

West stared at another puff of smoke rising above the chair. "Then what are you doing here growling at everyone like a wounded bear?" He walked to the fireplace and turned to his brother, who sat, legs sprawled out in front of him, slumped low in the chair. West's chest felt suddenly queer as he looked at Jared and saw in his face something he'd seen once before: a man who had lost hope. "Christ, Jared, what the hell happened?"

Jared lifted his eyes, and West saw that haunted, hunted look that sucked the breath from his lungs. Jared sat up suddenly, drawing his legs in and resting his elbows on his thighs. He took a puff on his pipe, not noticing that the embers had gone out. He let out a bitter laugh. "Don't be so dramatic, West. She still loves her husband, still looks for him. For all I know, the man is still alive."

West shook his head. "I don't believe that. And neither do you."

Jared shook his head. "You're right. I don't believe he's alive. But he might as well be."

"What about Rachel?"

"She'll be fine. Ever hear the expression 'Out of sight, out of mind'?"

"Homer was no romantic," West said.

"Neither am I." Jared, finally realizing his pipe had

gone out, laid it aside with some disgust, as if it were more proof that nothing in his life was right. Jared stood abruptly and looked about the room like a wild man who desperately needed to tear something—anything—apart. West took a step back.

"I want to break something. Give me something to break."

West grabbed the first thing he saw, a pretty flowered vase that he knew his mother liked but felt was worth the sacrifice.

"No. Not that, you idiot. It's Mother's favorite." He looked around the room. "That," he said, pointing to a figurine. He stalked over to it, grabbed it up, and made to heave it across the room. Then he stopped.

"Damn!" he yelled. Then he let loose a series of foul words that West hadn't heard since he'd been on the *Julia*. Jared slumped down onto a sofa and dropped the figurine onto the floor, where it landed unscathed, and he buried his hands in his hair. Jared stayed that way a long time, until West shifted uneasily on his feet and wondered if he should leave his brother alone.

"How close is the *Huntress* to being outfitted?" Jared demanded.

West grew instantly wary. "Captain Ferguson says she'll be ready in a week or two."

"I'm taking her out."

"No, Jared, you're not."

Jared looked at him hard, and West felt the hairs on the back of his neck rise. *Oh, hell.*

"West, I can take any damned ship in our damned fleet any damn time I want."

West looked down and let a out a sharp puff of air. "It'll kill you this time."

Jared shrugged.

"I can't let you do it."

Jared blinked at him, as if he truly couldn't believe he was attempting to defy him. Well, he was. *Damn it.*

"You cannot stop me, West," Jared said, smiling, delighted, it seemed, by his younger brother's courage. "I'd like to see you try." He stood up, looking invigorated by the prospect of going head-to-head with his brother.

"Hell, Jared, I'm not going to fight you."

Jared looked flabbergasted. "Then how do you plan to stop me from captaining my own ship?" The question started out pleasant, but quickly disintegrated into something ugly and hard.

"You can't run away this time," West said, wondering if he had a death wish. He'd never seen his brother as angry as he was right now. Jared's nostrils flared, his hands fisted, his body looked about to explode.

"You walk dangerous ground," Jared said with quiet menace.

"I don't care," West said rashly. "I watched you try to kill yourself. I watched you put the barrel of a pistol in your mouth and beg me to pull the trigger." He was so damned angry, so frustrated, that he felt as if this time, just this once, he could pummel his giant of a brother. "You will not take that ship, Jared," he said, his voice breaking. "I swear to God you will not."

Jared jerked his head away from the pain and anger he saw in his brother's eyes. He'd held at bay for two days the pain that was ripping him apart. He'd even fooled himself into thinking he would come out of this thing with Rachel unscathed. But now, with his brother's interference, with his pitying looks of concern, it hit him with the force of a whale fluke. He closed his eyes and concentrated on breathing. He'd wanted to die that night on the *Julia*. He'd wanted to die when he lay in that whaleboat, the cold Atlantic rolling beneath him.

He wanted to die right now. God, how he hated this weakness, this curse to have a heart that could so easily be filled by a woman, that could hurt so damn much he wanted to tear it from his chest.

A strange sound erupted from his throat, which had become clogged and painful, as if something hard and sharp were lodged there. His body became racked with pain, with something awful, with a hurt so deep he couldn't contain it. Something wet was on his cheek. He lifted a hand to his face and wiped, bringing his hand down to look at the wetness. Another sob escaped his throat. And another, no matter how he fought it, no matter how tightly he clenched his fists, no matter how he tried to close off his mind from the torment he was feeling.

Jared felt a strong hand on his shoulder and he tried to shake it off, but his brother simply tightened his grasp.

"Goddamn me," Jared said, his hoarse voice betraying him. He decided to suffer his brother's hand there on his shoulder.

"Not yet, Jared. Not yet."

Jared breathed deeply, trying to rid himself of this ridiculous weakness. It worked, slowly. He got control of at least the weeping part, if not the pain, if not the fear.

"I'm all right now," he said, half believing himself. In his heart he knew he'd never be right without Rachel.

Rachel kneaded the soft, cool dough on the flour-covered table, and stared hard at her mother's back. The unspoken words between them could have filled a volume. When she'd told her parents that Jared had to go home to New Bedford, they'd looked at each other and exchanged the oddest look. Her parents, for whatever reason, had fully expected Jared to propose. And he probably would have if she hadn't thrust a knife into his back that day on the beach.

She wished she could stop thinking about it, but if anything, that moment had become more clear, more agonizingly vivid. Over and over again she would picture herself standing in front of him, her hair whipping about her face, her smile, her eyes bright with anticipation. She could see him looking down at her, loving her. And then, in one horrifying moment, something on the beach drew her eyes away, pulling her from his beloved face no matter how she tried to resist. She could see her body stiffening, her eyes widening, her mouth opening in disbelief, her heart pounding, pounding when she recognized Richard. And then she heard the small gasp, felt the cool sea air enter her lungs the tiniest of seconds before she realized how foolish she'd been.

How she tried to rewrite what happened in her memory, tried to stop herself from looking—or at least from thinking Oren was Richard. God, they hardly looked alike at all, which only went to prove how ridiculous her reaction had been. But she could not push away the terrible look in Jared's eyes—the same look she'd seen when she first saw Jared open his eyes after he'd been rescued from the sea. How frightened she'd been by that look then, that vast nothingness she'd seen in his beautiful eyes. His voice, so cold—as cold as her heart felt now. A lump of misshapen ice, jagged and piercing, sat heavy in her chest.

They didn't come right out and say so, but she could tell by her parents' stiffness, their furtive glances, that they blamed her for his leaving. Of course they'd liked him. What parents could object to such a man, one who was kind and strong, intelligent and loyal—and wealthy, if what Donald Small told them was to be believed.

Rachel shaped the dough, plopped it on a flour-dusted wooden tray, and began work on a second lump. In all her memory, Rachel could not recall her mother being angry with her. She was angry now. Rachel could tell by the angle of her back, her quick, efficient movements as she chopped carrots for the soup they'd have for supper.

Rachel let out a little huff. "Spring's early this year." She said it as if she were challenging her mother.

Mabel let out a noncommittal sound.

Rachel stared long and hard at Mabel's back, pursing her lips, kneading the dough so hard her fingers ached. She pounded it into shape and placed it none too gently next to the first loaf. "Is there something you'd like to say, Mama?" There. It was finally out. Rachel watched as her mother's shoulders sagged. Mabel turned slowly around, a look of guilt or shame on her lined face; Rachel couldn't tell which.

"You hurt a fine man," she said.

Rachel dipped her head. "I know."

"Richard is dead."

She closed her eyes. "I know that, too."

Mabel stalked to the table and stood inches from Rachel. "Do you? You tell me why a fine man like Captain Mitchell, a man who so clearly loved you, would suddenly up and leave not a day after asking permission to marry you. You tell me that, daughter."

Rachel lifted her head, her eyes, already burning from unshed tears, filling and blurring her vision. "He asked Papa for permission to marry me?"

"Well, of course he did," Mabel said, her voice infinitely gentler. "Didn't he ask?"

Rachel stared blindly at the unformed dough in front of her and pushed her fingertips into the cool mixture. "Oh, God."

"Oh, honey." Mabel hugged her daughter close, her eyes filled with worry. "We thought he'd asked and you'd said no."

Rachel could only shake her head, for her throat hurt too much to speak.

"What happened?"

Rachel's body heaved silently as she tried and failed to take a breath. Finally she took in a great, gulping sob. "Oh, Mama," she said, flinging her arms about her mother's waist. "I thought that's what he was going to say. But then . . . but then . . ." Rachel dissolved into tears.

Mabel, apparently having had enough of such nonsense, grabbed her daughter's head firmly and made her look up. "What happened?" she demanded.

Shame filled Rachel as the memory of what happened washed over her. "We were on the beach," she said dully. "Oren was walking toward us. I saw him and for an instant—he was still quite far and you know that Richard and Oren had similar builds. Oren is not as fair as Richard, but anyone could have been mistaken. Why, I've heard of widows who think they recognize their husbands long after they're dead."

"Oh, no."

"It wasn't my fault. Not entirely. He wouldn't listen to me. He accused me of thinking Richard was still alive, or of wishing he was, and I . . ." She closed her eyes at the memory of what she'd said. "I yelled that Richard could still be alive. And then he told me he was going home."

"Do you?"

Rachel scrunched her face up in confusion and sniffed loudly. "Do I what?"

"Do you still think Richard is alive? Do you still love him?"

She could hear Jared asking the same thing, and she gave her mother the same answer. "He was my husband. My God, everyone expects me to simply forget him. But he's been gone only six months."

Mabel shook her head sadly. "You can't even say it now, can you? You can't bring yourself to say that Richard is dead. 'He disappeared, he's gone,' you say."

Rachel pressed her jaw closed. "You don't understand."

"What don't I understand? How hard it is to accept that someone you love is dead without seeing a body? Is that what you're saying? I planted two plaques in the ground for sons without seeing proof."

"That was different. You knew how they died."

Mabel threw up her hands.

"If someone had seen him, if just one person knew how he died, then I could accept it."

Mabel was silent for a long moment as she looked at her daughter with infinite sadness. "It's good that the captain's gone," she said finally.

"How can you say that?"

Mabel's expression grew fierce. "Because I love you, because I loved Richard, even with his flaws, and the good Lord knows he had plenty of them. But he's gone, Rachel. *Dead*. I don't know why you won't accept it. Why? Why won't you?"

Rachel swallowed hard and curled her hands into fists. "I have accepted it. Truly I have. In here," she said, bringing her fist to her heart. "Oh, Mama, I love him so much."

"Let Richard go, honey."

"I wasn't talking about Richard," Rachel said on a sob. "I hurt Jared so much. I'm so stupid. Stupid, stupid, stupid." She pounded the table.

Mabel chuckled. "It takes a smart girl to know when she's been stupid, I'd say."

"He deserves more than I have to give him right now. He's the most wonderful man. Brave, honorable. Oh, I know he's a bit rough. But he loves Belle. Oh, Mama, did you see his face when he said goodbye to Belle? He was so brave, and I know his heart was breaking when she begged him to stay." She began sobbing anew when she recalled how Jared had gently pushed Belle away and into her arms, his jaw set, his eyes filled with unfathomable sorrow.

"That's enough tears, daughter, unless you plan to go out and water the garden."

Rachel gave her mother a teary laugh.

"Now. Do me a favor. Wash your face with cold water, then go out and find that father of yours and tell him his lunch is nearly ready. I think I saw him out by the shed."

Feeling like a little girl again, Rachel pushed herself up from the table and did as her mother asked. She paused to look in the small mirror her father used to shave in and grimaced when she saw her puffy, red-rimmed eyes. No doubt her father would ignore the obvious sign of tears. Such emotional displays sent him running from the house every time.

Rachel headed toward the back of the house and the large shed where her father worked on his boats and fishing gear. He'd taken to repairing nets for fishermen to earn some extra money. It broke Rachel's heart to watch him do the intricate work with his gnarled hands, knowing how painful it must be for him. On fair days Ambrose worked outside, but in foul weather she knew she could find him in the shed, squinting to see in the dim light. A fine mist swirled about her, and Rachel closed her eyes against the wonderful feel of it.

"Papa," she called before opening the door. She

peeked inside, but he was nowhere to be seen. Later Rachel couldn't have explained what made her step inside. The shed was always a happy place where her father would work, where they would sometimes have one of their rare father-daughter talks. Rachel did most of the talking, but she didn't mind. She liked the shed, with its smells of wood, fish, beeswax, pipe tobacco, and linseed oil. Long after her father was gone, Rachel knew she could come into this shed, close her eyes, and her father would return, vivid and alive in her mind.

Shaking away that melancholy thought—she'd had enough such thoughts recently—she looked about fondly, her eyes resting on a ledger tucked up on a shelf filled with spools of hemp and jars of screws and nails. It was so out of place, so different from what was usually in the shed, that Rachel reached up and pulled it down. Her father, in all her recollection, had never kept records of expenses—not even when he was captain of his own fishing vessel. She flipped through the book and shrugged when it appeared that every page was empty. Perhaps her father intended to start keeping records of his net repair earnings. She was about to give up when she spotted some writing in the very beginning of the ledger. Curious, and feeling a bit as though she were snooping, Rachel opened the page and saw her father's handwriting.

At first it made no sense. It appeared to be a brief listing of sea conditions, tides and dates, ships and cargo, similar to what she'd seen Donald Small record. Rachel's brows knitted as she recognized the ships as ones that had foundered near Truro in the past three years. She could tell immediately that it was not a complete list of wrecks. Her heart nearly stopped when she saw, underlined heavily, the words *Merry Maiden, August 4, payroll shipment.*

It was the ship that had foundered the night Richard disappeared. And then, next to that entry, far in the margin, her father had written words that made her blood run cold.

Chapter Nineteen

◁~~~~▷

Rachel's first sight of New Bedford crystallized the anxiety she had been feeling for four days into stark fear. She stood at the rail of the Martha's Vineyard steamboat she'd been lucky enough to book passage on and let out a long sigh. "What am I doing here?" she whispered, her eyes pinned to the harbor and the city beyond that rose above it.

In all her twenty-two years, Rachel had never left Truro—and that she found herself at the rail of a ship, far from home and alone, somehow made real the horrible truth of what she'd found that day in her father's shed.

After finding the ledger, she'd managed to push away the panic that threatened to send her running and screaming from her parents' home, and plodded through the three torturous days in which she'd pretended a broken heart was to blame for her sudden and overwhelming desire to take a trip to New Bedford. Belle, who had been withdrawn and unhappy since Jared's departure, had looked at her with stunned disbelief when Rachel had told her she would be gone for a few days. Then she'd become oddly silent, returning her mother's good-bye hug with a listlessness that made Rachel's heart ache even now. But Rachel forced herself away from her daughter, just as she forced herself to act as if her father were the same man he'd been before she'd gone into that shed.

Her first thought when she stepped out into the bracingly cold air from that shed was, *Jared*. Her eyes immediately went to the small cottage, her mind forgetting for an instant that she had sent him away with her careless words. Round and round she went, finally concluding that the only person who could help her was Jared—the one person who might refuse her. She thought about sending a telegram, but what would she say that wouldn't sound as if she'd gone completely mad? This need to see him became almost desperate, nearly supplanting all else—including the true reason for this journey.

And it *was* a journey for a woman who had never traveled farther than Provincetown, who had never seen a building taller than a tree. Who had never stepped upon a paved road or into a building made of stone.

Now, as she looked at the forest of masts that clogged the harbor, all the fear she'd been holding at bay rushed back, making her almost ill. Nowhere to be seen were the gentle bluffs of home, the golden richness of the coastline. Here was a city, massive and breathtaking, with so *much* to be seen, it almost hurt her eyes. Just then the wind swirled about her, driving the mist from the steamship's wheel onto the deck. She stepped back inside the spartan cabin and sat among a handful of other passengers on a hard wooden bench. And watched as New Bedford loomed ever nearer.

Rachel looked at the mansion in front of her in awe and disbelief. It was the most magnificent structure she'd ever seen. Surely this was not where Jared lived, and she resisted looking down again at the slip of paper she held in her hand where Jared had hastily scrawled his address. She'd kept it in her pocket, proof that he had never intended to cut all ties.

She could not place her rugged sea captain in this elegant, pretty home. No, not a home—a mansion. It was a huge, solid fortress of white granite, with four Doric columns that supported a third-story portico. It was something out of a storybook, this great house sprawled behind a high iron fence that sat high on a hill above the city. French doors opened to the portico from which, Rachel suspected, one could see the harbor and beyond. The windows gleamed from polishing; its granite face was clean and unblemished. It was a house for royalty, or a spectacularly wealthy sea captain.

Rachel walked casually up to the iron fence, trying not to stare too openly. When she spied a gardener raking away the winter leaves from beneath the shrubbery outside what appeared to be a solarium, Rachel stepped away, her cheeks burning, as if she'd been caught trying to break into the house instead of simply looking at it. The quiet street was lined with towering elm trees, now bare of leaves, and sturdy walls and iron fences that protected the rich inhabitants from the riffraff that might venture up to the hill, away from a harbor that stank of rancid whale and rotten seaweed.

She felt like riffraff.

Never before had Rachel been more aware that she was poor. It had simply never occurred to her until this moment that she was. She'd never wanted more than what she had. Her dreams didn't include ball gowns or a great house on a hill—they were much simpler dreams of sunny days, baby smiles, and cozy winter nights. She was hit by a wave of homesickness that was nearly strong enough to send her running down that hill and to the harbor. Here not even a day and Rachel was already longing for soft sand beneath her feet, a tangy scent to the air, and the homey and weathered houses tucked behind the dunes. She found walking on the slate sidewalks jarring and awkward; her feet hurt. She'd read about cities, about buildings that crowded each other, streets bustling with pedestrians. But she'd never imagined the noise, the general confusion that it all produced. It was all so foreign, this city with its hard-packed streets that were nicely lined with strategically planted trees that soared high above her. But more foreign was this house—Jared's house—with its grand columns, its expansive lawn, its mullioned windows that winked in the sun.

Rachel was afraid of it, afraid it all meant that Jared wasn't the man she'd thought he was, that he'd come home and realized he'd missed this place, these people. How foreign Truro was, and how very far away.

Back home there were no fine carriages or French dressmakers. She was dressed in her best—a plain white bodice and simple brown brocade skirt that contained not a single flounce nor bit of lace or trimming to brighten it up. Her Sunday best was shabby compared to the dresses she'd seen the women of New Bedford wearing. She had no fur collar on her coat or ermine muff to protect her hands. She wore her old green coat with the black velvet collar that wasn't nearly warm enough.

Oh, what was she doing here?

When she'd first run from her father's shed, she could only think that she needed Jared desperately. Now she began to doubt whether he would be pleased to see her. She'd broken his heart. She'd let him leave without telling him how much she loved him. Would he throw her from the house? Or would he drag her into his arms?

Suddenly she wished she'd taken more care with her appearance. Her hair was in a simple braid, a practical style she thought would be perfect for such a long trip. Her simple dress, her old green coat, her worn cotton gloves, had all made her feel safe and secure. Now she realized how foolish and naive she was. How could she walk up to that massive front door and knock? She clutched her carpetbag even tighter and fought the urge to turn around.

When she noticed a man walking toward her from the other side of the iron fence, it took all of Rachel's resolve not to turn and flee. His expression was more polite and curious than hostile. He was young but balding and he wore no tie. It was the gardener she'd seen from a distance.

"Can I help you, miss?"

Rachel raised her head and nodded, thinking she ought to impress this man with her calm demeanor. "Yes, sir. I'm here to see Captain Mitchell."

"Which Captain Mitchell?"

Rachel was momentarily flustered. "Oh. Jared Mitchell. The oldest." She bit her lip and smiled an apology, giving up the pretense that she was a lady of quality come to call on the Mitchells. She didn't know the first thing about being a lady. "I'm here to see Jared Mitchell."

The man gave her a look, up and down, that made Rachel distinctly uncomfortable. "If you're looking for work, you can go on back to the kitchen and ask for Mrs. Wilcox."

A blush stained Rachel's cheeks. "No. I'm . . ." Her nervousness returned, and she felt ridiculously hurt that this man automatically assumed she was a servant, even though she admitted to herself that that was what she looked like. Why not assume she was something more important, like Jared's fiancée?

"I'm his fiancée," she blurted out, and immediately

crossed her fingers behind her back, praying God didn't decide to strike her dead for her lie. It was *almost* true. Well, she silently amended, it could have been true if she hadn't been such a ninny and thought Oren was Richard.

The man actually let out a short burst of laughter. "Is that what he's calling it?" His gaze had gone from polite to decidedly impolite. Rachel had no idea how very improper it was for her to come to the front gate unescorted. She had no idea what she looked like to this man, how foolish she sounded. But she was beginning to understand at least that she should have telegrammed Jared and told him she was coming. Back home it had all seemed so urgent.

Or perhaps it was her very real fear that if she'd warned him of her visit, he would have sent someone to the wharf to send her packing.

"I am his fiancée," she said softly.

Something in her voice must have convinced him—or evoked a bit of sympathy—for his demeanor instantly changed. His eyes softened, and he gave her a look of pity. "You go on to the front door and ask for Mrs. Mitchell. Captain Mitchell is at the counting house this morning. I'm Connor. The gardener."

Rachel nodded and gave him a tentative smile. "Rachel Best." He gave her a look she couldn't quite interpret. Finally he nodded toward the open gate and stepped back. Rachel walked to the gate, hesitating a moment before walking through, as if she would instantly become a different person when she stepped onto the graveled drive. She began walking purposefully toward the house when Connor called to her.

"Miss," he said, taking a few steps toward her before stopping. "You have family? You have a place to go?"

Dread settled in the pit of Rachel's stomach. "Yes."
Connor nodded, then turned away, leaving Rachel
staring at his back and again fighting the terrible
urge to run. Did she look so out of place that even
a gardener could be concerned about her? She gazed
up at the mansion, at its white granite walls, and felt
her throat close up. *If he doesn't love you, if he never
did* . . . She would deal with that when it happened.
All those daydreams she'd had on the steamship of
him rushing toward her with that wide grin on his
face seemed ridiculous now. She had taken his love
and thrown it away. A man like Jared would not fall
to her feet and forgive her. He would help her, she
knew that in her heart. He might not want to, but
his honor would take him back to Truro. And then
he would return here, to his world.

Rachel took a deep breath and walked toward the
door that loomed larger and larger the closer she got.
Her feet crunched on the gravel and she imagined
they said, *rich-rich, rich-rich.* At the bottom of the
steps, she removed her coat and draped it over her
arm. She walked up the wide stone steps, her eyes
pinned to the door. Then she searched for a knocker
or bell to ring. In the middle of the massive door
was a small keylike device that could be a ringer,
but might also be used to lock the door. She stared
at it a long time trying to decide whether she should
give it a twist. What if she locked the door? She gave
it a tentative half turn and heard a satisfying ringing
sound. Before she could ring again, the door opened.

"Yes?" The woman stared at her, taking in her
windswept hair, her plain brown dress. "Yes? Can I
help you?"

"Mrs. Mitchell?" she croaked out.

The woman smiled, but it wasn't the sort of smile
that made a person relax. "No. I'm Mrs. Wilcox, the
housekeeper."

Rachel blushed. "Oh. Sorry. Is Mrs. Mitchell at home?"

Mrs. Wilcox pushed the door imperceptibly toward Rachel. "Who may I say is calling?" Her tone was polite, but somehow condescending.

"Rachel Best," she said, half expecting Mrs. Mitchell to have no idea who she was. In fact, she mentally prepared herself for such an event. The housekeeper closed the door after asking Rachel to wait. Rachel didn't know enough to be insulted, and the fact that she didn't told Mrs. Wilcox she had chosen correctly by having the girl wait outside.

Rachel turned and looked across the vast yard, breathing in air that was only slightly tainted by the smells of the harbor below. It was quiet, with only the sounds of birds to break the silence. The gardener was nowhere to be seen, and Rachel felt a tinge of disappointment, for he'd seemed so ordinary in this vast temple of the unfamiliar. She looked up and noticed a large beveled-glass lantern hanging above her head, a sturdy chain suspended from the stone entryway. Everything around her was so sturdy, so opulent. So different from everything she knew.

The door opened behind her and Rachel expected to see the unpleasant Mrs. Wilcox standing there and pointing a sharp finger toward the gate. Instead, she saw a lovely older woman, her violet-blue eyes filled with kindness and a small bit of concern.

"Mrs. Best," she said. "Please come in. I apologize for keeping you outside, but we were not expecting you, and I'm afraid Mrs. Wilcox was unaware you are a . . . friend of my son's."

Rachel felt another sickening twist in her stomach at that telling pause Jared's mother gave. What had Jared said about her? she wondered as she walked into the grand entrance hall, her eyes taking in the sweeping marble staircase, the large grandfather clock directly in front of her, the soaring ceiling and glittering chandelier. "Then Captain Mitchell has mentioned me," she said, unable to keep the relief from her voice.

"Yes. Of course, Jared never has been very talkative." Something about the way she spoke, her hesitant manner, put Rachel further on edge. "He didn't mention you would be visiting." She could hear the question in the older woman's voice and dread blossomed inside her. Rachel had the distinct feeling that Mrs. Mitchell, while polite, was fiercely protective of her son.

"No. He didn't know I was coming." Rachel pressed her lips together, feeling more uncertain than she had her entire life. Clearly this woman didn't know what to make of her visit. She was polite but exceedingly curious, and too much a lady to question her outright.

"Jared isn't here at the moment, but I expect him to return before dinner." Mrs. Mitchell turned to look at the clock. "That's less than an hour. Why don't you wait in the parlor and I'll send him in to you as soon as he arrives?"

Rachel gave Mrs. Mitchell a brittle smile and followed her down a hall, fighting the urge to flee once again. Worse, she realized she had the need to use the privy, but was too embarrassed to ask where it was. Rachel hadn't gone in the steamship, for that facility had been so foul she simply couldn't bring herself to use it. She knew that modern homes had privies installed indoors, some with toilets that flushed. But she'd never used one and had no idea how to operate such a device.

After Mrs. Mitchell departed with a polite nod, Rachel found herself in a lovely room decorated all in yellow and green. The floor beneath her was covered with a thick pale green carpet, the walls yellow silk, the furniture a clever mix of green and yellow and was so delicate-looking, she hesitated to sit down for several minutes. On one wall was a fireplace with yellow-tinged marble that looked too pretty to be real. On the other wall was a large painting of a beautiful woman seated next to a man. Rachel's eyes widened and her heart nearly stopped. It wasn't just any man. It was Jared. The woman must be his first wife.

Rachel walked toward the painting, her heart thudding painfully in her chest. The woman was stunning. As delicate as a china doll, with a rosebud mouth, winged brows, and the palest skin Rachel had ever seen on a woman. Abigail had been her name, she remembered. Jared stood looking young and brash, his feet spread like a man of the sea, one hand behind his back, the other resting on the back of the chair. His fingertips brushed his wife's shoulder, a hint of a touch but somehow so intimate Rachel had to look away. Abigail wore a stunning gown of mint green, a softly feminine creation that would have looked ridiculous on Rachel, she thought. Tiny yellow bows decorated the modest neckline, and Rachel wondered if this room was fashioned to match the painting, or the painting to match the room.

Suddenly heat suffused her face. Why had Jared's mother asked her to wait in this room? They had walked down a long hall, passed half a dozen rooms before coming to this one—the one with the portrait of Jared and his wife. Was it a pointed reminder of the sort of woman Jared had loved? Rachel sat heavily, her back to the painting, but its image was seared into her memory. She was the opposite of the girl in that painting. Her cheeks were flushed from the sun and wind, her hands dry and slightly rough from washing clothes and dishes and cleaning fish. Her hair was light and Abigail's was a lustrous brown.

Rachel sat, her back stiff, for what seemed like an

hour. Her bladder was aching, and she could not ignore it any longer. She went to the door and peeked out, hoping to see a maid walk by. Lord knew she did not want to encounter Jared's mother and ask her where the privy was. She moved down the hall, tiptoeing softly like some burglar, when she heard footsteps behind her. Stifling the urge to run back into the parlor, Rachel turned and smiled when she saw a young maid, her arms filled with a pile of linens.

"Excuse me. I wonder if you could direct me to the necessary."

"You've found it," the girl said, pointing to the door directly behind Rachel. She moved off down the hall, humming beneath her breath. Thank goodness, for Rachel wasn't certain she could have walked the length of the house.

When she was finished, Rachel eased the door open and silently closed it, her body tensing when she heard voices coming from the front of the house. Her heart slammed against her chest. It was Jared. She knew his voice, that angry tone, down to her toes, felt her body hum with sharp memories. Her gut twisted. Why would he sound angry? Because she was here? Staying close to the wall, Rachel moved toward the foyer, feeling ridiculous for her stealth, but driven by rampant curiosity. She was well hidden from him, and so moved closer until she could clearly hear what was being said.

"Is she pregnant?" It was an angry, impatient question.

"Not obviously so." Mrs. Mitchell's voice was soothing, concerned.

"Good Christ, why else would she be here?"

Rachel could picture his face, could imagine him pulling at his chocolate brown hair, fisting it painfully in his grasp. She heard the sharp, angry strides of an irritated man.

"Would that be so terrible?" Another man. West, she thought.

"Yes." He let out a foul curse, and his mother let out a gasp of outrage. "Damn me. *Goddamn me.*"

Rachel stood there, her body suddenly gone hot with hurt and humiliation—and pain, an ache that made her heart feel as if it were tearing apart. What a horrible mistake she'd made. What a foolish, awful mistake. Her knees began to tremble, a quaking that moved up her body until she shook with it, her body clammy. Hot tears pricked at the back of her eyes, and she shoved her hand in front of her mouth to stop herself from sobbing aloud, squeezing until her cheek hurt. *Don't cry, don't cry.*

"I thought you loved her," West said in that calming way of his. "You do, don't you?"

Rachel held her breath, awaiting his answer.

His deep voice rumbled through her; she could *feel* it. "No. No."

She turned and fled silently down the hall back to the parlor, bile rising to her throat. *My God. What am I going to do?*

Jared felt as if his head would explode first, then his heart. "No. No," he said, nearly choking on the pain in his throat. "That's not it," he said finally. He looked up at his mother's worried face, his brother's confusion. "I love her. God above knows I love her."

"Then why . . ." Julia began, her brow knitted with worry.

"If she is pregnant, I will marry her. You know that, Mother. But it is not what I want, to be a kind of consolation prize." He was angry, down to his soul furious that the only way he could entice her into marriage was by impregnating her, that she should come to him only because she was desperate. When he was still in Truro, he'd harbored a ridiculous hope that Rachel would beg him to stay, that she would run after him, confess her love, her foolishness. But she had not. She had let him say his good-byes, dry-eyed and dispassionate, and all the while he was using all his strength not to drag her into his arms and beg her to give him her heart. An idiot was what he was. But he'd not make a jackass of himself over a woman—at least he wouldn't let her see him bray out his sorrow like a wounded animal.

He took a deep and cleansing breath and braced himself, like a captain turning his wheel into a tidal wave that would surely capsize his ship.

"Where is she?"

"In the back parlor. I didn't know where to put her. You never said . . ." His mother made a fluttering motion with her hands, one that was slightly accusing.

"The parlor with the portrait of Abigail and me?"

Julia closed her eyes briefly. "I didn't think," she whispered, then put her hands on her hips. "And you never told me a thing about this girl other than that she nursed you to health. If I had known who she truly was to you—"

Jared held up his hand to stop his mother's tirade, a gesture as effective as a gag. "She is nothing to me now. You acted entirely appropriately."

He hadn't told his mother what Rachel meant to him. He hadn't told anyone but West. And now she could be carrying his child. His son or daughter. He closed his eyes against a wave of pain and joy and began walking toward the back of the house.

Rachel felt almost frighteningly composed for a woman whose heart had just been broken. *He doesn't love you*, she thought over and over until they simply became words, an abstract thought that had no particular meaning to her. She realized she had come to

New Bedford not only to enlist Jared's help, but because she had foolishly believed Jared would immediately forgive her. Clearly he would not. She also knew she still needed him desperately, for she could trust no one in Truro with what she'd discovered. Despite everything, she knew she could trust Jared.

When he walked through that parlor door looking breathtakingly handsome, her heart hardly reacted. This wasn't the man she remembered, this cosmopolitan businessman in his fashionable suit and short-cropped hair. He wore a charcoal gray double-breasted coat with silk braid around the pockets and collar, and a lighter waistcoat with matching braiding around the edges. Trim-fitting trousers made him seem even taller than she remembered. Taller and more imposing—more like the man she had heard in the hallway who had heatedly declared he did not love her.

Well, she wouldn't love him either. Not too much. Not so much that she would forget her pride and beg his forgiveness. And really, she hadn't done anything all that wrong to begin with. He deserved to suffer as much as he'd made her suffer—thrusting himself into her life, making her heart feel things she wasn't ready for, making her realize how empty her life with Richard truly had been. He hadn't the vaguest idea what he had done to her life, how he had, with his smile and his strength, turned her topsyturvy. She wasn't ready to fall in love, she wasn't ready to say good-bye to Richard when Jared had floated into her life that October day.

And yet she'd let Jared into her heart. He was there still, elbowing his way deeper and deeper into that secret part of her that was reluctant to let him in, embedding himself so deep that Rachel knew there was no way her heart would ever get rid of him. He held a place that Richard never had. As her eyes swept over him, she knew she was completely, utterly lost. Of course she loved him. With all her heart. Every last bit of it.

Except now it was too late.

Before that realization had a chance to ruin her resolve, she smiled a greeting, managing to look pleased as well as sad. With a touch of nervousness. Perfect. As if watching from above, she moved toward him, a small smile on her lips, her hands extended as if she were greeting a well-liked acquaintance.

"Jared. You are looking well." How odd her voice sounded. Hollow and echoey. Oh, this was very strange. Rachel almost giggled. Shouldn't she be railing at him, pounding his chest with her fists, pulling his hair and demanding to know why he didn't love her?

He remained silent, but his eyes darted to her flat stomach, and she had a moment when she fiercely wished she were carrying his child. Then he would be forced to marry her, forced to love her.

"Are you pregnant?" he demanded.

Rachel lifted her chin, but her hands strayed to her stomach. "No. I'm not."

He looked slightly confused. Nothing more—not disappointed, certainly. And Rachel realized with a wrench that despite what he'd said to his mother and brother, she'd wanted him to be disappointed.

"Then why are you here?" he said as he walked toward her. "Ah, is it that you've had a change of heart? You've suddenly realized that your long-departed husband is indeed dead?"

His words were ugly, his tone mocking and just as ugly. Rachel shrank away from him. "Stop it, Jared. You know I never meant to hurt—"

"Yes, yes, you never meant to hurt me. Is that what you were going to say?"

"Yes." She didn't like this man in front of her—his clothes, his voice, the sneer on his face. Her mind shut down; the only thing echoing in her head was his voice, saying, *No. No. I don't love her.*

He didn't. She hadn't believed him, not truly, until this moment.

"Why are you here?" he repeated, this time with weary impatience.

Rachel stared at him, trying to see the gentle, kind man she remembered. She shook her head. "I shouldn't have come." She backed up toward the door, but in two strides he was there, blocking her way. His eyes swept over her face, and for an instant Rachel thought she saw something in his eyes, something of the man she'd known in Truro.

"Perhaps you shouldn't have come, my dear. But you are here now. And as you are not pregnant, I cannot fathom a reason for your traveling all this way." Suddenly he blanched. "Belle." He grabbed her upper arms. "Is it Belle? Is she ill?"

"Oh, Jared, no," she said in a rush. "Belle's fine. Other than that she misses you desperately."

He dropped his hands immediately, shoving them deep into his pockets, and took a step away from her, as if embarrassed by his transparent display.

"Jared, I need your help. That is why I've come. You're the only person I can trust. I am sorry I hurt you." She wanted to tell him she loved him, but knew how foolish that would be, given that he'd just denied loving her. "I know I'm perhaps the last person you want to help. And my reasons for being here . . . well, I know you will not like them." She knew that even saying Richard's name would drive him away.

"For God's sake, Rachel, just tell me."

She smiled at his bluster, which she liked much better than his sneering condescension. Then she turned back toward the painting of Jared and his wife. "She was beautiful."

Jared let out a groan of disbelief. "Rachel, if you

do not tell me your reasons for being here I swear I will throw you from this room and bar you from this house. By God, spill it!"

Rachel winced. "You'll think I'm mad."

"You're driving me there this instant."

"All right." She took a deep breath. "I think my father murdered Richard."

Chapter Twenty

Jared let out a bark of laughter. "Good God and all the saints, this is too rich," he said, shaking his head. "First you deny that he's dead; then you come to me with some cockamamie story about how your father murdered him?"

She nodded her head, looking incredibly unsure of herself despite that affirmative gesture. "I think my father is a mooncusser. And I think Richard found out and tried to stop him and . . . Oh, I know it sounds insane." Rachel dropped down into the nearest chair and clutched her skirts in her fists.

"All right. Tell me why you think these things." Jared sat down across from her, drinking in the sight of her. God, she was beautiful. Was there ever a woman born who was more desirable, more lovely than this woman sitting before him? It had taken all his willpower not to drag her into his arms when he'd walked into the room. Something in the way she stood—stiff and unwelcoming—told him such a gesture would not be agreeable. Her eyes, usually as warm as a late-summer sunset, were frosty and empty of any tender emotion. He ignored the sharp stab of disappointment that she was not carrying his child and pretended an indifference he far from felt.

Gone was the cool disdain she'd displayed not two minutes before, replaced by fear and uncertainty. She began hesitantly relating her tale of finding the ledger in her father's shed.

"All those ships foundered in calm seas on moonless nights. Including the *Merry Maid*. My father was keeping a log, listing cargo and ships. And next to the *Merry Maid*'s entry he'd written 'Richard knows.' "

Jared leaned forward, intrigued by Rachel's story but still doubting whether her father had anything to do with Richard's death. "So you think Richard found out about the mooncussers, learned your father was involved, and your father killed him to keep him quiet. Is that right?"

"No. I don't want to believe that. But I don't know what else to think. What else could all that mean?" Rachel drew in her bottom lip and bit it. "And there's something else, something I forgot about."

"What is it?"

"I remember Richard and my father arguing about something. I could hear them shouting as soon as I reached the top of the dune above the house. By the time I got to the house, they had stopped, but Richard's shirt was wrinkled about the neck, as if my father had grabbed him. When I came into the house—my parents' house—they weren't speaking, but it was clear they were angry. That must have been a week before he disappeared. The only reason I remembered is that they never fought. My father and Richard were so close. I asked Richard about it that night, but of course he told me it was nothing. Now I think it must have been about my father's involvement with the mooncussers. I can't imagine what else they would have been fighting about."

Jared cursed beneath his breath. He had a strong suspicion what that fight had been about, and it wasn't mooncussers or gold shipments. More likely

Ambrose had been telling his son-in-law to stop cheating on Rachel. Could Ambrose have murdered his son over that? And what of those strange entries in the ledger? It was difficult to imagine a man like Ambrose, a man who'd made his living on the sea, who'd had two sons die at sea, luring sailors to their deaths. He didn't believe it, and he told Rachel so.

"I don't believe it either, not in my heart," she said, looking so distraught that Jared had to force himself to keep from comforting her. "But when I think of that ledger and their argument, it makes sense. I'd never seen my father so angry. When he is mad about something, he grows silent or grunts and walks away. My father doesn't shout."

Hell, thought Jared. He didn't want to be the one to tell Rachel that her beloved husband had been cheating on her for nearly their entire marriage. But it was either that or let her believe her father murdered Richard. Jared clicked his tongue against his cheek and gave Rachel a steady look.

"I think you ought to talk to your father."

Her eyes widened, and then she rolled them in disbelief. "Oh, yes, splendid idea. I'll just walk up to my dear father and say, 'Papa, did you murder my husband and are you a mooncusser?' And he will say"—she lowered her voice to imitate Ambrose— "'Aye, daughter, I did.' Of course I can't do that."

Jared let out a chuckle. "That isn't quite what I had in mind. I would begin by asking him what Richard and he were arguing about."

She shot him a look of pure exasperation. "And if he says he doesn't remember?"

"Then I will be there to remind him," Jared said levelly.

She lowered her head and looked up at him beneath furrowed brows. "You know what they were fighting about? How can that be?"

"I don't know for certain, but I strongly suspect I do."

"And it wasn't about the mooncussers?"

"No."

Her eyes flashed. "Tell me."

Jared shook his head. "I will not. It is your father's tale to tell."

Rachel stood abruptly and stalked over to him, her dander up good and high. "Tell me," she demanded with more force.

The wretched man had the audacity to lean back in his chair, cross his arms over his chest, and give her his most charming smile. Oh, what that smile could have done to her heart if she weren't so very, very angry with him. "No," he said, nearly singing the word.

She began pacing in front of him, so mad, so frustrated she wanted to scream. And then, abruptly, she stopped and looked at him again, at his eyes, his expression. When he noticed her intense scrutiny, Jared carefully schooled his features. Had she imagined the heat she'd seen in his eyes? She took a step back, her face as bland as his. Of course she'd seen nothing in his face but amusement with her predicament.

"All right, then, Captain. Can you tell me if you know whether or not my father is a mooncusser?"

"That I do not know, but I suspect he is not." Again he gave her a smile.

"Then what happened to Richard?" she asked, more to herself than to Jared.

"I don't give a damn about Richard," he spat, and lunged out of the chair. "Perhaps Richard was the mooncusser. Perhaps he was killed by one of the sailors he was trying to murder."

"Richard would never—"

"I told you I don't care about Richard," Jared

nearly shouted. He strode to a side table to pour himself a drink. Without a word, he filled a glass and drank, jerking his head back to send the liquor down his throat faster. He put the glass down with exaggerated care, as if what he truly wanted to do was smash it against the wall.

"You don't understand, do you?" he asked quietly. "You don't know that every time you talk about him, I want to strangle you." He hissed out a breath. "Or kiss you."

"Kissing might work better," Rachel said, her voice trembling slightly. She didn't know what to do when he was this way, a raging giant.

Jared dropped his head even lower. "Why did you come here?"

"I told you—"

He shook his head, his eyes still trained on the glass he'd just drained. "No. You've come to torture me. To stand there looking so . . ." He lifted his head, his gaze penetrating, disturbing in its intensity, his eyes saying what he could not aloud. "And you tell me that the reason you are here is to find out who killed your beloved Richard." His look was incredulous. "Have you no idea what you are doing to me?"

Rachel looked at him uncertainly. *You don't love me; you said you don't.* "You're the only person I can trust."

He let out a puff of air that was almost a laugh, but it was far too sad a sound for that. "All right, then. All right."

She dipped her head and tried to see his expression. "All right you'll help me?"

"Damn my soul, but yes. I'll help you."

She smiled, but her eyes still searched for some sign that he didn't still want to throttle her. "We can leave tomorrow. If that's all right."

"Fine."

She started to go, but turned around. "There's one more thing," she said, dreading what she had to say next.

"I don't want to know, do I?"

She shook her head and winced. "My mother has the idea that I came here to make amends with you. I had to come up with a plausible reason for coming here. I couldn't very well tell my own mother that I suspected my father of murdering my husband." Rachel let out a nervous giggle at the absurdity of that statement. "If you return with me, well, she might have the idea that all is well between us."

"Then she will simply discover that she is wrong."

"Well, yes. I suppose. She would be wrong if she thought that, wouldn't she?" Somehow the last came out as a question. Rachel fought the urge to yell out that she loved him, that she had cried herself to sleep nearly every night since he'd left, her heart breaking over him. But she could not make such a declaration to a man who not ten minutes earlier had said he did not love her.

"Very wrong."

Rachel swallowed, wishing she could again feel the nothingness she had when she first saw him. "Shall I meet you at the train station at noon, then?"

"Is that how you came here, then, by rail?"

"I took the steam ferry from Martha's Vineyard. Obed and Oren were heading out and they took me there. I don't think there's another ferry for at least a week."

Jared nodded and turned back to the side table, busying himself with another drink. "Where are you staying?"

"I don't know. I hadn't thought that far ahead."

He looked at her, studying her. "You really were frightened, weren't you?"

"I wasn't afraid my father would hurt me, if that's

what you mean. I suppose I was more afraid of knowing, of suspecting such a horrid thing." She gave him a helpless shrug. "I didn't know what else to do, where else to go."

Jared gazed down at his drink and swirled the glass slightly. "So you came here."

"Yes."

"I find that . . . odd."

"So do I." When his eyebrows rose in surprise, she smiled. "I knew my reception wouldn't be all that warm. I'm sorry to put you in such a position."

"And what position is that?"

"Of having to see me. Be with me."

He gave her a crooked grin. "Such a sacrifice." He took in a deep breath. "You should stay at the Parker House. It's on Purchase Street, just four blocks from here toward the harbor. I'll escort you there, if you don't mind."

Rachel immediately shook her head. "I walked past that hotel. I don't think it would suit." The Parker House was a monstrous building with liveried footmen standing guard outside and well-dressed patrons milling about the grand lobby. She knew she could never afford such luxury.

"You'll be my guest." When Rachel made to protest, Jared stopped her. "No arguments. It's the most respected establishment in the city. You'll be comfortable there. Consider it payment for saving my life."

"All right. I know I will not win this argument."

They walked in silence from the house, Rachel painfully aware of Jared's mother, who stepped into the entrance hall as they were leaving, a silent question in her eyes. She nodded politely, but Jared ignored her and continued out the door and down the steps.

In an almost reluctant manner, Jared took her hand and put it in the crook of his arm. At first it felt strange and formal to walk that way. But just touching him with one hand, just having his large, strong body so close, made Rachel feel safe. And for some reason it gave her heart hope.

Chapter Twenty-one

Dear Captain Mitchell,

I pray you remember our conversation regarding my retirement in June. I have assumed you are still interested in the position of keeper of the Highland Light, and as we discussed, I recommended you as my replacement. You may schedule an interview with Mr. Lewiston in Boston at your convenience. Mr. Lewiston awaits your reply. If he does not hear from you by February 25, he will assume your disinterest.

Donald Small

"What's this?" West asked, holding up the letter from Donald Small.

"None of your business, that's what it is," Jared said, dismissing his younger brother. At least he thought he was dismissing him. He stood there, still holding the letter and glaring at him. Hell, when did West begin getting too big for his britches, thinking he could intimidate him with a stare?

Jared ungently placed his pen in its holder. His office in the Mitchell Countinghouse was tucked away from West's, but obviously not far enough.

"It's February tenth," West said.

"Thank you."

West tapped his finger against the top of his desk. "Aren't you going to reply?"

"No." Jared crossed his arms over his chest and leaned back in his chair, giving his brother a brilliant smile. He knew from experience that his smile could sometimes be more terrifying than his frown.

West pulled a chair from against the wall, rotated it, and sat with his arms across the back, making himself comfortable and unconsciously putting a barrier between him and his irritated big brother. From the look on his face, Jared knew West was about to get preachy again. Being a father seemed to give him the mistaken belief that he was all-knowing. He dished out advice like an old woman, and Jared was getting damned sick of it. He was also getting sick of his mother skittering about him as if he were about to chop her head off. For God's sake, what was wrong with everyone around him? He'd been pleasant and courteous since his arrival home a week ago. For the most part.

"You're no good to me here," West said.

Jared was about to argue, but realized he loathed working at the countinghouse. The brothers were supposed to take turns operating the business side of their whaling enterprise. Thus far, Jared had escaped this tedious business, but he thought he'd come to grips with his lot. That was what he had thought until this past week. His mind drifted too much, and not back to his ship. His mind—his heart—was back in Truro. All week long as he sat behind this desk studying the list of existing and potential buyers, Rachel would invade his thoughts. When the small wall clock across from him softly chimed the hour, inevitably he would look up, and just as inevitably, he'd try to imagine what Rachel was doing just at that moment.

He had it bad, he did. He couldn't stop thinking about her, dreaming about her. Everything reminded him of her—even the damn pen he used. He'd remembered her brazenly changing his first telegram home after demanding the pen and scratching in her own little message. He smiled, then frowned fiercely when he realized he smiled. God, he'd missed her.

Part of Jared knew he was not being completely fair to Rachel. It was true that Richard had been dead less than a year. He told himself to be more understanding of how she was feeling. Understanding how she felt did nothing, however, except make him a little crazy. It didn't make her love him the way he loved her. It didn't wipe Richard's memory from her mind. It did nothing. What he needed, more than anything, was to forget her and Belle and Truro. To wipe them from his mind and heart. What folly to go back to the place where shreds of his heart still lay in the soft sand.

"I know I'm no good here," he told West. "Give me a ship." He would go to Truro and he would leave immediately, head to sea, let the vast waters wash away her memory.

"Go to Truro, Jared."

Jared felt the rush of anger and tensed his body against it. "Go to hell," he said as pleasantly as he could. He picked up his pen, letting out a curse when a splattering of ink hit his desk, and pretended to calculate their expenditures for the next six months. It was no use. West wasn't going to go away. "Though it's none of your business, I'm going to go to Truro tomorrow. With Rachel." Upon seeing the wide grin on West's face, Jared scowled anew. "Wipe that grin off your face. It's not what you think. I'm simply accompanying Rachel back to Truro; then I plan to return here. And take the first readied ship to sea." He thrust out his chin as if daring West to sucker-punch him. To his disgust, West's grin only widened.

"Oh, you'll not be back."

"Care to wager on that?"

"As a matter of fact, I will. If you come back, you can have the *Huntress*. You can sail her off the end of the earth. Just send the oil back first."

Jared crossed his beefy arms and narrowed his eyes at his younger brother's rash confidence. "And if I stay?"

"You authorize the sale of the company," West said, a brilliant gleam in his eyes. West had made no secret of his dislike of the whaling business.

"Done," he said easily, knowing he'd never have to pay his debt. "I'm afraid you'll be disappointed. Rachel and I are finished." He knew he was lying to his brother when he told him he had no hope of staying in Truro. Truth be told, it was what he wanted more than he'd ever wanted anything in his life. Certainly more than he wanted to climb aboard a whaler again. He couldn't stop this thing in his heart that exploded when he saw her. He couldn't stop loving her, could never stop wanting her, even as she ripped out his heart again and again. Jared knew Rachel was oblivious to the pain she was inflicting on him with her blithe request that he help solve her husband's murder. God, how he'd wanted to blurt out the truth of what kind of man Richard had been. It gnawed at him that the whole time he'd been making an idiot of himself mooning over her, Rachel's only thought had been of her husband. At least she believed him dead, he thought darkly.

"If you believe you two are finished, then why are you going to Truro with her? If you didn't care about her, you'd just let her go."

"I never said I didn't care about her. You know that."

"Aye. I know," West said, looking away from the pain he saw in his brother's eyes. "What happened this morning? Obviously she's not carrying your baby or you'd be marrying her."

"No. She's not pregnant. She thinks her father killed her husband. Can you believe it? And she came here for my help." He nearly choked on the words.

"Is it possible he killed him?"

"Anything's possible, but you've seen Ambrose. He's not much bigger than a mite. He thought of Richard as a son." Jared shook his head. "I don't think he could have done it, but Rachel did find some incriminating evidence." He shrugged. "Frankly, I don't care who killed him just as long as he's dead."

"Are you certain that's the only reason Rachel came here?"

Even that simple question hurt for the unwanted hope it made him feel. "She gave me no other reason." He let out an oath. "I'll not make an idiot of myself over her again."

"Don't bet on it. Women have the strangest effect on us. I ought to know."

"You've always been soft in the head and in the heart," Jared said, waving a dismissive hand at him.

West didn't argue, just gave him an irritating grin that told Jared his brother was thinking about his wife. West and Sara made loving and forever seem easy. Jared, who had lived through more than most men could imagine, had never felt so helpless as he did when he thought about loving Rachel. He'd sailed through hurricanes, he'd saved men's lives, he'd looked the devil in the face more than once. But he couldn't make Rachel love him.

Chapter Twenty-two

∽

I can't make him love me, Rachel thought as she tugged on her gloves, dropped her carpetbag by her feet, and commanded her heart to stop its hopeful beating. But if he felt nothing for her, certainly he would not accompany her back to Truro. Her heart a big lump in her chest, Rachel sat in an oversize, overstuffed chair in the Parker House's opulent lobby and stared at the entrance. This place, with its silk-covered walls and velvet furniture, made her nervous. She could have fit her entire cottage in the room she'd stayed in alone. The one luxury she found very much to her liking was the bathing room in the basement of the vast hotel. She'd taken a long and wonderful lavender-scented hot bath in the steamy, cavernous room early that morning.

"Rachel." She started at the deep male voice, and her heart began that instant and irritating pounding she was afflicted with whenever she saw Jared unexpectedly. What a fine gentleman he looked to be, with his knee-length navy coat and his curly brimmed beaver hat in hand.

"My carriage is out front," he said, holding out his gloved hand for her to take, another formal gesture of a gentleman to a lady. How easily Jared slipped back into this life, she thought, suddenly feeling cranky. Jared could stride upon a whaler, curse and snap commands. He could walk a sandy beach with a costen flare like a man born to the deep, soft sand of the cape. And he could don a dapper suit, plop a curly brimmed beaver hat upon his head, and stroll into a luxurious hotel as if he owned the place.

"We mustn't keep the driver of your fine carriage waiting," she said testily.

He furrowed his brow, but offered his arm and headed toward the entrance, doffing his hat at an acquaintance on the way out.

"Who was that?"

"A buyer in town. He is considering investing in one of our ships to cut down on his own costs."

"Oh." She felt stupid, frumpy, and completely cross. "New Bedford certainly is different from Truro," she said after they were seated in the carriage. Jared sat across from her, his legs splayed, his knees on either side of her legs. She pressed her fingertips into the soft leather of the seat and glanced out the window of the first carriage she'd ever been in. Outside she heard the driver urge the pair of horses onward, and the carriage jerked violently. Rachel clutched at the seat, her eyes widening in fear until she noticed that Jared was completely relaxed.

"That is a considerable understatement," he drawled. "New Bedford is one of the wealthiest cities in the world. It's crowded and modern and I wouldn't care if I never saw it again."

Rachel didn't believe a word of it. How could anyone live in Truro after living in an exciting city like New Bedford, with its theaters and libraries, hotels and restaurants? She didn't stop to think that given the same choice, she would live in Truro forever. "It's exciting," she forced herself to say. "All these buildings and people. You can go to balls and concerts. I read a notice about a lecture on Africa at Liberty Hall. You can't get that in Truro." Rachel had no idea why in the world she was defending a city she wished never to see again.

Jared chuckled. "No, I suppose you can't." He gave her a penetrating look. "I loved being on the sea. I loved that I could see forever, that the wind pushed at my face and pushed my ship toward more of the same. I think Truro suited me for that reason. When I return to New Bedford, I'll be taking the *Huntress* out again."

Rachel felt her stomach drop in disappointment. Of course he wouldn't stay in Truro. Of course not. She knew that. But to have him on a ship, to have him so far away, so . . . unattainable . . .

"I thought you were through with the sea."

His face was impassive. "It has its merits."

"But you said it would kill you. You said—"

His anger stopped her before his words did. "Enough! You have no right to lecture me about what I should or should not do. Once I am finished in Truro, I will do whatever I damn well please."

Rachel pushed back against the seat and stared at him, stunned by his sudden and unexpected fury. She could take his bluster, but the icy rage she now saw was almost frightening. "I don't want you to come with me. I can handle this myself. Stop the carriage." She stood as if to open the door. He pushed her roughly back to the seat, then leaned over her, his fists digging into the seat cushion behind her.

"I'm going to Truro," he said with venom, his face not two inches from hers.

Rachel clenched her jaw and narrowed her eyes. "You don't frighten me." She could feel his breath on her face, could smell the tooth powder he'd used that morning, could see just how closely he shaved, could dip her eyes and stare at the mouth that always made her blush.

"What are you doing?" he asked, his voice rough, but not with anger this time.

Her eyes darted back to his, and her cheeks burned. He moved slightly closer, a small jerk, as if he were waging an internal battle. "What are you doing to me?"

Rachel started to shake her head, but his mouth upon hers stopped the movement. He let out a strangled sound, a man forced to act against his will. He tilted his head, moving his mouth against hers, slipping his tongue against her sensitive lips. Rachel let out a small gasp, and her hands moved up to grasp his lapels.

In one swift movement he was gone, sitting across from her again, staring at her as if he loathed her. His hands gripped the seat, releasing it only when he noticed that her eyes were trained on his clenched hands. Rachel licked her lips, still moist from his kisses, and Jared looked away out the window at the city that was passing by.

Rachel had never held in what she was thinking, but she found she could not talk to this man who sat beside her—at least not about the thoughts that raged in her mind. The train that would take them to Hyannis would arrive in a half hour—a half hour of sitting in tense silence.

They sat on a wooden bench in a train depot the locals had dubbed "the tomb" for its resemblance to an Egyptian catacomb. Rachel was in such a morose mood, she thought it fitting to be in such a place. Why had he kissed her? And why had he looked at her as if she had forced him? *Cad. Scoundrel.*

She folded her arms in a huff and turned slightly away from him. She couldn't be certain, but she thought she heard him chuckle, and she let out a derogatory snort of her own. He ignored her, which only fueled her anger more.

He probably didn't even know about Richard and Ambrose's fight. How could he, after all, unless her father had told him about it? She couldn't imagine such a conversation between Jared and her reticent father. To her credit, Rachel managed to keep all the questions that bubbled up inside of her inside until they were seated in their private compartment. Jared had insisted on traveling first class even though it would be only a four-hour trip to Hyannis, where the tracks abruptly ended. From there they would take the tediously slow coach, packed like sardines and jostled about like pebbles in a baby rattle.

Jared sat across from her in the compartment, his long legs stretched as far as they could go—not far enough by half. Rachel took off her gloves and hat and laid them on the seat beside her. Jared stared at the items as if they were offensive, then stared out the window.

"If you don't wish to accompany me, I understand. I hadn't given a thought to the fact that you have obligations here, that you've been back only two weeks." Rachel tried to keep the anger from her voice, but failed.

"Twelve days."

"Yes. Twelve days. Truly, Jared, you must . . ."

He tore his gaze from whatever he'd found so fascinating out the dingy window. "I must what?"

Rachel let out a small puff of air. "I realize things between us are rather . . . strained."

He looked pointedly down at his pants and coarsely said, "Not at the moment."

Rachel knew she should have been insulted or affronted or any number of things, but she found herself laughing instead. "You are an awful man," she said between laughs.

Jared made a great show of trying not to smile, but in the end he chuckled, deep and low. After that the tension between them lessened considerably.

"You must think me ridiculous, coming here with such a tale."

"On the contrary. I think you are frightened, and perhaps with good reason. No, I don't believe your father killed Richard, but I'm beginning to think that someone else did. I've suspected for some time that Truro has been infested with mooncussers."

"Then you think my father—"

"No. I don't. But I think Richard was."

That tension between them was back tenfold. "What?" she asked, incredulous.

"I've said it before. I think Richard was a mooncusser."

Rachel could feel angry heat make her face flush. "Tainting Richard's memory will not endear you to me, if that is your reason for such slanderous words."

Rachel watched, her pulse beating rapidly, as Jared's face turned hard and tight. "You think too much of yourself," he said, his voice edged with barely controlled anger.

"*You* kissed *me*," she said, jabbing a thumb against her chest.

He ignored her. "If you truly want to discover what happened to your husband, you will have to cease being so blind to the man and his flaws."

Her eyes glittering with angry tears, Rachel stared at the narrow door that led to the hallway, thinking she'd rather spend four hours standing out there than with this insufferable man. "I know exactly the kind of man he was. If he wasn't the best husband, the best father, then so be it. But Richard would hardly murder someone for riches. He was a good, kind man." Rachel let out a bitter laugh. "Surely we would have lived far better than we did if Richard was filling our coffers with ships' cargo."

"Richard was on patrol that night. There was no signal when the *Merry Maid* hit that sandbar. Why do you think that was?"

"How do you know that?" Rachel whispered.

"Because I've asked. Because I suspected for a long time that something strange happened that night. You're right, Rachel; a man like your husband would not drown in calm seas. But wouldn't the man you know signal if a ship was foundering?"

Rachel swallowed past the aching lump in her throat. "He looked the other way. That's what you're saying, isn't it?"

Jared did not look happy to have his point proved. "Aye. That's what I'm saying. Or he could have drowned, could have struck his head on something. We may never know."

Rachel hugged herself. "It's cold in here," she said, more to explain the gesture than for any lack of warmth.

Jared reached up above her and pulled down a blanket, then tucked it around her, all the time pointedly avoiding her gaze.

"Do you have any idea who the mooncussers could be?"

"No. But your father might. I believe your father, given what you told me about that log, had been suspicious for months before the *Merry Maid* foundered."

"Is that what they were arguing about, then?"

A shadow passed over Jared's face and he again turned to look out the window. "Perhaps."

Jared watched as Rachel tugged the blanket around her. She looked so damn sad, he would have done anything at that moment to be able to comfort her, to hold her against him, kiss her brow. Her lips. But they'd just been talking about Richard, and his ghost loomed as large as ever. "It's going to be a long trip," he said.

"Mmm."

That sound rumbled through his chest. It wasn't anything like the satisfied purr he remembered her letting out when he kissed her, but it was close enough to make him think of it. Unbidden, his eyes drifted to her mouth, her delicious pink mouth. When he lifted his eyes, he knew he'd been caught, for he saw the flare of recognition in her eyes before she quickly looked away. While his heart cried out for her to love him, his body cried out for a much more carnal thing.

Had he said this would be a long trip? He should have said interminable.

"Have you had your breakfast?" She nodded. And licked her lips. He clenched his teeth against the surge of physical need that rushed through him.

"Well, I haven't," he said, sounding surly and not caring. "I'll be in the dining car. And for a good long time."

Rachel watched him go, relieved to be alone with her thoughts. Was it possible Richard had been a mooncusser? It was almost more possible to believe her mother was one of those scoundrels who lured men to their deaths. Thirteen men had died the night the *Merry Maid* foundered. Had those thirteen been murdered by someone she'd known her entire life? By her own husband? It was inconceivable.

They had grown apart, that was true, but the Richard she'd grown up with and fell in love with could never have raised a hand against another man. She'd admitted long ago that her marriage to Richard had been a bit unnatural. He hadn't touched her as a husband should since the day she had announced she was pregnant, nearly six years before his death. He'd been truly pleased when she told him about the baby, and she thought he was abstaining because he was being considerate. But after Belle's birth, months and months passed, and still he didn't turn to her as she longed for him to do. She'd asked him once, and never again. The memory could still make her turn hot with humiliation. He'd looked pained when he answered her, as if he knew he was hurting her. "I can't. I just can't."

And life went on. Day in, day out, they lived together. They talked about their day, they sometimes laughed, but it was always there between them. It hurt at first, that her husband found her so lacking, but eventually the hurt went away. Or at least was well hidden.

Richard had never looked at her the way Jared had, even when they were first married. His eyes hadn't lingered on her lips; his gaze hadn't seared the clothing from her back. Feeling suddenly overwarm, Rachel threw off the blanket.

"Damn you, Richard," she whispered, closing her eyes against the new wave of pain. She sagged a bit, deflated and sad. Richard wasn't to blame for her losing Jared. She was.

Jared stood in the middle of the small room, hands on hips, eyes shifting angrily from the bed to Rachel. "I don't like this any more than you do, but Mr. Jasper assumed we were married, and I wasn't about to argue. Besides, there's only one room left in this godforsaken town, and this is it."

Rachel flung her gloves onto the bedcover, a patchwork quilt made inexpertly by Mrs. Jasper. "I don't know why he would assume that. You could have been my brother."

"Perhaps it was your wedding ring that threw him off."

Rachel looked down at her hand as if surprised to find she still wore her ring, and immediately started fiddling with the gold band. "Oh. Yes."

"You wouldn't want to take it off. God forbid that Richard would come home and find you walking around like some jezebel without your wedding ring on." Jared's foul mood had grown decidedly more foul when he discovered that not only would they have to spend the night in Hyannis, but they would have to share a room. Most of the inns in town were closed for the winter season, and the one that was open was small and filled quickly with train passengers.

"Richard's not coming back. I know that," Rachel said, spinning around and showing him her back and attacking the contents of her small carpetbag. "I think my father murdered him, so obviously I believe him to be dead."

He heard her throat close up on those last words and he cursed himself for his callousness. He wasn't good at dealing with the complexities of a woman's mind. If it had been West standing there, he could have walloped him on the back and offered him a stiff drink. He knew he expected too much of her, knew she wouldn't fall into his arms the minute she finally realized the truth about her husband. But, damn it all, he wanted her to. He wanted her to turn around right this minute, her wonderful eyes laughing, and . . . what? Apologize for loving her husband?

"Rachel." He grimaced when her back stiffened. "I'm sorry."

"For what?"

"Hell, I don't know," he boomed out, feeling frustrated and aroused and so damn much in love he wanted to burst. "Just forget it. Just go to bed. I'll lie on the floor. Why don't you toss me one of those pillows."

She didn't move, and he had the horrible feeling she was standing there crying. *Hell.*

Sniff.

Damn and hell. He could tell by the way she held her arms, by the way her head was bowed, that she was fiddling with her wedding ring. He wished he hadn't mentioned the ring, but the fact that she continued to wear it had bothered him for a long time. She'd worn it even as he was about to ask her to be his wife. That alone should have told him she wasn't ready to fall in love with another man.

"You're not crying, are you? Because there's nothing to cry about. Nothing. Wear the damned ring. I don't care." Jared winced, knowing he sounded angry. He wasn't angry. He just wanted her to stop that sniveling. God, it was driving him crazy.

"Listen, tomorrow you'll be home, you'll talk to your father, and you'll find out all this was just in your imagination. Everything will be fine." *Sure, she'll feel just wonderful when she discovers her husband was having an affair for six years.*

Another sniff, this one louder.

"Rachel, honey, you've got to stop crying."

"I'm trying," she said, sounding all stuffed and slobbery. Then she let out a shuddering sound, as if she *were* trying to stop weeping with all her might.

Jared knew that if she didn't stop right away, he'd do something he'd regret. Like kiss her again. Kiss her until kissing wasn't enough. *Aw, Rachel, please, please stop crying.*

He took a step toward her, then another and another until he was right behind her. He lifted a hand and let out an angry breath when he saw that it trembled. *Christ.*

"Rachel."

She spun around and buried her head against his chest. "Oh, Jared, I'm so sorry."

Of all the things she could have said, her apologizing was the worst. It made his heart slow, then pick up painfully. With a small sound of surrender, he put his arms around her and held her tight. Then he lowered his head so that his cheek rested against her soft lavender-scented hair. "Sweetheart, you've got nothing to be sorry for. Nothing."

She clutched at him more tightly and he thought he'd die of happiness just to hold her in his arms again. He clenched his jaw to stop himself from telling her how much he loved her and instead dragged his head downward until his lips pressed against her cheek. Two inches to the right and he would be kissing her sweet lips. A few layers of clothing and he could bury himself inside her. She backed away a bit, then fiddled with her sleeve, pulling out a clean handkerchief, looking up at him with a bit of embarrassed good humor as she blew.

"Feel better?"

Rachel nodded, then tossed the sodden cloth to her bedside table. He thought she would move away, but instead she laid her head against his chest again and closed her eyes. His face was ravaged with pain and joy as he lifted it to the ceiling, beseeching God to give him guidance. He held in his arms the woman he loved, the one who could not love him, and he wanted her as he'd never wanted anything in his life.

"You make me feel safe, Captain Mitchell," she said, sounding sleepy.

Safe. Hell. He surely couldn't seduce her now. Now that she was feeling *safe* with him. He stiffened, and she stepped back, an apology in her smile, a blush staining her cheeks.

"Thank you," she said, then backed away even further.

His brows furrowed. "You're welcome," he uttered, not knowing what else to say.

"I'll try not to do that again." At his questioning look, she said, "You know, cry, throw myself into your arms." She let out a breathy little laugh. "Make an idiot of myself."

He shook his head. "Consider my shoulder available for crying on."

"Thank you, Jared. You're . . ." She licked her lips. "You're a grand friend."

Jared immediately set his features so she wouldn't see how her words wounded him. "Yes. Of course." He had to get out of his room, away from her and her *friendship*. "I'm going to the harbor to see if I can hire a packet to sail us to Truro. It'll get you home faster."

She smiled at him and he nearly ran for the door. What had he been thinking of when he agreed to accompany her back to Truro? He was like a moth that beat itself again and again against a window trying to get to a light. Being with Rachel was that futile, that painful.

"I'll probably be in bed when you return," she called just as he reached the door.

He turned and stared at her, hardly able to keep everything he was feeling from showing in his eyes. "I'll try to be quiet when I return. Lock the door behind me, will you?" Just before he clicked the door closed, he heard her call out good night. He leaned his head against the door and whispered, "Good night, my love."

Chapter Twenty-three

～～～

"Mommy, Mommy, you came back!"

Jared watched, his throat tight, as Belle hurled herself into Rachel's arms, nearly knocking her over. Her face when they'd walked into the house was a sight he would never forget. He'd missed this little girl, missed her bright brown eyes, her wispy blond hair, that high-pitched voice that made him want to smile.

"You're all wet." She giggled, then pressed more kisses against her mother's rain-slicked cheek. Outside, a storm was just hitting the coast, which had nearly delayed their homecoming. He readied himself for Belle to throw herself into his arms, but she simply stared at him, one hand clutching her mother's hand.

"Hello, Belle."

Wide eyes gazed up at him, then at her mother, a poignant uncertainty in their depths.

"Aren't you going to say hello to Captain Mitchell, darling?"

"Then he's real?"

"Of course he's real."

Belle turned again toward Jared and he smiled and tilted his head. Then he hunkered down, just in case his brave little girl had somehow suddenly become frightened of him. She looked scared standing there, so uncertain what to do, and his heart broke for her. He was about to rise, to gently tell her they could visit another time, when Belle burst into tears and walked toward him, her arms limp by her sides. She flopped into his arms, so overcome with whatever was breaking her heart, Jared had to keep her from crumpling to the floor. Over her head, he threw Rachel and her mother a look of total male helplessness. Belle sobbed sloppily for a full minute before sniffing loudly. He pushed her back to look at her, to give her a reassuring smile.

"I thought . . ." She hiccupped. "I thought you were dead," she said softly, then wiped at her face, leaving behind a little trail of dirt. Jared gave Rachel another panicked look, and she rushed to her daughter's side.

"Oh, no, honey. I told you the captain had to go away. He didn't die. See? Why would you think such a thing?"

Behind them, Mabel gave a snort.

"Because of Daddy. You said Daddy was still alive but he never came back and was dead and I thought that maybe Captain Mitchell was dead, too."

The lump in Jared's throat grew impossibly bigger. What was it about the Best women that unmanned him so?

"Oh, Belle, no. Captain Mitchell just went home. Daddy died and went to heaven."

"Daddy's never coming back," she said with authority, as if she were informing her mother of this revelation.

Rachel darted at look to Jared. "No. He's not. Not ever."

Belle gave Jared another hug. "I'm glad you're not dead, Captain."

"Me, too," he said gruffly before setting Belle away from him and standing.

"Well, Captain. I got the cottage all cleaned and ready for you," Mabel said in her no-nonsense manner.

"I thank you, Mrs. Newcomb, but I believe I'll be staying with Mr. Small for the short time I'm here."

Mabel glanced quickly at Rachel, a frown forming. "I see."

"Where is Papa?" Rachel asked, trying to quickly change the subject.

"In his shed."

Jared placed his big hands on top of Belle's head, then leaned down to kiss her soft hair. "You stay with your grandmother, Belle. Your mama and I have to go talk to your grandpa. I'll see you later."

Belle looked up at him solemnly. "Promise?"

"I promise."

"Because last time you went away, you wouldn't promise. Remember?"

"Aye, princess, I remember."

"But you came back anyway." She grinned.

"I sure did. Now go with Grandma."

At Mabel's questioning look Rachel shook her head. "We'll talk later, Mama."

Rachel ducked her head against the cold rain and wind and began walking toward the shed, glancing back at Jared to make certain he followed. She wanted more than anything to lean into him right now, to lay her head against his chest as she had in the inn room, but he seemed wary and distant—almost as if he were dreading this confrontation with her father as much as she was.

She knocked on the door, calling out for her father, and smiled when he gruffly invited her in. "Jared's with me, too, Papa," Rachel said as she stepped up into the gloomy room. The space was cramped with all three inside, but Rachel wanted to keep this conversation as private as possible.

"Mr. Newcomb."

"Captain," Ambrose said, setting aside the net he was repairing.

Rachel gave Jared a helpless look, then shook her head. She couldn't do it. She couldn't stand there and accuse her father of killing her husband.

"Mr. Newcomb, Rachel needs to know the truth about Richard," Jared said.

Ambrose's eyebrows snapped together in consternation. "What the devil are you talking about?" he said, giving Rachel a quick look.

"I've told Rachel nothing about this, but I think it's time you did."

"Told me what?" Rachel was getting more and more confused. As stunning as it was, it was clear that her father and Jared were keeping something from her.

"Nothing," Ambrose snapped.

"Hell, sir, she thinks you killed Richard."

Rachel gasped her outrage and immediately denied what Jared had said. "No, I don't!"

"Rachel." She heard the clear warning in Jared's voice.

"Well, maybe I did. Do. Oh, Papa, I don't know what to think."

Ambrose looked more bemused than angry or shocked by his daughter's accusation. He looked to Jared for an answer.

"You see, Rachel overheard you fighting with Richard about a week before he disappeared. She found a ledger that seemed to incriminate you."

Rachael watched in horror as her father's face first went pale, then turned red.

"She needs to know what that fight was about. And you might want to explain that ledger as well."

Ambrose scratched at his two-day-old salt-and-pepper beard, muttering beneath his breath. He started to reach for his pipe, then thought better of it. With a deep breath, he started.

"Mooncussers. That's what the ledger was about. Damn mooncussers. Never had enough proof and still don't, but I began to note a pattern and started keeping a log. I started noticing that the ships were foundering when Richard was on patrol. Now, sometimes he would be there to warn them away, and sometimes not."

Rachel felt sick. "You think Richard was in league with mooncussers?"

"No, I don't. At least not all along." He tucked in his bottom lip and licked it, then grimaced as if in pain. "You sure you want me to tell her this?" he asked Jared.

"Yes, sir," Jared said, not looking at Rachel.

Ambrose let out another string of oaths. "Richard, God rest his soul, was with another woman those nights. And that's what I was fighting with him about."

"What?" Rachel felt the world drop from beneath her feet. She shook her head. "What are you saying?"

"I caught him myself. Told him to stop seeing her. That's what that fight was about. Told him he was partly to blame for those three ships foundering, 'cause someone started to realize he wasn't on the beach some nights when he should have been and . . ." He stopped when Rachel whirled around and covered her face with her hands.

The two men looked at each other helplessly; then Ambrose jerked his head toward Rachel, telling Jared he should comfort her. Jared put his arm around her but she shook it off.

"Don't touch me," she spat. He backed away immediately. "How could you? How could either of you keep this from me?"

"We didn't want you hurt," her father said hastily. "Isn't that right, Captain?"

"That's right."

Everything suddenly became so clear. What a fool she'd been, loving a man who had betrayed her again and again. She choked on her grief when she realized with sudden, painful clarity that while Richard hadn't been faithful to her, he had been faithful to the other woman. The woman he'd loved. *Oh, God.* Her eyes grew wide and she gasped for air.

"I . . . I have to get out of here," she choked out, lunging for the door and heaving it open, letting the wind fling it out of her hands. She stumbled out into the storm and ran and ran until her lungs hurt, until she fell to the wet sand, her fingers digging in deep.

Back in the shed, Ambrose was in a fine temper. "Happy now?"

"She thought you killed Richard!"

"What does that have to do with him cheatin' on her all those years?"

"The ledger and the fight were tied together in her mind. You'd written something about Richard knowing about the *Merry Maid*, and she put the two together and was quite convinced you killed Richard."

Ambrose roughly tamped tobacco into his pipe. "Now what?"

"Now she knows her father didn't kill her husband."

"Yeah? Well, who did, then?"

"No one," Jared said, exasperated. "Or one of those mooncussers or his lover. Hell, I don't know."

Ambrose lit the pipe and puffed, squinting his eyes against the smoke. "Here's what I think. I think Richard, that last time, agreed to look the other way. I think he was going to take a cut of whatever they got. But when they all started the killing, he tried to stop 'em and they killed him." Ambrose stopped abruptly, as if not talking about it would stop his brain from going over and over it.

"Have you told anyone about your suspicions?"

"Nah. All this town needs is a witch-hunt because some crazy old man thinks there's mooncussers about. Besides, why drag a man's name through the mud?"

Jared gave him a thoughtful look. "That's why you denied there were mooncussers. You were protecting Richard."

"Maybe." Ambrose reached up to a shelf and took down a box. Inside was a half-full bottle of whiskey. "Drink?" he asked, offering Jared the bottle.

Jared grinned and took a swig, gasping at the strong liquor. "Damn, that's good." He gasped and his eyes watered.

"I figure you could use some liquid courage to woo back Rachel."

"I'm afraid that's not going to happen, sir. I just came back to be with her when she confronted you about Richard. I'll be leaving as soon as I can hop on the next boat to Boston or New Bedford."

Ambrose tipped back the bottle. "What about that lighthouse job?"

Before Jared could answer, the door swung violently open, slamming into Jared's shoulder. "Who was it?" Rachel demanded, her face fiercely determined.

The silence in the little shed was thicker than the smell of whiskey and tobacco. She glared first at her father, then at Jared.

"Now, what does that matter?" Ambrose asked, doing his best to give his daughter a calming smile.

She gave him a look that would have shriveled a lesser man on the spot. "It matters," she said between clenched teeth.

"Rachel, maybe it's better if you don't know,"

Jared said, talking like a man trying to soothe a growling dog.

"And look at every woman I meet and wonder if she's the one? I have to live in this town. I have to know."

"I just don't think it's a good idea," Ambrose said, his words slow and measured.

"I've a right to know who my husband loved."

"Maybe she's right," Jared said, his heart aching for her.

Just then, all three of them raised their heads, the frantic sound of the alarm bell carried on the wind over the dunes, cutting off their thoughts of errant husbands.

A ship was foundering.

Chapter Twenty-four

❧

It was a magnificent, horrific sight that met Rachel's eyes when she rounded the final bend to see the sleek clipper ship listing to its side and helplessly pounded against the beach. The sailors must have tried to tack away until the bitter end, for the ship's sails were still unfurled and snapping like thunder in the wind. She could see the outline of people clinging to the rail, their faces, stark and white against the bleakness of the sea, pointed toward shore. She'd seen many wrecks over the years, but still couldn't shake the sadness that set in when she saw a ship, sturdy and invincible in the roughest seas, sitting helpless on the beach. It was like watching a strong man weep.

She was almost glad of this wreck, if no one was hurt, God willing, for her heart and mind were ravaged by what her father had told her—by what he and Jared knew. Mingled with the anger was shame for suspecting her father of such a heinous act, and embarrassment for how foolish she'd been all the years of her marriage. She had time to think, walking alone toward the wreck, about that time when she'd finally confronted Richard about lovemaking. How he'd seemed so tortured. How she'd blamed herself, when all the time he'd had a warped sense of loyalty and fidelity to the wrong woman.

She wished he were alive so she could scream out her anger, her hurt. And for a fleeting moment, she was glad he was dead.

A loud bang shocked her from her dark thoughts. The beach cannon. A handful of men, her father and Jared among them, stood around the cannon watching as the heavy projectile arched toward the ship's rigging. She was close enough to see the weight wrap itself in the rigging, close enough to her the victorious shouts from those on the ship and beach. By the time she reached the wreck, the first of the passengers, a woman, her sodden skirts whipping in the wind, was being helped into the sling that would carry her to shore. Jared was among the men standing at the ready, his hands resting on the thick rope that the men would use to pull the woman ashore, a grand ride that would end on the sandy beach. He'd taken off his coat despite the cold mist that fell, looking strong and big enough to bring the woman in alone. Rachel forced herself to look away, not wanting even a smidgen of kind thoughts to touch her regarding Jared. She was still mad as a cat in water about how he and her father had kept their little secret from her.

Rachel looked instead to the woman, who was trying, even in this desperate situation, to pull her skirts down and retain her modesty. She hovered just above the crashing waves, her feet and legs dragging a bit when the waves surged high, and she would scream and clutch the rope ever tighter, her eyes squeezed shut as if closing them would end her nightmare.

It was only the second time Rachel had seen the cannon in use. Most of the time the stranded sailors simply jumped ship and swam to shore. Those who couldn't swim stayed aboard and waited for the rescuers to pick them up with boats. If the seas weren't violent, a ship could escape foundering unscathed and be floated at high tide. But this ship was being battered by seas that were rising around it, the solid *wump* of the waves hitting the hull sounding ominous.

As soon as the woman was safely ashore, the men wrapped her in a blanket, but Rachel could see she shivered violently. Her hair was plastered to her head and she cried in small bursts, as if she couldn't contain the fear inside for longer than a few moments. Rachel went up to her, wrapping another blanket about her stout shoulders.

"Is that better?"

The woman responded in another language, her eyes wide and desperate. Rachel smiled. "It will be all right," she said gently, hoping her calm tone would soothe the woman. The woman instead pointed toward the ship and spoke, moaning out words filled with fear and hope. Getting into the sling was a young boy, perhaps ten years old, who waved toward his mother with bravado before clinging to the sling.

"He'll be fine," Rachel said, as the woman moved stiffly toward the place where her son would be hoisted. Halfway to shore a huge wave pummeled the boy, who swung on the line, safe, secure, if suddenly very much afraid. The boy made it safely ashore, a wide grin on his face as the crowd cheered. But when his mother wrapped her arms about him, he started to cry, hiding his face against the blanket so no one would see.

More Truro residents were arriving, all laden with blankets and baskets of food for the sailors and passengers. Mr. Travist and his daughter arrived with a wagonful of whiskey and jars of food, and Rachel's

mouth watered when the scent of something savory
drifted her way.

Again the men pulled on the rope, sending the
sling chair back to the ship, their movements strong
and rhythmic, like men hoisting a sail. Another
woman struggled to get on the sling, a bundle
clutched in her arms—a baby's cry swept over the
crowd, and all eyes watched as the men by the cannon began hoisting the woman and her child ashore.

"The waves," Rachel whispered to herself, watching in horror as a large curling breaker moved
toward the ship, toward the woman who hung
clutching her baby to her. She rushed over to Jared
and pointed, crazily thinking that he could stop
something horrible from happening. She felt him
tense next to her, his eyes steady on the wave as if
willing it to dissipate before slamming into the ship.
When it did, the sound was almost deafening. The
mighty wave broke over the clipper, pushing it, making the line that connected the ship to the shore go
slack. The woman, letting out a scream Rachel would
hear in her head for months, was thrust into the icy
water. Then the ship righted itself and the woman
bobbed up. And the screaming became more horrible.

"The baby," Rachel shouted. Jared was already
leaping into the water as the men worked like mad
to drag the woman to shore. She struggled, horribly,
desperately, to escape the sling that kept her from
following her baby into the sea. Jared's head disappeared beneath a wave; then his feet appeared as he
dove to the sandy bottom, kicking and fighting to
move against the vicious current.

They stood watching silently but for the shrill
keening of the woman.

"He's got it," came a shout from the ship.

And then, like some great sea god rising from the
ocean, Jared erupted to the surface, a baby in his

arms. Men rushed into the water to help him, to grab the infant from him and bring it to safety. A sputtering baby's cry split the air, and a great shout followed. The woman ran to her baby, her face glowing, her arms outstretched.

Jared, forgotten in the joy of the baby's good health, trudged out of the surf and walked only a few yards before dropping to his knees. Rachel watched as Esther, a shy girl who worked at the Mews, went to him and covered him with a blanket. He clutched it to him and nodded his thanks.

"He'll go to hell for his sins."

Rachel turned, surprised by the vicious words, and saw Donald Small standing next to her, his small brown eyes trained on Jared and Esther. "What did you say?"

Small looked at Rachel, a strange light in his eyes, and he immediately changed, looking sheepish. "Esther's my girl."

Rachel gave him a small smile and wondered when Mr. Small had begun courting Esther. "I don't think you need to worry about Captain Mitchell."

"You two ain't together no more. That's what I hear."

Rachel darted a look to where Jared still knelt. Esther was offering him a jar of something steamy, and for just a second she felt a stab of jealousy and regret. She should have been the one to go to Jared, not someone he hardly knew. At least, she didn't think Jared knew Esther well. "No, we are not together, Mr. Small. But neither, I think, are the captain and Miss Travist. Here she comes now. Perhaps you can convince her to give you some of whatever she's brought."

He grunted, but moved back to the cannon to help the men hoist another passenger from the ship. Jared moved to go back to help them, but Rachel intercepted him, standing in front of him. She looked up at him, not knowing what to say, only knowing that whatever anger she'd felt had been swept away when he waded into the surf to save the baby.

He looked tense, the hard planes of his face taut. "The baby. It's all right?"

Rachel nodded, confused by this tightly coiled ferocity that gripped him. "Are you all right?" Gentle, tentative.

A slow smile spread across his face, confusing Rachel even more. "I think I have never been better." He breathed in deeply, his nostrils flaring, and he strode off to assist the men and the passengers.

It took hours to retrieve all the crew and passengers, but finally everyone, including the harried captain, was ashore. Negotiations had already begun with the local wreckers about removing the cargo from the ship, hauling it crossland to the bay side, and shipping it to Boston for the shipping company. Cold and despondent, the crew and passengers were divvied up among the townspeople, who would give them shelter until they could make their way home or aboard another ship. Four crewmembers would stay in Jared's old cottage, two more in the main house. Rachel watched as they walked dejectedly behind her father, who had yet to say a word to any of them except "Follow me." They did.

Rachel followed behind, not wanting to talk to her father or anyone else. Now that the excitement of saving the ship was over, her mind slipped back to her own misery.

"Rachel, wait." Jared ran to catch up with her, bounding in the sand as if he'd just sprung out of bed, refreshed and ready to greet a new day. He seemed annoyingly chipper and Rachel couldn't help but wonder darkly if it was Esther who put that spring into his step.

"You're not still angry, are you?" he said, all charm, dipping his head so he could see her expression. She had the distinct feeling that even if she were spitting mad he would have grinned at her.

"Of course I'm angry," she said, but her mouth jerked up into a smile despite her words. She couldn't scowl at him when he looked so utterly handsome.

Then suddenly she found herself flying through the air, her legs splaying out, twirling, twirling as Jared held her and spun her around. "Is this the most beautiful of days?" he shouted, laughing and spinning, his feet digging a hole in the sand as he whirled about. His happiness was infectious, and Rachel squealed and laughed with him.

He set her down, breathing hard, his eyes dancing with mirth. "I saved her," he said. "I saved that little girl." Jared closed his eyes as if overcome with emotion; then he shook it off and began striding down the beach. "Did you see her?" he shouted up to the sky. "Did you hear that lusty cry? Did you?" It was as if he were shouting up to God, and Rachel thought that was exactly what he was doing. Her eyes prickled with unshed tears.

Oh, Jared, you saved her, brought her back from the dead. Just as you tried to with your little girl. You didn't fail this time.

"You are a true hero among men," she said, and couldn't help adding, "even if you did lie to me."

He waved a hand at her as if it didn't matter. And it didn't. Not truly. But she couldn't let him think so just yet.

"Not a lie," he said. He sobered suddenly, and Rachel felt a twinge of regret. "Oh, Rachel, I would have done anything to shield you from learning about Richard. Except, perhaps, accuse your father of murdering him."

Rachel gasped. "Oh, goodness. I forgot all about that. I have to tell my father how sorry I am for accusing him of such a thing."

"You did so only in your mind," he said, tapping her head. "I think your father will forgive you. If you forgive him for keeping his secret. You know, he told Richard to break it off as soon as he found out. He was trying to protect you."

Rachel let out a sigh. "I realize that. I realized a lot of things today." To her horror, Rachel's throat closed up and tears threatened. She swallowed them down, angry that she would waste any more tears on a husband who was cruel in his misplaced sense of honor. He should have divorced her.

"Rachel, don't do this to yourself." Jared placed a big hand on her shoulder and it felt so good. She wanted to lean into him. A friend would comfort another friend, wouldn't he?

"I wasted so much of my life loving someone, trying to make him love me. Every year, every *day* of my life with him was a lie. I feel so . . . stupid."

"People do stupid things when they fall in love," he said, dropping his hand from her shoulder.

She shook her head, not realizing that Jared was talking about himself. "I never fell in love with Richard. I just always loved him. I can't remember him not being part of our lives, even before his father and brother died and he was simply my neighbor. All that time I never knew him. He must have felt so trapped. He must have hated me."

Jared swallowed down a stab of impatience. God above, he hated talking about Richard. He couldn't even bring himself to utter nonsensical comforting words, couldn't bring himself to say that Richard probably did love her. He didn't care. He just wanted Richard to be gone from her mind and her heart. He was about to turn and leave when she gave him the strangest look.

"Esther."

"What?" His entire body tensed, and he wondered wildly how she could have possibly figured out who Richard's lover was.

"Does she mean anything to you?"

"To me?" He was so relieved, he laughed aloud. "Good God, no. I mean, she's a nice girl, good-natured from what I could tell, but no. Not a thing."

"Not that I care," she said in a rush. "If you were to fall in love with her, it wouldn't matter. Of course, it *would* matter. To you. You are my *friend*, and I want you to be happy."

"What the hell are you talking about?"

Rachel bit her lip and he tried not to stare, tried not to imagine his lips brushing against hers. "I don't want you to feel you can't discuss such things with me," she said, a sick look on her face.

"Discuss what things?"

She sagged even more. "Falling in love. Friend to friend," she whispered.

He hated that she kept calling them friends. How could he be her friend when he'd kissed her breasts, when he'd sunk deep into her warmth, when he'd come inside her and screamed with joy? How could he be her friend when he loved her so much he couldn't imagine life without her? Actually, he could imagine such a life, one on a whaler, one filled with endless days of stinking carcasses, of whiskey, of cold days and colder nights. Anger replaced any lingering sense of well-being, swift and hot. "Stop calling me your friend. I am not your friend, nor will I ever be your friend." Damn if she didn't look like she was going to cry again. "And don't you *dare* cry."

Rachel looked stricken by his words, and he felt that old familiar panic bubbling in his gut.

"I can't help crying when you yell at me like that. And curse. When you tell me that you don't even *like* me."

"I never said that and I'm not yelling," he shouted, and watched with horror as she winced; then her face crumpled. "Good Christ, you are driving me crazy. Good night, Rachel. Thank you for destroying one of the few good days I've had in six years." He spun around and stalked away from her, sand flying up behind him. He could hear her run after him, her breath harsh, her skirts flapping and likely making running down the beach rather difficult.

"How dare you," she said when she reached him. She stumbled, saved herself, then ran and caught up again. "How dare you blame me for something of your own making. You lied to me. You're the one who said you didn't love me."

He stopped so suddenly she nearly hit him. "And when would that have been?"

She clamped her mouth shut.

He should have been angry with her, but she looked so adorably guilty having been caught in her own lie, he wanted to kiss her. "You shouldn't say things you cannot prove," he said, his voice low and silky. It didn't seem possible, but her mouth closed even tighter, her eyes glittering with anger.

He began walking down the beach again, his strides long and sure, not bothering to slow to accommodate her when he again heard her feet pounding in the sand. "If we are not friends, then what are we?" She'd stopped running and stood on the beach, the wind blowing her loose hair toward the bluff. He turned and studied her, clenching his jaw.

"Nothing. We are nothing."

It was nearly dark, but he could tell that her beautiful eyes glittered and he knew she was crying. "Before . . ." she croaked out. "Before you go, could you tell me who she was? Who Richard's lover was?"

His heart hardened and he knew he'd done the right thing. What a fool he would have been to again declare his love. He wanted to reach into her, to grab her heart and squeeze every last bit of Richard from it. No. They were not friends. "Esther Travist."

"Esther?" she said in a squeak, disbelieving. Then she blanched. "Of course. Esther. He would go there. Often."

Overhead, the first stars were beginning to appear, and the wind, so harsh all day, suddenly calmed even though clouds high above them skidded across the sky as if driven by a gale. He could imagine himself on his ship, wished he were there already instead of standing on this beach fighting the demons inside him who tortured him with images of holding Rachel in his arms. Maybe a better man would have gone to her, held her, but he couldn't do it. He couldn't bring himself to comfort her when her heart was ravaged by thoughts of another man.

"I'm staying at Mr. Small's for a few days," he said, his voice dull. "If I don't see you again, good-bye."

She dipped her head for a moment, then looked at him again, her eyes clear. "Good-bye. And thank you."

So this was it. A thank-you and a good-bye. "I hope you find happiness, Rachel Best." Christ, his throat hurt.

She hugged herself and nodded. Her fingers dug hard into her arms. "I want you to know . . . I have to tell you—" She clutched her coatsleeves tighter still. *I'll always love you.* "Good luck. That's all. Good luck and Godspeed."

Then she turned and ran up the bluff. He watched until she disappeared from sight.

Chapter Twenty-five

❧

The last of the sailors were gone from the Newcomb house and cottage, and life was slipping into its normal routine. Rachel didn't know whether Jared was still staying at the lighthouse and told herself she didn't care. She fought the terrible urge to take a walk along the beach that would lead her beneath the light in hopes she would see him. Every hour she had to tell herself he didn't love her, that life would be better without him.

Rachel watched as Belle scampered up a sandy hill and disappeared from view. She was going to the lighthouse again today, which must mean Jared was still there.

"When are you going to stop that infernal sighing and go see him?"

Rachel turned to find her mother standing behind her, scowling.

"Good Lord above, any fool would know why he's hanging around here so long."

Hope filled her heart so quickly it hurt. She shook her head. "No, that's not true. I don't know why he's still here, but it's not because of me. Mama, I heard him tell his brother he didn't love me."

"Probably just the anger speaking."

"He shouldn't be angry with me. He should understand how difficult it was, how difficult it still is."

"Maybe." Mabel sighed and sat down at the kitchen table. It was where they'd had their best talks, and it looked as though they were in for another.

"Did you know about Richard and that woman?" Rachel asked, sitting down across from her mother.

She shook her head. "No. I found out from your father the night of the wreck, and I wasn't too pleased he'd kept it from me. Guess he figured I wouldn't have been able to keep it from you. He was right about that. I would have told you."

Rachel gave Mabel a small smile. "Thank you."

Mabel waved a dismissive hand. "You told me once that Richard didn't love you. Well, you were probably right, and I'm sorry I didn't believe you then. I surely don't know what he saw in that Travist woman, though."

"She's very sweet. I thought she was sweet," Rachel said, clenching a fist and thinking of Esther wrapping a blanket about Jared's shoulders, of how she'd offered him her well-known beef stew. She'd defended that woman to poor Mr. Small, but now she wasn't so certain that Esther didn't have designs on Jared. *Conniving hussy. Sweet indeed!*

Ambrose burst into the room just then, his face glowing with excitement. "I was right!" he shouted, then stomped over to Mabel and gave her a big kiss on her cheek. "Mooncussers right here in Truro."

Mabel and Rachel gasped in unison.

"What's happened?" Mabel asked, clearly anticipating a good story.

"The government arrested a boatload of 'em from Nauset, including one of our own. Earl Waterson, the devil. He was cryin' his eyes out at the town hall, chained to the wall until the coach arrives." Ambrose suddenly sobered, and he gave Rachel a wary look.

"Richard," she whispered.

"He wasn't involved with them. Not really. Leastwise that's what Earl claims, and I believe him. Richard was known to sometimes shirk his duty on patrol." Ambrose's cheeks turned ruddy at his veiled reference to Richard and Esther's affair, and he shuffled his feet.

"It's all right, Papa. Go on."

"Well, the first two times they tried to lure a ship in, Richard was there to wave his costen. The third grounded, but he sounded the alarm. That was the *Gypsy*, remember? Came ashore on a black night, calm seas? No one got hurt, but Earl and those fellows got quite a reward for shipping the cargo bayside."

"Were they involved in the latest wreck?" Mabel asked.

"No. But they were involved with the *Merry Maid*." He stopped and squeezed the back of his neck, then felt his front pocket for his pipe. Finding nothing there, he scowled. Then he looked at his daughter, his eyes filled with sadness and regret. "Richard was involved, too."

"No, Papa!"

Ambrose put up two hands. "Now, now, don't go getting all in a tizzy. He was just going to look the other way. Earl said Richard didn't know anything about any killin' planned. But it seems the cargo was a bank shipment, and those men decided they didn't want any witnesses left."

"They killed Richard," Rachel said with certainty.

Ambrose shook his head. "According to Earl, Richard never showed up at the wreck and never came to divvy up the prize."

Rachel's head suddenly ached, and she pressed her fingertips against her forehead. "Why? Why would Richard do such a thing?"

"Now, remember, I'm getting all this from Earl." Ambrose felt for his pocket again, as if he'd somehow missed feeling his pipe the first time he'd looked for it. "He told me Richard was planning to run away that night and needed money. It makes sense, given that I'd told him to break things off with that woman."

"Oh, God," Rachel said softly. She felt as if she'd dropped into a nightmare and had yet to awaken. Every word out of her father's mouth was like a cold shard of metal to her heart. Just when she'd thought Richard's sordid story couldn't get worse, it did.

"He agreed to not sound the alarm. Well, that night there wasn't any alarm." Ambrose scratched his head. "Earl swears up and down Richard wasn't there that night. But it's possible he tried to stop the killing and got killed himself by those Nauset boys."

"And he obviously didn't run away with Esther." Ambrose's eyes widened in surprise.

"Yes, Papa, I know who she was and I know she didn't run away with Richard, because she's still here."

"Jared," he said, frowning even more.

"I'm glad he told me. Everyone else knew." Rachel closed her eyes briefly. "I don't know what to believe. Did you think Earl was telling the truth?"

"No reason he wouldn't. That boy's facing death. Don't see why he'd lie about something like that."

"To spare you?" Mabel asked, twisting her hands in front of her. Her face had gone pale.

Ambrose gave his head a jerk. "No. I believe him when he says he didn't see Richard that night. But that don't mean he wasn't there. Must have been one hell of a scene." Ambrose clenched his jaw and his eyes got hard.

"Richard did a lot wrong, Papa, but I know he never would have gotten involved with those boys if he knew they were intent on murder. We couldn't have been that wrong about him. If he was there, he tried to stop them; I know he did."

"What else could have happened?" Mabel asked.

"He must have been killed by those mooncussers. Nothing else makes sense."

"Maybe he changed his mind at the last minute and Esther killed him," Rachel said, knowing she was being absurd. She stood abruptly and walked with purpose to her coat.

"Don't be ridiculous," Mabel said. "And where do you think you're going?"

"Earl's likely gone by now," Ambrose said, eyeing his daughter warily.

"I'm going to have done with it and talk to Esther Travist."

The Mews Tavern was crowded, loud, and smoky. Men stood two deep at the small bar, and all the tables were filled with everyone from the town council to fishing hands fresh from a trip to George's Bank. A few women even sat among the men, clearly not trusting their husbands to return with the proper amount of gossip. Town clerk Barney Smythe had just happened to overhear Ambrose Newcomb's interview with Earl Waterson, and within hours the juiciest story to hit Truro in a generation got even juicier.

Jared walked in with an unusually quiet Donald Small, not surprised to find the place jammed with townspeople. Esther was nowhere to be seen, and her father behind the bar looked like he might blow a cork any minute. He served up drinks and took his customers' money, but looked like a man about to get his teeth pulled. No doubt he was overhearing some less than nice things about his daughter.

Jared had trodden softly on the subject of Esther with his friend. He knew Small loved Esther, and suspected the lightkeeper had also known about her long affair with Richard Best. He recalled Small telling him that Esther's beau was gone, and Jared had

assumed the man had left town. Now he realized
Small must have been referring to Richard; Ambrose
was at the lighthouse when he discovered the affair,
so it made sense Small knew as well. As the two
walked silently to town, Jared said, "The tavern's
bound to be crowded. And I've a feeling Miss Travist
won't be about this night."

Small's face was pinched and drawn. No doubt the
older man was beside himself with worry for the girl.
He only wished Esther had shown Small even the
tiniest bit of interest. Small's concern in light of Esther's indifference was pitiable. They were quite a
pair, the two of them, two lovesick swains pining
away for women who didn't love them.

When they entered the tavern, Jared was not surprised when Small went right up to the bar, pushing
his way through, and whispered something into Sam
Travist's ear. Travist put two beefy fists on his bar,
gave Small the scariest frown Jared had seen in a
good long time, and shook his head.

When Small returned, looking frustrated, Jared
said, "Things will calm down a bit, you'll see. People
will forget. She'll survive the gossip."

"So you're concerned, are you, then?" Small bit
out. "Maybe she'll agree to see you."

Jared gave him a crooked smile, and decided to
overlook that bit of nonsense, deciding Small was
angry about what Jared guessed was Travist's response to his request to see Esther. "Of course I'm
worried. I've a feeling I can't get any of that fine beef
stew tonight."

Small gave him a disgusted look, then took up a
position near the door that led to the kitchen, clearly
hoping Esther might show her face. Jared nearly
groaned aloud when he spotted an angry-looking
Travist coming up toward them, and he wondered
just what Small had said to the man. Poor sap; all

Don needed was for the father of the woman he loved to throw him from the tavern.

Jared was surprised, then, when Travist came up to him and said, "She wants to see you." Jared felt Small stiffen next to him, but when he turned to him, the older man's face was bland.

Jared leaned toward Small's ear so others nearby wouldn't hear him. "I'll let you know how she is and tell her she has a friend out here," he said. Small just looked at him and nodded. As if he suddenly didn't give a damn about Esther.

For so long now, she'd felt as if she were teetering on the edge of a cliff, fighting the horrible desire to throw herself off and end the pain. But she'd no idea just how awful falling would be.

That was how Esther Travist felt—as if she were finally falling, falling toward the jagged rocks that would end the pain that started the day Richard Best married Rachel Newcomb. She could hear the unusually loud rumbling of voices through the door that led from the Travist residence to the tavern. It was a rare night that the sound of bar patrons carried upstairs to the four rooms where she'd lived with her parents her entire life. She knew why they were there, could guess what they were saying about her: it was only what she'd deserved.

Esther closed her eyes and thought of Richard. She did that when things got too difficult, when the yearning got to be too much to bear. All her life she'd watched him, secretly admiring him, too shy to say more than a quiet hello when he passed by the tavern on his way home. When Ambrose decided he was old enough to frequent the tavern, it was Esther who had served him. But it was Richard who drew her in, discovered that behind that shyness was a wit and passion for life even she didn't realize she possessed. Of course, she fell in love with him long before he even thought of her as anything more than Esther, the tavern owner's daughter. Richard would spend an inordinate amount of time in the tavern, slowly drinking a single beer, and talking with her between customers. She thought he might care for her, but then he married Rachel, and her heart broke and broke and broke each time she saw him.

Later, Esther learned that Richard had been miserable about his marriage. In a whispered confession, he'd once told Esther he'd believed Ambrose when he told him one woman was as good as another, that he'd forget about Esther and grow to love Rachel. Any feelings he had for Esther would die when he was married to Rachel. He loved Rachel, didn't he? Ambrose, the man who lifted him from despair, who gave him a home and called him son, had asked him to marry his daughter. How could he say no? He'd told Esther that in that first year of his marriage, making love to his wife was duty only, a way to slake his need, while his mind and body cried out for Esther.

He remained faithful to Rachel for a year, reminding himself over and over of the wedding vows he'd taken. He even read them to himself while shutting out the incessant chatter of his ever-cheerful wife. That first year, he would visit Esther at her father's tavern twice a week. He would sit in the same chair at the same table and watch her, making Esther's blood sing, and her heart ache in misery. They hardly spoke a word to each other beyond his telling her what he wanted to drink and her polite answers. It took him one hour to drink a single tankard of beer. To anyone else in the tavern, he appeared to be a quiet man, a contemplative one, who kept his eyes on his tankard and his thoughts to himself. But they were keenly aware of each other, of each word spoken. He'd lift his eyes and let them follow her, his gaze burning with love and desire, and Esther feared someone would surely see what seemed so blatant to her.

Twice a week for a year he'd sit in that tavern, tearing Esther's heart in two. The day after Isabelle had been born, he visited the tavern and saw her eyes glittering with unshed tears. She hadn't cared about finally showing what was in her heart. She wanted him to know she was dying inside.

"Congratulations, Best," her father called over. "Too bad not a boy. Next time, eh?"

Richard's smile had seemed forced, his eyes darting, as always, to see Esther's reaction. She'd kept her face averted, but the glass she was wiping was dry as a bone though she kept on wiping at it. How many times had she wanted to tell him to stay away, to spare them both this agony? Richard later revealed that he did not intend—ever—to tell Esther his feelings. Certainly he did not plan to touch her. But the night his daughter was born he sat in the tavern waiting for Esther to return to the serving room. When she did not, he left.

He was perhaps a stone's throw from the tavern when he turned and saw her sitting on the hill behind the building. She watched him from her perch, her arms wrapped around her knees. She never knew why he turned; he never had before. But this time he did. He walked toward her, and all the while her mind screamed for him to go home. *Wrong, wrong, this is so wrong.* Her heart's pounding was louder.

She stood as he climbed the hill, and thought about fleeing. Without a word he dragged her to him. For the longest moment he simply stared into her upturned face, his nostrils flaring, his teeth bared, as if he were being tortured and didn't want to cry out. And then he kissed her and it was over. He kissed her soft, pink lips, her pale cheek, her chin, her nose, her eyelids. He kissed her hair, her ear, all the time saying over and over, "I love you. God, I love you."

She was crying and laughing and kissing him, and saying over and over, "I love you."

They made love in the grassy sand behind the tavern and afterward held each other tightly, knowing they had sinned, knowing they would sin again and again.

Richard and Esther were excruciatingly discreet after that. They met alone once a week, but Richard continued his innocent visits to the tavern when he would sit and drink his tankard of beer and devour his love with his eyes. They never talked about Rachel or Isabelle or their sins. They pretended they each only had one another, and in their hearts that was no lie. It was their one heartbreak that they could never have children together. On that they were careful, knowing that a child would end their time together.

Esther would never forget the pure joy that shot through her when he came to her just six months ago and said they were running off together. "Damn them all," he'd said, his eyes bright with anger and excitement. "I'll get an annulment, a divorce; I'll be a bigamist. I don't care. I just want us to be together. I want your baby, Esther. Say yes, darling."

She had, laughing and crying, fiercely pushing away the decent part of her that said no. They were to have met at the mouth of the Pamet River and then sail to Boston. From there, they didn't know where they would go and didn't care. They only knew they would be together at last.

But Richard never showed up that night. Fear tangled around her heart as she had walked home slowly, keeping the smallest bit of hope in her heart that she would meet Richard on the way. When she heard of the wreck, of Richard's disappearance, she knew he was dead. For nothing else would have kept him away that night.

Esther hugged herself and waited for Captain Mitchell to come to her. She didn't have the courage to face Rachel herself, but she wanted to let her know she was sorry for the hurt she'd caused her. A small smile played about her lips and she closed her eyes, a vision of Richard filling her, making her warm.

Soon, my darling. Soon.

Jared followed Travist back through the door that connected the tavern to the family's living quarters on the second floor. Esther was waiting in a dimly lit narrow hallway that led directly to a set of curving stairs. Her eyes were red-rimmed and wide and she looked the very picture of misery. Despite that her actions had hurt Rachel, Jared felt sorry for her. Her father grunted, nodded, and backed out.

"How can I help you, Miss Travist?"

She closed her eyes, and for a moment her face crumpled. He watched, feeling quite helpless, as she struggled to maintain her dignity, and he breathed a silent sigh of relief when she did. "I wanted you to give Rachel a message for me. Tell her I'm so sorry. I never meant to hurt her. Or Richard."

She swallowed and pressed her lips together, fighting to maintain her composure.

"She can tell me herself," Rachel said from the landing above them. Esther whirled around, gasping. "Your mother told me where to find you. Hello, Jared."

"Rachel." He looked up at her, trying to gauge how she was taking all this. God, she'd been through so much these past months. And here she was, confronting her husband's lover, looking beautiful and composed. Strong and lovely.

"What did you mean, you didn't want to hurt Richard. Did you kill him?"

Esther backed up against the wall, looking first to Rachel above her, then to Jared who stood next to her. And for just a moment, Jared thought they'd discovered Richard's killer. Esther looked frightened to death, filled with guilt and remorse. Then Esther slid slowly to the floor until she was sitting, her knees up, her arms about her legs, hugging them fiercely. Jared hunkered down to look at her, then motioned with his head for Rachel to come downstairs.

"Did you kill him?" he asked, gentle, persuasive, like a man trying to coax a nervous hound into a cage.

Esther shook her head. "This is so awful," she said, looking up at Rachel.

"Yes, it is." Rachel's voice was hard, her face harder still. "You haven't answered the question."

"Rachel," Jared admonished with a slight shake of his head.

"Do not *Rachel* me! This woman . . . this woman . . ." Her lower jaw thrust out a bit and Jared knew Rachel was trying not to cry.

"I know what you must think of me," Esther said woodenly. "I never meant for any of this to happen, but we loved each other so. And when your father went to him and demanded that we stop . . ." She shook her head. "He was insane. He didn't want to defy his father. But he couldn't leave me."

"How honorable of him," Rachel said with little inflection.

"He was honorable." She bit back a sob. "Oh, I know how awful this must sound."

"Do you?" Rachel asked, as if she were truly curious.

Esther ignored her, or was too wrapped up in her

own misery to hear. "We planned to run away that night. And when he didn't come, I knew something awful had happened to him."

"Did he discuss his plans with you? Did he tell you about the *Merry Maid*?" Jared asked, his voice low.

Esther shook her head. "If I had known, I would have talked him out of it."

"So you didn't kill him," Rachel said flatly.

Esther looked up at Rachel. "I thought you did, at first. Then I realized you couldn't have. I knew you loved him, too. I wanted to believe he died trying to save those men. But in my heart I don't believe it. He wasn't supposed to patrol that night. He was supposed to come to me. But he must have gone. He must have realized what was happening."

Rachel suddenly sat down upon the bottom stair.

"Well, now we know who didn't kill him," Jared said. He ignored the dark look Rachel shot him.

Esther looked beseechingly at Rachel. "I wanted to tell you how sorry I am. For everything. It's my fault Richard died. It's my fault you were betrayed. I know that. I could have stopped it. I could have just gone on. But . . ." She pressed her lips tightly together. "For so long after he disappeared, I wanted to tell you, but I couldn't. I know what they're saying out there about me. I know what you must think of me."

Rachel stared at the bare wood floor for a long moment. "I think the one person who is to blame is dead. And if he were alive, I'd kill him," she said fiercely.

Jared wanted to laugh, but knew better.

Rachel stood. "I guess that's it, then. We'll probably never know who killed Richard, or if he drowned, or stepped off a bluff and knocked himself senseless." She rubbed her forehead and suddenly looked beyond weary. "I don't hate you, Esther, but I wish I did. You were my friend when we were girls and you stole from me the one thing in my life that was good."

Jared felt his chest tighten. He didn't want to hear any more, especially not about how much Rachel loved Richard.

"He was a good man," Esther said, her throat closing.

Rachel shook her head. "No, not Richard. You stole my innocence. I *liked* it. I liked thinking the world was good, my husband faithful. Perhaps I am naive, but I wanted my world bright and happy. That's what you stole from me."

If possible, Esther looked even more miserable. "I'm sorry," she whispered brokenly.

Rachel shook her head slightly, as if disbelieving that any of this could have happened. "Good-bye, Esther." She gave Jared a long look before silently ascending the stairs.

Chapter Twenty-six

～

The night air was bracing, head-clearing, welcome. As Rachel walked along the winding path that would eventually lead her home, the sounds of the town grew muffled, then faded away, overtaken by the rustling of the wind in brush and grass. A rabbit burst from the path in front her and she gasped. Her heart was still pounding when she heard someone running behind her.

"Rachel. Wait."

Rachel tamped down the little thrill she felt at the sound of his voice and turned. He slowed when he saw her turn, his long strides eating up the distance between them. He stopped in front of her, slightly out of wind, and she could see his breath in the moonlit night.

"Rachel."

Before she could anticipate it, before she could even think of uttering a sound of protest or of welcome, he'd pulled her to him and begun kissing her. She tasted him, she breathed him in, she filled the hollow place in her heart with him, wrapping her arms about his neck and drawing him close. She opened her mouth when his tongue pushed against her lips, letting out a sound of pure pleasure. They dropped to their knees, and she could feel the cool sand through her dress. He pressed his arousal against her, letting her feel him, how much he wanted her. His hands, rough and gentle, moved over her body, to her buttocks, her thighs, her breasts, molding her to him. And she just clung to him, lost in the wonderful feeling of having Jared kiss her, touch her again.

It was not like in the train, a battle to fight against this thing between them, the hot, smoldering need that consumed them. They welcomed it, relished it, moaned and touched and kissed until her face was burned red from his beard, until the ache between her legs seemed almost painful.

"I can't fight you. I can't, I can't," she said, kissing his lips, chin, neck.

He let out a sound, animal and deep, a sound that might have frightened her before, but now thrilled her. *He must love me,* she thought. *He must. He would not make me feel this way if he did not.*

"I want you, Rachel," he said, kissing her hard nipples through the layers of wool and cotton, biting gently and then wonderfully ungently. "God, I want you now." He pressed her harder against his arousal, letting out a groan, then thrust a hand between them and down, so he was cupping her heat, pressing her and making her want to take him inside her.

Rachel was no longer aware of the cold sand, of the colder wind. She knew only that she wanted what Jared wanted. Now.

"Yes. Now."

He unbuttoned his pants. She lifted her skirts, and sharply cold air hit her between her legs where she was wet from wanting him. It made the air seem colder. It made what she was doing suddenly wrong. She sat up and lowered her skirts in one fluid motion, watching as Jared's hands stilled on the last button. He looked up, then sagged, and began re-buttoning his pants without a word.

"I'm cold," she said. *And I want to hear that you love me. I want to hear it, Jared.*

"I lost my head. I didn't intend to—"

"Ravish me?"

He let out an irritated puff of air. "Aye. You are so very ravishable."

"That isn't a word."

She could see the flash of his white teeth in the darkness, glad she could still make him smile. She hugged her knees, trying to stop the cold night air from penetrating her skirts, from reminding her just how ready she'd been for him.

"I want you," he said, his voice rough, forceful. "We can go to the cottage. I'll light a fire."

"No."

"Ah, Rachel, I need you with me tonight."

Need. What Jared needed was a cold swim in the Atlantic. "I can't do this. I can't make love with you. It's all a lie."

He drew back slightly, and she could tell he was getting angry with her. "A lie."

"It would just be fornicating and you know it. It wouldn't be making *love*. And I can't do that. I can't be a loose woman. I know I did before but that was before." *Before, when you loved me.* "Do you under-stand?"

Jared stood, shoved a hand into his pants, and ad-justed himself rudely in front of her. "You've been quite clear," he said, his voice as cold as the wind blowing in from the ocean.

Rachel, still sitting awkwardly in the sand, slowly began buttoning her coat. She looked up and saw he'd held out a hand for her to take. She laid her hand in his, not wanting to let go, but dropping it as soon as she gained her feet.

"I'll walk you to your house," he said, as if talking to a maiden aunt.

Rachel swallowed the ever-present lump in her throat. This had been a god-awful day. She wanted to curl up and cry, then sleep for a month. "Thank you."

She walked in silence for a long time. It seemed like an eternity to Rachel, who was brimming with things she wanted to say, to ask. She wanted—oh, how she wanted—to ask him if he loved her, but was so afraid of the answer, it was one thing she knew she'd never be able to utter.

"Are you leaving soon?" she asked instead.

"Aye."

"Make sure you say good-bye to Belle."

"Of course I will."

"You're definitely going to go back to sea?"

"Aye."

Rachel was walking just slightly behind Jared and fought the urge to jump on his back and pummel him with her small fists.

"Do you love . . . whaling?" she said in a rush, closing her eyes at how close she'd come to disaster. *Do you love me?* How pathetic that would have sounded.

He stopped, turned, and glared. "What I don't love is being talked to right now. If you don't mind."

Rachel took a step back, and didn't follow until he was several yards in front of her. "I *need* you," she muttered, just under her breath. "I *want* you. Kiss me, Rachel."

He whirled around, anger emanating from him. "Are you speaking to me?"

She glared at him, completely unfazed by his angry stance. "No." And she brushed by him, telling herself she wasn't disappointed when he let her go by.

*   *   *

Jared stared at her back, at the shapeless coat that hid her curves, and fought the ungodly urge to pick her up, fling her onto his shoulder, carry her to the cottage, and ravage her as his body demanded. He didn't understand women, or at least this woman. Abigail would never have spoken to him in such a manner. Of course, he never would have treated her the way he'd treated Rachel either. He never would have made love to his wife without a wedding.

He'd make Rachel love him. He'd make her scream out her love for him; he'd make her say it again and again. He'd touch her, bring her to the edge, make her see how foolish it was to deny her love. He'd . . .

He'd do nothing and he knew it. He wondered when he'd turned into a woman, obsessing the way he was about love and tender feelings and all sorts of flotsam that had no business washing around in his veins. He'd told her he loved her and watched her eyes light up for another man. He'd made love to her knowing she withheld her heart, knowing she was thinking of her husband. He couldn't force her to love him. Dammit, he wanted to, but he knew he couldn't. He could make her want him, he could make her body respond, he could bring her pleasure, and that was all. But she didn't even want that. She was not, as she so succinctly put it, a loose woman.

They reached the fork where he would turn left to the lighthouse and she would continue toward her home.

"Thank you for walking me home," she said politely.

He looked up at the sky, at the millions of stars scattered above him. A cloud, fringed with gold, drifted across the moon. It reminded him of her eyes, and he cursed that he'd never be able to watch a cloud pass over the face of the moon without thinking of her. Not that he'd ever stop thinking about her. He was already feeling nostalgia for a place and a time he hadn't yet left. But he knew that in one month he'd be at the helm of his ship waiting for the boy in the crow's nest to shout, "There she blows. She blows to leeward!" For the first time in his life, such a thought only left him feeling despondent.

"I think I would have liked it here in Truro. I've been happy here, Rachel. Happier than I've been in my life."

"I'm glad," she said, her voice sounding strange.

"Good-bye, then."

"You're leaving?"

"Aye. I am. Tell Belle to come by the lighthouse tomorrow, will you?"

"Then this is good-bye?"

He looked up again at the sky, to that cloud moving slowly, revealing the bright, nearly full moon. "It is. And I think forever this time."

Rachel's heart felt as if someone were beating it with a hammer. The air was sucked from her lungs, and she found she couldn't breathe, never mind speak the words she wanted to say. *Tell him. Tell him tell him tell him you love him. Tell him.*

Instead she walked up to him and put her hands on either side of his beloved face. She moved her thumbs to the corners of his mouth, down to his chin and under his jaw, then brought his head down for one final kiss. *This is it,* her heart cried. *This is the last time you'll touch him, the last time your lips will press against his. Make it last, Rachel Best, make it something you'll always remember.* She kissed him softly, with just the slightest amount of pressure, brushing her lips back and forth once, twice, before withdrawing.

"I'll never forget you," she said, uttering the closest thing her heart would allow to the love she felt. "I know that's not what you want to hear, but it's true."

He looked at her a long time, and Rachel imagined she saw his eyes turn brilliant before he turned his head.

"I shall hold you forever in my heart," he said low, then turned and walked away.

Chapter Twenty-seven

"Been busy?" Small spat as Jared walked into the tiny cottage at the base of the light. Small stood by his stove, stirring something that looked bad and smelled worse, and Jared hoped for the lightkeeper's sake that he'd ask Esther to marry him so he wouldn't have to eat his own cooking anymore.

"Don't feel up to talking tonight, if you don't mind, Don," Jared said.

"Yeah. Don't do much talkin', do you? All action. Ain't that right?"

Heaving a sigh and knowing he was in for a long night, Jared sat on the ladder-back chair and rested his elbows on the table. "You got something stuck in your craw?"

"You love her, don't you?" His voice was tinged with sadness.

Jared furrowed his brow in confusion. "Well, hell, Don, you know I love her."

Don's face reddened, the skin around his compressed lips stark white. "She won't have you," he said finally, almost challenging Jared to deny it.

Jared let out a humorless laugh. "This I know. She's still obsessed with Richard."

"But he's dead." He turned back to whatever he was cooking. "Dead and gone."

Jared slapped his palms lightly atop the table and heaved himself up. "I'm ready to hit the hay, Mr. Small. Good night, sir."

"Good night," Small said distractedly.

Jared ducked his head to enter to hall that led to two tiny bedrooms, then withdrew. "I forgot to tell you that Miss Travist seems to be holding up well. She's understandably upset, but she seems like a strong woman to me."

"Yes. She is. Good night."

After Jared left the kitchen, Small clenched his fists tightly until the knuckles turned white, until the veins protruded and his hands shook.

The next day, Belle, her heart in her throat, ran as fast as she could to the lighthouse, praying the entire way that the captain was still there. He'd promised to say good-bye before he left, and she believed his promises. Not like Papa, who'd said good-bye that night. She remembered because Papa never kissed her, and that night he had. And hugged her, too.

"I'm going, baby, but I promise someday I'll come back."

He broke his promise and that was bad. Except, if he really was in heaven, then she supposed it was okay. Grandma explained all that to her. Maybe Papa shouldn't have made that promise. Sometimes adults did that, made promises they couldn't keep. Especially if they had to go to heaven. Once you were there, you were stuck.

She'd thought that was why the captain hadn't promised he'd come back. She'd thought he knew he was going to heaven just like Papa had. But he hadn't. He'd come home even though he hadn't promised he would. Belle grinned when she saw her captain standing outside talking with Mr. Small. She liked Mr. Small because he always had rock candy or cider for her. But she liked the captain better. He let her climb up on his lap, and when he laughed she could feel it right in her tummy. The best thing, though, was being on his shoulders. She could see the whole wide world from way up there. Captain said it was like being in a ship's crow's nest, and when she told him she wanted to be a captain someday, he said she could. He didn't say she couldn't because she was a girl. She would be a girl captain. And he'd said, "I bet you will be."

She had wished last night on every star she saw, a thousand wishes at least, that Captain would decide to stay with her and Mommy. She knew the Captain liked her mommy, and she also knew that Mommy liked him. A lot. Grandma explained that was why Mommy cried all the time, though that didn't make much sense to Belle, because she loved the captain and that made her happy. Except he was leaving soon. That was why Mommy was crying this morning.

"For Christ's sake, Don, the girl means nothing to me."

"That's not what I was hearing last night."

Jared gritted his teeth. "Good God, man, I was talking about Rachel."

"You knew which girl we was discussing. You knew." The wiry little man poked a vicious finger into Jared's chest. Jared simply looked down at that offending finger, bewildered.

"Don." His questioning tone was mildly menacing. Small stepped back, his cheeks flushed, but his eyes flashed in anger.

"Captain! Captain! Hello." Belle came bounding up, all windblown rosy cheeks and scattered blond hair.

"Hello, darlin'," Jared said, smiling and placing a big hand atop her head.

"Hello, Mr. Small. Got any rock candy? Please?"

"No, I don't," he said absently. "You stay away from her, that's all. Esther isn't your whore." Small turned and walked away with one final glare to Jared, who gave Belle a shrug and a smile, hoping to lessen the lightkeeper's awful words and anger.

"He usually gots rock candy," she said in a small voice. "You leaving today, Captain?"

Jared hunkered down, pulled up a bit of grass, and fingered it before tossing it aside. "Tomorrow." He'd planned to leave this day, but the sky was heavy and threatening rain.

"Will you ever come back?"

Jared felt something squeeze at his heart. "No, honey. I won't ever be back."

"That's why Mommy was crying, huh?"

He took a fast, deep breath. "Mommy was crying?"

Belle nodded solemnly. "Grandma said she was crying because she loves you so much. Do you think that's why?"

Though hope soared, he shook his head. "Your mommy has had a tough few days."

"Cause of Daddy being dead?"

Smart girl. "Yes, honey."

She shook her head. "I think Mommy used to cry because of Daddy, but now she cries because of you." She tilted her head and squinted her eyes. "Want to know what she said?" She didn't wait for him to answer. "She said, 'Oh, Mama'—that's Grandma—'Oh, Mama, he's leavin' an' he doesn't even know I love him.' You know Mama loves you, don't you, Captain?"

Jared had grown very still. "Belle, are you telling tales?"

"You mean fibbing?" She looked so stunned, Jared knew immediately Belle was telling the truth.

"No, no, you wouldn't fib, would you?"

She shook her head vigorously back and forth, blond hair slapping her cheeks.

"What did your grandma say to your mama?" Jared said, feeling not the slightest bit guilty for interrogating a five-year-old.

"Grandma asked why in heaven she didn't tell you."

"And your Mama said?" he urged.

"She said how could she when you didn't love her." Again that little tilt. "That true?"

Something inside Jared gave way; something hard that had surrounded his heart for months snapped. He remembered suddenly her accusation that he didn't love her, the way he'd dismissed it as Rachel being angry. How could she believe he didn't love her? He'd made a fool of himself walking around with his heart on his sleeve; he'd ravished her twice, given her looks that she couldn't possibly have misinterpreted as anything other than love. Or lust. He cringed inwardly, thinking about the previous night when he'd said over and over, "I want you, I need you." He'd been too much of a coward to tell her he loved her.

"Shit."

Belle's eyes widened. "That's a naughty word."

"You're right. It is." He squinted his eyes and smiled at Belle. "Can you keep a secret, Belle?"

She nodded, her eyes bright with excitement.

"I love your mama with all my heart. How's that for a secret?"

She gave him a smile that could have lit the lighthouse behind them on the coldest night.

"Are you gonna tell Mama?" she whispered, as if Rachel were standing beside them.

"I just might." A wave of doubt hit him. Rachel had always claimed to love him, but he'd known her heart was not his—not all of it. And he wanted all of it. Every last beat. If that was selfish, then so be it.

"Then you're not leaving?" Belle said, her gap-

toothed grin making Jared's heart twist painfully. It
was best that Belle thought he was still leaving.

"I didn't say that, Belle. I'm coming by tomorrow
to say good-bye. Do you understand?"

She shook her head. "No. If you love Mama and
she loves you, then why would you leave anyway?"

Hell. Damn and hell. "Why don't we just wait and
see what happens." He'd discovered from Rachel
that that sort of nonsensical reply worked to soothe
Belle when she really wanted something that Rachel
wasn't certain she could give her.

"Okay. Come on. Let's go for a walk on the beach.
Maybe we'll find some treasure." She tugged on his
hand and he followed, a lumbering giant pulled
along by a little fairy princess.

Esther stood at the mouth of the Pamet, waiting.
Not since that day when she'd allowed herself to kiss
Richard had she felt so much at peace. She'd left the
tavern that morning knowing she would never return, knowing she would stand at this place where
she had waited in vain for Richard all those months
ago. This time she would be with him.

It was a beautiful spot on the bayside, especially
with the sun setting low. The heavy clouds that had
marred the day gave way in the early evening to a
bit of sunshine and a promise that tomorrow would
be lovely and warm. The water was molten calm,
and a few early spring gnats danced near the surface.
The still water offered a perfect reflection of the red-
yellow sunset, and Esther thought it nice that one of
her last sights would be of this glorious vision. A
snowy egret lifted its dainty legs out of the water,
its yellow eyes searching for prey. It was so quiet
here, she heard the tiny splash the egret made when
it stabbed into the water and captured a tiny, flop-
ping fish.

She wanted to die here, not in the icy Atlantic. She wanted to slowly slip away, to imagine herself walking toward Richard's waiting arms. Esther walked into the water, wincing at how cold it was, and frowning. She didn't like the disquiet that struck her suddenly, the realization that this wouldn't be the comfortable, peaceful death she longed for. But it would be death, an end to the pain. An end to her parents' humiliation. Poor Papa, who couldn't even enjoy the best business his little tavern had ever generated because his daughter had brought him such disgrace. She'd never seen her father's face so weary and drawn, and her mother had never looked at her the way she'd looked the past few days, as if she were ashamed and frightened of what her daughter had done.

Esther began to shiver, but set her jaw and continued walking deeper into the bay to her knees, her thighs, feeling with horrible awareness the steady rise of the frigid water on her body.

"Miss Travist, a mite early for a dip. Water's cold."

Esther closed her eyes and cursed. She knew many curses, having picked them up over the years from the tavern's patrons, though she'd never said one aloud. She pressed her lips together, willing herself to ignore the man behind her. Obed Cobb, who'd said nothing to her in years but "beer, please" and sometimes "thank you," had discovered her. She took another step into the bay, her body tensed from cold and the awareness of the man behind her who would surely object to her plans.

"Miss Travist, it will pass," came his words, filled with quiet strength. "You don't think it will, but it will. That pain you feel right now, that's eating up your soul, it'll never be gone. I won't lie to you. But it won't be so raw; the ache will fade."

Tears filled Esther's eyes and her head slumped. She'd never have dreamed in a million years that

Obed Cobb could be so eloquent. She turned just her head to look back at him, a man she'd known all her life, as familiar to her as this bay. He was lanky, without a scrap of extra flesh on his bones, his face long and rather homely. He was the kind of man who worked hard and went unnoticed until he passed from this earth. Like her.

Except now, no one would ever forget Esther Travist, the woman who'd had an affair with Richard Best. "Go away," she said, her voice strong. "Please, Mr. Cobb."

Obed let out a beleaguered sigh. "Can't. Come on out now. I surely don't want to get all wet and salty."

Esther's dress felt heavy around her legs, dragging her down. *Please go away, Obed,* she prayed, even as she knew he would not. The fear hit her hard that tomorrow she would lack the courage to do this. Or somehow find the courage to live. She buried her head in her hands. "I don't want to go home. I can't. I can't face them."

"Then you come on home with me and stay if you want. Ma could use a bit of female company since my sister got married. She's been lonesome when Oren and I go fishing. You come on out and have a nice warm supper. It'd please Ma; I know it would."

He made it sound as if she would simply go over for a friendly visit, as if she weren't standing thigh-deep in this water wishing for death. She thought of the note she'd left her mother in the sugar tin, a note she wouldn't find until the morning when she was spooning in heaps for her father's coffee. She couldn't let them find that note now, but couldn't bear to go home. Suddenly she was so, so tired, and she swayed in the tide's soft current. Obed immediately started forward, but she turned and raised a hand to stop him. "I'll come out," she said, and dragged herself toward the beach.

They stood and stared at each other a long moment before Obed finally spoke. "I come down here every evening," he said, a subtle warning in his voice.

Esther was so drenched in sadness, she could not speak. But when he held out his work-roughened hand to her, she grasped it tightly. "I wonder if you could let my parents know I'm all right," she said.

He smiled down at her, letting out a long sigh of relief. "Woman, you right scared ten years off this life."

"I'm sorry."

"It's all right. Didn't need 'em anyway."

Obed Cobb had just made a joke, and Esther felt the strange sensation of laughter bubbling in her throat. Imagine, Obed Cobb joking.

"Just gave 'em back with that little laugh," he said, teasing her lightly.

Esther stopped suddenly, fresh tears springing into her eyes. "You're a good man, Obed. I thank you."

His ears turned red and he screwed up his mouth, clearly not used to hearing such words. "Let's get you home," he said gruffly. But he squeezed her hand and held on tight as he led her away from the water.

As the sun dipped low, turning the brown and gray landscape golden with the day's last light, Donald Small stood at the exact spot where he'd been standing when he had seen the two of them all those months ago. Even though they were so far away, he'd recognized his beloved Esther immediately, her long, long brown hair trailing down her slim back. They were walking side by side, her hands clutched behind her, her face uptilted as if she were listening intently to whatever the man was saying. They stopped, and for a moment she looked toward the light, and he imagined that she was looking for him, looking to see if he were there, and he half expected her to wave in greeting. His heart had tripped over itself with that hope, then sunk, hard and low, when he saw her turn her lovely face for the man's kiss.

Impossible. It couldn't be. He recalled that feeling, that sinking dread, that rage that filled him when he imagined her lips pressed against another man's. He let out a small sound, gaining the attention of Ambrose, who'd come for a visit. Ambrose watched the romantic little scene with slightly less interest.

"Who's that?" he'd asked, squinting toward the couple. He grabbed up the spyglass Small always kept in the light and trained it on the couple. "I'll be goddamned," he said. "That bastard." He snapped the glass downward and clutched the rail tightly with his free hand.

He could still recall taking the glass from Ambrose's hand, tugging it free, as though Ambrose were reluctant to give up his secret, and looking through. The roaring in his ears, the sound that stayed there like a raging sea in his head, began the moment he moved the glass to focus on Richard Best ravishing Esther. There could be no question that they were lovers, no question that if he and Ambrose were to stay there and watch, they would see proof. The man's hand was on her breast; her hands were clutched around his neck, her head thrown back as he kissed her neck, as he unbuttoned her dress.

"I can't believe what my eyes just saw," Ambrose said, full of outrage and embarrassment that his son-in-law would be so foolish.

Small couldn't look away, even as the roaring in his head became almost unbearable.

"For God's sake, man, give me that," Ambrose said, snatching the glass away. When Small looked to where the couple had been standing, he saw nothing, and that sickening feeling in his stomach grew until he had to swallow down the bile forming. They were there, hidden by the brush and grass, making love. Richard was touching her, kissing her, tasting her. He broke out in a cold sweat.

"Right there. Right where Rachel or even Belle might see them. What the hell is he thinking?" Ambrose turned to him. "I'm sorry you had to see that, Small. I hope I can trust that this stays between us. I'm getting home." He cursed all the way down the iron stairs, leaving Small behind to stare out the window, to wonder and imagine what Richard was doing to his beloved Esther. Rage, hot and swift, filled him, and he vomited. Then a calmness stole over him, the same sort of feeling he now had.

Esther Travist had disappeared. He'd just been to the Mews to see her, and her father had been beside himself with worry. Had Small seen her? Had anyone? Small had not, but he knew who had. Jared Mitchell was leaving tomorrow. Esther had disappeared. It was happening. Again.

It was so obviously clear what he would have to do.

Again.

Chapter Twenty-eight

❧

"Mama," Belle called as she continued to draw on the back of a piece of water-warped wallpaper that had washed up two seasons ago. It had been ruined for walls, but worked nicely for drawing.

Rachel bent over the dining table to study the picture, moving the oil lamp closer. "It's the lighthouse," she said, glad her daughter had drawn something so easily recognizable. "Is that Mr. Small?" she asked, pointing to the stick figure standing near the almost-lighthouse.

Belle scowled. "No. That's the captain." She quickly drew two more figures. "That's you," she said, her pencil-smudged finger pointing to the larger of the people. "And that's me."

"Very nice," Rachel said, trying to keep the sadness out of her voice. It was so hard pretending her heart wasn't in pieces. That morning, she knew Belle had seen her crying. She didn't want her daughter to know she was brokenhearted.

"We're a family," Belle said, then drew a sun in the sky.

"Baby, Captain Mitchell is going home tomorrow."

"We're a *pretend* family," she explained, as if her mother were the one confused.

"Oh. That's fine, then. It's a very nice picture."

"Mama?"

"Yes?"

"What's a whore?"

Rachel nearly choked. She knew immediately that somehow Belle had overheard someone talking about Esther. She'd wanted to shield Belle from what was happening by keeping her from town, but apparently the gossip had touched her. "Where did you hear that word?" she asked, keeping her voice mild.

Belle screwed up her face as she attempted to draw some flowers. "Mr. Small. He was grumpy today. He said that word to the captain and the captain didn't like it. I don't think. I can tell when the captain's mad. Can you?"

"Yes," Rachel said, thinking that it was the one emotion Jared was quite poor at hiding.

"Mr. Small was mad, too. He didn't give me any rock candy even though I know he gots some. I saw it just the other day. He had lots, and I don't think he would have ate it all. He was so mad he didn't give me any."

"Who was he mad at?"

"Who was mad at who?" Mabel asked, marching into the kitchen. "Finally finished someone's birthday dress," she said, giving Belle a wink.

"Really, really? Can I see? Can I?" Belle said, jumping from the table and grabbing her grandmother's arm.

"Belle, who was Mr. Small mad at?" Rachel asked, trying not to let the frustration she felt show.

"Oh. The captain. Really mad. Mr. Small got all red and stomped off. And he didn't give me any rock candy." She whirled around. "Can I try on my dress, Grandma?"

"Now, why would Don be angry with the captain?" Mabel said.

"Grandma."

"Belle!" Belle jerked, and Rachel was immediately repentant. She took a breath and softened her voice. "You can try on your dress right after supper. After you wash before bedtime. You can go look at the dress now. But wash your hands first; they're full of pencil."

Belle ran to the sink, giving the pump a few pulls. She showed her hands to her mother before dashing up the stairs.

Rachel went to the window, pulled back the curtain, and looked in the direction of the light. It was lit. For a reason she couldn't quite touch upon, she was filled with uneasiness, as if the beacon had suddenly become menacing, not the comforting light it had always been. A tiny bit of something tugged at her consciousness as she stared at the light, something about Mr. Small and Esther and Jared. Perhaps she was simply bothered that Mr. Small had been angry at Jared, or that he'd used such an awful word in front of Belle. That must be it.

"The days are getting longer," she said.

"People will get busy with the warm months coming. They'll have more to do than to sit around gossiping about their neighbors."

Rachel turned her head and smiled at her mother. "This is more excitement than this town can take," she said wryly. "Things will never be the same. Never." Lord, she felt glum. She almost caught herself wishing that time would sweep her back to two summers ago, before Richard disappeared, before she had discovered he was a wretch. Before, before.

But it had all been a lie, and not such a good life, after all. There had been no real joy, nothing real, she realized. What a sad state of affairs. She'd loved a man who'd loved another. And all the while, Esther had been loved by Mr. Small—the other broken heart in this mess. She remembered Small's reaction when Esther had helped Jared after he saved the baby, how angry he'd been that Esther had shown concern for him. He'd been jealous, hotly, bitterly possessive of a woman simply because she'd offered another man comfort. How long had Small loved Esther?

Suddenly the hairs on the back of Rachel's neck prickled uncomfortably.

"Mama, where's Papa?"

"Where he always is these days. In his shed. Why don't you go get him? It's near suppertime. That ham smells about ready to carve."

Rachel walked to the shed, her mind whirling, crazy thoughts making her stomach flutter. Her father stepped out of the shed before she reached it, looking surprised to find Rachel bearing down on him. "Papa, who else knew about Richard and Esther? Not now, but when you found out."

Ambrose immediately looked uncomfortable, and patted his pocket for his pipe. Rachel reached out and grasped his wrist. "Papa, who? Did Mr. Small know?"

Ambrose's bushy eyebrows rose in surprise, and Rachel's stomach fell like a block of lead. "He knew, didn't he?"

"I was up in the lighthouse when I saw them. Don was with me. How did you know?"

Rachel grabbed his other wrist, more to steady herself than to keep her father from wandering away. "He's in love with Esther, Papa. How did he react when he saw them? Do you remember?"

Ambrose studied the sand, his face screwed up in concentration. Then he shook his head. "I was so danged mad, I don't remember anything Don said. I remember him lookin', but that's a natural thing. What's all this about?"

Rachel let go of her father's wrists and hugged

herself. "It's probably nothing. But Belle said this morning that Mr. Small was very angry about something, and I think it was about Esther. He was angry with Jared. And now I think . . ." She took a shaky breath and squeezed her arms tightly. "Oh, Papa, do you think Mr. Small might have killed Richard? Is it possible?" Rachel pressed one shaking hand against her temple, grateful that her father didn't immediately dismiss her insane thoughts.

"Heck, anything's possible. Something happened to Richard that night."

"Oh, God." Rachel had only one thought: that Jared was staying with Mr. Small, and that the lightkeeper was angry—angry about Esther. "Mr. Small thinks Esther is sweet on Jared."

"Now, now, Rachel, don't go jumping to any crazy conclusions."

"He must have found out about their plans. He must have killed Richard." Rachel scrunched up her face. "That sounds impossible. Of course Mr. Small wouldn't. I've known him my whole life." She let out a laugh. "If he knew what we were saying about him, he'd likely laugh with us."

Ambrose rubbed his jaw and shook his head. "Can't imagine it. Richard wasn't as strapping as the captain, but he was a big lad. Big enough to whup Don if Don went after him."

"Of course." But fear ate at Rachel. "Papa, I know you'll think I'm crazy, but where's your old flintlock?"

"I've got no powder and no balls for that old thing, and you know it."

"I know, but I'll feel safe if I have it with me."

This was too much for Ambrose. He scowled at his daughter and went about filling his pipe and lighting it. It was only after he'd taken several puffs, all the time studying his daughter with a scrutiny that made Rachel want to squirm, that he spoke. "Now that I think of it, Don's been moonin' after that Esther for as long as I can remember. Didn't take it seriously, though. I'll go with you, girl. Now you got me all riled up." He ignored Rachel's bright smile. "I don't know what we're going to tell your mother, trooping over to the lighthouse at this hour."

"I love you, Papa," Rachel said impulsively, and gave her father a quick kiss on his beard-roughened cheek.

"Then you love a fool," he said, all gruff, but his cheeks were tinged with pink. "You know, we'll likely find them eating their supper, like we should be doing."

"I know. But I'll go crazy until I know Jared's all right."

Ambrose took another puff on his pipe and looked toward the light. "That man know how much you love him?"

"No."

"Then I think it's about time you told him."

With that, Ambrose meandered back to the house, Rachel following in his wake.

Jared was glad to be leaving this place. The pleasant interlude he thought he'd have with Small would never materialize. There was just no talking to the man, no reasoning with him. He'd gone about his business, not asking for Jared's company, disappearing up the tower to light the lamps without a word. Jared had stayed in his room watching from the bed as one by one fans of light cut through the darkening sky as Small lit the lamps. A slice of light went through his window to illuminate the foot of the bed where he sat. He felt a stab of regret that he would never see Truro again. Never see Rachel again.

His life was going to hell.

Jared didn't want to think about the next few days, or months, or years. His lifetime stretched out before him, feeling more like a sentence than anything else. A life without Rachel. It was a physical ache in his gut, a sickness. Perhaps, he thought, he could come back someday, when all this was over, when her heart was empty, when she was as lonely as he was now. Perhaps he should marry her now anyway, forget that she still loved Richard. She might even tell him she loved him, but Jared knew, deep inside, that a vital piece of her was closed off to him.

Jared heard Don moving around in the kitchen, banging pots unnecessarily hard. Jared chuckled beneath his breath. He could remember Doc on the *Huntress* doing much the same thing when he'd criticized his cooking. It was lousy, watery, unpalatable stuff he'd laid before him, and Doc knew it was awful. But he'd still gotten all in a huff about Jared's comment that the slop looked like something that had already been chewed and swallowed. Ah, what a life to look forward to, he thought glumly, wondering if Doc would return to the *Huntress*. Probably not. After a voyage that lasted nearly five years, it was unlikely any of his crew would be willing to sign on again. Another crew, more training, more coddling the greenhorns, punishing the thugs, more nights, endless and cold. And lonely as hell.

Jared heaved himself off the bed, making the wood slats beneath the straw-filled mattress groan. He ducked his head and entered the kitchen, feeling absurdly wary of the little man whose back was to him. Small was muttering to himself, unaware that Jared was in the same room.

"What's for dinner? Smells good."

Small jerked, then continued stirring silently.

"Hell, Don, I'm leaving tomorrow."

"I know. I know what you're doing," Small said low.

Jared furrowed his brow. "I'm going home," he said slowly.

Small let out a laugh, but said nothing.

"If I ever sail by here, I'll lower my mainsail as a signal."

"Told you already, I'm leaving. I'm through being lightkeeper. Told you that. You don't listen." Small was like a tightly coiled spring ready to burst, and Jared was tempted to go to town for the night. He was rapidly losing patience with the older man, but Jared felt a certain amount of loyalty to him. Hell, he liked the old guy—at least he had until Small decided he was stealing Esther away from him. Jared didn't have the heart to bluntly tell Small that Esther hadn't the vaguest idea that Small was in love with her.

Small dropped the spoon onto the stovetop, tiny drops of chowder spattering to the floor. "Where is she? That's all I want to know. Where is she?" He kept his back to Jared, but he could tell from the man's stance that he was fiercely angry.

"Who?"

Small whirled around and gripped the edge of the tiny table. "Esther," he said. "She's gone. You know where she is."

Jared felt a niggling of fear, then immediately realized how ridiculous it was to feel anything but perhaps irritation with the man. But the look in his eyes was feral, a look he'd seen before in men made mad by endless days in the doldrums from the scorching sun beating down on them. Men would suddenly turn on a friend, bloodlust in their eyes. They could turn dangerous, and nothing short of throwing them overboard to cool them down would stop their rampage. Jared, on more than one occasion, had had to heave a man into the tepid sea, then fish him out when he promised to behave. On ship, he was king. Here, in this kitchen, he was just one man facing another.

"If Esther is gone, it is because she wanted to escape the gossip. I don't know where she is; neither do I care," Jared said, keeping his voice even.

Something flickered in Small's eyes, and for a moment Jared saw a bit of sanity return before he glared again. "Best denied it, too. Even after I saw them together. He denied it. But I knew . . . I knew he was running away with her. He was leaving that night, and she was waiting for him somewhere." He blinked rapidly. "I told him it wasn't right, what he was doing. I told him that. But he wouldn't listen."

Oh, shit, Jared thought. *Mystery solved.* Without moving, Jared tensed his entire body, ready to spring at the smaller man.

"You killed Richard."

"He . . . he touched her," Small said, shuddering.

"Don. Listen to me, man. I never touched Esther. I don't love her. I am not running away with her."

Small shook his head. "You were with her," he said on a sob. "She asked for *you*. And now she's somewhere waiting for you. If you just tell me where she is, I'll go to her. Explain things." He sounded almost petulant, a teenage boy lamenting about a schoolboy crush. He'd always sounded that way, Jared realized, with his boastful stories, his need to impress.

"Rachel was there at the tavern last night, Don. Rachel's the one I love. Remember?"

He sneered suddenly. "That's just what Richard said." He took up a wickedly long knife from the stovetop, and Jared gave the older man a look of exasperation.

"Aw, hell, Don, I don't want to hurt you. Put the goddamn knife down."

"You'll never touch her again."

"If you were planning to kill me, you should have tried to surprise me," Jared said calmly, even as his heart beat hard in his chest and a surge of adrenaline made him want to wrench the knife from Small's hand. He had to be cautious, or the little guy just might cut him. He had no concern, none in the least, that Small would actually succeed in killing him.

Small blinked, taken aback by Jared's composure.

"Put down the knife, friend. You don't want to kill me."

"I do."

"No. You don't. And I don't want to hurt you, either. Put it down."

Small swayed where he stood, his eyes filling with tears, before he pointed the knife to his own chest and looked up at Jared.

"Don. Your heart's on the other side," Jared said with a small, disarming smile, right before he lunged and punched Small hard in the side of the head. The little man flew across the room, the knife pinwheeling out of his hand to stick into the door, just as someone knocked on the other side. Don lay moaning at the base of the door as Jared calmly shoved him aside with his foot and let whoever was on the other side in.

Rachel, hearing the commotion, rushed inside, closely followed by Ambrose, who wielded a pistol, his eyes wild, his hand shaking.

"Come to save me?" he asked, lifting one eyebrow.

Rachel glanced down at the still-moaning light-keeper, then up at Jared, who was grinning at her like some kind of fool. Then she took in the knife embedded in the door and gasped. Ambrose sauntered in, dumping the useless pistol on the table.

"Ain't loaded. Didn't really think we'd need it."

"I appreciate the gesture," Jared said, and Rachel wanted to groan out her frustration. Obviously Don had tried to kill him, and there he was, all manly and smug, acting as if it were an everyday occurrence that someone tried to murder him. Though she knew he was fine, her eyes swept over him just to be certain. Knowing Jared, he could be bleeding to death and not say a word before he fainted from lack of blood.

Ambrose stepped over to Small and squatted down. "What the hell were you thinking, you old fool?" Small curled up into a ball and wept. Ambrose gave him a couple of hard pats that weren't quite a gesture of comfort, and stood.

"Was he really trying to kill you?"

"Apparently," Jared said, jerking the knife out of the door. He gave it a cursory look before tossing it on the table next to Ambrose's old flintlock.

"Because of Esther?" Rachel asked.

From the floor, Small's sobs became a bit louder, and Ambrose shook his head in disgust, muttering about old fools and old friends.

Rachel stared at the knife a long time, her face so tight her head ached. The words were there, the question she had to ask. "He killed Richard, didn't he?"

"Aye, he did."

The strangest thing happened. Rachel felt as if she were riding a cloud, rising up and over the world, light enough to be pushed by the softest spring breeze. *It's over*, she thought. Even though she knew Richard was dead, she realized that it was not until this moment that she *believed* it. How odd. How wonderful she felt, and despite everything horrid that had happened, she wanted to whirl around, arms spread. She felt, she decided, very much the way Jared must have after he saved that baby. Now she knew what it felt like to be free.

She covered her mouth with her hands, and above her fingertips her eyes filled with tears. She saw through blurred vision Jared tense. How he hated tears, she thought, wanting to laugh.

And then she did laugh, and it took a moment for Jared to realize the odd sound coming from her wasn't sobs, but laughter.

Her father looked at her cautiously, and even Small stopped crying. Rachel pressed her lips together, trying with all her might to stop the happiness that bubbled up inside her. Oh, goodness, was she actually happy that she'd just learned who had murdered her husband? *I'm mad,* she thought.

"I can't help it," she said. "I know it's inappropriate. I know." She turned to Small, who was struggling to sit up and eyeing Rachel cautiously. "He killed Richard," Rachel said, knowing she sounded deliriously happy about it. She wasn't; she knew deep inside that she would weep for Richard. But at the moment, she was just so glad to have it *out*. To *know*. To have it all over. She just wanted to laugh. So she did.

"Oh, you must think me quite mad," she said, sobering abruptly, then letting out another chuckle. She looked from her father to Jared, both men equally ill at ease. "I'm fine. Truly fine for the first time in years." She turned to Jared and put her hands on his upper arms, taking the time to enjoy the massive strength she felt there. "I know how you felt that day you saved the baby, Jared. You felt free, didn't you?"

He looked down at her, and she nearly drowned in that beautiful green-eyed gaze. Oh, how she loved him. She loved, loved, loved him. It was nearly bursting from her, but even in her delirious state she knew now was not the time to make such a declaration.

"Aye," he said, and he swallowed hard and moved his arms as if to embrace her. Behind them Small stood, and Jared's attention was immediately drawn away from her.

"Stay right there, Don."

The lightkeeper swayed, woozy from the blow to

his head. He shuffled slowly to the kitchen chair and sat down heavily. Ambrose quickly moved the knife and gun away from him as Small buried his hands in his thinning hair.

"I just love her so," he said. "He was going to take her away." He looked at them for understanding, the woman he'd made a widow, the man who'd loved Richard as a son.

"I'll take him to town hall," Jared said. "I'll be back to look after the light tonight."

"Forgot about the light," Ambrose said. "I'm sure the town would be grateful for your filling in until the service can send us another keeper."

Jared grasped Small's arms and heaved him up. Darting a look to Rachel, he said, "I'll think on it." Then he walked out the door, pulling Small with him.

Chapter Twenty-nine

Rachel had cheated, but she'd be darned if she could figure out how to build anything in a bottle without breaking it open first. It had taken four bottles before she'd broken it just so, and even with her cheating, the thing inside was hardly recognizable. Belle had helped by creating stick figures that looked like giants next to the sugar-cube lighthouse she'd tried to create. A bit of yellow paint for the light, black for the shutters, red for the roof, and it almost looked like a building.

"It's beautiful, Mama," Belle said after Rachel had cemented the two halves of the bottle together.

It was not beautiful. But it was so awful that perhaps Jared would like it. She'd poured sand into the bottom of the bottle, then sat the sugar-cube lighthouse on top. Every time she jostled it a bit, the lighthouse would fall over and clink against the bottle, and Rachel would have to jiggle it until it was upright again. Rachel stared at her creation, and her insides felt as if she were being attacked by a swarm of butterflies.

"Courage," she whispered. Lord above knew it would take more courage to tell Jared she loved him than it had to barge in when she thought

Mr. Small planned to murder him. She would not allow herself to imagine that he did not love her. Yes, he'd said as much not two weeks earlier, but she didn't believe it. She couldn't believe it. How could a man not love her and look at her the way he did?

She hadn't seen Jared in three days except from a distance, when she just happened to be sitting atop a bluff within sight of the lighthouse when he'd gone outside. Of course, she'd just happened to be sitting there for two hours, her eyes trained on the light. He'd spied her and waved and she'd waved back; then Rachel had pretended to be busy studying the bayberry bushes that wouldn't bear fruit for another two months.

"Mama," she called out. "I'm going to the lighthouse to bring the Captain a couple loaves of bread." *And a sugar-cube lighthouse.*

"Why don't you bring him a crock of butter while you're at it," Mabel called down from the second floor.

Rachel filled a basket, aware that it looked as if she were trying to bribe him into courting her. She knew it was only a matter of time before Jared received more female visitors, all plying him with their best pies, jam, and smoked hams.

She took the path that meandered along the bluff, where the sand was firmer and walking was easier. She realized that although she'd walked the entire distance with the blue Atlantic beside her, not once did she look out to sea. The night after Small had been taken away, she had cried for Richard, but they were quick tears and not filled with the despair she'd once felt. Freedom was a wonderful, giddy thing, she decided. Almost as wonderful as love. She took in a deep breath, savoring the sharp tang of the ocean, the sweet, fecund scent of spring, the crisp white of the lighthouse against the brilliant blue sky.

As she stepped into the clearing that contained the lighthouse, Jared emerged from the tiny cottage where he'd been staying. Rachel lifted her basket to show why she was there, and she resisted the urge to press a hand against her chest where her heart was threatening to burst through.

"I've brought some provisions," she said, and handed the basket over to him. He took it without looking inside. The wind swept the hair across his forehead, a waving strand teasing his long lashes before he jerked his head to get rid of it. He needed a haircut and a shave, but he was dressed immaculately, richly, in a crisp linen shirt, tie, and deep blue silk waistcoat.

"You're a sight," he said with a small smile.

"Oh!" Rachel looked down and took in her old coat, her scuffed boots, her dull brown skirt, and turned crimson.

"No. I meant a sight for sore eyes."

She smiled, feeling shy. "Oh."

He cleared his throat. "Why don't you come in and I'll put these things away. Then you can have your basket back."

Rachel followed him silently into the small kitchen. For some reason, it didn't seem strange that Mr. Small wasn't about. Already the former lightkeeper was in a Boston prison, having confessed without remorse or hesitation to murdering Richard. Jared loomed large in the tiny space, making Rachel intensely aware of him, of his warmth and salt-and-fresh-air scent.

"What's this?" he asked, pulling out the bottle, knocking the lighthouse over in the process.

"It's nothing. Just a silly something I made for you." She took it from his hands and tried to jiggle the thing upright. "It's supposed to be a lighthouse. It's awful, I know, but Belle wanted you to have it." *Coward*.

"Belle made this for me?"

Rachel flushed, then laughed. "I did."

He lifted one eyebrow. "It's . . ."

"Sugar cubes."

"No, it's nice. Thank you." His voice had grown gruff, and he turned away to study the bread and butter crock.

Rachel stared at his broad back and took a fortifying breath. "I love you," she blurted, the words feeling like a rush of water held back by a dam that finally broke under pressure.

He went still, then turned slowly toward her. "I've heard those words before," he said, caution in every syllable.

"I know. I know it's difficult for you to believe me. So I've decided to show you." Rachel had never been so forward in her life. But she so wanted to make him believe she loved him. She wanted to rub her hands on his chest, feel his hard body against her, kiss his mouth. She wanted him inside her, moving slowly, then roughly. She wanted his hands and mouth on her breasts, his fingers touching between her legs. She wanted to thrust her tongue against his. She wanted him.

It must have shown in her eyes, for his breath caught and his eyes swept over her possessively. "Show me?" he nearly choked out.

"We're alone," she said. "And I need you, Jared. Very much."

Rachel had planned a slow seduction, but things got away from them. Perhaps someday Jared would submit to the casual caresses, the long, sensuous kisses she had imagined before bed each night, but the minute their lips touched, it was as if someone lit an explosion between them. They were wild for each other, and for the first time in her life, Rachel understood how passion could sweep a person away, how the earth could spin out of control. Every touch, every kiss, set her afire. Every word he spoke made her move urgently against him. He felt so wonderful, so hard and firm and strong and hairy. So wonderfully like a man.

They moved to the small bedroom and fell to the bed, half-undressed and urgently tearing at their own clothes, laughing at each other's haste. When he fell next to her, naked and warm, Rachel nuzzled her face against his chest, loving the way his soft hair felt against her cheek, breathing deeply, pressing close, wanting him to be a part of her. She ran her hands up and down his body, touching him, watching her hands skim over his muscles, delighted when he sucked in his breath. She took him in her hands and squeezed and watched, her eyes dilating, when he threw his head back and moaned, his entire body becoming taut. Oh, she liked this. She liked being free.

Jared moved between her legs, muttering about her torturing him. He pressed his thumb between her legs and slipped a finger inside her, and Rachel shuddered with desire. He looked down at her, his beautiful eyes hooded, and smiled. "I love it when you look like this," he said, his voice gruff and low.

He moved his thumb and finger and she squealed. "More."

"More." He grunted. "More and more and more."

He entered her then, hard and swift, and she arched into him, crying out with happiness. Rachel wrapped her legs around his waist, squeezing him into her, and he cursed, then laughed.

"Wait!"

Jared's eyes shot open in disbelief. She'd become tense beneath him and her hands pressed against his chest to stop his motion. His breath, harsh and rapid, caught. "What?" he managed to utter.

She smiled at him, a vixen's smile. "Do you love me?"

He moved slowly in and out. "Do I love you?" he asked, forcing himself to sound casual, forcing his movements to slow when he wanted to lose himself again. "Now let me see." In and out. "I think . . ." In. "I'll have to say . . ." Out.

Then he stopped and stared hotly into her eyes. "I think I would die without you. I think every day we were apart I lost a little bit more of myself. I think, my darling girl, I shall love you until the day I die."

She smiled up at him and his heart stopped for just a second. "That will do," she said softly, then pulled his head down for a soul-wrenching kiss.

The sun was getting low in the sky, turning the whitewashed walls of the tiny bedroom a pinkish yellow. They slept, turned toward each other, crisp white sheets tangled about them. One large and hairy leg had escaped the sheet and was draped heavily over Rachel's hips. She slept anyway. They awakened slowly, sweetly, opening their eyes to see the one person in the world they wanted to see. Every morning, every night for a lifetime, they would open their eyes to each other. Rachel smiled at the thought.

"I love you," she said, and her eyes filled with tears. "Sorry. I know how much you hate when I cry." She smiled and wiped away the tears with her fingertips.

"I don't mind happy tears. It's the scared, mad, angry tears I can't abide," Jared said. "Those *were* happy tears, were they not?" He used his best captain's tone.

"Yes, sir."

He squeezed her closer to him, closing his eyes, an odd sensation in his throat.

Her hand moved idly up and down his arm, and he knew she was thinking about something—and would surely speak it aloud any second.

"I know you love me," she said.

"I do."

"Then why did you say you did not?" she asked, pulling her head back so that she could look into his eyes.

He smiled and shook his head. "And when did I say that?"

"I was eavesdropping. At your house. You told your brother that you didn't love me."

He nuzzled her neck. "I didn't."

"I heard you," she said, giggling at the way his beard felt against her sensitive skin.

"Then you heard wrong." He furrowed his brow and looked down at her. "What exactly do you think you heard?"

"West asked if you loved me and you said no."

Jared shrugged. "I can't recall precisely what was said, but I can assure you it was a misunderstanding."

"Oh," she said, kissing his jaw. "You're assuring me."

"I can assure you of a great many things," he said, loving the hell out of the way her lips felt against him.

"Such as?"

"I can assure you I love you. That I'll love you forever. That I'll love Belle and all the other children you'll give me."

She let out a sigh and he felt her soft breath against his neck. "I suppose you'll want to get married."

"I can assure you we will." And then he kissed

her and looked down at her again, liking the way the setting sun made her glow pink and soft. Setting sun . . . "Hell. I've got to light the damn lamps," he muttered into her neck.

"Go on, then. I'll be right up."

She watched lazily as he got dressed, enjoying the play of muscles in his buttocks as he pulled on his drawers, making a mental note to pay more attention to that particular part of his anatomy the next time they made love. He kissed her before he left the room, a kiss that left her breathless and stunned. *Oh, my.*

After he'd gone, Rachel stretched like a cat after an afternoon nap in the sun. She pulled on her clothes that were scattered about the bedroom, hall, and kitchen, blushing when she found her dress tossed negligently atop the small kitchen table.

By the time she reached the iron stairs that led to the light, the sun was touching the horizon and Jared had all the lamps lit. She could smell the oil and smoke, and was about to ascend the stairs when she heard Jared coming down. When he reached the bottom, he swept her up into his arms in a bear hug that left her breathless. Oh, how she loved him.

"Do you think, with all that's happened, you could live here?" he asked, his hands interlocked behind her back. She tilted her head to look up to him.

"I love Truro. But I love you more."

He took her hand and led her outside. They walked to the edge of the bluff, the wind buffeting their faces. "I can't leave this place, Rachel," he said at last. "It saved me."

They stood, arms about each other, looking out at the Atlantic, watching the waves come endlessly to shore, the sun's last light glowing red behind them. Above them, two seagulls hovered gracefully on the breeze, as if keeping watch over them. Never had they seen anything so lovely. Never had they been so happy, so much in love as they were that moment. It was a gift they would treasure in their hearts for all the days to come.

Another gift from the sea.